Vision on a French Battlefield

Bluefeather looked at the dud eighty-eight. There was his spirit guide, Dancing Bear, squatted down sitting on the shell. Bluefeather started to scream a warning at him before the dawning of who it was stilled the cry.

"That's perty fair fightin' goin' on around here, dear brudder," Dancing Bear said.

After what Bluefeather had seen and survived in this single day, he was qualified to make a year-long speech if he so desired, but because he felt too weary to work his vocal cords so heavily, he simply said, "Hey, I learned something, Bear. Ground war made me realize that one can breathe blood . . . and nothing is unbearable." He was silent for a while, then he finally overcame his weariness enough to try to be angry. "Where the hell have you been?" He motioned at the carnage around him. "Can't you see this is the worst day of my life? What good are you if you aren't around when the going is tough? Answer me, Bear."

Dancing Bear did a friendship dance around the shell and followed that with one of his famous toe dances right on top of the murderous object. "You are right. Going is tough all over around here."

"You been around here today?"

"Oh, for sure, dear brudder. I been working my ass off for my clients on both sides."

"You been consorting and consulting with the enemy?" Bluefeather was mortified. "I shoulda known that's why they had us zeroed in all day. That's treason, Bear. You oughta be hanged."

"They are your enemies for now. Not mine. I don't have any of those. That's not the way it works when you crash through to this side of the river."

BLUE*f*EATHER

FELLINI

MAX EVANS

BANTAM BOOKS
NEW YORK · TORONTO · LONDON · SYDNEY · AUCKLAND

BLUEFEATHER FELLINI

A Bantam Book / published by arrangement
with the University Press of Colorado

PUBLISHING HISTORY

University Press of Colorado edition published 1993
Bantam edition / November 1994

ISBN 0-553-56539-7

Published simultaneously in the United States and Canada

Bantam Books are published by Bantam Books, a division of Bantam
Doubleday Dell Publishing Group, Inc. Its trademark, consisting of
the words "Bantam Books" and the portrayal of a rooster, is Regis-
tered in U.S. Patent and Trademark Office and in other countries.
Marca Registrada. Bantam Books, 1540 Broadway, New York, New
York 10036.

PRINTED IN THE UNITED STATES OF AMERICA

OPM   0 9 8 7 6 5 4 3 2 1

One From the Heart
For

My wife, Pat, my number one critic, who also suffered safely through all those long decades of my taking notes, thinking and figuring on *Bluefeather Fellini,* and then the five and a half years of actually writing it down. My profound and ever-lasting thanks for surviving with me the roller coaster from poor to plenty over and over and—on occasion—actual deg-radation, as well as sharing the few glorious times of a trea-sured sense of accomplishment in our other stories.

For

Federico Fellini, the great director who taught me to feel the color, see the sound and hear the unsaid in such great films as *La Strada, La Dolce Vita,* and *8½.*

For

Burt Kennedy and Ed Honeck, who always kept the faith long past its due.

For

Those deeply loved and influential amigos and amigas who have gone on the "Long Adios," including my mother, Ha-zel, who taught me to read, and love it, before I started school. Wiley (Big Boy) Hittson, whose brief life of daring, courage, total loyalty and sudden shocking death by gunfire inspired my novel *The Hi Lo Country.* Luz Martinez, the "Santero" who followed me to Taos and carved cedarwood into permanent beauty and dignity. Woody Crumbo, the great pioneer Pottawatamie Indian artist, who became my artistic and spiritual mentor and whose spirit is in every chapter of this book. And finally to our little dog Foxy, who came to us as a stricken stray and stayed to love and be loved through the last, forever-long months while we sought the proper publishers of the words and feelings inside these cov-ers.

MAX EVANS
Albuquerque, New Mexico

CONTENTS

PART ONE

~

SENSUAL YOUTH—FIRST REAL LOVE

THE SCENT OF GOLD

ONE

IT WAS THE TIME OF YOUTHFUL JUBILATION, AND BLUEFEATHER Fellini—the chosen one—knew that never, never, never before had anyone his age been so blessed. In just a few days, they would be rich—rich as bankers, rich as doctors, rich as movie stars, rich as kings. Grinder the Gringo was giving him this wondrous opportunity, and if he lived a thousand years, he could never show his ample appreciation for the golden opportunity afforded him by this generous genius sitting with him in the woods at this moment.

He sat across the campfire in Twining Canyon north of Taos, New Mexico, watching the toothless old prospector, Sam Grinder, with respect. He could hear the voices of the night birds in the forest as clearly as violins, and feel the very earth vibrate with other more muted sounds of walking and flying life. The campfire flickered on the rump of the burro feeding contentedly from a feedbag and swatting, from habit, an imaginary fly with his tail.

Now that they had eaten, Grinder took off his hat, pushed at his gray, stringy hair and took a large chew of tobacco from a paper container. He chewed with long-suffering gums until the tobacco was soft and ready for spitting. He turned his head and exuded a stream into an empty coffee can.

Bluefeather thought, "What a gentleman." All the prospectors and hunters he had known before spat into the fire to test their accuracy and enjoy the little explosions from the moisture. Grinder looked up at him, somehow knowing the young man's thoughts were too complimentary.

For decades the old prospector had walked the sizzling southwestern deserts, climbed the jagged mountains, chewed the dust, dodged the blizzards without complaint or defeat. He had joyously spent his occasional discoveries on women, beer and chewing tobacco. He was always grinding on forward just as his name implied.

Grinder studied his new partner with respect, friendship and a learned cunning. He observed Bluefeather through slitted, knowing eyes. The quality he looked for was definitely there. It flickered from the young man's large, black eyes and was obvious in the alert, almost regal, manner he carried his head and the way he climbed the Taos mountains with a long-stepped, but smooth, attacking stride.

Yes. Yes, Bluefeather Fellini was from the people of yearning. Whenever one walks or rides with yearners, the world becomes generous with great gifts of almost ceaseless adventure—and makes one pay terrible prices for the ultimate joys. Grinder knew this to be a fact, for he was a yearner himself. Now, right now, he must start his time of testing. The time of teaching. It must come from him naturally, without plan or precedence. Bluefeather was worth the effort—or worth nothing.

"You know, kiddo . . . ?" he said.

Bluefeather, his large, dark eyes absorbing the flames and projecting them back even stronger, waited as Grinder thought over his next statement.

Then he got it in order and went on, "God is supposed to have made us in His image, but He didn't engineer us too good. When I was about fifty-five all my teeth fell out. Now I ask you, why didn't He take my balls instead? I really need my teeth." He spat again, "kerpluk, kersplash," into the can and slapped a hand on one over-all-covered knee, saying, "Get the idee?" A great boom of laughter exploded from him.

Bluefeather laughed as hard as he could to show his appreciation. The noise made the owls quit hooting, a mountain lion quit stalking a deer, a bear quit digging under a rotten log and the burro stop chewing oats and turn his head to stare at Grinder and Bluefeather with curiosity and a tinge of superiority.

"You know, son, I never hired anybody I couldn't whup." He gave a quick pause and a knowing glance at the well-muscled, half Taos Indian, half Italian young man who watched and listened, then added, "When I was younger, that is."

The aspen wood fire, slow-burning and almost smoke-less, reflected its orange light on Bluefeather's olive-red-dish skin and chiseled features as he listened intently to every word the old man said.

"Well, except maybe once 'er twice." Grinder continued, "I remember this one particular time. This feller just begged me for a job. Said he'd do just about anything in the world for a chance to go prospecting with me. Well, I was so dang broke he wound up having to pay me for the privilege of getting to work for me. I worked him so hard he fell down flat on his face from exhaustion. And guess what!" Grinder paused for effect. "He found us a nice little placer deposit before he could recover and get back up. Get the idee?"

"Yeah. Yeah, I get it."

"Well, sir, that ain't all there is to this story." He spat

into the can before continuing, "It was a profitable little find. With his percentage he bought a hardware store, and I been paying him money for supplies ever since." Grinder slapped both bent knees and almost fell over laughing.

Bluefeather joined the mirth mostly out of respect and the old man's contagious sense of the ridiculous.

"Well, Blue, this feller has put two kids through college. The boy's a dentist, the girl's a schoolteacher. Now, all that was good for him, for his kids, for the community —even the country. Hell, he's a deacon of the church, a member of the town board, a pillar of the community."

He stared at the campfire a moment before continuing. "Me? I just went on prospecting, having fun, living outdoors with the rabbits and skunks most of the time. You see, son, those things is what's good for me, but if him and Old Grinder hadn't taken a gamble on one another, way back there, he might not be so deeply admired, so damn respected—even feared, . . ." he grinned grandly, "and the miserable son of a bitch he truly is. Get the idee, kiddo? You either got gold running through your veins or you ain't."

Grinder paused and stared off into the darkness. "Ah, robin piss, nobody ever hears these stories, 'specially young boys like you—and 'specially from an old man like me. You gotta make up your own mind where you're goin' in this world, then get after it and stay with it like a badger after a prairie dog."

Bluefeather smiled, but his dark eyes showed concern as he tried to interpret all the old man's messages. There was no way he could know that it was part of his initiation fee into Grinder's final trust. Now, Bluefeather made a mistake but had no way of knowing so in advance.

He said, "Well my Indian blood tells me one thing, and my Italian blood tells me another."

"Now, there you go—I've noticed it before. Ever chance you get it's, 'I did this 'cause I'm part Indian; I didn't do that 'cause I'm part Italian; that's my Indian blood talkin'; that's my Italian blood talkin'.' That's very tiresome. What do you give a shit whether anybody knows about your bloodline or not? There ain't a damn one of us ever lived who can do a single thing about our bloodline. Not one ever born. Not one in all history. You think you're the only one who's dark, light, short, tall, goofy, smart, crippled or was ever cut down by your blood mixture? Haw. I say shit again and then again once more. Think. Go back millions of years, a minute at a time. Don't never be one of them self-bleedin' excuse inventors."

Bluefeather was stunned, paralyzed. For a moment he thought about knocking Grinder in the head with an ore sample, but control was definitely one of his strong points —one his Indian mother had deeply instilled in him. But he wasn't supposed to think about that, according to Grinder.

Grinder went on, "Now, listen up with very big ears. You want to talk bloodlines. Me? I'm a bunch of things: part Scotch-Irish, part Black-Dutch, Welsh, Choctaw, Po-lack and no doubt some Mexican, Jewish and colored blood has probably crept into the brew, and I know damn well, for sure, I'm part burro and a tad of coyote. We're all Americans, goddamnit, and we all got to grit and groan to earn our place here. Make it ours alone for just a little while. That's the only freedom, by God—getting your little spot on earth to work for you and you working like hell for it. There ain't no more than that, and I don't never aim for you to bring it up to me again, kiddo. Now go to sleep. Tomorrow's gonna be a long and great day for us Americans. Especially the very first ones like you."

Grinder chuckled himself to sleep, as young Blue-

feather gritted his perfectly rowed, white teeth to keep
his tongue silent and his muscles frozen. Soon he decided
not to kill Grinder until morning, and his breathing
slowed to normal.

He slipped into his bedroll and rubbed his hand across
his forehead. His fingers automatically followed the thin,
almost undetectable, scar that coursed at an angle on his
forehead across the upper bridge of his nose between his
eyebrows. At the touch and memory, he smiled. Then an
even bigger, sparkling smile came. By the Great Spirit's
worship, he would never bring that "breed" subject up to
Grinder again. He had not been conscious of his using his
bloodline as an excuse. He determined that perhaps
Grinder the Gringo mongrel had just done him another
"great" favor.

As the fire flickered down and he rubbed at the suddenly itchy sliver of a scar, he thought of how he had
received it and about his childhood at Raton, New Mexico, where he was born.

The town hovered up against the mountains, which
contained the coal seams of its livelihood. The famed Raton Pass north into Trinidad, Colorado, brought a few
overnight travelers; the grama grass-rich ranchlands to
the south and east fed thousands of cattle; but the coal
mines were the black fossil lifeblood of the town.

Bluefeather's Italian father, Valerio Fellini, had married a Taos Pueblo Indian girl named Morning Star Martinez. He had met her while joining in the Friendship
Dance at an open ceremonial at Taos Pueblo. She was
delicately, darkly beautiful, and Valerio had fallen hope-
lessly in love with her.

It created a time of chaos, this marriage, for the family
clans of the Taos Indians were just as strong as those of
the Raton Italians. But enough authority can settle even
the most entrenched disputes—even those of blood.

Morning Star's father was a powerful shaman, and it was his position that determined the final acceptance of the marriage and mating from the Indian side. There also had been no argument when he gave his newborn grandson the spiritually strong Indian name of Bluefeather.

It had taken a little longer for the Italian family to come around, but after the birth of baby Bluefeather, both families were reconciled.

Valerio was a mine superintendent. He had earned this position by working underground since he was seventeen. His status in the community was greater than the mayor's. Besides that, he had the reputation as a fair man among the underground miners and one to respect in a barroom brawl. Around Raton he was considered in the league of Jack Dempsey and Jack Johnson.

Bluefeather grew up as an only child. The thought did cross his mind that this may have been chosen because of the mixed blood. He would never know. All his aunts and uncles had birthed multiple cousins for him to grow up with—to play with, fight and love.

Morning Star was a caring, gentle mother who wanted her son to have the kind of education that she reasoned would keep him occupied and interested in life aboveground and out of the coal mines. She didn't want him "down in the hole." Her deep beliefs came from people who respected all that the Great Spirit had created—the whole earth, its animals, birds, insects, its all. She felt it was unnatural to scar the earth's beauty for wealth—wealth that always vanished in the end. She respected her husband and his family's heritage, but she pursued this goal for her son with a strong will.

She taught Bluefeather early on how to read and whetted his curiosity for varied, fine things. Valerio reinforced her when it came to Bluefeather's school studies. There was no shirking. Later Bluefeather would thank his family and his gods for this most priceless of gifts.

With all these blessings, Bluefeather's doting aunts, female cousins and grandmothers almost convinced him he had one too many—he was almost too pretty to be a boy, and he hated it. From the time he could remember, all he had heard from them was: "Isn't that the most beautiful child you ever saw?" "Look at that hair, thick and shiny as a girl's." "What a girl wouldn't give for those eyelashes." "He's just too pretty to play baseball. What if he got hit in the face?"

By the time he was sixteen, his six-foot height, his wide, lean shoulders and his expertise at sports made him even more attractive. His father had taught him, along with the studying, how to hide his chin behind his shoulder, jab a left fist, fake another and follow up with an overhand right that simply dropped whoever took the blow, like a sack of low-grade coal.

He overheard girls talking about his good looks and took advantage of it in a callous way, for a while. How was he to know if the young ladies cared for him for himself or because he was handsome? This became very important to him. He began to think that a few nicks and scrapes might change his image enough for him to discern the difference.

At first, he started friendly fights outside his family clan, over mostly nothing. Things such as someone not moving aside on the sidewalk fast enough, or someone looking at him the "wrong" way. He had a physical altercation with Eloy Gomez because he stepped on his shadow twice in one day. Unforgivable. Although he received many blows, bruises and contusions, they all healed, and he was as handsome as before.

His second cousin, Guiseppe "Hog Head" Fontano, who was twenty-five years old, weighed 248 pounds and worked as a "collector" in Chicago, came to town to visit his kin. He loved card games of all kinds—mostly because he was a cheat and won a great percentage of the time.

Bluefeather was in a jokers-wild poker game with Hog Head and three other cousins. He noticed that his Chicago kin always won when he dealt. Always. Bluefeather knew no one could do that without rigging the cards. The odds were just too high against it.

He stood up and called Hog Head a liar, a cheat, an overgrown ape and a disgrace to the family. His tactics worked. Hog Head hardly looked up, and he certainly didn't argue, as that would have been wasting time. In one motion he arose, reaching over the card table and slapped Bluefeather across the side of his cheek and head with a huge open hand. He hadn't formed a fist out of respect for youth.

Bluefeather was knocked backward, whirling and falling face-first into the beveled edge of a dresser top. It split his forehead at an angle between his eyebrows. The flesh was peeled back and blood flowed wondrously into his eye and down his cheeks. He checked all this out after struggling awhile to get his rubber-soft legs under his body so he could look in the dresser mirror. At first he was very sobered by the sight. It's true, he had wanted his features altered, but not quite that much. But it was too late; it was done. He might as well think of it as a difficult chore easily taken care of by his cousin Hog Head Fontano. He was suddenly very pleased.

Hog Head was dealing the cards again, uttering softly, "Don't nobody say I'm a disgrace to the family."

The betting went on as before. Bluefeather rejoined the game, wiping at his face with a red-stained handkerchief, saying, "Hey, Hog Head, would you teach me to deal someday?"

"Sure, kid. Anytime."

The old mine doctor had sewed him up so skillfully that only when Bluefeather got angry or highly emotional did the scar show. He resented the good doctor's skill for a while but soon found that when he sat almost directly under a light the thin scar invariably showed up. He had tried it from every angle with his mother's hand mirror. It would be there for as long as he was. Young Bluefeather was satisfied that now he could get on with his life in a normal fashion.

Soon after Hog Head's addition, he was disappointed to overhear his grandmother Fellini tell her closest friend, "Poor Bluefeather is so handsome, he'll be handed much without any effort on his part. Those Olympian eyes will bring him many delights and probably doom, for he is so naturally generous, he'll give all his earnings away."

"But they're such kindly eyes," answered her friend. "How could he not be a sharing soul?"

The cousin who overheard this with him later told a friend, "Yeah, he'll kindly knock you on your ass and kindly pick you up and generously do it to you again if you kind of don't like it."

As soon as he graduated from high school—to his father's delight and his mother's worry—he went over Raton Pass to Trinidad to work as an oremucker (shoveler) in the mines. His father's heritage was readily visible in his work, and rapid job promotions were forthcoming. He made shift foreman faster than anyone in the area ever had. His future seemed to be as vast as a cloudless sea. At first this success distressed his mother. She wanted him to go to college and pursue some other endeavor. His mother's expectations for him were yet to come.

Then, oh yes, then, he met the old gringo prospector who told enchanting tales of lost mines in Twining Canyon north of Taos. The old man seduced his young mind with a simple trick of yellow sorcery. Grinder the Gringo had revealed a glass vial full of nuggets from the size of sand grains to the scope of a pencil eraser. He showed old geological reports and drew maps with authority and expertise. Bluefeather was properly entrapped.

It was natural that Bluefeather's immediate family and other kin tried to dissuade him from this foolishness; but toothless Sam Grinder could chew tobacco and drink beer at the same time and continue through many hours of dedicated conversation without any apparent injury. This amazed and convinced young Bluefeather that a man of such unique accomplishments should be followed, listened to and learned from. All this and more would inevitably occur.

At first the Fellini family was more than a little upset with young Bluefeather for what they considered a very rash decision. Aside from his leaving the safety and security of home and friends, his joining up with a gold prospector was, in their minds, sillier and more risky than the venture undertaken by another ancient relation, Christopher Columbus. Bluefeather's leaving also threatened the future marriage plans of the Bertinoli family to their beautiful daughter, Margaret.

Bluefeather finally reasoned with everyone by pointing out that, in truth, he was simply going over to the other side of the Rocky Mountains. The Fellini family took some consolation from his being near the maternal side of his family at Taos Pueblo. They reluctantly gave their blessings, but not without many messages to relatives throughout the multistory adobe structure advising them on the manner in which the promising young company man must be guided back to his true and practical future. It was a wasted effort. The genes of gleaming dreams had been unleashed from his head. Many things might slow them down, but nothing could stop them now.

Bluefeather loaded up his gear in the back of the old prospector's battered Ford truck, and they headed toward what Grinder referred to as his "great hacienda."

The Gringo's great hacienda in Taos, just a mile from the plaza, turned out to be a four-room, slab (slabs being waste-wood strips from a sawmill) shack, the cracks filled with mud, with no electricity and no indoor plumbing. There was a well with a bucket on a pulley in the front yard and an outhouse in back. The hacienda did, however, sit on three acres of subirrigated pasture.

The old man explained as they emptied the last of Bluefeather's gear from the vehicle, "You see, son, a gold huntin' man has always got to own him a little headquarters somewhere. Then between strikes he'll have a place to plan and think about his next go. Cain't nobody shame and starve him plumb out. Get the idee?"

The first thing he did with Bluefeather—after introducing him to the house—was to take him out in the pasture and make him acquainted with his burro, Tony.

"Now another thing . . . always keep a burro or mule —mules, if you can afford 'em—and some feed. That way, no matter what, you'll never be afoot and at the mercy of functional folks—the vault stuffers. It's those functional folks that do in men like you'n me. We make 'em uncomfortable."

Bluefeather learned a great lesson standing there in a Taos, New Mexico, pasture. By necessity he found that he really could shake his head "yes" and "no" at the same time without breaking his neck. This ability would come in handy throughout his life. He also learned to be a good listener, mainly because he had no choice.

Grinder the Gringo ground on, "Now let's get on back to headquarters. We got things to discuss."

They walked the seventy feet back to the house with purpose in their footsteps. Grinder opened them each a beer and began to show Bluefeather ore samples from the entire Rio Hondo mining district—chunks of rainbow metallic copper; bornite from Frazier Mountain, shining with an iridescent patina as it was turned in the light; oxidized malachite and azurite, the grass-green and ocean-blue coppers, from Bull of the Woods Mountain—until Bluefeather's eyes and sense of color would be forever linked to chunks of rich ore samples.

Then came the clincher. The yellow metal would forever be imprinted on, and in, his entirety when Grinder showed him a fist-sized piece of white quartz with visible gold, some pieces as big as his thumbnail, splattered through it. Grinder placed the glass vial right next to the quartz rock and handed Bluefeather a magnifying glass.

"Now look carefully. The placer gold is the same as that in the quartz. It's the same color and grain. That rock is from the mother lode. No question about it. And that ain't no float rock neither. You can tell by the sharpness of its edges and the white shininess of the rock that it was just recently broke out of the mother lode vein."

Bluefeather asked, "Do you know the location of this?"

Grinder chose to ignore the question. He continued, "All great discoveries have come from finding jist one rock. Jist one and this'n here is it." He was chewing and swallowing the tobacco and beer with much enthusiasm as he pushed the white, shredded hair out of his little pea-sized, milky-blue eyes and walked around the room two or three times muttering to himself as if he were nearing the answer to all creation.

Finally he stopped, standing close, but just to the side, so he could look at an old, faded print of Christ on the cross where it hung crookedly on the wall. "I swear to the Almighty, I dug this here gold with my very own hands."

"Then we're ready to start our mining operation right off, huh?"

"Well now, son, I don't know how to tell you this, but after I found the placer and the vein—there they are right there on the table—I musta' fell off a bluff and knocked something loose in my head, 'cause all I remember is waking up here at headquarters with a big knot and a three-inch cut in my scalp and a whole case of empty beer bottles layin' about."

Bluefeather's strong young stomach did a little hula dance inside his ribs. He had not yet learned to handle the enormous changing of directions and gears that occurred so suddenly in the world of gold seekers.

"You mean . . . you actually mean to tell me you can't remember anything about it?"

"Well, it ain't 'cause I haven't tried. I've spent nearly a year now straining so hard my head sometimes felt like it spun off and rolled all the way to the Rio Grande. It sure ain't 'cause . . ." Then Grinder showed what makes a good mineral mountain man. "We'll find 'er, kiddo. And we'll be rich far beyond the greediest of dreams. Don'tcha worry 'bout that. Look here." He pulled a cigar box from a shelf and took out two neatly folded, official-looking documents. One was a geological report by a prominent, consulting geologist dated Albuquerque, New Mexico, November 2, 1900. He had written it for the now defunct Rio Hondo Mining Company. The other made for Messieurs Frank C. Smith and Son, Denver, Colorado, by Colonel L. S. Judd, mining engineer of Vicksburg, Arizona, dated December 14, 1907.

"Read 'em and you'll see what I'm talking about."

Bluefeather read about dikes, transverse veins, andesite porphyry, mica schists, incline shafts, crosscuts, estimates of ore bodies and values, and quotes from assay reports.

Grinder had waited patiently. "Well, kiddo?"

Bluefeather just sat and stared at the reports.

The old man said, "See, there's plenty of clues in those reports about enriched zones. All we gotta do is check ever' one out till we find our lode. Get the idee? Oh, yes siree, you are one lucky young man to be afforded this lifetime opportunity of adventure and riches. Riches, I say. Riches aplenty to buy all of Taos County, were you a mind to."

Bluefeather suddenly felt the need for "just one more" beer. He had five just one mores before he slept from several kinds of Taos exhaustion all occurring in his first night in the little mud village. It was a good thing he didn't know that this would seem like a placid night later on as he and the gringo explored the mountains, the saloons and the artists' society gathered here from all over the world, and he would meet his greatest temptation so far—Lorraine Friedman from New York City.

TWO

IT WAS THE TIME OF HARVESTING EARLY SUMMER HAY IN THE fields and money on Taos plaza. Bluefeather sensed that it was going to be a good, solid summer in the little mud village.

The winter snows had been heavy in the mountains, assuring an abundance of water for the irrigation ditches and the fishing streams that moved toward the Rio Grande a few miles west of town. Daily afternoon showers now kept the air crystal clear, and the dust settled on the unpaved streets of the plaza.

Heavy history had visited the village of Taos and stayed to mesh with the new that was always forming. The savage Pueblo uprising—which had forced the Spaniards all the way back to Mexico, and their ensuing bloody, permanent return—echoed through the adobe walls. From those of fame and power, who had once lived and loved here, there remained many historical, "spirit" presences. Kit Carson was one of the prominent trappers buried here. Hundreds of other mountain men chose Taos as their rendezvous place after trapping for furs in the Rocky Mountains. It was a town accustomed to fame. Names such as the late Governor Charles Bent and the deceased Padre Martinez were as familiar in the village as the name of the current mayor.

To Bluefeather and other casual observers, Taos seemed like a normal, unhurried world, but deceivingly so, for underneath and mostly hidden was a creative force, like artillery explosions taking place in selected spots in the mountains, in unseen art studios and occasionally along the curving side streets of the adobe town.

The tiny mud settlement was like a magnet. The artists and their colony attracted visitors and buyers from around the world. People came and rented homes for a month or the summer to paint, to take photographs, to try to absorb a mystique that mostly defied their attempts at description.

People of worldly import like Georgia O'Keeffe, Leopold Stokowski and many, many more would visit the matriarch of Taos (and possibly matriarch of American art and artists), Mable Dodge Luhan, and her Taos Indian husband, Tony. The Taos masters, Oscar Berninghaus, Bert Phillips, Ernest Blumenschein and others, were all painting, enjoying growing sales and recognition around the world.

The Pueblo Indians tolerated the visitors, posed as artists' models and allowed photographs in designated areas, both at the multistory adobe dwelling and in town. Their images, including many of Bluefeather's kin, were being hung in homes, buildings and museums across the United States and in other countries. Unimpressed by their fame and attractiveness, they went about their farming, horse and cattle trading, fishing and mostly private ceremonies just as they had for hundreds of years. They accepted the invasions of varied peoples with astounding grace and dignity, as long as the visitors didn't interfere in their ancient religious ceremonies without invitation.

Almost the entire east side of the plaza was a large,

vacant lot surrounded with hitching rails for saddle horses and wagons and teams. Bluefeather loved and belonged in this place of unhurried activity. The Indians, blanketed like bedouins, would come and go and gather in colorful groups to wait, talk, trade and drink or just enjoy the warm sun as did the old men—*los viejos*—of the Hispanic world.

The sparkling atmosphere gave the great bluffs and forested canyons of the sacred Taos Mountain—north of the village and the pueblo—such a clarity that it dominated Taos, its people and all the wild creatures as if it were the first and largest cathedral built by the gods.

It was on the other side of this massive prominence, up Twining Canyon, that Bluefeather and Grinder started their search. To form their main camp, they pitched their tent by the creek at the foot of Frazier Mountain.

They could see the green malachite, oxidized stains of copper, painting the bluff above them. It was real, but still an illusion, because the fifty-yard-wide stain was just that. Many a prospector had been lured up those bluffs thinking the stain was a massive deposit of solid ore.

As they started their search for Grinder's lost mine, he told his new protégé, "Remember son, everybody in the whole world is a treasure hunter. Most of 'em never find much 'cause they haven't got the guts to take the extra steps. Anyway, you gotta have the smell for gold. I can smell it like it was a skunk. I can sniff it out no matter where it hides. I ain't no rock hound. I'm a pure and sure gold-dog."

Bluefeather would have followed him unhesitatingly off a thousand-foot bluff if he had said the vein was at the bottom. He wasn't sure, yet, but he felt he was gonna be a hell of a gold-smeller himself.

THREE

BULL OF THE WOODS MOUNTAIN IS JUST ABOVE TIMBERLINE, over twelve thousand feet high, in the Sangre de Cristo Range just north of Wheeler Peak, the highest point in New Mexico. They moved their camp up there with the help of the burro, Tony, right by the headwaters of Twining Creek.

As they packed to climb, Grinder said, "Don't worry. It's just three whistles and a fart to the top of this mountain."

After eight hours, on a trail suited only to the agility of mountain goats, they finally reached their intended campsite just at dusk. Bluefeather was a tired young man marveling at the old man's stamina but questioning his mathematical calculations.

They soon found the porphyry outcrop mentioned in the geological report, just forty or fifty yards east of the highest point on the mountain. There were flowerlike crystals of malachite and azurite copper in it. They found other rich-looking samples of ore in many old tunnels scattered over the sides of the mountain, but no visible gold.

They cut samples of the best prospects, and Grinder

showed his young protégé how to thoroughly mix up the rock cuttings in a sack, quarter them on a tarpaulin and then quarter them again. They reduced the weight of their load enormously by following Grinder's advice: "One of the great failings in prospecting is high-grading yourself when you know the values are not there. You ain't cheatin' nobody but yourself."

Bluefeather and his Raton relatives were miners, but black coal was always easily identifiable. Over and over he had felt the bloodswell of discoveries that turned out to be yellow, shiny iron pyrites (truly fool's gold) or chalcopyrite copper that was an even duller yellow and closer to the hue of real gold.

After he had excitedly shown these discoveries to Grinder, twenty or thirty times, the old miner sat him down and said, "Look," handing Bluefeather the ore glass and a nugget from the vial. "Now look at the pyrite. See. It's shinier. It's like glass. It's fake gold. Raw gold is more loosely grained, and that takes the luster off it. You getting the idee, kiddo?"

"I'm beginning to, I think . . . just a few more days and I'll . . ."

"Well now, I'll tell you the secret of this wondrously malleable metal. See this here nugget? A jeweler can hammer that so thin it would reach halfway to the bottom of the mountain without it separating. Now ain't that a wonderful thing?"

"Yeah. Yeah, it sure is, but what's the secret you were gonna tell me?"

"Oh, that. Okay. If there's any doubt at all about it being gold . . . it ain't."

Bluefeather soon learned the truth of this and thereby saved much time throughout his life for better, more productive activities.

They worked downward now to the many caved-in tunnels on Frazier Mountain, sampling the outcroppings above them, digging, chipping, looking for the twenty-foot-wide brown dikes where they intersected with much narrower quartz veins, hoping every second to finally look upon the spot of Grinder's rich lode.

Bluefeather slithered into tunnels that were still open, sometimes almost getting trapped. In case there was a hang-up or a cave-in, the rule was that one man always waited outside any tunnel entered by the other.

The insides of the tunnels were hauntingly beautiful with the damp copper glowing in all its varied blues and yellows. Most of the tunnels on Frazier Mountain slowly leaked water from the heavy winter snows through their minute cracks and perforations.

Bluefeather finally learned that one could become entranced by the silent beauty; the sound broken only by his own chipping or the occasional dripping of water.

Grinder had to tell him again. "Hey, you're gettin' carried away with the purty and wastin' valuable samplin' time. I know. I did the same thing when I was your age."

Bluefeather heeded the advice. They had covered every visible prospect on Frazier Mountain that they felt had any merit, when they suddenly discovered a streak of ruby silver on the edge of a tiny hole. Bluefeather bent down and shined a flashlight down into the darkness. There was a huge hole under them, and their weight was on very thin rock. They retreated quickly, walking ever so softly.

"That's a stope. Miners drop ore from above when they find a rich pocket. Those guys came upon an enrichment of ruby silver and just let it drop."

Lower down they saw where the tunnel had been blasted under the vein. Bluefeather began digging furiously at the portal. Grinder sat down to cut a big chew of tobacco. He stuffed it into his cheek and worked his gums in amusement at Bluefeather's wasted efforts.

"Well, he has to learn it all," Grinder thought to himself. "Might as well let him chance a look."

It turned out to be a hell of a risk. The minute space he had dug suddenly opened so big that the light barely reached the top, revealing the tiny opening they had almost stepped into earlier. Bluefeather had some difficulty enticing Grinder to join him for a look. With their carbide lamps and the flashlight, the massive stope was revealed. They could see scatterings of silver still hanging above, absolutely unrecoverable.

"Somebody took a wad outa this stope. I'll bet there was high gold values along with the silver, but they ruined the mine forever," Grinder said with a sad hurt in his voice.

Bluefeather didn't need this explained. He could see it would be impossible to timber the hole where tons of rock hung loose, ready to fall. The mine had been raped and plundered so drastically—for a quick gain—that it could no longer be worked. The previous miners had ruined it for anyone who followed.

Bluefeather had already been in several tunnels on Bull of the Woods that were in the same condition. These were the first undeniable physical signs of the waste of human greed that he had witnessed. As he thought of the long-ago miners, he was stunned and enraged. Then he wondered if he would do the same when he and Grinder found their place to stope. He swore he wouldn't, no matter what Grinder did. But of course, he was young, and his elders had told him that ideals were either thrown away in youth or kept and expanded in old age. There was no in-between. Hell, he didn't know for sure what he might do.

He was relieved to hear Grinder's voice say, "Let's get

out of here. A strong thought could send this mountain crashin' down on us, kiddo."

"Kiddo's got the message," Bluefeather answered as they started for the opening, the nervous sweat curling his dark hair and running down his face so the salt filmed his large eyes with tears.

The assays came back and told a story that verified the validity of the old geological reports. So far the veins revealed in the tunnels and the surface cuts showed an average of one and a half percent copper and a little gold and silver by-products—too low-grade to mine without a huge, expensive mill. The intersection of the veins and formations showed an enrichment, but nothing to compare with the placer and rock Grinder had found; and most of these had already been usurped by tunnels and stopes underneath them.

Grinder put a confident voice to it, explaining, "Lookee, son, we've narrowed it down now. There's a lot less to prospect, so that means we'll be finding her soon."

Grinder walked stiffly but recklessly about the mountains, weaving, wobbling, moving on as carefree as a blue jay. Bluefeather knew that the crazy gringo's equilibrium had been knocked askew ever since his fall at the discovery point, and he worried every second they were climbing, even though the old man rarely fell hard enough to break the skin.

Then early one evening Grinder got up from the campfire to empty his tobacco juice can, stumbled and fell in a little rocky wash not two feet deep and broke his left leg below the knee.

"Now don't that scald the hog. We're gettin' close to the find, kiddo, or the devil would never have tripped me like that."

By the time Bluefeather hauled Grinder into town, got his leg set, delivered him two cases of beer and a carton

of Beechnut chewing tobacco, made a trip back to the
camp to get Tony and all their gear, he was ready for a
small vacation. He could afford to take one, since a
widow who lived three houses away from Grinder,
Maude Cisneros, would visit, comfort, cook and drink
with him. Bluefeather decided to go visit his relatives at
the pueblo.

Maude assured him, "Now, boy, you take all the time
you might need for a good visit with your grandpapa. I
sure enough take care of the gringo here. We been
amigos for seventy million years."

A friendship that old could mean nothing but good
company for them both. Bluefeather was totally relaxed
with her now.

He motioned for Maude to follow him outside where
he handed her nine dollars, saying, "Maude, we want that
leg to heal properly, so you be sure he gets some meat
and eggs and try to get him to drink some fresh milk
along with all that beer."

"No worries," she waved a heavy arm in the air. "No
bother. I take care of him like leetle baby boy." She
smiled so big her cheeks rose up and almost hid her dark,
happy eyes.

"I'm sure you will, Ma'am. I'll drop by in a week or so."

"Now you stay right over there at the pueblo long as
you like, and don't worry yourself none. Get the idee,
kiddo?" And they both laughed at her mimicry. She had
obviously done a lot of careful listening to the gringo in
the past.

He left feeling free of responsibility. His natural-born,
coyote ears heard the two old friends talking inside the
house as he readied to leave.

"Hey, you beautiful old Spanish woman, get us a new
beer."

Maude answered, laughing with him, "Only the rich

are Spanish in Taos. I'm a Mexican because I'm poor. Better you call me Mexican. Don't you savvy nothin', you toothless old gringo? Huh?"

Bluefeather moved away smiling for them. He felt good because his friends did. That's the way he was.

FOUR

It was the time of things that moved about the earth at Taos Pueblo. Bluefeather eagerly pitched in and helped his grandfather and uncle make the first cutting of grass hay in their allotted pasture. It was a good crop from plentiful summer showers this year.

Two horses pulled his grandfather on a mower that cut the long grass close to the ground. Bluefeather drove another team pulling a rake and piled up the long windrows to dry. When it was cured enough they would stack it next to his grandfather's barn to feed to the livestock throughout the long, harsh winter.

They worked in the fields all day, skipping the noon meal. By evening they were ravenous, but the long day seemed a little shorter for the field hands because of the feast they anticipated at the end of the day. They knew Bluefeather's grandmother would have beef and corn, or sometimes a stew made from soaked venison jerky with several kinds of vegetables and chiles. And always, she would have many loaves of fresh bread she baked in the *horno* (outdoor oven). Bluefeather had missed her bread with its thick crust and tender insides. Just the thought or smell of it made him dizzy and caused saliva to accumulate in his mouth. Then his absolutely favorite thing was the dessert she would serve made from fresh fruit, when it was in season; if not, she used dried apples or apricots.

The little time that was left after the cutting and the stacking was spent repairing barns and equipment and looking after the livestock. Lots of visiting went on with his kin in the Bear Clan. However, his grandfather, the shaman, was always on call to those in need of spiritual or physical healing. They were a team, his grandparents, because during the time he spent in the cedar-burning ceremony to rid the body of bad spirits, she would prepare whatever combination of herbs it took to benefit any fleshly illness. Bluefeather was constantly amazed that they made no discernible signs to each other or conversation as they worked so perfectly as a team.

He remembered when he was about seven years old and his family had been visiting here while his father hunted deer with his uncle Stump Jumper. After the hunt Bluefeather recalled watching them dress the deer out when a signal, unseen to him, came from atop the highest level of the mud building from a kiva chieftain denoting "the time for staying still." (For forty days, beginning December 12 and ending January 20, the pueblo occupants do not chop wood or dig in the earth. They can, if needed, ride horseback only at a normal walk, to care for the livestock, but they cannot drive a wagon and team. For this period of time, they try to become as close to dormant and as in rhythm with the earth entering deep winter as possible.)

When the quiet time would come upon the pueblo, Valerio always loaded his family in the car and eased off the reservation and back to Raton to hold down his job in the mine. Bluefeather could never forget the sudden switch in tempo of his two worlds. There was no concern this summer, though, for he soon adapted to the pueblo ways as his mother once did.

Although visitors are allowed to attend the Turtle Dance, Corn Dance, their very special Deer Dance and a couple of other ceremonies, the core of Taos religious events is rigidly protected from anyone outside the pueblo. The kiva and Bluelake rites are the most carefully guarded.

Just the year before, Bluefeather had been honored with participation in both. So it was no surprise to him when his grandfather advised him one evening that they would be going to the sacred cave on the northwest side of Taos Mountain. He was allowed no supper that night and no food the next day.

They were all elders of the Bear Clan who rode through the foothills to the Mother Mountain. They wore varied colored blankets of fine weaves, used only in ceremonies. While doing ordinary work the elders wore Arab-style blankets made of plain cotton from the local J.C. Penney department store and folded them to cover their heads and the sides of their faces as well as their bodies.

Bluefeather was riding in the center of the group and knew that he was the focus of this trip. He was not afraid, nor did he question the hunger of his empty stomach but instead looked forward to whatever would occur with confidence and a feeling of warm and total trust.

They rode across a canyon and up a trail on its side and tied their horses. It was just sundown. His grandfather took his medicine bundle. The others carried skin drums and a large blanket. They walked the final distance to the cave. There was a neat stack of twigs and larger sticks piled near its entrance waiting for them. They would replace them when they left.

The youngest member present of the Bear Clan was his uncle Stump Jumper. He was allowed because he was a shaman-apprentice to his father. He was in direct line after uncounted centuries to carry on the sacred traditions. He built the fire as the night swallowed the last sunlight.

Bluefeather's grandfather, Moon Looker, motioned him to sit in the middle of the blanket and watch the fire. He performed the cedar-smoke cleansing, spreading the smoke in all directions with an eagle feather. The drums beat softly. The shaman walked into the cave alone for a few silent moments then returned to the circle. Chants were sung. The fire flickered and danced to the beat. Drum. Drum. Drum. Chant. Chant. Drum. All was one.

Bluefeather saw a rabbit jump out of the fire. It leaped playfully on the far end of the blanket, then another and another rabbit played there until there were six. They were cottontails, fat with full, soft fur. They paid him no attention as they moved about touching noses. Then four of them ran swiftly in different directions toward the four winds. One dug swiftly down into the rock, and the last leapt straight into the sky. They all vanished.

Now a stranger stood between the blanket and fire smiling at Bluefeather and speaking, "Well, hello there, dear brudder Bluefeather. I come to meet you, for sure."

"Who are you? Where did you come from? What are you doing here?" Bluefeather asked.

"Just like other white feller, asking three questions at same time to be answered. Okay, all right then. One. I'm Dancing Bear," and he did a little dance that did indeed imitate an upright bear. "Two. I come from other side. Three. I been called up on assignment to be your guiding spirit."

"I don't think I need any spirit guide. I'm doing just fine."

Dancing Bear did a fast step that might have been part Deer Dance, Turtle Dance and the Texas Two-Step, say-

ing, "You don't need me this time right now, but things
change from one sun to the other. Maybe so, you could
use a little professional help someday. Maybe."

Bluefeather jumped to his feet, and Dancing Bear flew
up on a rock to avoid possible attack and great danger.
He squatted there on the precarious perch smiling at
Bluefeather, with flickers of firelight washing back and
forth across his face and looking like a big sitting bird.

"What kind of Indian are you anyway?" asked
Bluefeather, studying the beaded moccasins, the soft
buckskin suit, the featherless band around his head that
held his loose, iron-gray, shoulder-length hair, mostly in
place.

"That is one good question. One. I'm proud of you for
being brief already."

"You still haven't answered my one question."

"Well, now lookee here, then," and Dancing Bear leapt
from the rock, whirling in the air all the way down next to
the fire. He did dances so fast that Bluefeather thought
his legs must break off—Cherokee Stomp Dance, Apache
War Dance, Ute Rain Dance, Creek Eagle Dance, Taos
Deer Dance and on and on—until Bluefeather's eyes
were dizzy and his hearing impaired.

He shouted, "All right. That's enough. Stop it, you
hear? Stop it."

Dancing Bear stopped with both feet several feet off
the ground, arms outstretched, motionless as if he were
carved from the magic mountain itself.

Bluefeather took a deep breath, staring wide-eyed at
his guide. "It may come to pass that I need a spirit guide
someday, but I don't need a cockeyed whirling dervish
telling me what to do."

"Oh, oh, oh, hi, yi, yi. I never, for sure, advise my dear
brudders. I let 'em build their own trails."

"Well then, what good could it possibly be if a guiding spirit doesn't guide?"

"One good question. Thank you. Maybe we are titled wrong. Maybe we should be addressed as pointers, like bird dogs. Huh? What you think of that, dear brudder? Maybe you can call me Dancing Bear the pointing spirit. That please you more?" He proceeded to dance around bent halfway over, pointing first with one finger at parts of the mountain then doing the same with the other and then into the star-speckled heavens. Then he whirled like a scared cat, pointing both index fingers at Bluefeather's heart, and laughed until he could no longer hold his arms out. Anyway, he needed his hands to wipe the tears of mirth from his eyes, shiny as little black diamonds.

"I got to go now. Authority is calling me. Remember, dear brudder, you don't own no earth here. It on loan, see? See?" Bluefeather tried to speak, but Dancing Bear paid no mind and spoke on. "Same thing 'bout you. Nobody around here on this earth own you either. Fair? Fair? Huh?" And he was gone.

Bluefeather's yell traveled across the western foothills and miles of sagebrush-covered desert all the way to the Rio Grande Gorge. "Hey, come back here . . . you deserter, and tell me what I'm supposed to do. You can't just start me out with dances and talk that wouldn't make sense to a corncob and then leave me. Hey! Hey, you!" But Dancing Bear was gone. In his spirit mind, he had done all that was necessary.

The fire was low. The elders encircled Bluefeather again. He lay on the blanket and slept deeply like a played-out puppy.

FIVE

Bluefeather rode in the wagon beside his cousin Smiling Dog, who drove the gray team past the Manby house on North Pueblo Road and on down to Taos plaza. Smiling Dog tied the team to a hitching post near three saddle horses. Several of Smiling Dog's friends were standing about in twos and threes waiting to visit. Bluefeather knew if Smiling Dog got the chance, he'd get drunk today. Even though it was against the law for Indians to buy whiskey, those who wanted it did so surreptitiously out back doors of saloons and from bootleggers. Since the Indians were constantly afraid of being caught, fined and jailed, the pints were emptied as fast as possible. This sudden jolt of alcohol to the brain could have made even an elephant stagger.

Bluefeather wasn't interested in drinking today. In fact, he drank only occasionally, and only when the situation seemed to demand it. He loved to explore Taos plaza—the center of the village, a permanent local stage. It often held a sampling of the entire world. Bluefeather loved to watch the kaleidoscope of colors—the blankets, clothing, jewelry, hair and skin. He was fascinated by it all. The shops held beautiful paintings, Indian pottery, religious *bultos* (upright crucifixes) and *retablos* (paintings on flat wood to hang on a wall), Navajo blankets and every other southwestern art and craft.

There was always a generous mixture of colorfully blanketed Indians from various pueblos present on the plaza. Then there were the Spanish Americans or Mexicans (as some preferred to be called). Most of the town's public officials, city and state, plus the police force were of this nationality. Then there were the mongrelized gringos, some with bloodlines beyond research.

A few tourists were taking photos of the adobe architecture, but their main interest seemed to be the Indians. Boom! It struck Bluefeather that he had adapted so well to the pueblo life, he'd forgotten that he, too, was wearing a faded pink blanket and had allowed his hair to grow into two respectably long braids. What would he do if a tourist approached him for a photograph? Would he be a fakery if he posed as a full-blooded Indian? If not, how could he explain? The problem lasted only a moment, for the passing of scattered conversations made him forget. He relished just walking along overhearing bits and pieces of all the varied conversations. He rarely looked at the speakers. It took strong will not to, but this was part of the game. He wanted his mind to picture the person, not his eyes.

"That lady in the curio store said the governor is coming tomorrow to give a speech here on the plaza. Shall we stay over?" one male voice said.

"I can't imagine why you would think we'd like to hear a political speech while we're here. This plaza says all the things I'm interested in," another male voice replied.

Then Bluefeather heard a female voice join the two male ones so strongly he almost broke his neck to keep from turning his head.

She said, "The tourists don't come to New Mexico to

see politicians. They come to see the Indians, the cowboys and the artists that inhabit these adobe buildings."

Then, on a few more steps, he heard, "Did you folks
come through Amarillo, Clayton and Raton?"

"No, we came down from Denver."

"That's also a beautiful drive. We came that way two
years ago."

More walkers and talkers moved perpetually along the
rectangular boundaries of the plaza.

"I know that the greatest thoughts are never told or
written, but let me try and explain this dream I had last
night . . ."

Bluefeather really would have appreciated hearing the
rest of this and was tempted to follow them—even if it
was against his eavesdropping rules—but the voice
moved on, diminishing, as another floated into hearing
range.

"He always picks the dumbest women."

"Yeah, but boy are they lookers. Give him some
credit."

Bluefeather moved on, stopped in front of La Fonda
de Taos Hotel and turned to look across the center of the
plaza.

He heard a hurried voice that didn't seem to fit Taos
but was of the village just the same. "Terrasita read the
cards for me yesterday. I've just got to tell you all about
it."

"I have something to tell you, too. Mabel has insisted
we come for cocktails before dinner tonight. She has this
artistic genius she wants us to meet."

"Introducing genius is Mabel's business. We should go.
Let's go into La Fonda and have a drink and catch up on
our visiting."

Bluefeather saw a young couple crossing the corner of
the plaza in front of him. This time he watched them as

he heard the Anglo man say, "Taos is as mysterious and indecipherable as knowledge itself. The more you feel the mountains and mysticism, the wider the cavern of the unknown becomes."

The pretty girl, holding her mate's arm, leaned her head into his shoulder and said, "Oh, I know, and I don't want to leave here. I wish we could just stay here forever."

He watched them while their voices trailed off into silence as if caught in a vortex of crosswinds. Bluefeather thought they were strangers, but somehow they were also his kin. Maybe the young man's thoughts were felt deeply enough and spoken honestly enough that they would always be part of Taos plaza.

The next voice he heard was as melodious as a great song, youthful as the first sunflower bloom and vital as water.

"Excuse me, but may I please take your picture?" He didn't move while he waited for another voice to answer her. None came. Before he realized she was speaking to him, there she stood, camera in hand, directly in front of him.

He turned his blanketed head slightly to stare at a golden young woman. How could it be? Had Grinder the Gringo mesmerized him with visions of the precious metal to the point that everything he saw was impregnated with it? Her blonde hair was streaked with golden strands. Even her wide, hazel eyes contained little, sparkling gold nuggets. The sun had caressed her skin and carefully brushed it in even strokes with the color of its rays.

She moved directly in front of him, looking up intensively as if she was trying to read his mind—his very soul.

"Will it be all right?" she asked, suddenly relaxing, exuding vitality and eagerness.

"You're speaking to me? I . . . I . . . uh, well okay."

"Oh, gladness," she said.

Gladness? Bluefeather thought, What kind of woman is this who uses the word "gladness"? Well, whatever, she doesn't hesitate once she gets your attention.

"Hi, I'm Lorraine Friedman."

"Good to meet you. I'm Bluefeather Fellini."

"What an unusual name."

She looked at him through the camera lens and snapped a couple of shots. Then she stopped and studied him as if he were a new dress she might consider buying. She backed off, her eyes never leaving his face, and stood by a shiny, new 1935 Buick roadster. She said to him around the windshield, "Everyone takes pictures on the plaza. Do you mind if we go somewhere different?" She didn't wait for him to answer. "Okay. Get in."

Bluefeather couldn't believe what was happening. He removed the blanket from his head and wrapped it around his waist. He walked slowly, half hypnotized, to the other side and got into her car without saying another word.

She drove expertly around the plaza and headed east to Taos Canyon. It was a short drive of five or six miles. She parked by the creek and directed Bluefeather in many poses in the sunlight and shadow, totally absorbed, instructing him with many "pleases," "move here," "move there," "tilt your head up," "look at the mountain," "look at the creek."

"Good. Good. Perfect. Ah yes, delightful. Beautiful. Beautiful. Now look straight at me. Hold it." Click. Click.

All the time she was posing him, she was intermittently explaining that she and her divorced mother had rented a summer home here; that they were from New York City; that her mother owned and operated both a modeling and advertising firm, but she was not one of her mother's photographers; that hers was a different calling with the camera, although she wasn't sure what it was yet; that she was filled with gladness that he was so kind to pose for her; and would he please call her "Lorrie," and she would like to call him "Blue."

"It seems everyone—professionals and amateurs— wants to take pictures of the older Indians whose lives are written on their faces and in their eyes. You see, Blue, I want to try something different. I want to capture that fragility of youth looking forward to a life not yet formed . . . like watching the pyramids going up."

Bluefeather thought that was sure a fine ambition, but his head was overloaded with all this sudden posing and bountiful information. He'd asked for none of it. How had this happened?

He had been on the verge of getting testy when she said, "That's enough for today. I've imposed on you far too long. Could I express my thanks? We'll go back to town and have drinks and dinner on me."

Now he faced something else he had never before experienced. His long hair and his Indian attire posed a new problem. He did look like a full-blood now. Earlier, Lorrie had thought he was joking when he told her his father was a full-blooded Italian.

He blurted it out, "Don't you know it's against the law for Indians to buy whiskey?"

Lorrie suddenly became still where she was sitting on a log putting her gear in a camera bag. Then she lifted her face up to his with a mixed-up emotion emitting from her eyes and said, "Oh, I'm sorry."

Bluefeather knew she meant it. He said, "It's all right. I really don't care that much about drinking, but if we want it, it's easy enough to get. There are bootleggers all over town."

"Well, I'll feed you then. There's no law against that."
They laughed.

They laughed for the next few hours. Bluefeather
would never be able to remember at what. He was rapidly being enclosed in the sweet-scented cocoon of young
love.

It happened on the mesa west of town where they
parked and watched the sun go down across the Taos
desert. So many people had tried to paint this happening,
and most had failed. It was just too much. The sky was on
fire, with streaks of purple clouds fracturing the sun's rays
so far into the clear sky that it seemed as if it would take
the whole universe to dissipate them. The suddenly
brassy oranges and violets glowed momentarily like a gift.
Then there were the last rays that flared up as a good-bye
before the day and night blended in a profound stillness
and quietness.

They talked and caressed there in the desert, walking
about in the twilight smelling the sage that pungently
perfumed hundreds of square miles. They kissed and
closed their eyes so that all this was integrated into their
nonthinking, purely feeling moment of magic. They understood the coyote that howled in a draw near them,
because on this evening they were as much a part of their
surroundings as the animal. Youth. In fluorescence.

She drove him back to the plaza to see if Smiling Dog's
wagon was still there; if it wasn't, she would drive
Bluefeather to the pueblo. It was a good thing the team
was still tied there. It was difficult for them to go their
separate ways. They kept holding on to one another as if
they would be parted forever. Finally, after agreeing to
meet the next day, Bluefeather gathered the will to part.

She reluctantly backed the roadster onto the plaza
street as he untied the team's lines and crawled up on the
wagon seat. There was Smiling Dog, lying dead or passed

out, in the back of the wagon. As Bluefeather backed up the wagon and reined the horses around toward the pueblo, Smiling Dog sat up, pushing at his eyes with the backs of his hands as if to be sure they would still open.

"I got too much fun goin' over there at Taos town. I think maybe it's a good thing to own some of this fun stuff."

Bluefeather agreed, guiding the horses toward a moon-burned Taos Mountain, breathing wine, feeling heaven, moving on a road of rapture. It was the time of no thinking.

SIX

YESTERDAY BLUEFEATHER HAD INTENDED TO SPEND A COUPLE of hours exploring Taos plaza and visiting his partner, Grinder. Instead, he had spent from just past noon until almost midnight with Lorrie Friedman, Taos summer resident and photographer from back East. Of course, Taos being the absolute and only center of the universe, everything else was "back there," "over there," "down there," "up there" and especially "out there." Golden lady Lorrie Friedman was the center of the center.

Bluefeather drove Grinder's old Ford truck slowly away from the pueblo, for his mind was dangerously elsewhere. He was pleased that Lorrie liked to drive, because in truth, he didn't. While riding a mule or walking, he could think. A mule would not deceive him and run off the road or into any oncoming traffic. Walking was such an ancient instinct that he could descend a mile-deep shaft, climb a two-mile mountain or make love along the way in his picture-mind, without falling or crashing into objects. Driving a car was an entirely different matter, and it was particularly dangerous in his present state of mind. He woke up this morning to find himself so in love with Lorrie that he would certainly die if he didn't hold her again soon.

It felt just like first love, but it wasn't. No, Lorrie was actually his third love.

First love had struck Bluefeather's heart at age eleven, as suddenly as lightning bolting a tall tree. She was Leesa Curry, a petite, soft-spoken blonde in her early twenties. Miss Curry was his fifth-grade schoolteacher.

It was the third day of the fall school term. Billy Martinez had brought a garter snake to school in a cigar box, and it was causing a considerable amount of girlish squealing in the back of the classroom. Miss Curry, unable to get the class to come to order, straightened herself to her full five-foot-one-inch height and marched to the scene of the excitement.

She calmly reached over, took the snake in hand, held it up for the rest of the class to see, explained that this harmless little creature did a considerable amount of good in its natural habitat and asked Billy to please set it free during the lunch break so it could get on with its business of ridding the world of unwanted pests.

When she gently returned the snake to its captor's care and returned to her desk, Bluefeather was almost blinded by the dizzying surge that passed through his being—it stayed with him all year.

It was, in the end, a very productive happening. He did all kinds of extra schoolwork, and his homework was always handed in on time and done as neatly as possible. He read many more books than were required of him and found that reading was just as exciting and rewarding as Miss Curry had said it was. Zane Grey and Jack London showed him vistas of deserts and snow, action and adventure, even beauty that he had looked at without seeing before. He became more open now to everything. Aware. His major goal in life was to gain her smiling approval and a gentle hand on his shoulder, and he received them both.

His second love had come at the age of sixteen when one day, in one second, he had noticed that Margaret Bertinoli had the longest black eyelashes, the biggest dark-brown eyes that danced with mischief and mirth, and the shapeliest long legs of anyone in high school. He spent over half his time thinking about rubbing his hands over them. Then he found himself finally thinking about the rest of her, most of the time, and would have gone uneducated and frothing-mouth mad if he hadn't decided that the only answer for him was to eventually marry her.

Once he declared this to be his lifetime commitment, both families were pleased. After he graduated and went to work in Trinidad, Colorado (only eleven miles away), his anticipated progress in the mines and ability to start a family were proven.

The day he received his second promotion at the mine, he decided to start the formal proceedings of asking Margaret's father for a meeting that would determine how he would spend the rest of his life. Before this could come about, though, Grinder the Gringo and his golden rocks had come crashing into Bluefeather's world.

His decision to follow a golden dream to Taos, thus leaving his intended bride and his glowing future in the mines, sent waves of despair and anguish, mixed with anger, among the planners and plotters of his entire future. He did not blame them, and he felt much agony and shame before they were finished with their admonishments. He could not stop this terrible move any more than he could block the blood flowing through his veins.

He thought of the long-legged Margaret often with aching and deep regrets, but such thoughts slowly receded into the mists of Twining Canyon. There was no doubt in Bluefeather's soul that Miss Bertinoli would marry a mine owner's son and become part of those two families, bearing lovely and talented children for all to love and admire.

Bluefeather had broken all family tradition and was becoming excitedly mired in this new world that he himself was inventing as he raced along—second by minute, by hour, by day here in Taos.

Now, this third love, Lorrie, walked out before the imagination of his misty eyes. Her perfect legs moving so gracefully, he expected her to break into ballet steps at any moment. When she pushed the long, thick ponytail of sunshine hair from her face and smiled at him, bells clanged, the lame became well all over the world and dogs had pretty puppies. It was indisputable to Bluefeather that never had there been anyone as intelligent, humorous and beautiful as Lorraine Friedman. She was a genius at photography, and her kisses would have caused Cleopatra to expire from jealousy. Besides that she had 20/20 eyesight and perfect hearing and smelled like a pasture full of spring flowers. Bluefeather was to be complimented no less, especially since he had acquired all this knowledge of his love in less than one day.

Bluefeather was just as surprised on his second date as he was on his first. Lorrie took him home to meet her mother.

The Friedmans' summer house was located at Ranchitos just above Taos Creek on the mesa. The meandering dwelling seemed to have sprouted out of the ground from an adobe seed. All the mountains to the north and east as well as the entire valley were visible from this high point. On the west side, the patio offered a full panorama of the sunsets.

"Mother, this is Blue. Well, I should be more proper; Bluefeather Fellini."

Lorrie's mother moved forward and extended a slender, soft hand with two large, turquoise rings and said, "Hello, Blue. I'm Candi Friedman."

The young prospector was suddenly glued to the floor, and his eyes were surely lying to his brain, for what he saw was a woman so striking she would have turned heads at the Resurrection. Candi Friedman was almost six feet tall and moved like a walking python. Her dark green eyes were even larger than Lorrie's, and her almost blond hair was pulled back in a bun so smooth it made her creamy cheekbones as prominent as an Indian's. Her neck was long, slightly curved and elegant under a small but firm chin. Her face was delicately and softly colored except for the brilliant vermilion she wore on her full lips. Her nose accentuated all these attributes, precisely placed and shaped, to finish off a truly classical beauty.

Bluefeather did not remember any more of their introduction. He found himself sitting in the patio with a drink of Scotch in his hand, astounded that there existed two such females in all the world much less a mother and daughter in the same house.

Candi, who sat in the chair across from him, wore a long, gathered, red-print "squaw" dress with a Navajo concho belt around her waist and a heavy, squash-blossom necklace hung about her neck. Two long, thin slivers of silver dangled lightly from her earlobes. She smoked from a silver cigarette holder, waving it and punctuating sentences with it like the director of a symphony orchestra. She had, in fact, directed the conversation so smoothly, without obvious interrogation, that Bluefeather never realized he had been played like a zither.

Candi had found out his reading preferences, his current ambition as a potential mine owner, his bloodline and his immediate madness for her daughter, and had made him feel comfortably at home while doing it.

"Now then, darlings, shall we have another drink? You

know, Lorrie dear, your friend Blue could make a top model with the proper grooming."

Lorrie went to bring another round of drinks, saying, "Oh Mother, please. Can you just forget the agency for now? All right?"

Candi spoke to Bluefeather so confidently in a voice so strong and smooth that he felt they had been coconspirators for life.

"Of course, dear Blue, you can see what a fine model Lorrie could be, but she'd rather tinker with a camera instead. She won't even use her little hobby in the agency. A pity, don't you think?"

"I don't know anything about that kind of business, Ma'am," Bluefeather said with much sincerity.

"Of course, how silly of me. I forget that people have other interests. It's just so lucrative to loll about for a few hours a week with the photographer doing all the work. There are many fringe benefits to be had for the asking as well."

Before Bluefeather could be made aware of all those fringes, Lorrie returned with the drinks. He had lost count of the number consumed. Bluefeather was floating in the ancient Taos mist of vast mountain green, desert sage, adobe walls, paintings, books and an old, old mystical air that both exhilarated and calmed, with all the edges knocked smooth from booze, beauty and conversation. There was a feeling he had never dreamed existed. This mellowness would surely continue through eternity, since a million years had been enjoyed already, this second day with Lorrie.

They watched the sun go down and the glorious colors rise, catching on the clouds and filling the sky with quickly changing beauty, then they had dinner. Bluefeather was amazed that Candi and Lorrie had pre-

pared the meal so casually while visiting, mixing drinks
and absorbing the stunning sunset.

They had roast leg of lamb, green beans, potatoes, a
green salad and for dessert, a spiced bread pudding. The
red wine was dry and smooth.

Bluefeather Fellini enjoyed the food, the company and
all the world that evening. After giving them each a kiss
on the cheek, Candi Friedman bid them good-night.

"It was so good to finally meet you, Blue. You will
come back often, won't you?" she said with a powerful,
smiling gaze that seemed to push his eyeballs into the
back of his skull.

"Well . . . thank you very much . . . I sure hope I
get to see you again sometime." Bluefeather suddenly
realized that Candi had said she was so glad to "finally"
meet him. It had seemed like many generations since he
had met Lorrie, but the word "finally" made Bluefeather
aware, for an instant at least, that he and Lorrie had been
acquainted for something a little less than two days.

Lorrie walked him out to his car and gave him a good-
night kiss, pushing him away as he felt his hormones and
adrenaline mix with the booze in a truly lustful manner.

"No, no. Tomorrow. We have tomorrow."

With the strength and will of a war elephant,
Bluefeather drove away. He was so extremely charged up
that there was no way he could quit now. He wanted to
go to a saloon but couldn't until he got his long hair cut.

He drove to Grinder's house and was thrilled to see the
glow of the kerosene lamp that meant Grinder was still
up. He went to the open back door and found Grinder
and Maude sitting at the kitchen table drinking beer.

They listened to him go on and on about the
Friedmans. In his elevated state, the young man thought
they were having a normal conversation; however,
Grinder the Gringo and Maude Cisneros could easily dis-

cern otherwise. Bluefeather never stopped talking except to go to the outhouse occasionally.

During one of Bluefeather's outdoor trips, Grinder spat tobacco juice into a tin can, took another swallow of beer and said to Maude, "There's only one thing that'll take a prospector's mind off gold even for a little while, and that's brand-new love."

Maude agreed. "Seems like he's got both kinds of fever real bad."

Bluefeather came back inside, speaking as he closed the door. "Say, did I mention that Lorrie's a hell of a good cook? I never had a better meal in my life."

A few hours and many empty beer bottles later they all slept. Bluefeather enjoyed his dreams on the kitchen floor, where Maude had tossed a Navajo rug over him.

SEVEN

BLUEFEATHER GOT A SHORT, NEAT HAIRCUT AND BOUGHT SOME new clothes. He shaved every day and took a bath in the number-four washtub so often that Grinder remarked, "Son, if your hide springs a leak you're gonna drown."

Bluefeather and Lorrie were together most of each day and night now. They had picnic lunches in the mountains up Twining and Taos canyons. They walked in the desert and studied the lizards and insects. Lorrie was taking pictures all the time in such a casual, unhurried way that Bluefeather was mostly unaware of it. He took her often to see Grinder and Maude and Tony, the burro. They all liked one another right off.

Lorrie and Bluefeather drove over Palo Flechado Pass to explore the now-vacant gold workings at Elizabeth Town near Eagle Nest. It was only a short drive from there through the canyon to Cimarron then northeast to his hometown of Raton. He ached to show her off to his folks, but somehow never brought it up. He did not want to face the scorn and possible retaliation of having deserted Margaret Bertinoli. He had given no promises about his future intentions toward Margaret, but somehow his thoughts had escaped, giving the relatives of two good Italian families a different idea.

Bluefeather admitted to himself that he just did not have the courage to make such a bold and tradition-insulting move as taking a beautiful New York lady into the family lair. Not yet.

He took her to Twining often, where they would sit and listen to the emerald water sing and chant and whisper old stories. Once they climbed up Frazier Mountain. He showed her mineral outcroppings and broke off richly colored specimens for her.

Then she wanted to go into the main tunnel and was momentarily shocked when he said, "Oh, nooo. A woman can't go inside a mine. It'll cause a cave-in."

She looked at him with many questions on her face, but she did not ask him why. Bluefeather was so relieved at her silence, and felt so guilty at his abruptness, that he broke all rules and told her about Grinder's lost quartz vein. He was very pleased when her attitude was one of shared excitement. He had feared that she would ridicule their search.

They went out for meals and drinks a couple of times, and no one even questioned serving him liquor. The short haircut and the new clothes had made him someone else. Just a few weeks back he was a pueblo Indian, and now he was a young Latin squiring about a classy lady from Manhattan. People stared and whispered to one another, "What a handsome couple those two make."

With this freedom, Bluefeather could wait no longer to take Grinder, Maude and Lorrie to the Don Fernando for a party. Not all the plans worked out. Maude's youngest son had an upset stomach. She felt he shouldn't be left alone, so she missed the revelry.

After a fine Mexican dinner, Grinder said, "Let's take a table near the bar so we can get down to some basic lying and drinking and have some serious fun. Get the idee, kiddos?"

Once they got Grinder off his crutches and his busted leg propped up, he began to stuff his lip with chewing tobacco. Bluefeather felt a twinge of apprehension about how Lorrie might react to seeing Grinder gum tobacco on one side of his toothless mouth while drinking beer with the other. His concern was unfounded. If it bothered her, which he was sure it must, she did not allow it to show.

They had already consumed several beers. Bluefeather and Lorrie danced many dances to the jukebox music and were feeling uninhibited and full of play. When they went back to their table, Lorrie gave him a smile that would have candied acid. Her eyes poured almost visible emotions into his chest, of such warming and primal opiate that he truly thought he would explode. So he decided to express the special joy he was feeling by leaping upon their table, with the agility that a leading ballet dancer would have envied, and performing some of the dances that his guiding spirit had created and initiated. He was certain his rendition would meet with Dancing Bear's approval.

Grinder shouted and pounded his crutches on the floor, trying to help his exuberant protégé any way he could. The bartender watched tolerantly. As long as they were spending money, and there was no great damage or overwhelming disapproval from the other patrons, he would allow the extra exertion of fun. Some of the other customers actually smiled and yelled encouragement. Only a few seemed to resent joy being carried to this extreme.

Lorrie marveled at his dexterity, although it took a few beats to acquire such a sanguine attitude as Grinder had accepted as perfectly natural. The beer glasses shook, but none were touched, and not a drop was spilled. Bluefeather made what appeared to be a misstep and Lorrie was quick to chime in, "No teetering on the table, Blue. 'Tain't allowed."

"Don't worry, precious one. I've already drunk myself completely weightless and I'm almost floating."

Grinder understood this perfectly and said, "Hell, that's nothing, kiddo. I can drink myself invisible. Like right now. I bet nobody in here can see me—maybe the crutches, but not Old Grinder."

Bluefeather sailed gracefully to the floor then sat down and suddenly became profoundly serious, looking all around with great concern. "Where's Grinder? When did he leave? I hope he didn't miss all of my dance."

Lorrie pitched right in, "I don't know. I didn't see him go."

"Well, he'll be back in a minute or he wouldn't have left his crutches dancing all by themselves."

"Of course," Lorrie said, slapping her hands on the tabletop, "I hadn't thought about that." Then she said, "Oh look, Blue. He's come back," and she pointed in exaggeration at Grinder.

They all laughed as freely as three-year-old children, raised their drinks in a wordless toast and then had a moment of quiet seriousness.

Grinder seized this opportunity to launch into one of his adventures about hunting Maximilian's treasure on the Yaqui Reservation in northwestern Mexico. He was on the part where some of his crew had—against his strict orders—tried to mess around with some Yaqui women. The resultant little war had left seventeen bodies for the buzzards. He was not quite to the juicy part of his story when he was interrupted.

A very large young man loomed over their table, cleared his throat and with the tiniest crooked grin said,

"The old man's messy mouth is making my wife sick," and pointed to the table where a very pretty black-headed woman sat glaring at them with dark eyes of disgust.

Grinder was so busy setting up the geography of his private Yaqui war that he did not even notice the man. He talked on with a little stream of tobacco juice making a muddy creek from the corner of his mouth and on under his chin.

One thing Bluefeather's father had told him was always to try joking his way out of trouble before taking extreme actions. Bluefeather said, "Tell your wife not to worry. He'll swallow the cud any minute now."

The man put two hands, big as a fence-builder's gloves, on the table and hovered over Bluefeather like a lightning-burned thundercloud.

"Get that filthy old man out of here right now or I will do it myself."

"He's got a broken leg and he's a little deaf. It might take till about closing time."

Lorrie was watching the mean interloper and trying to hear Grinder's tale at the same time. The fun was beginning to be drained out of the evening.

"You gettin' smart with me, feller?" the mean one roared.

People at other tables stopped visiting, their mouths open from partially finished sentences, and were quiet. Some froze with drinks tilted to their lips while other drinks remained in midair.

"Please, sir, we don't . . ." Bluefeather started to say.

The man put his hand on the back of Grinder's neck and started to speak, "Say, you old . . ."

Bluefeather had slipped his left foot behind one of the man's legs. He smashed his right foot into the knee with all he had. The trip and the kick were supposed to flip the mean man backward so hard his head would bounce off the floor, and his knee should be so damaged that upon regaining consciousness he would be in no condition to leap up and create harm to innocent people.

He did go backward and crash into his own table, knocking his wife upside down so that her full skirt flipped up, giving the bar patrons a brief floor show. He scrambled up growling and sounding beastlike.

Bluefeather was a little late. He threw a punch that had all his 170 pounds behind it, but it didn't land solidly on the moving face. The blow that grazed along the side of the jaw and connected somewhat with the cheekbone did turn the 220 pounds around and halfway over another table, where three occupants fell crawling on hands and knees, swift as lizards, trying to escape the turmoil.

The agitator did a surprising thing for an overgrown adult; with mighty arms spread to grab and crush Bluefeather into syrup, he ducked his head and charged like a Mexican fighting bull. One hand did manage to close on Bluefeather's shirt as the youngster swiftly and wisely leapt out of the way. The man's head hit the adobe wall after passing through the glass covering a watercolor of the Ranchos de Taos Church. As he staggered back with a four-inch, bleeding gash, along with many small slivers of crushed glass in his skull, he dropped the remains of Bluefeather's shirt on the floor. This irritated the young prospector since it was the first time he had worn the garment, having saved it for this special evening with his special friends. It was his turn to roar, although the actual sound was more like a piglet shrieking. There was no denying the sincerity of the highly creative words that went along with it, however.

Bluefeather frothed out, "You dirty no good, second-rate chicken plucker," then he took a heavy swing and connected. "You . . . overgrown, fuzzy-brained descendant of an inbred tax collector," and he struck again.

Everything had been a blur before. Now it was all a red haze, and the two men rolled over and over knocking things out of the way, smearing blood like paint. Bluefeather was kneeing, hitting and occasionally biting. Nonetheless, he wound up with his back on the floor, and the man of many names was sitting on his stomach pounding on his neck, shoulders and chin. His inaccuracies were preventing total destruction, so he decided to choke Bluefeather to death.

The long darkness was descending on the valiant but outmatched young warrior when relief suddenly came. He gasped wonderful smoke-filled air into his desperate lungs as the massive hands slowly released his throat.

Lorrie, seeing her lover beginning to lose the fight and maybe his life, had jumped on the man's back and was reaching over and ripping at his face and then his eyes with her sharp fingernails while screaming sensible things like, "You vile beast. Take your filthy hands off my man."

At the risk of permanent blindness, he released his grip. He fell over on the floor, rubbing blood from the top of his head and other spots into the furrows of fingernail tracks across his eyes, crying, "Oh, my God. I'm blind. Oh, my God, I can't see. Oh, my God."

Bluefeather stumbled up, not caring about his several cuts and purplish lumps, just thankful to have his breathing intact. Now the pretty black-headed, black-orbed, pale-faced wife with the weak stomach who had started the entire thing was bent over her husband, wiping at his face with the remains of Bluefeather's new shirt, saying, "Oh, my poor, poor darling. Oh, my precious, what did . . . what did these terrible people do to you?"

Grinder precariously crutched his way forward looking at Bluefeather's abrasions as he stood there with no shirt and one blood-smeared arm around a now-shaking Lorrie. Grinder's gaze dropped to the messy people on the floor.

"Well, looks like you folks been having a whole pile of fun," he said, taking out the paper Beechnut container. Leaning expertly on his crutches, despite the many beers he had consumed, he took out a fresh wad of tobacco. He now swallowed the last chew just as Bluefeather had promised he would. Timing is everything. The fight had all been for nothing.

EIGHT

GRINDER INDIRECTLY COMPLIMENTED BLUEFEATHER THE NEXT day. "I admire your courage, son, but question your judgment. That bastard you fought was as big and dangerous as a runaway train." He spat a wad of tobacco juice out of his unmarked face into a coffee can and continued, laughing, "I've found that honor is often extremely expensive . . . but sometimes dishonor is more so. Huh, kiddo?" He was, of course, proud as a dominant stallion of his young and very active protégé.

Bluefeather had many points on his body that were a mixture of greenish blue to varied hues of purple. There were places and tissues, stiff and throbbing, that he had never felt before. They nursed along a couple of bottles of beer easy and slow, afraid to make any rash or sudden moves that might cause an imbalance of mind, or flesh and bone.

"You gotta admit, Grinder, that Lorrie is one hell of a woman."

"I admit. I admit," Grinder said throwing his hands up. "And by jingos, I'll never know how she talked those cops outa taking the whole bunch of us to jail."

"Kind and smart cops, I'd say, Grinder." Bluefeather

laughed softly, "You did get a good look at what she did to that bastard's face, didn't you?"

Grinder was feeling no hangover. He was charged up because he would be able to take the cast off his leg in another week, and he could not control his eagerness to get back on the trail of the lost vein that had birthed the one rich offspring of white quartz and yellow gold.

Grinder was entering the ancient gold-fever zone now. He took out his vial of little yellow nuggets and set it on the kitchen table. He intermittently tapped its bottom on the wood and turned the precious rock to view its multifaceted fractures and light reflections.

Bluefeather opened them each another beer and slowly sipped. He watched Grinder's battered, big-boned hands moving the gold as delicately as a mother touching her new firstborn infant.

Grinder was talking, but the beat-up young man was not his usual, attentive self. Somehow the gold and his thoughts of Lorrie had become mixed together like a pattern of sun shining on wispy clouds—vaporous more than real. He felt a warmness that came from far away. It washed and numbed the pain of his bruised flesh, and he was totally enveloped in a veiled cocoon of fuzzy rainbows. There was no hurt here, no danger, no turmoil; only a soft, even cozy peacefulness, a blessed euphoria. He never wanted to leave it. If he did not move or think, the glorious transparent shroud might stay with him, protecting and consoling him with a delicate nothingness.

Then Grinder's voice penetrated the enveloping shield. "You know what a gold prospector is, son? He's a bullshitter of truth. Never forget this, my boy. Never. Gold is the aphrodisiac of power and greed."

Grinder looked at him sideways across the neck of his beer bottle, which just missed the tobacco in his mouth. His eyes were bright and glowing with laughing sparkles as they studied his young protégé for reactions. He was pleased to see that his words had penetrated for a brief moment, but then the longing look of young love transposed the knowledge he had so freely imparted. Grinder had seen that look many times and had felt it a few himself. He was sure it was the one power capable of overcoming that of gold, but of course only temporarily, at most.

Grinder was not consciously dredging up these words and thoughts. They just came forth from the special caring he had for the young man. If the old man had bothered to analyze his feelings, he would have admitted seeing much of himself in the lad across the table from him who was so engrossed in his feelings for Lorrie.

He pushed a few strands of the lank, gray hair out of his eyes and got up saying, "I feel like cooking. What do you want? Bacon and eggs or eggs and bacon?"

"I'd really like some plain bacon and eggs if you don't mind."

"That's exactly what I was thinking, too."

NINE

BLUEFEATHER HAD NOT YET LEARNED HOW TO GET OUT OF unwanted social obligations. So he went to the Friedmans' cocktail party.

It started in midafternoon and lasted until after midnight for him and Lorrie's mother. He was amazed at Candi Friedman's casual easiness as she entertained. The only help she had was the eighteen-year-old-daughter of her neighbors, the Archuletas, and a bartender borrowed from La Fonda de Taos.

Guests wandered in and out of the patio and settled in varied-sized clusters. Unlike at most cocktail parties, there were more sitting than standing. People drifted around, ate hors d'oeuvres, refilled their glasses and then sat down somewhere to have conversations.

The adobe hacienda was regal without arrogance. Magic enfolded. Replete. Paintings by many local artists decorated the walls. They ranged from the realism of E. Irving Couse to the abstracts of Emil Bisttram. Primitive cedarwood carvings of Patricino Barela and colorful pottery from the Zuni and Santo Domingo pueblos were placed in shelves and on tables with deliberate balance in mind. Old wooden church crucifixes and *retablos* joined company on the walls. Well-worn Navajo rugs softened the floors, while the midafternoon magical sunlight of the high desert cascaded in slanting patterns of tender yet strong designs across the patio and through the large window and open doors.

The serene beauty of this atmosphere, the softening effects of the booze and the rush of adrenaline began to give Bluefeather a feeling of sublimity and confidence. He had not felt comfortable at first—perhaps even out of place. But why should he feel that? No one could be out of place in Taos unless he or she was far beyond ordinary offensiveness. The gathering here was proof of that. The guests ranged from the world famous, to those wanting to be, to those not caring about either but enjoying the repasts and the greatly varied companionships. There was no escape from the dominant outdoors with its almost arrogant skies, the reserved, sometimes awesome, mountains, the sagebrushed desert—more changeable in color and mood than any ocean—that penetrated the thickest adobe walls and permeated the living beings like ectoplasm, or hot syrup on pancakes. There was no escape. Either the ambience was absorbed and enjoyed or a person was shrunk to a body of walking dust.

Whether it was the drinks, Lorrie's beloved presence or the fact that half his blood had been here around a thousand years, Bluefeather felt robustly at home. All doubts of his personal bearing vanished in the warm haze of the time of Taos. It was his now. Forever his.

The attending age-groups ranged from the nineteen-year-old Lorrie all the way up to the next-door neighbor, eighty-five plus, Doña Archuleta. Eclectic.

There was the accountant, Rodriguez, and his wife, Mary; a famed writer and painter he had yet to visit; a designer of squaw dresses for a shop on the plaza; a banker; a restaurateur whose establishment specialized in chile rellenos; a remittance man from Saint Louis and a remittance lady from Syracuse; an ex-cowboy now in the automobile business; and others just as varied in their occupations and preoccupations.

Everyone was dressed in elegant, casual comfort with an emphasis on bright colors. The black, formal look was not popular in Taos. Long pleated squaw dresses dominated the scene, with their wearers usually weighted down with turquoise and silver jewelry. Cotton slacks or even faded Levi's were enhanced with the richness of handmade and embroidered Mexican shirts.

The mingling and murmuring grew to a certain pitch and then slowly subsided as some guests left. There were no loud protestations about either leaving or staying. Restful excitement. Some overloaded on hors d'oeuvres while some preferred to drink. Intellectual conversation, if desired; fortuitous meetings, if one wanted. Even solitude amongst the multitudes, if desired. It was a typically successful Taos social. A pleasurable gathering of old and new bloodlines in a mystical unawareness of time.

To young Fellini, however, it was a wondrous occurrence, even though he had resisted yelling like a pack of coyotes several times, and his legs had felt betrayed when he'd done only a couple of little jigs instead of a wild original dance of great invention. Although he was totally unaware of it, he had been watched the entire evening by Candi Friedman. Her daughter had appeared, and reappeared, by his side, touching him on the back, grasping his hand for just a moment, sometimes joining in his conversation with someone else, and yet never in an intrusive way. She just let him know she was with him—there.

Spud Johnson chose a spot at the end of a couch and stayed. People came and went, visiting and serving him the little food and drink he desired. If there was anyone who represented the sociability of a Taos party, it was

Spud Johnson. He was special, even in a village that specialized in a concentration of special people. Formerly a writer for the *New Yorker,* he had wound up in Taos by way of visiting his friend, the poet and writer Witter Byner of Santa Fe. The indefatigable Mabel Dodge Luhan had convinced Spud to move to Taos. He did. Forever.

Spud wrote a little journal called *The Horsefly.* It was a newspaper insert of Taos's main weekly paper, *El Crepusculo,* or as the locals called it, *El Creeps.* He was a bitingly humorous writer, and no one who did anything escaped his penetrating attention. This, of course, included his many world-famous friends, such as Frieda and D. H. Lawrence, Georgia O'Keeffe and many other notable personalities. He could, on rare occasions, be generous in his praise of a book, a poem, a painting or a worthy incident of any kind. In person, Spud had a kindly acceptance of people's foibles and was good humored as a bonus. Nevertheless, most people were afraid of him because of the little journal he wrote.

Spud had a cadaverous face, even in his youth. This made his brownish black eyes prominent indeed. At first glance Spud's eyes said they had seen too much and done too little about it. They could be interested, amused and in agreement, with moods changing so fast that the projections could be lost on the viewer. Today he sat in the corner of Candi Friedman's couch and held casual court, sponging in almost everything, as he occasionally sucked on his curve-stemmed, usually unlighted, pipe. Few knew that in addition to his journal and his poetry, he was the editor and typist for all of Mabel Luhan's writings. His indirect contributions to Taos were as great as those of Kit Carson or Padre Martinez.

Candi took Bluefeather by the arm saying, "Darling boy, you must meet our Spud." Bluefeather's olive-brown face was enhanced with burning crimson and she said, "Spud, this is Bluefeather Fellini. I'm sure you've heard of him. He and my daughter, Lorrie, are the barroom brawling champions of Taos, New Mexico."

Spud smiled out at Candi's lilting, easy laughter and said, "That is quite an honor to hold in a place known worldwide for its savage little wars."

Bluefeather was guided to a seat next to Spud and joined in the best his amateur cocktail party talk would grant.

"I hope we're not so overrated that someone else issues an immediate challenge," Bluefeather said.

"Not to worry, my boy. In Taos the gossip is altered daily by swiftly changing sins."

Bluefeather was surprised how comfortable he was with the small legend of Spud Johnson. They visited easily on many subjects. He was pleased even more when Spud discussed the mining history of Twining Canyon and Frazier Mountain with far more knowledge than he had heard from anyone who had been there before— even Grinder the Gringo.

They were interrupted often by someone paying their respects to Spud's little power structure. He invariably introduced Bluefeather as a friend of the Friedmans' and a mining entrepreneur. Sitting by Spud this length of time, and being a Friedman friend, gave Bluefeather an immediate respect that most people could spend a lifetime desperately seeking but never achieving. Candi Friedman was aware of this even with her back turned all the way across the room. She was very pleased.

Finally, Lorrie came and excused herself to Spud as she led Bluefeather away saying, "Blue, I want you to meet one of my favorite Taos people ever. She never stays very long, so we have to go see her now."

Now, Bluefeather had a remote knowledge of the Honorable Lady Brett's importance in the history of Taos and beyond. She was born of royalty and had chosen art, as well as D. H. Lawrence, as her calling. Her following Lawrence and his continuously growing entourage to Taos had appeared puppylike to many, but she didn't care what people thought about it. Brett's art studies at the exclusive Slade School in England would have little use in the way she wanted to portray Pueblo Indians. No matter. She was beginning to be noted for her combination of primitive and classical interpretations of the Indians.

When Bluefeather was introduced to Lady Brett, he felt awkward, not only because of her world-famous associates, but also because of the curved metal horn she was using as a hearing aid. But when the large woman with frizzy, whitish hair and a long, wonderful nose that came to a little, almost beadlike, point gleamed forth a natural heart-grabbing smile, Bluefeather's uneasiness disappeared.

Lawrence was once asked why he liked Brett and he replied, "Because she lights things up." This she did like halos turned into holograms.

Bluefeather didn't remember their conversation, except that she knew his grandfather, Moon Looker, and had hired him to model for one of her paintings. He was puzzled at how easily Brett and Lorrie were discoursing. He felt that this particular meeting had been a failure, but of course, it hadn't.

He excused himself to go get another drink, leaving his love—his destiny—communicating freely and with exuberance. He took a longer look at two of Brett's paintings on Candi Friedman's wall and felt a trueness to one half of his ancestry in spite of his current, amateur knowledge of painting. He felt something emanate beyond the frame. He would forevermore judge any work of art by this sudden discovery and unsolicited gift from Lady Brett.

Between the two paintings hung a framed short poem. He stepped closer to read it.

AUTOBIOGRAPHY
One of my dreams is very old
And never has been or will be told
But three of them have long been sold
And ten have caught their death of cold.
Spud Johnson

He was strangely touched by the little thoughts of the kindly man he'd just visited. He had another drink and became more gregarious.

Candi managed to join Lorrie in her bedroom where she was combing her hair, each stroke reminding her of Bluefeather's loving caresses.

"Darling, I must ask a favor of you. It's for your own welfare, of course."

Lorrie dropped the comb in front of her, holding it in both hands as she turned wordlessly to face her waiting mother. She was long familiar with the sincere but authoritative tone of her mother's voice when her mind was glued to a certain thought.

Candi continued, "As you know, our little gatherings are over when I say they are, and I addressed everyone to the fact it would be from six till eleven. They'll all soon be gone—even the drunks. They know my rules."

Lorrie waited, then said, "Well, Mother, what is it?"

"I want to keep Blue for just a twinkling. One brandy perhaps."

"Please, Mother, don't interfere. He's too intelligent not to know what you're doing. Please don't."

"He is, of course, well-read and smart, but he doesn't

have the experience, you see, the background—certain advantages must be pointed out. Now don't you worry a second, darling. Have I ever let us down?"

Lorrie could easily have begun a debate that might possibly have risen in volume and extended time. She gave in, trusting that Bluefeather would reach his own decision with her in mind.

"I suppose you just want me to disappear?" Lorrie asked.

"Just for convenience' sake, dear. We must not clutter his head in advance. Now that's a good—and wise—girl." Candi kissed her daughter on the cheek and reentered the little, temporary Taos world she had created. Lorrie followed a discreet forty seconds later.

Spud motioned for Brett to bend closer to him, and cupping his hand around her best ear he said, "Candi is going to acquire young Fellini for Lorrie—and her advertising firm."

Brett whispered back, " 'Tis a pity to remove such a handsome and charming young man from this valley—from his roots actually."

"Not to worry, Brett. He will return. You and I always have, you know."

"But, we, dear Spud, were not born here. We came here at Mabel's bidding."

"Nevertheless, our roots sank here in spite of all our travels."

They chatted on in private about memories and experiences that only those who are wealthy and famous, or those who associate with them, can conceive.

Bluefeather emptied his drink and gathered Lorrie into his arms and danced her around and around the kitchen. Her warm blood flushing her skin and the smell of her, the glorious smell of love and excitement and the physical totality of holding her against him moving, mov-

ing as the whiskey did in his brain, disturbed a center of
his being he could no longer control. He tilted his head
back and yelled all the way through all the walls and
ceilings of the adobe house. It was coyote. It was lion. It
was eagle and owl. It was Bluefeather. It was of such loud
and exuberant suddenness that an almost unseen shock
washed over and through everyone present, but they controlled it and acted as if it had never happened. One
could not show resentment toward someone who had
been anointed by Spud, Brett and the hostess, Candi
Friedman.

Bluefeather danced on wildly with Lorrie, who laughed
as she said, "Blue, you crazy idiot. I love you."

A couple more twirls and Bluefeather suddenly
stopped, saying, "What in hell has happened? I've drunk
myself sober."

Then Lorrie quietly poured him another. The crowd
started leaving, offering both real and obligated compliments. Then, without anyone actually realizing it, Candi
and Bluefeather were alone. Just as Candi had planned.

Lorrie, now sitting rigidly in her nightgown facing her
bedroom mirror but not noticing her reflected image,
combed furiously at her hair.

The sun had long ago gone to light other worlds; the
moon came up, replacing the yellow glow with soft blue
across the green sagebrush and painting the sides of the
adobe houses in the same settled softness. The valley had
a scattering of tiny artificial suns peeking from the windows of the homes in the village. Somewhere in the valley
a dog barked, and the distant hum of a pickup motor
diminished, and it was quiet in the night.

Bluefeather hadn't remembered much of his limited
conversation with Lady Brett, and he couldn't figure out
how he had ended up here sitting across the kitchen table
from Candi Friedman. But here they were.

Lorrie's mother had just served them an exquisite, supposedly "good-night" brandy. She smoked as elegantly as ever from a long, slender, inlaid-turquoise holder. He would never forget the beauteous force of her strong, green eyes looking through him as easily as through steam from a teakettle. He might someday forget their color, but he would always remember their intelligent strength.

"You get along well in mixed crowds, young man. I'm sure Lorrie is proud of you. Of course, she's prejudiced, being so damnably in love with you."

"Where is she, anyway? She's been gone quite a while. Has she gone to bed?"

"Oh, to tell the truth, Blue, it was at my insistence. We must talk, you know? You and I."

They looked at one another, the olive and the cream. The powerful, green eyes of experience stared into his misty, ebony ones that were almost as large. Although younger, they drew on other abilities, such as instinct and long-past experiences buried deep within his genes.

Bluefeather became extremely calm now and sipped his brandy slowly as it was made to be enjoyed.

"She's a child-woman of great potential as both a wife and a photographer . . . or whatever else she might take a fancy at becoming. I don't want her hurt any more than necessary in this world of uncalled-for pain. Do you understand?"

"I think so. I'm pretty sure I do."

"Well, let me put it to you, dear Blue, as clearly as words can express. She loves you passionately and with reasonably good sense. You have the looks and a proven social ability to fit in beautifully as a top model for my company. The benefits for you would be numerous. To name a few—the pay . . . the position . . . yes, even the surface glamour . . . plus, my lovely daughter."

Bluefeather tried to say something, but she continued on with such determination that he politely held back.

"You two could have a wonderful life . . . free from financial wants . . . a creative life, if you please, and you'd have sufficient time to figure out what other pursuits might call you . . . all the while living in and with beauty and abundance." Then she struck with her well-planned clincher, "Manhattan is full of gold that's already been mined."

It was then that Bluefeather realized he could never explain to her that piles of yellow bars in a bank vault were not his goal. Never in a million aeons could he get through to her that it was people like Grinder who made it possible for bank vaults to fill up at all, or that what Bluefeather and Grinder shared in the mountains could never be calculated by a genius a thousand times more intelligent than Einstein. It was so precious and private that words, maybe even thoughts, were inadequate. Feeling, absorbing it silently was the best anyone could do.

So, silence now.

She poured them each another but smaller brandy, looked him directly into the eyes and said, "Well?"

Bluefeather could not comprehend how the next words could come out of his mouth, but they did.

"I never would have believed in ten zillion years that a little half-breed like me would be made so grand a gesture." In his imagination, he genuflected an apology to Grinder for his last statement and smiled so enchantingly at Candi Friedman that it turned her experienced soul—calloused and formidably shielded to the core—to warm-stirred Jell-O. She smiled formidably back, taking his words as total acceptance of her just-verbalized wishes. Those two mighty smiles met and resounded silently in beauty, and in both, but in different ways, love for Lorrie. It was not yet known which one had diffused first.

• • •

Grinder and Maude Cisneros had partied all night, cele-
brating the removal of his leg cast. Bluefeather joined
them for a while. He just wasn't up to their enthusiasm,
so he soon excused himself and went to bed. Candi
Friedman and her daughter had him feeling indecisive.
This was against his nature. He was a young man who,
after asking himself two or three questions, made his
choice and acted on it.

Maude, after entertaining her boyfriend until three in
the morning, had gone home to take care of her chores.
Grinder was sleeping in. It would be his last party before
returning to the mountains and resuming his search.

The next morning, Bluefeather walked out into the
pasture to think things over and visit Tony. The subirrigated grass was as thick as beaver fur and about a foot
tall. It was a grand day with the air so clear it seemed to
squeak. The mountains stood out against the northern
and eastern skies so clearly that they appeared to be only
a mile away. He did not notice these goodly enchant-
ments as he rubbed Tony's neck. Candi Friedman had
offered him a piece of the world that nearly all people
would lie, rob and cheat their brothers to attain. Some
would certainly commit murder for the position he had
been offered last night, all because his unique bloodline
had so profoundly affected his physical appearance.

Then there was the main reason for all this—Lorrie.
She, too, could not help the physical and material benefits bequeathed to her by her father and mother's joining
of flesh. The fact that she was pursuing one of her many
gifts through photography and had overcome all her birth
advantages to be a loving, caring and celebration-of-life
lady made her very special indeed.

He cared for her so much his very eyeballs ached. His
chest was about to explode, and his toes were frozen al-

most for certain. So what the hell was the quandary about? He could almost grasp the reason, but then it melted and dissolved into an unreachable mist. "God uh mighty," he thought, "is love always such terrible, sweet agony?" How could he know that this was one of the prices of youth? The main one, in fact.

The burro dropped his head back down to the luxury of the earth and casually grazed at the bounty of the grass. Then Bluefeather was startled to see Dancing Bear sitting a few yards in front of him chewing on a grass stem. Dancing Bear stood up smiling. His hair was braided in the double Taos style. That first night on the mountain his hair had hung loose under his headband.

"What kind of spirit are you anyway?"

"Same as always, dear brudder. The helping kind. I fit the needs of my clients the best I know how. 'Course, I'm limited by the knowledge of the subject."

"What kind of talk is this anyway? You sound like a combination preacher, lawyer and cop."

"Now you catching on. Dear brudder, I see you are in turmoil. Allow me to dance for you. Your choice. Greek? Yugoslavian? Scottish? Irish? Swiss? Maybe German or French?"

"Stop. Stop all that." Then, seeing the rejected look on Dancing Bear's face, he changed his mind. "Greek . . . Greek will be okay."

Dancing Bear certainly danced. His beaded Cheyenne moccasins whirled in the grass. His hands were above his head, fingers snapping as loudly as castanets, then he slowed down and sang something that sounded Greek, yet moved on and on, with the fringes of his buckskin suit slapping in time with his stylized movements.

Bluefeather glanced around quickly, embarrassed that someone might be witnessing such a crazy Indian of un-determined origin doing Greek dances in an open pas-

ture with a young man and a burro as his audience. When
he saw that Tony grazed unconcerned and unaware of the
activity, he was enormously relieved.

Bluefeather clapped politely, hoping no one would notice, and whispered as loud as he could, "Thank you.
Thank you. That is enough for now . . . I feel better
already."

Dancing Bear smilingly stopped, obviously pleased, his
dark brown face happy with achievement and his body
poised for more consoling. "Maybe Russian dance?"

"No. Later, please. Thank you."

"Ah well, I suppose we have to talk now."

"If you wouldn't mind."

"Why, dear brudder, that is a good portion of the business I'm in, . . . this talking stuff."

"Well, these people, these women, I don't know how to
say it, they're just fine people, both of them, and they
want me to go to New York and become rich and famous
and all those kinds of things. They're pretty and nice
and . . ."

"You say that already before."

"I'm sorry, but you see . . . it's the mountains. I think
Lorrie might stay here with me in the desert and the
mountains, but I'd be gone most of the time on my business. It wouldn't be fair. My business seems so unpredictable; of course, if Grinder and I find the mother
lode . . . well that would be . . ."

"Whoa. Whoa," said Dancing Bear. "Whoa, too much
talk at one time shrinks the space for thoughts. Now, let's
see here once more. Maybe you go to mountains and
somebody done robbed 'em. Huh? Huh?"

"Goddamnit, talk so I can understand. I thought a
guiding spirit was supposed to give guidance."

"That is too true. Guidance. Not doing. Guiding spirits
ain't mamas. Men cain't nurse babies. Great Spirit put

teats on 'em by mistake. What you think anyway? Experience is still a stranger to you. You haven't even had the clap or ever been in jail yet or fought in a big war and here you are thinkin' I'm gonna do everything for you. You gotta pay for the trip, dear brudder, whether you enjoy it or not."

"Jesus, you're gettin' worse. I wish Great Spirit would send me another, smarter guide. You talk like you been eating peyote buttons and locoweed soup for a hundred years." He fervently wished that Dancing Bear didn't cause him to say such rude things. He vowed to control himself better.

"Not near that long, dear brudder, and now we say to you the truth. A feller told me once—when I'm still on your side of the river—'Hey, Dancing Bear,' he says, 'step lightly on the strongest mountains and harshest deserts, for they have delicate skins.'"

Now Bluefeather ran this last statement through his addled head several times. It made sense for everybody else, but what in holy hell could it possibly mean to him right now?

"I tell you true, dear brudder, you shouldn't do it, but the mountains will stay 'round awhile even if you treat 'em badly. Say, before I go, you want a nice Norwegian dance?" And he whirled and dipped and dallied right out over some cottonwood trees along an irrigation ditch and went somewhere else.

Bluefeather, being as yet unadjusted to the company of spirits, was startled, then angry. "Hey, please come back. Dear guiding spirit, come back here and tell me things I can understand. Hey, please, I say. You didn't tell me a single thing worth hearing. I'm gonna report you . . . you hear?" He didn't, however, have the slightest notion of where to turn in his complaint.

Bluefeather suddenly turned and strode with purpose

back to the house. Grinder had arisen and was haltingly cleaning up beer bottles, ashtrays and stale dishes. Neither one uttered more than two or three grunts.

"I have to go make a phone call. Do you want me to get gasoline while I'm at the filling station?"

"Yeah, fill 'er up."

Bluefeather went to the telephone, which felt like acid-coated steel produced by the devil, and managed to call his love. "Lorrie, I love you. I've got to go to the mountains and help Grinder set up camp. I don't want to go, but . . ."

"You have to go now? Right now?" she asked.

"Yes. I've got to, honey. His leg is still stiff and sore. Believe me, darling, I don't wanna go. God, I want to be with you, but I'll be back at noon in three days."

"Well, I love you, too. And Blue, . . . I'm really glad you're coming back on Saturday because we're leaving Monday for New York. We're already doing some packing."

This last comment brought misty, sticky, pointed pains back to certain parts of his body.

They said, "Good-bye," "I love you," and "I'll miss you," three more times. It was with bone-aching difficulty that Bluefeather hung up the instrument of bad news into silence. He stared, tempted to pick up the appurtenance from its hanger and call again. He shoved his hands in his pockets and turned away.

TEN

THE TWO PROSPECTORS WERE ANXIOUS TO SET UP CAMP AND GET about the business of finding the vast wealth assigned to them by the Great Spirit. They were convinced it was ordained. They had to leave the pickup with Grinder's friend Pacheco in Arroyo Hondo, and pack in using their strong backs and Tony's much superior one. They were close to the last place near Twining Canyon that might gift them with rocks that matched the single precious one that drove them on and on.

They pitched tent near an old tunnel about a mile and a half northeast of the village. The tunnel had collapsed about forty feet in, but with a half-day's digging they managed to scramble over the top of the fill and get to the ore face. They were disappointed that it had little quartz—and no gold.

Somebody had found enough values to drive a 180-foot tunnel here, so Bluefeather agreed that they must work the area carefully before moving on.

On the second day, Grinder found a piece of quartz float rock that slightly resembled the precious one. Its edges were worn smooth and its luster was dulled, indicating its movement atop the earth for aeons. Grinder excitedly broke it open with a prospector's pick, and the fresh edges did resemble the gold-laden one. However, there was no gold visible to the naked eye, and the glass revealed only quartz; but not all rock, even in the richest of veins, carried visible gold. Their excitement rose.

The next day they carefully worked up the rough little canyon toward an outcropped bluff where there was scant overburden.

That night after supper Grinder pulled out a piece of parchment with a crudely drawn map on it.

"I been meaning to show you this for a couple of weeks. Ol' Paul Burch came by the house the other day, and knowing what prospectors he and his brother, Elmer, are, I showed him our sample rock. He liked to of fell over. He told me he'd seen the same kind of gold-bearing rocks several years ago. Sheepherder had sold them to him. Paul's crippled from that car running over him, you know? So he drew me this map describing where the sheepherder said he'd found them."

The map showed a line that traveled off Twining Road across Twining Creek on a logging bridge, up the South Fork Creek to a small lake where several springs converged to form the headwaters of the stream, and up a steep game trail to the west, perhaps half a mile. Thirty or forty feet along the trail, where it curved back south, the sheepherder had slipped and fallen down a steep eastern slope and had accidentally found the small pieces of gold-filled quartz.

"Now, Blue, this copy is for you in case anything should happen to me." Bluefeather tried to protest, but Grinder would have none of it. "We gotta play as close to a cinch as we can, you know? I done bumped the point of discovery out of my brain before I met you, and I've broken my leg since. We gotta split up this information.

Hellfire, I might break my goddamned ol' stiff neck next time."

"It might be me who falls. Who knows?" said Bluefeather, staring into the red, orange and yellow patterns of the piñon campfire.

"Naw, hard-peckered boys like you don't get hurt so's it lasts. Especially you, Blue. You got too much livin' of life to get in yet. I can tell these things. You're gonna do wonderful things 'fore you're through, son."

They sat on their bedrolls, sipping coffee, staring off into the purple night. The fire crackled loudly and a night bird chirped as if to say "the prize is here"—the same as the mountains way down below seemed to whisper it.

They could see the dim lights of two small houses on the rim of Arroyo Hondo Canyon, struggling to be seen in the seemingly limitless space of night around them. Bluefeather stared at the lights trying to imagine the occupants inside one of the houses. The mother would be putting three kids to bed while the father smoked his pipe at the kitchen table listening to a song on an old battery radio. The woman was still young, and she bathed in an iron tub by the cookstove. She dried her smooth, olive body, rubbing it even after the wetness was gone. Now she became Lorrie in Bluefeather's scenario, and he was the man who turned off the radio and led her to the fresh covers turned back on the ancient, carved bed. Lorrie stretched out under the low, flickering light of a kerosene lamp. Fresh as clothesline-dried sheets, fresh as springwater, fresh as virgin life. He was nude himself now and was lying beside her. After caressing her breasts, he was moving his hands up her smooth spreading thighs when three things happened: Grinder reached for his coffee can, missed and spat a saved-up mouthful of tobacco juice into the fire that caused a minor explosion of sparks and spittle; a single coyote howled as loudly as a

dozen in the canyon just below them; and the staked
burro decided to bray into the moonless night.

When these sounds broke the nocturnal silence,
Bluefeather's inner being was turned all around and
moved on past the great Taos Mountain south to the village and on to the Friedman hacienda. It would not stop.
He didn't sleep that night until almost daybreak.

Lorrie had been all over and through Bluefeather no
matter how he twisted in his bedroll, and her mother's
great green eyes were turned on them like circus lights,
following their every move and thought, pulling them
both along with her, all the way to New York. They
screamed, kicked and cried, but she dragged them on
without ever touching either one.

Grinder also had a restless night. He dreamed of
Bluefeather leaving by train, on foot or mule and even
flying off without wings.

When daylight awakened Bluefeather, Grinder had the
fire going, his face washed and his hair combed. He
threw some sourdough into one Dutch oven and some
bacon and the last of their fresh eggs into another.

Grinder's fine, later-than-usual breakfast helped
Bluefeather only a few moments. The hot coffee was
swallowed but not tasted. Yesterday by this time, Grinder
would have had at least two hours of earnest labor done,
but today he busied himself feeding oats to Tony, studying maps and geological reports and cleaning up around
the campsite.

Bluefeather just sat on his open bedroll and stared into
clumps of trees, searching their shadows for an answer.
None came. None.

"You know, Blue, I hate to admit it, but I just can't call
up the location of that damned vein no matter what I do.
I've tried conjuring it drinking whiskey, beer, wine and
water. I've tested out starvin' myself into a trance and

eatin' until I could barely breathe. I've rolled over a thousand times a night and spent another thousand hours staring at the universe. I've prayed to God and cursed Him. I've tried to sell my soul to the devil and even threatened to castrate the horned bastard if I didn't get a fix on the gold's location. So far nothing has worked, and if I had any teeth I'd uh ground 'em to chalk by now."

"We'll find it, Grinder, don't worry anymore. We're getting close. I can feel it."

Grinder was both amazed and pleased to see and hear Bluefeather escape his reverie, even for a moment. Grinder had stayed in camp that morning to make his last speech, knowing that something about Bluefeather's new love was tearing at his guts like a ravenous hyena.

"Well, I'm sure glad you got that feeling, Blue. Makes me feel better already. Say, it's none of my business, but when is that Lorrie and her mama going back to New York?"

"Monday."

"Monday?"

"Yeah . . . I gotta bring it up one time or another, Grinder. I promised I'd meet her tomorrow at noon. Is it all right if I leave early tomorrow? I'll be back Sunday to see you, even if I'm . . ."

Grinder's tough, old guts twisted up like a den full of freezing rattlesnakes, but he said casually, "Sure, son. No problem at all. I think we'll just hang around camp today so we'll both be in good shape to tend our chores tomorrow. I can't wait to get that country prospected up to that bluff. I'll bet that's what you're feeling . . . the vein is right there in that bluff. I'm close to smelling gold, son. Real close."

"There's something else I gotta . . . well . . . no use waiting on this either. Grinder, I . . . that is, they've offered me all kinds of rich folk's stuff to go back to New York with 'em."

"Well, son, you're free to go, far as I'm concerned, if you think it's best for you . . . for your whole life. Even though I'd sure hate to lose you, you got ol' Grinder's blessings." He remained dry eyed, but the tears inside almost caused them to explode.

Bluefeather went on. "I sure appreciate that, but I just can't make up my mind. I can't sleep or nothing. I think I'm going to go flat-ass crazy if I don't decide soon. I never could take much indecision, anyway. I love that damned woman as much as I can, but I love that mountain there, too." And he pointed at the north slope of the magic Taos Mountain where the sun was waking it up with caresses of warming orange light.

"Hey, son, we all seek the truth that pleases us."

Bluefeather really thought this one over before he spoke. "You're just as correct as you can be, but I've been trying to figure what's really right for me instead of what pleases me."

"Yeah, sometimes it's sure enough damn near impossible to figure out what we're supposed to do—which could be what we really want to do . . . if everything is in balance and our luck's runnin'."

There was silence for a couple of minutes as they both watched the sun changing and enlarging the light and shadows on the sacred mountain.

The old man hid, with practiced care, his fear of having lost Bluefeather. He had just now reached a point of total trust after having risked both their lives in old tunnels of rotten rock. They had laughed and played together, cementing the other side of a total friendship—one for which a man should be willing to die. He hid the ache that numbed his heart at the vast loss of a companion— the one he had chosen to share his upcoming fortune. A true partner was rarer than all the gold he had pursued his entire lifetime.

Bluefeather was suffering the same emotional struggle. His young mind jumped back and forth from Grinder to Lorrie until the confusion caused him to eradicate, on the surface at least, the deep hurt he was going to feel either way he decided. He thought of trout fishing, timber, bears and his grandmother's *horno*-baked bread.

Then Grinder sort of mumbled to himself, "A feller's got to make up his mind about problems and then kick one and piss on the other with all he's got. Right or wrong, kiddo?" He spoke louder now and with much certainty, still staring at the mountain. "It's true that the sun comes up every single day, but it comes up one time less for me and thee each morning." He hesitated a moment and broke wind so loudly that the burro raised his head and turned to check out the disturbance. Bluefeather was so shocked that he fell back on his unmade bedroll and laughed his indecision right out into the mountain air.

Grinder jerked the floppy, greasy, old hat from his head and fanned his fanny, laughing so hard he could hardly boast out, "Knocked a hole plumb to bedrock with that'n. Right, kiddo?"

Tony went back to grazing.

ELEVEN

He met her on the plaza in front of Skeezix Rodriguez's drugstore. He disliked unnecessary driving, but today he asked Lorrie if he could take over the wheel of her car. She seemed pleased at this sudden change in him. He drove south to Ranchos de Taos and turned left on Talpa Road. They passed the house of modern artist Andrew Dasburg. Both commented on the young cottonwood tree next to Dasburg's adobe studio that seemed to have grown with perfectly balanced limbs and leaves just to please the artistic sensitivity of its owner.

Bluefeather drove on in silence with no conscious plan. Finally he turned southeast up the winding gravel road into the heavily timbered forestland toward Little Pot Creek.

Lorrie slumped down in the car seat watching the twisting stream as it caught light and shadows, sparkling, yet dull, like an old Navajo silver necklace. But her mind wasn't there with her eyes; it didn't even seem to be in the car. She was not with the wilderness either. She was in some blank, unseen, unfelt place she had never been before. Today a decision would be made and her natural courage was failing her. It would be up to Bluefeather to bring up that which she had anticipated, longed for and yet feared the entire summer. Words. Yes, words must be spoken from his tongue now. The time of young passion and heartwarming love must be put aside for a brief spell.

Although Bluefeather, too, was distracted and introspect, he tightly gripped the steering wheel and kept the roadster on the proper side of the road. He was only slightly aware of the wooded scenery, like a man knows a chimney is on the roof of an old house. Well, he could drive on and on for over a thousand miles to Brownsville on the southern tip of Texas on the Mexican border and it wasn't going to change a thing. He had to face it.

He glanced at Lorrie—his Lorrie—where she had scooted down even further, so her eyes were now barely level with the dashboard. Lord, oh Lord, how tender and helpless she looked. Of course, she had proven in many varied ways, including her saving him a terrible beating in a barroom brawl, that she could be as tough as large razors when the chips dropped from the ax blade. But at this moment, he wanted to hold her against his chest and tell her everything was all right—now, later and maybe forever.

He choked a little, swallowing frequently, pushing back the moisture that was trying to ooze beneath his eyelids. They arrived at the top of a pass overlooking the vast new world to the east. He stepped on the brakes awkwardly. The stop jolted Lorrie up and returned her to the now of things. Yes, now. Here.

"Lorrie . . ." He could not go on for a moment. Then he put his hand out and touched her on the shoulder. He started again, "Lorrie, you want me to go to New York, don't you? You want us to marry, don't you? Well?"

She looked at him with the eyes of a doe who had just given successful birth to her first fawn and caught the scent of a lion on the cooling breeze. "Yes. More than anything."

Bluefeather was tempted to question the "anything" bit. Anything, after all, could mean her staying here in the great Southwest, waiting month after lonely month, year following longer and longer year, while he pursued his own peculiar and particular madness with the earth-blessed rocks. It wasn't right to terrorize her into agreeing to suffer this fate just out of his desperate need for them to be joined. It would not be fair to either of them. There was no sense now in being altruistic. Charging straight on with the lance, hoping it would glance off some piece of invisible armor was the only way. Rough.

"Oh, Jesus, how it hurts to say it, Lorrie, but I can't do it right now. I can't go to New York with you. Not now."

"Don't you love me?"

"Yes, oh God, of course I do. But I've got this sudden feeling—I don't know where it came from—that the love we speak of is not enough."

"It would be for me. I'll do anything you want. Anything."

"I know that's what you think. I know you even mean what you're saying, but I know better, because I keep getting the same feeling. Then . . ."

"What are you telling me? That I wouldn't be able to give up New York and all the things my mother has in mind for us? Blue? Please tell me the truth. What are you feeling? I can't take it any longer. Just say it and get it over with."

"Well, I don't know exactly how to say it. I don't know if you'll understand. I don't want to hurt you. That's the last thing I would ever want to do, Lorrie."

Lorrie already knew he was saying "no" to her. Every word pained her more. Still she was hoping, grasping for the component that would make them cohesive. "Is it the modeling for Mother's firm that bothers you?"

"No. It's not the modeling. Hell, some of my Pueblo kin have been modeling for Taos artists for years. No, it isn't that. Maybe it's because I had already made a decision, before I met you, about what I have to do next in my life. And I have to stay right here in Taos to get it done. That's the way I am once I've made up my mind. I hope you can understand. My parents sure didn't. But I am doing it anyway. It's just that everyone has to have his own work. . . . It finally becomes more than . . . ah, hell, it's just the way I am."

Bluefeather was not thinking of these words in advance, and he didn't speak them as knowledge either, but they came on out anyway.

"Damnit, darling, I can't marry you and your wondrous mother. It would be bigamy. I'm already committed to Grinder and that mountain," he said as he waved back over his head in the general direction of the mighty, rocky bulk that dominated Taos Pueblo, the Spanish village and the rest of the canyons and deserts for hundreds of square miles.

"Well, I guess it just comes down to the fact that you can't go there and I can't stay here," Lorrie said as she blotted her tears. He realized how she hurt, from the way her body jerked as she sobbed as quietly as her emotions would allow.

He was numb. His emotions were dry. He knew this had to be finished as quickly as possible.

There were few other words between them as he drove back down toward Taos. As he circled the plaza he felt none of Taos's sometimes glorious, sometimes infamous, history. The only history that mattered to him at this moment was the one that was ending with Lorrie.

He drove her to the front of the Friedmans' hacienda,

got out and walked around to open the door for her. He was hurting to touch her one last time, to feel her heart pounding against his chest and push his face into her soft, blond hair so he could smell it and her essence just once more, but he didn't. It was done.

Candi stood on the porch wearing a turquoise dress that emphasized her colorations and exquisite, rich form. The welcoming smile dissipated as her daughter numbly opened the front-yard gate and walked quickly toward her. She took Lorrie in her arms, pushing her face between her breasts, and stared after the strong, young figure walking away toward the edge of the mesa down the road to town. She stood and wordlessly held her daughter. Her chest was pierced with a sudden, but ancient, pain of knowing.

The figure of Bluefeather could only be seen from the waist up now, then the head, and then nothing. Gone.

Bluefeather drove north out of Taos toward the village of Arroyo Hondo. Breaking up was something like boiling one's soul in carbolic acid. There was this feeling of far, faraway loss combined with a short breath of relief. Yesterday his vision seemed hypnotized by the road, and he couldn't even look at the land. Today the blindness had cracked open to let in light, color and form.

He glanced off to the right at Taos Mountain. The evergreen and sagebrush foothills sloped down like great stone roots. There was his part-time home, Taos Pueblo, at the bottom of the looming prominence. What an irony that its five-story main structure was the tallest building in northern New Mexico. Even so, it was barely visible, like a few grains of sand on the arm of a giant.

He pulled off the road and stared at the huge sacrosanct upthrust. Then he spoke aloud, alone, as if imagining a conversation with a close friend, "I salute you, oh precious, perverted, eminence, sister of powerful spirits and first daughter of the gods." As he crisply saluted, the shape of his face was slightly altered by a small smile.

He drove down into the tiny village of Arroyo Hondo, gateway to Twining Canyon. The land hovered on both sides of the life-giving creek that traversed all the way from the top of Bull of the Woods Mountain and other nearby peaks. The controlled turmoil of a lost love was barely subdued within him. His youthful exuberance to get to the mountains and start the adventurous work of seeking lost gold with his partner was almost more than he could handle. No matter what his aches and desires might be, he had to visit with Grinder's old friends, the Pachecos.

He drank coffee. He talked politics—although he knew little of this pastime. That was the way of the blood of Spain mixed with that of the mighty Mayan civilization. He bounced little Juanita and Adelina on his knees. He honorably thanked the quiet and solid wife of Gilberto Pacheco for the libation, and he told Gilberto how much he and Grinder appreciated being allowed to leave their conveyances on the Pachecos' property.

Everyone had been properly honored and pleased. He left, walking with much strength and agility up the swiftly steepening slopes to their prospecting camp.

It was midday when Bluefeather arrived breathing deeply, sweating some, but with plenty of strength to spare. He spoke to the burro and told him he was going to seek his master.

In the soft bottom of a little draw perhaps fifty yards from the bluffs, he found his partner's tracks. They moved erratically back and forth searching thoroughly for evidence on the surface of the earth. After a while Bluefeather decided that the tracks were certain to lead to the bluff, so he just walked as straight as the treacherous terrain would allow to their private landmark.

He was excited now, for he would soon rejoin his partner in the hunt. Maybe he could share in the excitement of discovery. All other concerns vanished. There was a freedom of choice tingling through his surging blood. He was home. Home to the mountain. Joyous. Thrilled. Pure.

He stopped as he saw Grinder's tracks approach the bluff and looked up in search of his form high in the deceivingly rough and creviced rock face. He strained, but could not see, or hear, anything of his friend. His eyes moved on down.

Then he saw the upraised hand sticking out through a tall clump of bunchgrass. The handle of a prospector's pick lay across the open palm. Grinder had slipped somewhere up there, concentrating so hard on the hunt that he had missed a step. He had crashed swiftly to the ground to have the life broken and jarred out of his body by one of the mountains he had loved so very much—that had given him his reason for breathing.

Bluefeather hauled the old prospector's body down the mountain on Tony's back. He would retrieve their camp gear later.

He and Maude Cisneros buried Grinder at her family plot at El Prado on the northwest edge of Taos. Only Maude and her children; one bartender; the two prospecting Burch brothers; Patricino Barela, Grinder's friend from Canón; and Bluefeather's uncle Stump Jumper and his cousin Smiling Dog were at the graveside. About a dozen in all.

Bluefeather spoke the eulogy: "Grinder the Gringo's earthly run is over, and I will always feel humble that he shared part of his life with me. He was full of wisdom and fun. He was loyal to his few friends and ignored his enemies. He was not an observer of life. Grinder was a participator in love and sorrow and the wondrous mixed adventures it gave him. He was a true walker of deserts and climber of mountains. We miss you already, ol' pardner. Good traveling to you, amigo. Amen." Bluefeather made the sign of the cross and briefly raised his arms in a burial chant.

He poured a knapsack of their mineralized rocks into the grave and turned and walked away with the others, leaving Maude alone with her last love. She stood there motionless in her black dress, veil and shawl seeming to grow smaller and smaller as if part of her was already joining Grinder. Bluefeather was stunned by the loss of his two main loves within twenty-four hours. It would take a special gathering of will to lose no time grieving for those already gone. He didn't.

Bluefeather was surprised that Grinder had left a recent will. Maude got his house and land. Bluefeather got all his mining equipment, his old truck, Tony, his vial of gold and his prized rock specimens, among which were five more large vials of nuggets.

Bluefeather smiled and mumbled, "The wonderful old digger had put away enough gold to provide for himself, Maude and over a year's worth of prospecting. He had just practiced his survival con on me and then decided he enjoyed the company." Bluefeather laughed aloud with abandonment. He felt good, just as he knew his friend had arranged. Then Bluefeather remembered that just two days earlier Grinder had said he might break his neck. Revelation.

Bluefeather took care of all the legal details with a wise, old Spanish lawyer. He delivered the necessary papers to Maude and enfolded her in a crushing, silent hug. He gave Tony to his grandfather at the pueblo, then came back and began loading his things into the old Ford truck.

He wrapped the rock that had driven Grinder to make his last climb and the Burch brothers' treasure map in waxed paper and put them both in the cigar box in the bottom of a footlocker with the rest of his special rock specimens. He planned to sell the vials of raw gold to Candelario's Curio Shop in Santa Fe for a nice wad of cash. He drove around Taos Plaza and turned right toward other worlds yet to come.

Before the highway dropped down into a horseshoe curve, where the Taos country would vanish from sight behind him, he pulled over to the side of the road, got out and swept his eyes back across the world's greatest panorama of big sky, big earth. He could see all the way west to Tres Ritos where the sagebrush fused into infinity. He moved his eyes back across the vast sagebrush desert to the curved malpais gash of the Rio Grande Gorge creating a volcanic scar seven hundred feet deep. Then his gaze moved on to the blur of the scattered mud rectangles of Taos and on up across the Sangre de Cristo Mountain Range.

It was already late enough in the day that the color of the blood of Christ was tinting the mountains' open spots. At last his eyesight was pulled to the limitless sky above it all. For the first time in his life he could not find a single cloud there. His orbs raced back and forth across the immense sky, but there were no clouds. None. There was something else. Something that he had never seen before in the limitless forming and reforming of the sky above the divine mountains.

He strained to discern its form, its dimension, by squinting his eyes and alternately opening them wide, like someone looking at the color and form of a painting. Something alive, pulsating, was there! It hovered above the vast upper spaces centered over Taos Mountain. It floated and poised like a giant transparent stingray of the sky. One instant it was billions, trillions, of gold specks, then it turned red and violet. During the tiny time of a single, swift glance, it became colorless to the point of near invisibility. It was there! Then streamers dropped down from the massive form like slowly writhing, silent tornadoes. Some of the tendrils from the sky were as light and delicate as a sleeping fawn's breath, and a few darkened and appeared to be shadows in the sky. Threatening and tender, raw and refined, all at the same instant. He knew that the thin, diaphanous feelers touched the earth of the Taos land and all its creatures in an energy that was filled with creation. The dominant thing was the ephemeral penetration of the light that shimmered as nowhere else in any other sky.

Then suddenly it was removed from his perception. He stared, straining. He could not make it return. Beyond being embraced in awe, he was humbled at the great privilege of the vision just gifted to him. He felt guilty he'd been given this omnipotent honor. Why him? Then it came to him, straight out of his heart, that the floating "Taos energy evolution" surely had been seen by others, but they, like he, would never be able to describe it. And if so, how, or why? Far beneath the fabled mountain, massive plates of rocks rubbed against one another embracing, making a humming music that a few could hear. Bluefeather was one who could.

He drove on around the horseshoe and then soon alongside the rock-churned Rio Grande south to Albuquerque to reorganize his life. The Taos days of both earthly and inexplicable "other" experiences were behind him but would always be a splendiferous virus in his blood. Young Bluefeather Fellini would soon be ready to run, ears back and head down, toward many other wondrous and magic worlds.

TWELVE

BLUEFEATHER HAD WANDERED FOR A SPELL FROM THE BIG Bend country of Texas to the Superstition Mountains of Arizona, half-heartedly prospecting, wholeheartedly drinking, dancing and accepting the attention of several women. The last was against his true nature. He was, in fact, a one-woman man.

Then, in Nevada he met Nancy, a fancy dancing girl who turned out to be much more. It seemed to him that every young man, at one time or another, had wanted a saloon dancing girl. This one, though, wanted him.

Nancy said to him, "Now, look, Blue, I've been everywhere and done everything. I know all men intimately. But I don't know you. You ask nothing of me but my love. Well, here it is, Blue. Take it, but don't throw it away. Come with me. I'll show you the tricks of the cards and we can tour the world. Just you and me. You'll never have to worry about a grubstake again. It will be better than it would be if you made a big strike. You will have all you ever need and more."

She made it sound so good, so easy, so sure. He enjoyed her talk and her love, and decided to give their relationship a mountain of a try. Unlike Lorrie Friedman of New York, Nancy was from this harsh land and worked it with skill and tenderness. He was influenced by this.

Many times Nancy would hold and tenderly, slowly, stroke Bluefeather's face, running a fingertip along the thin scar on the bridge of his nose. She was constantly amazed that he could be so perfectly sculpted and still have so little vanity and so much kindness to give, so much thoughtfulness to offer.

She taught him how to work the gambling cards and was patient while his hard-rock hands softened so he could finally manipulate the cards and deal to win. He cleaned their living quarters. He looked after her needs beyond anything her jaded life had known. She could not keep her hands off him, not knowing that this eventually would repel him.

He finally fell for the "easy way home" routine and began to thoroughly enjoy it. Nancy slowly had gathered together a talented burlesque company. Combining this with her notable singing voice and her lusty figure, the group was quite a draw. They traveled all over the West, with pleasure and profits growing all the time.

She was pale skinned with black hair and gray eyes, full figured for such a fine and light-footed dancer of exquisite invention and skill. Even so, there were women more beautiful than she in her dance group. There were women everywhere he went who were more handsome, but it was Nancy whom his young body was in heat for and his young mind fantasized after.

They had accrued enough savings to make a down payment on their own place. It all came together, and then apart, at Tonopah, Nevada. Tonopah was a mining town, and Bluefeather felt comfortable there among his own kind. Nancy's show was a yelling, stomping sellout twice every evening. Bluefeather kept all the gambling tables moving and paying.

How could he complain? She managed it so they could go to San Francisco together every two or three months. They drank the best whiskey, ate the finest foods in the most elite restaurants and stayed in the luxurious suites of stately hotels. She dressed him like an Oxford dude or an imperial prince by tailors of her personal acquaintance. They attended every worthy show in the city that was boiling with lust and life and illusion. The opera, the cabaret performances and the myriad of single and group entertainers who had come here to blend into the excitement of grand adventures and tragedies of the same scope were appreciated and rewarded with applause and generous tips by the two lovers from Tonopah.

These trips became a narcotic—a warm, sensual, ever-moving, eternally changing, other place. Then, after indulging several times in all that money and young bodies could desire, the first stale taste entered his mouth and the first slight sullying of overused nerves set in.

He told Nancy, at last, that he appreciated all the operatic indulgences, but the truth was that changing his outdoor nature was "like asking a piss-ant to play a trombone."

Nancy answered, "Lincoln was born in a leaky log cabin, but he learned to love living in the White House."

"But you see, Nancy, my darling one, Lincoln never watched the vision of a Dancing Bear nor did he climb mountains with a man who could chew tobacco and drink beer at the same time."

She ignored these retorts as simple jesting and said, "Your dried-up desert will still be there just like it is when you're old and made of sandpaper. Now, while your skin is smooth, we must enjoy our bounty."

But just as he would start to consider getting his two mules from the stable and scuttling into the night mountains and rocks, Nancy would trap him again with caring thoughtfulness and velvet deeds. A man could stay in this bejeweled cocoon and die of benign contentment.

Her bookkeeper and confidante, Rosalie, told Nancy, "Don't get your heart set on a 'forever deal' with this man. He's looking way off at something none of us can see—not even him."

"Since you're so clairvoyant, dear, explain why he can hardly wait to bed me, explain his thoughtfulness, his gentleness," she paused a second, "except when he has a rare spell of anger. Oh, Rosie, he'll stay because I'm giving him all any man needs."

"Believe me, honey, he ain't *any* man. He's . . . he's, oh, I don't know. I just know that I don't want you hurt again, that's all."

Sensing his growing lack of enthusiasm during their last trip to the West Coast, Nancy had a true and impressive surprise waiting for him upon their return home. In his private room, where he kept his unused prospecting equipment and his treasured mineralized rocks, she had had shelves built and carefully lined with black velvet and special lights to spot his displayed rocks. He appreciated her gesture of understanding where his true soul was hidden, and he felt humbled and obligated. That was part of the problem.

True, his gambling skills had been considerably refined under her expert guidance, since his earlier experience with his second cousin, Hog Head the collector, in Raton. He also had learned to dress and act the part of a gentleman gambler, again through her knowledge. He felt a combination of gratitude and resentment toward her. One good thing, though, all these things were forgotten in bed. In fact, after all this time of easily earned luxury, he was afraid their lovemaking was what had pulled him to her and held him, even now, instead of all the easy living. More and more often, he pondered this.

Slowly, like water rising in a large lake, he was becoming jaded with the "foreverness" of luxury and soft flesh. He would not deny that he enjoyed her touch, her careless laughter, her generous gifts. Damned right he did. But the chefs of this particular life had served up sweet delicate pastries far too often. He longed a little more each morning for the lonesome hunt, for the singular search and for the thrill of possible discovery. He longed for the things hidden by the wary earth; little clues to search for; tiny pieces of float rock; looking with the glass at stones for the first time with one's heart aware of the possible beauty, a hint of riches that might magnify before his eyes; the company of the mules, the deer, the eagle, the bear . . . ah, and that was another thing—his guiding spirit, Dancing Bear, had never once visited him here in Tonopah. He must get up from their bed, scented with lovemaking, early the next morning and call him up. He had tried to evoke the dancing one many times since he had arrived in Tonopah. Nothing. But today?

In a half-vision he lay there and "mind-talked" to Dancing Bear. "Look at me, ol' pardner, I'm so loved out I'm limber as a rotten rubber band. I'm as thoughtless as a sick chicken, and I haven't got any more dreams left than a rusty bucket. My spine has turned to worn-out rope, and my mind is as dead and worthless as a used eggshell. Please, dear Dancing Bear, come and give your meek and desperate subject help. Please beautiful, attentive Bear. Assistance, please, now. What good is all this silver and gold that's already been found and is handed to me at the mere turn of a card? Where is the accomplishment? The fulfillment of successful struggle? You don't need to dream of lovely women when you're sleeping in a whorehouse. Huh? Huh? Answer me if you can. If not, show me a sign. Just one. Please . . . please . . . please."

As the half-vision cleared away to instant reality, he sat up in bed and turned to see the strong, delicious figure of Nancy spread wide open before his eyes, with her head turned over one arm, breathing steadily so that her breasts moved just enough for him to feel the same stirring that had become a mink-lined jail.

He almost went down to her. In her natural knowing, she would raise her legs around his hips and moan love sounds at the ceiling before she even opened her eyes. Temptation. Indecision. Decision.

He dressed, acquired one of his mules and rode out through the mineralized blue and dull purplish hills of Tonopah. It was against his nature to ride and not search the ground for special rocks and colorations of the earth, but this time he ignored the earth. He looked out ahead, searching for the exact, right ridge.

The mule walked with brisk confidence, and Bluefeather could sense the feelings of escapement and discovery in the mule's muscles just as his own lungs relaxed and tasted the desert air scented like wafting caviar. After a while the town of mined metal from beneath the earth, with its silver dollars sliding across green-clothed tabletops, was gone. Now he could see folding and unfolding, obtruding and intruding, large bulks of rocks and earth bluing off into the distance. Oh, how he craved to go and explore their sides, canyons, crevices and sandy wrinkles that Nancy had so casually dismissed. If he had properly supplied himself and brought his other mule, he knew he would have ridden on without looking back.

Then they stopped, the man and the mule. Here he could see in a complete circle. Bluefeather reined the mule around a little so he could scan the entire panorama. He could hear two birds talking way off somewhere and see a soundless pair of buzzards circling far to the southwest. Quiet. Ah, what beauty. What peace. He felt his soul settle perfectly into the form of his body from where it had been dislodged by all the cards, booze, over-indulgence in rich foods and Nancy's lush body, as well as the adrenaline-pumped, stomping crowds who thronged the casinos searching for all of the above. Winning was the quick fix; losing the quick sad. Starting up again; the sudden surge of new hope. The old, old cycle.

All was forgotten the instant he saw Dancing Bear sitting on a cactus.

"I'm going to rename you Smiling Bear," Bluefeather said, spreading his own lips over his teeth in mirth like his spiritual mentor. "I thought you had deserted me forever when you didn't answer my half-vision."

"Dear brudder, I wonder why it is that apes and humans are the only creatures that pull their lips from their teeth when they are both happy and angry. What do you think of that, dear brudder? Tell me, please."

"There you go, Bear, asking questions when I'm so desperate for answers. Didn't you hear me talking to you, begging you like a man condemned to hanging, of my limited time? Huh? Huh?"

"But you haven't asked me a single question yet."

"I haven't had time."

"Take all of that time you wish, dear brudder, I got many minutes for listening. Maybe years, eternities even."

"Okay then. Listen, Bear. I'm gettin' mixed up about all that stuff over there at Tonopah."

"How's that? Isn't Tonopah a mining town? Aren't you a mining man?"

"Say, you really haven't been paying any attention to what's been going on with me, have you?" Bluefeather let out a deep breath and started to remind Dancing Bear that he had already broken his word and was proffering questions instead of answers just as before. He decided it

was no use confusing the rare meeting even more, and he
went on again. "That is true what you say, Bear, but it is
all the other things—all that money and fun, and the
women, well, a woman, and everything else a feller could
possibly want. I just don't know how much longer I can
take it. Nancy's a fine lady, and I don't want to hurt her
feelings or anything like . . ."

Dancing Bear yelled, "Whoa, whoa, whoa," just like
Bluefeather had at him once before. "Well now, we got a
brand new one here. I got clients complaining all the day
throughout the world about not enough money, not
enough food, not enough women. To tell you a sure-
enough truth, most of my clients are crying, screaming
and just plumb overrun with 'not enough.' This here is
one damn brand-new one for this old Bear. Hold it right
there. I got to go higher up for consultation and advice."
Dancing Bear zoomed up out of sight faster than a fiery
comet.

Bluefeather leaned back on the mule, looking up,
wanting his guide to return with advice from above.
Dancing Bear returned swifter than sight, for certainly
Bluefeather heard him before he saw him. "Dear brudder Blue, the One on the high horizon says He's too busy
right now over at Beijing to bother with problems at Tonopah. His associate tells to me this . . ."

Bluefeather interrupted, "I don't want to hear any of
your lame-duck, weasel-whining, secondhand blather. I
want first-cabin stuff or nothing. Right now. Right here is
when I need to hear words of wisdom. You hear me,
Bear? You hear me begging you like a kid wanting permission to go to the bathroom? I beg you like a street
corner pencil peddler."

Dancing Bear was leaping as light as a fruit fly from
one cactus to another. He was whirling around on one toe
yelling gleefully, "Wheeee, whoopee, pisseroni."

Feeling helpless, Bluefeather jumped from his mule and vigorously started throwing rocks at the dancing spirit. But the rocks ran together, creating a figure of two stone apes, one chasing the other with a stick in its hand. The ape sculpture just grew larger with the heavier rocks that Bluefeather hurled at his untouched guide. Finally he had thrown all the rocks within reach and had not even touched the spirit who danced like a swift ghost. Not even a single glancing blow had dusted Dancing Bear.

Bluefeather shoved enough breath from his lungs to shout, "Quit playing those magic games on me. I want the pure truth. You hear me? The pure truth." He gasped the frustrated air back into his lungs for a few moments then continued, "You know I love and respect you like my grandfather, the pueblo shaman. So treat me good and kind and thoughtful and do it real quick like he would."

Dancing Bear quit dancing, squatted down and started drawing pictures in the dirt with his trigger finger, saying softly but firmly, "A sunbeam penetrating a great forest mist in the canyons of Taos Mountain, an antelope giving birth to twins, lightning bouncing across a great lake. That is all magic. Magic, you hear? Even a mirror is magic, but real to the one making the image. What I do over on this side of the river is real. You hear, dear brudder? Real!"

Bluefeather was upset again, ornery upset. "There you go spouting all these highfalutin things at me like . . . like that. You're no good to me this way."

"Listen careful, dear brudder. You are lucky to have me around sometimes. Most people don't ever get to see their spirit guide. Only a few get to feel and a few get to hear, but most people have the insides of their heads squeezed so tight they never know we exist. Poor, poor people. Lucky, lucky Bluefeather. Huh? Huh?"

Then he cocked his head, listening far away, and said as he danced an Icelandic shuffle across the scorching desert out of sight, shouting, "Have a good Thanksgiving when you finish carving the big, wild turkey."

Bluefeather sighed. "Here it is only April and he speaks of Thanksgiving."

He stared for a time at the empty place from which Dancing Bear had vanished, then he looked at the statue of the two apes hovering in midair. He watched it slowly descend to the ground, then turn into a sculpture of a little man carrying two mules. By the time he had remounted his mule, the figures had become a pile of sand, and the next breeze, before he reined away, had started scattering the grains of the statue across the desert.

He went back to work as was his nature. Reluctantly.

Bluefeather had refused, even with Nancy's protestations, to take money from the underground miners in head-to-head games; however, the owners and the professional drifters were another story. He deliberately started the game that would bring about his turn at disaster. He didn't even know the man he was to finally beat.

The game of five-card stud went on all day, all night. The stakes rapidly had grown too big for all but the best. By three o'clock the next afternoon, only Bluefeather and the stranger, who called himself Grady, were left playing. There were a score or so of losers watching, taking sides. Many thousands of dollars were now on the table. This same situation was probably happening somewhere else in the West at this same instant, but one thing was turned around: Grady had caught Bluefeather dealing the second card, but he had said nothing until Bluefeather went for the third selected winning card under.

Nancy had warned Bluefeather that very few men in

the gambling world could smoothly go that deep into the deck, so the other pros seldom looked for it. All Bluefeather's years of practice went to hell in a glance; Grady called him on it. He knew he was caught, but professional honor would not allow an admission of guilt, or rather, of making a blunder. At Grady's cursing, he felt his skin tighten where the back of his neck joined his skull, and a searing of swift heat prickled his nose scar. Then, Grady's words and knife came at him all in a blur of motion and diffused sound.

Bluefeather deflected the knife from his heart, and it sliced along his ribs cutting a sudden little red overflowing creek that bottomed out against bone. He shattered and tore Grady's elbow over the edge of the card table, but Grady used his other hand to put a lock on Bluefeather's neck bones. He kneed Grady in the groin, gouged at his eyes with both thumbs and bit his right ear mostly off. Grady's fingers stayed locked as if they had been cast in solid bronze.

Bluefeather's vision was turning into a whirling gray mass as he fell. He was not aware that he had secured Grady's knife until after it was over. Later he remembered the feel of the blade slicing between Grady's cervical vertebrae. He choked and coughed away the violence, desperately seeking air until he could see again. Grady's throat was cut open all the way back through his cervical bones. Only a couple of tendons attached his head to his body. For just a last, heart-pumping moment, the blood spurted almost up to the high ceiling, then its spray dropped to a seep, like a suddenly dry courtyard fountain.

Nancy, her fellow entertainers and almost everyone in the Tonopah area had tried consoling Bluefeather, assuring him that it was self-defense. Some came forward with true tales of great and evil deeds Grady had committed in other states to many helpless folks. None of the words worked on the heart of Bluefeather Fellini. The rightness or wrongness no longer mattered to him. If he had stayed in the mountains where he belonged, it simply would not have happened. That's the way he felt.

So he left the fine wines, big steaks, the feather bed where he and Nancy rubbed skins, and all the other delights. He went back to the mountains. Riding one mule and leading another, he left Tonopah that night just as Nancy and her girls started their show.

He rode across the moonlit desert until the sun came kissing him with kind warmth at first, then searing him with savagery by midday. He had a canvas bag full of water and a wide-brimmed hat. Nothing could stop him from reaching the coolness of timbered country somewhere toward New Mexico.

THIRTEEN

Bluefeather rode down out of the southern Colorado mountains toward the town of Breen. He brought his saddle mule to a stop in the foothills overlooking this place of humans. The pack mule pulled beside them and tried to graze at the long bunchgrass.

He surveyed the setting and saw that there was a good-sized waste dump to the west and some movement around an ore mill below it. He reasoned there would be some action in the town since at least one mine was working.

To the south of Breen, he could see where the sagebrush of the high desert mingled with the thinning timber of the high country. This had always been his favorite kind of land—timber to the north, sage to the south. The Rio Bello edged the town in a half circle, sparkling blue-green where it was banked with cottonwoods golden as egg yolks and oak brush red as fresh blood. Little gardens and orchards that tempted his taste buds were visible even from this distance. He could see the activity on the main street. Several saddle horses and a few wagons and teams were mixed in with a few automobiles. There were even some new mid-1930s models. This was a good sign of local prosperity.

The houses were mostly wood and rock with steep, sloped roofs to more easily shed the heavy winter snows. On the southern edge of town, a scattering of adobes hinted at the Spanish influence of New Mexico.

Yes, he felt good about this town. The terrain suited him—rolling foothills, high desert, timbered mountains, water that had to be good fishing and even an operating mine. It was the right size for its surroundings, too; he figured Breen's population was about fifteen hundred.

But there was something else he felt. Something waiting for him that was good. He sensed this the way an old hunter knows there is a deer behind the oak brush before he sees it.

He smiled and spurred old Jackknife on down the trail. Nancy followed taking quick, short steps to keep the pack balanced. As the mules picked up their gait, there was a smile in the rhythm of their hooves as well.

Bluefeather's sense about Breen was correct. He tied his mules at a hitching post next to the little courthouse square and followed the allure of a sign across the street: MARY'S PLACE—HOMEMADE PIES—THE BEST IN THE WORLD.

Although he always took dried apricots and apples whenever he went on long prospecting excursions, he never seemed to get enough sweets.

After a fine plate of roast beef with steaming brown gravy, Mary handed him an ambrosial quarter of an apple pie as thick as a two-by-four, with crust as delicate as a spring cloud and a flavor as delectable and lasting as first love.

Bluefeather said to himself, "Now that's a pie worth digging for."

Mary smiled at him from her naturally rosy face under her red-blond hair that could match the fall colors of the mountains. Her blue eyes sparkled like polished turquoise and with the same expression of pleasure that danced around her full, pink mouth.

She asked expectantly, "Could you eat another slice?"

Bluefeather looked at this face of womanhood knowing that the body underneath was both strong and elegant like her cooking. "Yes, Ma'am. I think I could. I surely do."

The patrons—miners, drifters, a few cowboys and diverse others—were all a simple blur. He could not force his eyes to focus on anything but the little cardboard sign by the cash register that said, HOUSE FOR RENT. 10 ACRES. INQUIRE HERE.

Mary delivered Bluefeather's pie. He sat straight back in his chair rubbing his powerful, rock-digging hands tenderly back and forth on the red-and-white-checked oilcloth covering the table.

He looked back and forth from the pie to Mary's eyes. Back and forth.

She stood away from the table rubbing her hands lightly on the sides of her apron just below her hips. Neither one could think of anything to say that would break the spell of their transfixion.

"I'm Mary. Mary Schmidt O'Kelly."

"I'm Bluefeather Fellini."

Finally, Mary, feeling her face flare hot, turned hesitantly, looked at the kitchen and muttered something about "biscuits burning." She went to her iron range and became very busy.

Bluefeather sliced off a bite of pie so large it nearly choked him. He was saved by swallowing what was left of his water and coffee. He needed to gasp for breath but somehow got his lungs working before he turned blue or made any embarrassing noises. After that he kept his head tilted down over the pie and took very small bites. He ate it all, even picking up his spoon and scraping the remaining crumbs of the crust into it with the fork until the plate appeared freshly washed. He faked taking another bite of invisible pie as Mary hurriedly filled his coffee cup. She knew he was staring after her as she walked back to the stove.

Suddenly, Bluefeather felt a presence behind him, oppressive, and projecting disturbing vibrations into his back. It came from a table of four men, but he didn't have to look to know exactly where this uncomfortable feeling was coming from. It had happened many times before during his lifetime and was always right in its invisible warnings.

One of the men—big, with wide shoulders and heavy hands, a nice-looking face, except his eyes were somewhat close together—came over and politely introduced himself.

"I'm Stan Berkowitz."

Bluefeather knew this was the man whose presence he had felt and he said, "I'm Fellini."

"Pleased to make your acquaintance. I see by your mules," and he motioned out to them, "that you're a mining man. I'm the mill foreman here. If I can do anything for you, all you have to do is ask."

"Well . . . thank you, Mister . . . ?"

"Please, just call me Stan. The widow Mary and I have been dating for some time now. She makes some kind of pie, don't she?" He smiled like a braying mule.

Bluefeather somehow knew that the man was going to do something to him. He had met a few gracious losers in his time but never a joyous one. He must watch his back for a smiling dagger. If, of course, he decided to stay in Breen a spell.

* * *

Bluefeather wandered around the town for a couple of hours, then returned to Mary's Place to inquire about the house that was for rent. He had decided this was where he wanted to be. Maybe for the rest of his life.

Things moved so smoothly it caused a slight blur of memory. Somehow he had joined Mary in the kitchen to help clean up after closing. Then her elderly father, Ludwig Schmidt, had limped over to walk her home.

Bluefeather couldn't recall all the things they said that night of their first meeting in the cafe, but it left a sweet melancholia like a fine mist of honeyed air. He knew he would carry the scent of her, the feeling of her, through many dimensions of moving time.

At Ludwig's insistence, Bluefeather had joined them, after getting his mules and introducing them as Miss Nancy and Señor Jackknife as formally as if he were introducing royalty. Ludwig examined the mules and their packs in the moonlight with an experienced eye. He approved of both. Mary smiled fleetingly, knowing that her father had just accepted Bluefeather as the new tenant.

"Almost as fine a pair of mules as my last ones," Ludwig said.

Bluefeather was happy to unpack, brush down, feed the mules some oats and turn them loose in the corral. There was a nice shed for a stable, and the ten acres of grass were ungrazed and seeding out.

As he stepped up on the porch he noticed a small sign above the front door: LUDWIG SCHMIDT—ASSAYER. Great spirits alive! His new landlord was a mining man. Nancy would have said, "The cards are falling for you, darling. Push your luck."

Ludwig stayed in the main house while Mary showed Bluefeather his new home and helped him get set up. She lighted the lantern hanging on the back porch and two kerosene lamps inside. The house was spotless, even though Mary kept apologizing for not having it cleaner. Bluefeather wanted to laugh at this. If the place had been more polished, it would have been too smooth to stand or move about in without falling. He was really pleased with the three rooms. There was a kitchen, a bedroom and a supposed sitting room.

He threw his bedroll on the floor by the bed and pulled it open.

Mary said, "Oh, no need for that. Here, I've kept clean sheets and covers ready." She pulled off an old spread that she used to keep the undercovers dustproof.

Bluefeather said, "Ahhh, well if you don't mind, I'd rather get a bath before I use such a special bed."

"Well, in that case, there's firewood and a washtub on the porch." She demonstrated the hand water pump over a galvanized sink and got a couple of pails and set them up on the stove. She looked around hesitantly, holding her hands together in front of her as if there just had to be something else she *must* do.

Bluefeather said, "Now don't fret. Everything is fine. I'll just heat some water, take a bath and I'll see you both in the morning."

"Are you sure there's not something else you need?"

"No. No, you've already been too kind."

"Well, I'll be going then. Papa likes a bourbon and hot milk before he goes to bed." She started out the door and then hesitated. "Papa fixes his own breakfast about half past six or so, because I have to get to the cafe for the early birds. Good-night then."

"Good-night, Miss . . . Miss . . ."

"Actually it's Mrs. I'm a widow. But call me Mary," she said with almost an order in her voice.

"Mary it is."

And she was gone. He missed her before she had reached the back door.

Bluefeather slept later by far than he had intended and felt a little guilty. The sun was over the trees by the river when he arose. He fixed his breakfast from his prospecting supplies but vowed to get fresh eggs, potatoes and much more for the next meal.

He fed the mules a coffee can of oats before he even thought of feeding himself. He looked again at the pasture of lush grass and knew he had not needed to worry. Even in deep snow the mules would enjoy digging down to the grass because they would know there was plenty of oats in the barn. It would just be exercise for sunny days. It suddenly hit him that he had been so pleased with the entire situation that he had forgotten to pay Ludwig. He blushed until his face felt singed.

"Jesus H. Christmas Christ," he muttered to himself, "what a rude, thoughtless bastard I am." Well, he had cash, but because of his unforgivable oversight he decided it would make a better impression if he paid in gold dust. He knocked on Ludwig's door and after a while he heard the old gentleman limp to it.

"Ahhh, good morning to you, Mr. Fellini. Come in. Come in. Did you sleep well, Mr. Fellini?"

Bluefeather said, before he realized he was imitating Mary, "Blue. Blue, it is."

"Ah, yes."

Bluefeather apologized for neglecting to pay the rent, and although he was offered coffee, he insisted on getting business over with first. Ludwig led the way into his assay room. There were great rock specimens everywhere as well as old and relatively new mining claim maps all over the walls.

Bluefeather was stunned and highly pleased. Ludwig

was not just an analyzer of other men's labors, he had been a seeker himself.

Ludwig, seeing Bluefeather's expression, said, "Ah, yes, Bluefeather . . . Blue, I've been far more involved in prospecting than assaying. I've wondered many times if I've wasted my degree in chemical engineering. No. I suppose not. The money I've earned has allowed me to follow my . . . my dreams. Can I use that word with you, Blue?"

Bluefeather was thrilled even more than he could have hoped for. Here he had a landlord who was not afraid to be labeled a dreamer, and say so. After weighing out three months' rent in gold dust, Ludwig told him the history of many of the rocks. Bluefeather recognized some of them from mountain ranges he had visited himself. All green malachite copper might look the same to the casual observer, but to those who breathed it, every location had a slightly different cast—a differently hued host rock. Only true professionals had this capability.

It was midafternoon when they realized they had been lost in their worlds of hard earth and rainbowed minerals. To Bluefeather it had seemed like only a second ago since he had knocked on the back door; now he must leave. He suddenly felt that he had most certainly overstayed his welcome.

As Bluefeather apologized and opened the door to leave, Ludwig said with a strong voice that somehow gave confidence and comfort, "Oh, sir, never apologize for having true adventures and fun. That's what rocks are made for."

Bluefeather walked out into the late sun of the wondrous southern Colorado fall weather and talked to his mules.

"Say, kids, we've found us a home at last. Now don't you worry. There are hundreds of thousands of acres to prospect next spring right near here. We'll have a lifetime of that and a home too. Now, how do you like them pinto beans? Huh?"

They both listened, looking at him as they moved their ears to catch the special resonance, but then simultaneously they dropped their heads and started grazing again. This move was not done out of disrespect for their partner, but they knew that now was the short time of easy grass. They grazed accordingly.

In the next few days Bluefeather and Ludwig made many new discoveries about each other. For one thing, they were both avid readers. Bluefeather was pleased that they shared a love for Balzac and Dostoyevski. The Schmidt family room had been turned into a library, a music room and a place for contemplation. A great bay window looked out over thousands of acres of high timber and desert combined.

Before Ludwig realized that Bluefeather was staring at the rows of books with joy, rather than insecurity, he half apologized, "Well, you know, Blue, many of the mountain men read Shakespeare as a religion."

Sometimes they would talk for hours; then there were times when silence was the rule as Ludwig played his beloved Wagner records and the works of other composers on the Victrola. Occasionally he would play a Strauss waltz and, limping slightly on one lame leg, dance to the music. A quick change of mood might call for Beethoven.

A surprising cultural bond was developing between these two men of mountains, but they didn't spend all their time together. Every day, Bluefeather had gone to lunch at Mary's Place, and every day, he had helped her clean up the tables and dishes. He soon learned that she had taken on the restaurant business so her father could afford to spend time with his music and books during the fall and winter months.

Mary was very pleased that her father had someone to share his rocking-chair adventures with, but a different, strong emotion tore at her now. She herself wanted more time to spend with the new tenant. Being a practical person, she trained additional help so that she and Bluefeather could be together a great part of Wednesday and all day Sunday.

They fished the cold, Prussian-blue waters of the Rio Bello, and Bluefeather was amazed at how dedicated and skilled she was. Unbeknownst to Bluefeather, she was just as pleasantly surprised with his abilities.

On their third outing together she wandered downstream from him about a hundred yards and cast out into a deep, dark hole of twisting water next to a fallen log. The sun came bouncing across the ripples of the current and created a vibrating halo around her red hair. The shimmering rays cast little dancing lights over all her body, delineating her femaleness so strongly that Bluefeather missed two good strikes in a row. He jerked so hard at the third fish, while his head was still turned enraptured with the highlighted vision of Mary, that he slipped and fell into the water. Fortunately he was mostly below a cut bank so that Mary could not see his embarrassment, as long as he stayed bent over almost double.

He hooked a six-pound brown deep in the throat. The fish showed much resentment at this, diving, jumping and shaking with all its watery strength. Bluefeather finally landed it. He had fought the fish in his bent-over position so long that he couldn't straighten up to show it off with the proper shouting and bragging—the key element when fishing with a companion. When one is in the company of the most beautiful, intelligent, kindliest and best baker of pies in the entire world, it is an absolute requisite. Shame. Instead he lay down on the grass in a curiously bent position with the water squishing in his shoes and his clothes sticking to his skin.

He extracted the hook from the fish's throat with some difficulty, saying, "Forgive me, you flopping bastard." He hid in a circle of bushes until the slanting sun had him mostly dry. Then he went looking for his Miss Mary.

Mary caught three ten- or twelve-inchers, providing them with enough fish for a feast, and indeed, they had one that night.

Bluefeather had a little more bourbon than usual before the repast, and later, after the great meal, he had an extra two or three glasses of wine. He finally gathered the courage to tell Mary and Ludwig the whole truth of his fish story. Mary laughed so hard her eyes watered, and Bluefeather swore he could hear her entire body tinkling like a thousand ceramic bells.

Ludwig roared and shook. His face, strong as a lion's and chiseled from granite, turned a little softer with his mirth. Even so, his broad-knuckled hands that appeared strong as a rock crusher shook the room as he alternately slapped his good leg and then the tabletop.

Good people. Good times. Simple.

FOURTEEN

IN THE MEMORIES OF ALL, THERE HAD NEVER BEEN SUCH A long-lasting fall season in the Breen, Colorado, area. Everyone said so. The yellow-gold of the aspens and cottonwoods and brown-red of the oak brush stayed in the leaves that clung and quaked on the trees for extra weeks. Precious weeks.

Bluefeather and Mary rode the mules high into the mountains several times. They looked out over little streams at an occasional bear, deer and even elk. Once they caught a glimpse of a reclusive mountain lion. It must have been old, because its back was swayed so that its belly appeared to almost drag the ground.

Bluefeather enjoyed spotting tracks of all the wild creatures and showing them to Mary. He pointed out the varied shapes of a wild turkey, a coyote, a bobcat, a raccoon and a porcupine. He explained how the distances between tracks and the depths of indentations told stories of haste, slow walking, or even attack. She would ask questions and smile at his answers, as excited as a child at a frog pond.

Their last trip before winter was celebrated with a meal of fried chicken, potato salad and sourdough bread

with goat cheese, heightened by a bottle of red wine.
They chose a little highland meadow for their picnic,
where the thick, cured grass was surrounded by spruce
trees and a few aspens. These kept the wind to a teasing
breeze.

They could see for almost a hundred miles to the south
into New Mexico, across colorations of timber thinning
into the sage and cedar of the high desert. Richly colored
mesas twisted across the vast area like waves on a mighty
sea of dirt and stone. Then on and on, purples and blues
as the land broke and reformed. Finally the horizon and
the sky met, creating different shades of blue to every eye
that had ever looked upon their joining.

The sun was low in the sky, even at two o'clock in the
afternoon, but warmed the little park just enough to take
the bite out of the sharp, thin air.

Bluefeather felt at home where he sat and the same as
far as he could see. The two mules grazed contentedly.
He reached over and touched Mary on her temple and
twirled a flaming lock of her hair.

She turned her face to him, took his hands in hers and
held them to her lips. Then with a little glance of wide,
blue eyes at his dark ones, she moved his hands between
her breasts and squeezed them with some force. They
loved. Later she slept.

After a short time, Bluefeather got up and stepped
away, as quietly like the Indian he was, into the timber.
He sniffed the sharp evergreen scent and felt the nee-
dles, leaves and twigs crunch softly under his feet. This
was his first choice for a home. At this thought he needed
to touch Mary again.

He moved quietly out into the clearing and stood looking down at her where she lay. She was so lovely, so at
rest and at peace, that he was totally entranced. Immobile. Even though her breasts lifted up and down in slow,

deep breaths, the flush and touch of love still pinked her face.

He had no idea how many eternities he stood there absorbing her, but suddenly he realized her great, blue eyes were staring up at him, and he could read their message. He felt warmer than the sun that would bless them for only a few more minutes.

He was suddenly as drunk as a bottle of bourbon, as weak in the legs as a very old granddaddy spider. Then an instant surge of energy and exaltation possessed him. He bent and lifted her up, carrying her over the little meadow to a gap in the trees looking south.

She was awake when he let her feet down in the grass. They stood shoulder to shoulder staring at the southern panorama all the way across the invisible Colorado state line into New Mexico. She leaned her head over on his shoulder and he put his arm around her back. There was a stillness now. A silence to hear, and air so pure it breathed itself. Their outer vision joined their inner vision as Bluefeather raised one arm sweeping wide in front of him.

"We belong to that," he whispered.

"Yes. Yes, we do. Always."

In three days the leaves lost their yellow and red brightness and turned brown and gray. In two more they started drifting toward the earth's eternal gravity, delayed in their descent a fractional degree according to the cold gusts of wind.

Bluefeather felt some guilt. He'd been so absorbed in being with Mary, he had postponed crucial winter chores as he had never done before. At least he had put an old wagon in good shape earlier. Now he and the mules must get busy hauling wood for both houses—piñon for the fireplaces and cedar for the cookstoves. Cedar was better suited for the contained cookstove because it creates a quick, popping heat; piñon, which burns steadily, emitting a rich, earthy smell, would give much comfort and delight in the fireplaces the entire winter.

After hauling the wood down out of the mountains, he chopped it all into proper lengths and stacked it in neat rows. He worked furiously, sweating in the early winter winds, his strong, young body enjoying the extended exercise.

The snow held off even though the winds were icy from heavy, white moisture farther north. He caulked doors and windows and nailed down anything that was slightly loose. He saw to it that the grain bins were filled with sufficient oats and corn. He had already bought plentiful supplies of grass and alfalfa hay; he liked to mix up the grains and the roughage for his animals in the cold months. They would come out of the long winter in good shape, ready for the heavy work of spring. This thought brought others to Bluefeather's mind.

He had had only a few long visits with Ludwig when the old gentleman brought up what he called his "great secret." Bluefeather would never be so foolish as to take him lightly. If Ludwig chose to describe something in this manner, Bluefeather *knew* it was great. Even though the word seemed so overused almost everywhere, he did not doubt the quality of Ludwig's secret to any degree. Ludwig had promised to tell Bluefeather at the right time. Well, when would that be? When he was ninety?

It was very difficult for Bluefeather to admit to himself that he craved—yes, ached—to ask Ludwig what the hell it was all about, but he knew he must be patient and refrain from any questions until Ludwig chose to tell him. Even though Bluefeather was taught early in life—like most Indians, cowboys and mining men were—not to ask personal questions, it was still going to be very hard not to break the rules. It was the code. Oh sure, it was fine to ask people questions about the welfare of their spouses, or their children or even their parents. Also, it was permissible to ask someone about his crops, the weather or how his arthritis was getting along. But the great secret? Never.

He realized that when Ludwig felt like it, he would tell him, without any impolite questions being asked. If he didn't, then Bluefeather guessed it was just no one's business. Bluefeather was suffering great pain wanting to know. But damn the code—it held.

Again and then again he played over in his hearing-mind what Ludwig had promised: "I'll tell you, Blue . . . at the right time, of course, dear boy . . . I shall reveal to you a great secret. Your wildest fantasies are nothing at all. Nothing, I say. None of your dreams could touch my revelations, unless God made them for you personally at the right time."

As Bluefeather was saying, "Yes. Yes . . . ?" Ludwig's voice faded and he fell asleep.

Bluefeather repeated, "Damn the code!"

His curiosity kept him awake for three days and nights. He made medicine, chewed peyote and had natural hallucinations, but no answer came.

He finished storing the apple crop in the cellar, wrapping each apple tightly in newspaper or pages from the Montgomery Ward catalog. He saw the long shelves loaded with vegetables and fruits that Mary had canned all spring and summer. Now he rearranged the jars of apricots and peaches in bunches on the wooden shelves. To his joyful anticipation, there was a whole winter's worth of pies in those jars—enough for the restaurant and plenty for them personally.

There seemed to be only one thing left that he felt he

could add to the winter food supply. They needed a buck deer to hang in the meat house.

If only he could get Ludwig's secret off his mind, everything would be just rosy. Why? Why did Ludwig have to use that word "great"? Why couldn't he have simply kept quiet until the right time, or at least have said something like, "I have something to tell you in a few days, or . . . in the spring or . . . in the summer or . . ."

He decided to force himself to quit thinking about it. Anyway, he knew it would have something to do with a mining secret. He was sure of that. What else could the two of them share that deserved such words?

Bluefeather saddled Nancy, took his .30-30 and rode into the mountains. He wore a sheepskin coat and chaps, and had his hat tied down with a bandanna. When they got to about eight thousand feet, it was blowing so cold that he tied another scarf around his face just under his eyes so he could breathe warmer air and still see. If the snows had come on schedule, the deer would have been in the foothills, and hunting would have been easier.

Today he had seen some old and some recent signs of both bucks and does. Tracks and droppings were plentiful, but so far he had spotted nothing fresh. His young eyes could see fine from the top of the mule, but even so, at every clear patch of earth he would stop Nancy and lean over to carefully examine the ground. He figured the deer would be on the east side of the slope out of the wind and in the sun if possible. He was right. He saw where the larger tracks of a single buck had followed a trail and then left it just ahead of him. He had a choice of getting down, tying the mule, following the tracks and eventually coming at the deer from a downwind direction, or he could stay in the saddle and save a lot of walking and time.

He reined Nancy out after the deer. He watched her

ears work. Soon they came to the easterly edge of an open meadow heavily circled by spruce and some pines. He pulled the mule back and rode all the way around to the east side as he had planned. In a spot where the trees thinned a bit, he pulled up and carefully looked across the opening to the other edge. No matter how hard he tried to conjure up a deer in the varied shapes of scattered dead timber, he just could not make one appear in the flesh. Well, he had figured wrong. The buck must have moved on farther than he had figured. He would just have to ride higher to the north in hope of cutting the sign again.

They moved out and up now. Bluefeather was in the netherworld of doubt. He was in that highly charged condition that comes after one finds evidence of the immediate presence of prey, and then the sense of loss, or of a vacuum, when the prey seems to have vanished. Bluefeather was determined to conquer the spell.

He slipped the .30-30 from the scabbard and decided to gamble entirely on Nancy. She stepped delicately but surely through the scattered trees as only mules can do. Her long ears worked back and forth, listening. Her head was up, she was alert, sensing with all her body.

On they moved, and now, even as quietly as Nancy walked, Bluefeather felt that the noise was as loud as a landslide and that all the deer between southern Colorado and northern Canada could hear them. But that was sometimes the wisdom of hunting from the saddle—the wild animals heard the rhythm of four legs walking instead of two.

Bluefeather felt the mule's muscles tighten under the saddle and her steps shorten as she turned her head to the side with both ears pitched forward. She came to a stop like a bird dog on stand. There. About eighty to a hundred yards away stood the four-point buck. Its head was up, and it was looking in their direction. There was an open space to aim the rifle, and he could shoot to the side so the noisy explosion of the cartridge would not hurt Nancy's sensitive ears.

He took a deep breath and held it as he lowered the barrel down so that the sights entered just behind the deer's shoulder. It was the best he could do at that angle. He squeezed off the shot, his spirit going out the barrel with the lead, through the trees and the heart of the deer. Then it zapped back into his body as the majestic creature seemed to float just above the ground for an unmeasured instant, then fall dead without time for pain.

He reined toward his prey, the ancient hunters' genes within him causing his blood to flow like a flash flood. He dismounted, put the palm of his left hand on the forehead of the deer and said softly, "Forgive me, kind and generous brother."

He gutted the deer then swung it across the saddle. With leather thongs, he tied its feet to each stirrup. Then with another thong, he secured the stirrups under the mule's belly. It was done.

He mounted behind the saddle and headed home with the game, as men had done for uncountable time. There was no gloating here, and there would be no bragging later with Bluefeather Fellini, just a warm, pleased feeling at having done his job right. The cold mountain breeze went unnoticed now. He thought of a warm Miss Mary and hot peach pie.

FIFTEEN

ALL THE TOWN'S ROADS WERE OPEN AGAIN. THE COLD DROPPED down and surrounded everything but flame. Some days were the coldest ever recorded in the United States. Even so, the people adjusted and simply went on with their work the best they could. It was the time of acceptance.

Ludwig was delighted at the news of the engagement, asking Bluefeather, "When?"

"We've decided to do the deed when all the snow is gone from that long hill behind the house. The one Mary calls 'Clock Hill,' " and he made a northerly gesture.

"That is good, sir. That is splendid. It'll be some day in April or May then. We'll watch closely." Ludwig started making all kinds of plans. "Durango. We must go to Durango for the wedding. We'll stay in the Strater." The latter was a four-story, brick hotel built in 1887 and one of America's finest. After his pleasurable tirade, Ludwig added solemnly, "That is, of course, if it's the desire of you kids."

A few days after his initial elation, Ludwig became quieter and more withdrawn than Bluefeather had ever seen him. Bluefeather's first honest thought was a fear that

Ludwig was ill. He had grown so fond of the old man that he would be greatly troubled if Ludwig missed the great day because of an indisposition. He talked over his concerns with Mary, and she said he was always like this before a moment of meaningful decision.

She was right.

Bluefeather fed the mules and walked on the path he had shoveled through the snow over to Ludwig's to have some coffee.

Ludwig fussed and limped about, insisting on fixing and pouring the steaming liquid himself. He drank only half a mug. Then he brought a bottle of Napoleon brandy from the whiskey cabinet and, without a word, poured them each a portion large enough to fill their coffee mugs.

Bluefeather was surprised that the old man would drink brandy so early in the day. They sat, staring into voids, these two men linked together by their love of the precious rock from the earth and a lovely lady called Mary. They sat in silence, each waiting for the other to speak.

Finally Bluefeather came out with a cliché as he set his mug back down on the table. "This really hits the spot."

"Yes. Yes, the spot. Certainly. Certainly does." Ludwig twisted in his chair and looked out a frosty window, turned his mug on the table, looked at Bluefeather and grinned. He scratched in the white shock of hair on his large head as if he were cultivating it. He cleared his throat and glanced at Bluefeather, smiling so quickly an eagle would have missed it. He cleared his throat. Again. Then again.

He emptied the coffee and brandy in one mighty swig. Then he stood up on his bent and battered legs, straightening his spine, stuck his chin out and headed for his workroom with hardly a limp.

Bluefeather half expected a drumroll or maybe the music of a military band to blast forth. Ludwig returned carrying a leather-covered box perhaps ten by twelve by fourteen inches and placed it on the table right in front of Bluefeather. Then he inserted a key in the small lock secreting the contents of the box. He placed a massively boned hand on each end of it, hesitating as his old lungs moved his chest bones under the skin, in and out. Faster and faster, his eyes widened and brightened, and then with a flourish that would have done credit to most highly acclaimed illusionists, he raised the lid on the box. There it was at last.

Yes, finally Bluefeather gazed upon the great secret. It was a rock of rose quartz that almost filled the box. It was filigreed with wire gold as if sewn in by a large, magic needle. The snakes of gold seemed to twist and writhe around one another in ancient shining splendor.

Ludwig said, "Well . . . there it is," in a voice that could just as well have said, "Answer the doorbell. . . . God is standing on the front porch."

Bluefeather knew well that some of the greatest high-grade gold discoveries had been made in rose quartz, and he also sensed correctly that Ludwig would not be displaying this wondrous specimen unless he had found the mother vein that had given it birth. At a glance Bluefeather knew the rock had not been dug from the vein but rather that the elements had freed it. Then the float rock had moved a short distance downhill over many years. He knew this by its slightly smoothed edges. If it had moved a long distance, there would have been no sharp edges left at all.

At last he could give voice. "Thank you, Ludwig. Thank you for allowing me to gaze upon glory."

This pleased Ludwig immensely and he said, "Go

ahead, go ahead and lift it out of the box. Examine it with your glass. Go ahead, sir."

Bluefeather did as he was bid. He could barely lift it free in his fear of dropping the rock and smashing the lovely gracious container. He thought the specimen was well over half gold. He placed his prospector's magnifying glass close, adjusting it as the entire visible world turned to precious gold before his eyes.

"Ahhhh. Ahhhh," was what he said.

After a time he raised up, breathless, stunned, but before he could think of another proper comment Ludwig broke in. "I found it. I found the big dream. But I had to know if the vein carried any distance before I mined it. Naturally I called the claim the King Tut. As you will soon see, that part of the forest is covered with heavy overburden. So I took the strike of the vein, and sighting along it, I could see where the penetration of some rock bluffs must occur, perhaps a quarter mile up the mountain. If it did, I knew I would have the bonanza that all mining men seek—nay, all men and some women. There would be enough gold to buy a city, build a large lake or feed a million mouths. So, Blue—and I know you can understand my thinking—I climbed and slid, and climbed and fell, until I reached the edge of the jagged bluff. It sloped back slightly and had sufficient crevices and indentions to make an easy climb. It was not so. The gold had blinded me at about thirty or forty feet up. I'll never know. I slipped. I fell. I broke many bones, and my innards have ached now for these five terribly long years, but aside from my smashed and mangled leg, I am able to get along quite well, as you can see."

"Yes. Yes, of course," Bluefeather agreed. He did not know why, but he had thought that Ludwig had been crippled in the flash flood that had taken the lives of his wife and Mary's husband.

"Neither one of us knew it, but we have been waiting for one another, looking for each other. It was fated beyond recall that you'd ride your mules into this town and stop at Mary's Place exactly when you did, Blue, my son."

Bluefeather couldn't think of anything to say, but he believed, with all his being, Ludwig's every word. The old man spoke softly, always, but even so his voice was as powerful, smooth and penetrating as rubbing alcohol. It moved out in the air and surrounded him like a tent.

"Now, now, at last, you are here to fulfill my dream," Ludwig said. "Your dream. Mary's dream. Your strong, young legs will carry you—more carefully—to climb the cliff and uncover the vein. It is you, dear Blue, who will finish the dream for us all."

In this mesmerizing moment, Bluefeather gave his hand, his word, his vow, to Ludwig Schmidt, currently of the village of Breen, in southern Colorado. He was further thrilled when Ludwig showed him the map he had sketched out while recuperating from his fall. The vein was only half a day's mule ride from the room in which they now stood.

Late that night, Bluefeather stared from his bed into the darkness of the ceiling and smiled at the Great Spirit, voicing softly his thanks. He could have great riches, a loving wife, a father-in-law friend and his home, all right here. Here. Who had ever been so blessed? Who, indeed?

Bluefeather walked into Mary's Place in midafternoon. There were still two tables of coffee drinkers, cursing the government and talking hunting and fishing. Bluefeather spoke to them politely and they answered back only because of Mary. He did not, and had not, ever joined their tables for small talk. It just was not in his nature. When he had a friend, that person got his time, his attention

and his thoughts as long as they lived. Grinder the Gringo
had been one of those. Nancy had almost been a friend,
but Bluefeather's sudden departure had prevented it.
Now his number-one friend was old Ludwig. The fact he
was to be his mining partner and father-in-law was truly a
meaningless matter as far as their friendship was concerned.

So he chose a corner table like a regular customer,
which he intended to be before he shared with Mary the
churning tidings he held inside with such difficulty. It
took a tough man to control knowledge and feelings de-
sirous of exploding like a full case of old dynamite.

Mary sent him a smile of love and a little wave that said
she would be there in just a moment. Oh well, he could
handle it. As soon as the meal was finished he would take
her into the storeroom so he could share his elation with
the love of his life. Mary looked at him again as she was
finishing cooking something on the stove.

Ah, thought Bluefeather, how special that our warm
thoughts can cross the restaurant, ignoring the customers.
But suddenly her face seemed void. He could not see the
talking smile or feel love projecting like sunbeams
through a forest glen. What had happened? In one instant he felt alone in a deep canyon beyond the reach of
light. There was a stream flowing and roaring there, but it
had no fish in its currents and no animals came to drink.
No birds or insects would ever bother to seek its repel-
lent banks. What in hell was he suddenly doing there?

Then he saw Mary do a strange thing. She turned the
OPEN sign around to CLOSED and began talking to the other
customers. They were slowly standing, looking as confused as Bluefeather.

He heard her say, "No, no. It's all on the house. You'll
forgive me this inconvenience, just this one time, I hope.
Something has come up that must be settled. Now."

They shuffled out, glancing and mumbling lowly to one another. One of the most important daily rituals in their lives had just been disrupted. They were suddenly without a single thing to think or do before dinnertime.

Mary locked the door after them. She brought cups and a coffeepot to his table without looking at him or speaking. She poured the coffee and placed the large coffeepot in the middle of the table between them.

She took a sip, glancing across the rim of her cup at him as she did so. Then she set, or slightly slammed, the cup on the table just under the breaking point and said in a voice that would have charred fine oak beams and shattered knife blades, "He told you, didn't he? Well? Well, answer me."

"I . . . I . . . I . . . what do you mean? I don't under . . ."

"He told you about the King Tut. I could recognize that gold-mania stare all the way through the walls of a bank vault. I've seen that glazed look of greed since I was an infant."

"I thought you'd be thrilled that I'm to be partners with your father."

"Thrilled? Thrilled?" And now she stood up and walked to a wall before turning. "Thrilled at the chance to see someone else I love maimed or dead? My God, he's been crippled for years from trying to climb that bluff looking for more. More. Always more. He was an old man then. I'd just lost my mother and my husband, and he falls off that damned rock and nearly dies. Did you know he dragged himself for three days just to get down to the old truck? Three days. His hands and the rest of his body were a solid bleeding sore."

"It seems to me that Ludwig showed great courage and love for you to survive all that."

"Courage? Oh, he's got plenty of that. But consideration? None. When the gold takes over and becomes all . . . all, do you hear? Then thoughts of others are secondary." She hesitated a moment, pushing at her hair and wringing her hands as if she wanted to twist the blood out of them.

She finally started to talk again. "We had no one left but each other. Oh, maybe somewhere in Germany or Ireland, and then . . . then he goes and climbs in the rocks like a kid."

"It was just professionalism. You have to know if the vein is long enough to risk the expense of digging. That's the way it is."

"You sound just like him. There's always some excuse —some reason to perpetuate the obsession—the madness. I thought you were different. I thought you wanted to make a home here with me . . . with us."

"I do. I do. I love you, Mary, and I want to be with you all my life."

"Ha . . . haaa . . ." She stomped about, looking unnaturally awkward and repulsive for a moment. Then she was quiet and, still breathing heavily, cast her all-enveloping blue eyes on him, saying softly, "You'll let the mad dream go, won't you, Blue?"

"Well . . . I can't, Mary."

"What do you mean, you can't?" she screamed, her eyes suddenly turning green as malachite and hard as sculptor's marble. "Are you so weak that you simply can't say no? I thought you were a man. You're just a little, measly wimp. A joiner." This last hurt deeply, but Bluefeather made a desperate effort to understand.

"But I gave my word to your father. It's his last dream. I'd rather die than take that away from him. Don't you see?" He begged, "Mary, I'll be careful. I'm young. I'm strong. I'm experienced. We'll all be rich."

" 'Rich, rich, rich'—that's the word that never leaves

gold. They're glued together so strongly that families, friends, homes and lovers are ripped apart and destroyed, but not 'gold' and 'rich.' Oh, no." She was shaking now and beginning to choke to hold back her sobs.

Bluefeather had to reach her somehow and make her believe him. "I have never let gold possess me, darling. Please believe me when I tell you it never could, never will."

"Listen to you. Just listen. Empires have fallen. Millions upon millions of people slaughtered, tortured, until madness sets in on both the robbed and the robber. It's never stopped. It never will."

"But I'm different. Me. Bluefeather Fellini. I'm not the same as the others. I swear to you, I'll dig only what gold we need. That's all. No more. Ever. I give my promise to you on that, the same as I did your father. Both promises can be accommodated and honored."

"So you're going ahead with it? My father hypnotized you with his dreams. You're crazy. You're both crazy—filled with yellow madness."

"You are not hearing me correctly." Now he was shouting. "I said that I could keep both promises. I give you this vow on my soul. I will never let the gold obsess or dominate me in any manner that would jeopardize our love, but you must know that I have to keep my word to your father, or nothing matters—not friendship, not love, not honor, not gold."

He was exhausted and drained from the shouting, but not Mary Schmidt O'Kelly. She trembled even more, broke into sobs and moans of anguish beyond his reach, and then grabbed the coffeepot and hurled it at him. It splashed its contents about the room, clanging loudly in a strange tune with her own terrible angst.

"Get out. Go away. I hate you. I never want to see you again. Never, ever again."

With a pain so dull and deep it was not of his body but some other part of him, he tried to speak the right words to salvage something very special that was being lost— tossed away, like cold, winter ashes.

She scrambled for the kitchen, running into tables, and picked up a meat cleaver, still screaming things he couldn't or wouldn't hear. He barely got the latch to the outside door open before she attacked him.

He walked away in the snow path, his shoulders humped up like a cow's back in a blizzard. His heart beat erratically in fear and unspeakable sadness. There was no measurement for such a loss.

SIXTEEN

HE HAD WANTED TO STOP IN AND TALK TO LUDWIG ABOUT THE disaster, but it would not be proper. Mary was his only child. He had to face that. Now was the time he could have used another friend in Breen, but he only had a few acquaintances.

He thought about going to one of the three saloons and getting drunk. He discounted that thought faster than he had discovered it. Bluefeather didn't drink except for pleasure . . . for fun. So he went to the shed and fed the mules two hours early. They only smelled the grain and picked at the hay. They knew something was mightily wrong with their partner and moved about nervously, observing with both their large eyes and ears.

"Oh, cherished ones, my heart is in torment and my soul dangles over the escarpment of hell. We . . . we have lost our new partner. She has cast me out and beyond her, for reasons that are wrong but understandable. She has taken her tragic losses of recent years with much bravery and good cheer, but underneath she must have suffered the distress of the damned. I see it clearer now. She finally reached the point where she couldn't even think of any more losses of loved ones. Is that it? Am I

right, Jackknife? Is my thinking correct, Nancy? I see that
you feel I'm on the right track."

Bluefeather whammed the bottoms of his clenched
fists into the walls of the shed, shaking it and causing the
mules acute concern.

"What does understanding Mary's hidden feelings matter when the entire world has been ripped into frag-
ments. Huh? Huh?" He demanded a reasonable answer
from the mules and himself, but none came.

Bluefeather went to his house and built up the fire
until it roared and the iron stove seemed to bounce from
the floor. He tried to eat but threw up. He opened a book
and the words were all blurred and made him nauseous
again.

He stretched out on the bed and tried to sleep. Nothing worked. He saw Miss Mary. Her eyes washed him in
lustrous light, her voice soothed and excited him all at
once. Her body moved in rhythms that gave him pleasure
to the point of blankness, blindness—the nonknowing of
the ultimate intent of love and creation. Hours passed
before he moved.

He rebuilt the fire, but the room was still cold, so he
walked about, back and forth, like a newly caged coyote.
His stomach felt like he had been disemboweled and his
temples pounded as if he had competed in a head-butting
contest with a bull buffalo.

He was still up when the sun rose. By then he had
another affliction. Someone had extracted all the blood
and bone from his legs and filled them with water one
degree below freezing. His thoughts rattled around in his
head and made weird, uncontrollable sounds.

He craved to cry and sob aloud to relieve the rusty
barbed wire that was rapidly tightening around his heart,
killing him for sure. Had he known that Mary suffered
even more, he would either have started feeling better or

fallen dead. The pain from torn and lost love finally caused him to feel like he was floating around the room with a high fever.

At last, on the beginning of the third day, he fell belly-down on his bed and sobbed so long and hard he threw his back out of place. This bit of destruction hurt so badly, he only thought of losing Mary two out of every three minutes now.

Bluefeather had slept so hard from pure emotional exhaustion that he had forgotten about his dislocated back. He stood up and started to stretch. A pain that truly made him go blind struck his whole body, and he fell to the floor. He was afraid to move for a spell, but then, pushing himself slowly to a sitting position with the strength of his arms alone, he braced for the shock of expected misery from his lower back. It didn't come. Cautiously he eased to his feet. It was gone. The fall had knocked it back into place.

He was so relieved that he built a fire and cooked a big breakfast of coffee, sourdough biscuits, venison, eggs and milk gravy. And ate it all. Of course, it was his first meal in several days. He tried to count them. Two? Three? Five? A million? Well, somewhere in there.

He heated some water in a large pan, shaved and took a sponge bath. He put on clean clothes and actually combed at his tangled black hair. He raised one knee up and then the other. The back held. This gave him enough courage to actually make a decision. By damn it, he was not going to let the woman of his life get away.

He had just put on a heavy coat along with a muffler and was reaching for his hat when he heard the tentative knock. He hung the hat back on the hook and moved to the door. He could see the outline of a figure through the frosted glass as it tapped hesitantly again. Could it be . . . ? Was it possible that . . . ?

His breath was suddenly hard to find, even though it was strong enough to heave his chest up and down above his thrashing heart. He opened the door, close to fainting.

The air was turned to frost as her lips, red as her hair, moved and said, "May I come in before I freeze to death?"

"Oh . . . oh sure, come on in here." He stepped as far aside as he could when she entered, then swiftly but gently closed the door.

She untied the scarf over her head, unwound the muffler from her neck, then straightened up bravely like a Joan of Arc and said with much firmness, "I'll work the mines with you. Then we'll both know what is what. All right?"

Bluefeather could certainly be forgiven for stuttering and saying nothing clearly.

Mary continued in a businesslike manner that would have made the secretary of the Treasury proud, "I know all about the worldwide superstition of impending doom if a female enters a mine. It all started in Wales when a lady member of the royal family inspected a mine and immediately afterward there was an explosion and a cave-in, killing many miners. Yes, I know about that, and I also know that she had inspected several other mines that week where nothing of obvious danger occurred. You're not superstitious, are you, Blue?"

"Oh no . . . no, of course not. There's not a superstition," he swallowed hugely, "in my whole body. In fact . . . this will be just wonderful, because you and I know it is all foolishness." His excitement was escalating. "But all the other foolish prospectors will be afraid to come near our mine. Oh yes, Miss Mary, . . . why, it's just made to order for us." He was hastily removing his coat and saying, "Would you like some coffee?"

She hesitated a blink and said, "No. Not now."

Then, in a synchronized movement, their flesh moved together from the floor to the tops of their heads, and between kisses, Mary said with an infinite sound of relief, "Oh, Blue. Blue."

And he said, "Oh Mary. My Miss Mary."

Moving, still clinging together, they sought a more comfortable spot. They eventually found it and everything fit in its proper place.

The branches had been traumatically stripped from the pines, but the trunks had held strong. Now the branches grew back new, and even stronger, in an amazing few minutes.

SEVENTEEN

ALL THE DENIZENS OF THE BREEN AREA SUFFERED THE LONG winter of deep snows and iron-bending cold with commendable fortitude, but now that the patches of brown earth and vegetation were widening daily, they became irritable and fussy, issuing complaints at the slightest cause. It was the in-between time.

Mary and Bluefeather rode the mules, nearing home. The sun still slanted low, but nonetheless gave some warmth and a touch of promise to the ever-nearing, full awakening of the earth and all its seed. They had gone south for their outing where the mules could bypass the snow with ease. The last mile home, they dismounted to walk. It was warmer that way.

They led the mules and held each other's free hand. Their youth, health and love of loves awaited the green flush of spring with impatience. They felt like springtime, just as the weeks nearing would be.

Bluefeather chuckled to himself and said to Mary, "You know what? We'll have to name our first child America. Nothing else will do. He will be Indian, Italian, German and Irish. If that isn't America I can't conjure it up."

"America Ludwig Fellini. America . . . Ludwig . . . Fellini. Yes, it does have the ring of the nation."

They chattered on about spring, the wedding and the mine. As they neared their houses, both sets of eyes looked at Clock Hill, checking the evaporating snowbanks by immeasurable inches.

Bluefeather unwrapped the beryl crystal he had chiseled several years earlier from a pegmatite dike south of Taos near Penasco. Now he was glad he had not given it to Nancy. The six-sided gemstone was the most beautiful he had ever found. He put his glass on it. Clear, blue light radiated out of it like the birth of a tiny planet. To him, it was lovelier than a solid gold bar, more precious than a large well-watered ranch or a royal castle. He was sure the jewel had been invented by the Creator especially for Miss Mary, whose eyes were often the same color—with the same dancing lights. So he sent it off to Denver to be mounted in silver for a necklace, and he ordered a diamond wedding ring from a Saint Louis catalog. They both miraculously arrived at the post office on the same day.

He immediately rushed home to get a full view of Clock Hill. There were only two snowbanks visible in the shady portion of a long draw. The time of union was near.

His gold dust was gone and his cash was getting short. They would need money for the trip to Durango and the lavish party they were planning. After the wedding there would be the expenses of powder, dynamite caps, drills and just plain living to fulfill his promise to both his good amigo Ludwig and the other half of his bouncing, gleeful soul, Miss Mary of Breen.

He knew a way he could earn the money. It was his honor and his duty to do so. He would win it using the trade Nancy had so carefully taught him. Suddenly, he no longer resented the incidents at Tonopah so much.

Maybe the experiences, both delightful and deadly, could be transposed and used on a grand adventure of love. Maybe.

His footsteps became livelier as the idea became more acceptable to him. The purpose was very strong in his soul, and he began to appreciate the thrill that was beginning to stir in him. It was almost the same feeling he got when hunting deer, rabbits or other wild game for food.

The Breen Palace Hotel was small in room numbers, but it had a large bar with a dance floor. On Friday and Saturday nights a three-piece band consisting of a fiddle, banjo and guitar played there. The First Thought Bar, as it was called, had a steady clientele of miners, businessmen, salesmen and a few ranchers. On the weekends it howled with revelry. However, the most expensive action took place two doors behind the bar. Patrons had to pass through a large storeroom to get to the gaming room.

The bar was luxuriously appointed for this sparsely settled area. A fireplace with a five-foot open face had a large framed original oil painting of a reclining nude hanging above it. On one wall hung a print of Custer's Last Stand that was passed around the West by an alcohol manufacturer. It showed Custer standing, fighting gloriously, amidst thousands of charging Indians whose bullets, spears, tomahawks and arrows had somehow missed him.

There were several soft-cushioned leather couches and chairs. A walnut, glassed-in liquor cabinet, with accompanying front bar, held all the mixes of the time. Just beyond the huge fireplace was a green, felt-covered poker table. It was well-lighted and covered with ashtrays. It had been in almost constant use for twenty-five years now.

Skimpy Jones ran and banked the game. Although he played as an outsider, he took ten percent of each pot for the house. Even if Skimpy himself sometimes lost, the house always won. The players got new cards whenever they asked, and free drinks as long as no one got rudely drunk. If this happened, Skimpy, who weighed around three hundred pounds—a hundred of that was belly- and face-swelling fat—would escort the violator out in whatever manner it took. Admittance to this back room was gained only if one knew the bartender. Bluefeather knew him from his many meals at Mary's Place, so he was immediately passed through.

The first night he played, Bluefeather lost a little money and quit about midnight. He was studying the game and feeling his way. The next night, Friday, he felt the high voltage as he walked in. There was a lot of money in front of the five players. The game had started about two o'clock in the afternoon, and seven or eight players had already gone broke by six o'clock that evening.

Stan Berkowitz seemed to have the most chips, but Skimpy was a very close second. Wally Ward, the railroad super, also played. There was a mining promoter from Denver, who the players called Birmingham and who had a noticeable southern accent. The last surviving player was the owner of the light, telephone and utilities company of Breen, Saul Kahn.

Bluefeather mixed himself a light bourbon and water and told Skimpy he would wait for the next empty chair. In about thirty minutes Kahn stood up saying he had guests coming for dinner, and since he was nearly even he would cash in. Bluefeather took his seat. It was the nearest one to the fireplace, and he was directly across the table from his onetime rival for Mary's favors, Stan Berkowitz.

The game grew in intensity as the night deepened. They switched games often here. Instead of playing draw

or five-card stud all the time, they played hi-lo-split a lot
and seven-card stud poker. The house rules were dealer's
choice. So a player who was unable to almost instantly
adjust his mind to a new game could wind up a loser.

The players came and went except for Bluefeather,
Skimpy and Stan. In the fog of smoke and concentration
of Bluefeather's personal mind-clock, time ceased to exist. He had no idea whether the other players had sat in
for the jolting, high-adrenaline charge of a full house, or
for four of a kind, or whether some of them just needed
the money. The players changed like substitutes in a basketball game.

Bluefeather knew that he and Skimpy were playing for
a grubstake and a living, in that order. Bluefeather always
sipped his drinks slowly, very slowly, so that the players
who drank more heavily would not start watching him,
feeling he was setting sober traps.

So far it had been an honest game, except for the salesman who had tried to deal the second card but had done
it so awkwardly he never tried it again. Bluefeather deliberately had run a couple of bluffs on bad hands to get
caught so that later, when he did have a locked hand and
the pot was big enough, he would be able to suck the
other players in.

Sometime after midnight, a player from Taos sat in
next to Bluefeather. At two o'clock in the morning,
Bluefeather was two thousand dollars ahead. That was
surely enough to supply their needs for the trip to Durango and get the gold moving out of the King Tut.

Bluefeather played carefully now. Since he was the
principal winner, he knew it only natural that everyone at
the table was after his jugular. That's the way he liked it.

The last loser had said it was two o'clock in the morning when he gave up his chair, so Bluefeather guessed it
was now about three o'clock. That, of course, is the "ge-

nius hour" when drinkers—real tough drinkers—think they know everything in the entire world. That's when Bluefeather planned to knock them off. The kill.

There was just one problem: the man from Taos had somehow wrangled it out of Bluefeather that he had once lived there. Between deals the Taos man made unusual small talk, asking if Bluefeather knew this merchant, this artist, that remittance person. Since Bluefeather knew none of these people, the man obviously thought he was a liar and a phony and was making small hints to that effect.

"You must have been just a baby when you left Taos if you don't remember the artist Joseph Sharp. Everyone knows him. Ol' Joe is a legend in Taos and so is Long John Dunn."

"I'm sorry to say, I have heard of them both, but I never knew either of them personally."

"How could you miss Long John? He ran the stagecoach lines into Taos in the early days, and even at his age he's still dealin' at Mike Cunico's place."

"Just my bad luck, I guess." Bluefeather tried to dismiss the subject.

Everyone was staring at the two men now. Stan Berkowitz, who had been extra polite all night, now had that genius-hour grin on his face from boozing. The rising and falling of adrenaline over and over had left him somewhat narcotized. Skimpy was not much better off.

That's when the hand Bluefeather had waited for for two nights fell. Stan had dealt the cards himself. Four kings and a deuce. Bluefeather threw away the deuce and drew a queen. He was hoping they would think he was going for a straight and had missed. He started his bluff just as he had done before. He acted just a little overanxious as he immediately raised the pot a hundred, then two, then three. It was close to perfection.

Three opponents, Stan, Skimpy and Mr. Taos, must have drawn good cards, too, for they stayed. Mr. Taos was done and in for the pot on the second raise. Skimpy was in for another pot on the fourth. Then Bluefeather surprisingly checked. He figured there was six or seven thousand dollars in the pot. It was more than enough. He figured Stan would come at him with all his remaining chips, but Stan checked as well, sensing too late what had happened.

Stan turned over his three jacks and two tens. When he looked at Bluefeather's four kings, he got up and poured himself another drink and came back saying to Skimpy, "Deal 'em, Skimpy. If my check's good, this game just got started." He took a swallow of whiskey and said, "I can't let this newcomer beat me at everything."

Bluefeather felt the bristle hairs on his neck rise and speak to him in warning, but he knew he had to stay another hour or so. If he tried to leave, Stan would surely insult him. Even Skimpy, Taos and the other player would all know they had been suckered for their greed. No. He would play another hour and even more carefully lose a thousand or so back.

It wasn't working. The remarks from Stan kept coming and then Mr. Taos finally drove it all home with a direct question just as Bluefeather was shuffling the cards to deal. "Exactly where did you live in Taos?"

Bluefeather had been so totally involved in handling the game properly for Mary, Ludwig and their partnership that the question caught him at the wrong instant. "I didn't exactly live in town. I spent a lot of time at the Taos Pueblo visiting my grandfather."

"Oh, so he taught at the Indian school there, huh?"

Then Bluefeather really blew it. "No, my grandfather is a medicine man named Moon Looker. My mother is Morning Star."

"Then . . . then you're an Indian? A Taos Indian? You don't look like . . ."

"I'm half Italian."

"Say, it's agin the law to sell drinks to an Indian, and it's agin the law for you to buy one."

"I didn't buy any drinks. These were given to me."

Stan said, just as Bluefeather finished dealing and before he looked at his cards, "You bought into the game and the whiskey is part of it, huh, Skimpy?"

Skimpy looked around and added up the situation like any good professional. Mr. Taos was a very successful car dealer—not to be counted lightly. Stan Berkowitz was a regular player and steady customer with very strong local connections in the mines—where three-fourths of this establishment's business came from. The other player was the owner of a large cattle ranch with landholdings in both New Mexico and Colorado and was also a friend and strong supporter of the governors of both states. Skimpy was naturally respectful of such a powerful person.

He took a quick tally and said, "Stan's right. The Indian was deceiving us and breaking the law by buyin' in, because the whiskey sure as hell goes with the deal."

They all four, plus an onlooker friend standing behind Stan, stared at Bluefeather. The silence seemed extended through many changes of seasons and much eroding of rocks. He felt enclosed in a tight shroud made up of thoughts and eyesight so strong it could crush him into breathlessness.

A light somehow flickered in his brain. It was true, after all, there was always one son of a bitch to throw gravel in the gears. The man from Taos, who should have been his friend and compatriot, was that one.

Stan said as he looked around for support, "In a case like that, I reckon house rules would call for the Indian to return the money, huh, Skimpy?"

Skimpy nodded "yes" and clicked a stack of blue chips up and down in a hand so big and fat the chips were hardly visible. He puffed on the fat cigar between his thick lips, and the smoke clouded his face so that Bluefeather could not see his eyes already slitted and almost closed by surplus flesh.

The coldness of fear, of danger, emanated from Bluefeather's being, and the bristles of his neck were about ready to scream and leap out of his skin. He saw a year's worth of looking in just a few seconds. Hours ago, he had, out of habit and training at Nancy's establishment, spotted a sawed-off ax handle just behind Skimpy and the fireplace iron that was almost within reach. Bluefeather rubbed at the sudden burning of the thin scar between his eyebrows.

Skimpy was huge, experienced and mean but he would be slow. He figured to get Mr. Taos first. Stan was bigger than he was and, according to what he had heard, had a punch that would make a water buffalo cringe. Stan's friend's power was probably just under that or he would not be that close to the mine super. The rancher was totally unknown to Bluefeather. He was a year or so younger than Bluefeather, about five feet eleven inches and built strong all the way, except his hands looked a little delicate. He might be carrying a gun. Well, Jim the rancher was just about his size except for the hands, but he was probably a gouger, kicker and biter—anything to protect himself.

There were two out of the five, Stan and Skimpy, who had a chance to take Bluefeather if they got in an early blow. So he had it figured. He had to shock them so that their forces were scattered, and he, in truth, would be taking them on one at a time if—if he moved with enough speed. He knew without having to analyze that each man must go down wounded badly enough to stay down.

They waited for him to answer; all those staring eyes expecting explanations, a bartering suggestion or possibly even a bit of begging.

Bluefeather grabbed the ashtray in front of Skimpy, threw it and its contents in his face and at the same time whacked his left elbow on the bridge of Mr. Taos's nose. Taos went down screaming with the blood, struggling all at once for a way out of his badly broken nose.

While Skimpy was trying to scratch the ashes out of his eyes with one hand and reach for Bluefeather with the other massive one, Bluefeather got to the shillelagh and brought it down across the sixth cervical of Skimpy's neck as hard as he had ever swung a miner's pick. As Skimpy dropped to his knees bellowing, cursing, pawing at the air for something to crush, Bluefeather swung the ax handle so hard along Skimpy's jaw that he thought the piece of hardwood had snapped. He was wrong. It was the jaw that was broken.

Bluefeather saw a blur somewhere and punched his weapon at it like a sword. The blur moved back saying "Aggggh." There was another blur to his side. He ducked under it and swung the ax handle low with great force. It made a popping noise that felt good as it busted Stan's right kneecap in three parts, driving some splinters of bone between the joints.

Stan rolled, screaming and cursing right beside Skimpy, who now just frothed at the mouth, spitting out blood and teeth to keep from choking to death. Now Stan's friend, who had been knocked backward, came at Bluefeather with a chair. Bluefeather ducked the blow but it came down on one of his kidneys. His breath went as he dropped to one knee. As the man raised the chair for the coup de grace, Bluefeather drove the ax handle, with every last tiny fiber of strength he had, into the man's port of entry. The chair went sailing out over him right into the fireplace. While Stan's friend was bending over moaning and holding his pulverized privates, Bluefeather bounced the flat side of the weapon off the side of the man's face, fracturing his cheekbone, knocking six teeth loose and turning his nose forever south.

Bluefeather whirled to the side, and there stood Jim pointing a .38 special at his belly, smiling as if he had just sold five thousand head of steer for the biggest money ever paid. Ordinarily Bluefeather would have taken time to consider maybe making some kind of careful statement or cautious negotiation with a man who pointed a gun at him and grinned like that, but he was still full of mad.

When the chair burst into flames in the fireplace it popped exactly like a gun. Even one as sharp and watchful as Jim was fooled. He whirled pointing the gun at the new enemy. That's when Bluefeather, aiming to sidewind him in the jaw, hit him full in the ear so that it knocked the rancher spinning, and he dropped the gun.

Bluefeather kicked the gun across the room where it scooted under the whiskey cabinet. Jim came out of his whirl and kicked one of his fancy boots at Bluefeather. His aim was awry, as he was yet off balance from the blow to his ear. Bluefeather grabbed Jim's leg and twisted the ankle out of place, while at the same time jerking his foot as high as he could. He pounded one of his heavy prospector's boots right where the rancher was spread into a wide Y. Jim joined the others on the floor, but he had difficulty concentrating his moans on any one spot— he was wrecked from top to bottom. When he could talk, Jim gurgled out, regretfully holding his hurting places as much for protection as pain, "By the Almighty, I'll never, ever forget this shame. I didn't get to play a single hand of poker and still got the shit kicked out of me."

Bluefeather slapped him up-side the face again, and Jim became the quietest he would ever be for the rest of his life. Bluefeather turned and kicked the Taos man in the belly, saying, "You're the goon who started all this. You're gonna remember to keep your stupid mouth shut or I'm gonna empty it of teeth and fill it with a two-by-four."

The Taos man rolled over twice, stifling bad feelings and bad thoughts, and stared at the little stain of blood on the floor as if it had dropped from the palms of Jesus Christ.

Stan Berkowitz, the mining super, had never let up his bawling and bellowing, "My balls, my balls, my balls are mashed. What am I ever gonna do without my balls? I'll be helpless as a little baby. Oh, my God. My God."

Bluefeather gave him the most considerate, comforting answer he could think of, considering the activities that had led to his becoming indignant and resentful. "You got most of that correct, Stan. A great big, young and healthy man like yourself can't get a hell of a lot going without his balls. Even so, you're about the luckiest man in all the Southwest."

Stan stopped moaning for a second and, although his tongue could not utter the question, his tortured eyes expressed, "How's that?"

Bluefeather graciously answered, "Why that's obvious . . . I didn't scalp you . . . you lucky son of a bitch."

Stan was trying to stand up. Bluefeather kicked him precisely on the tailbone; this time he stayed down hurting so badly that he could only gasp out dull, moaning sounds.

It should have been over, but Bluefeather grabbed a chair and braced it under the knob of the door to the storeroom. He need not have bothered. The place had cleared out at half past one, and the last worker had left at least thirty minutes before the disagreement had set in.

Bluefeather hurled the ax handle into the fireplace where the chair looked like the skeleton of a small monster as it was engulfed in flames. Then he got the fireplace poker and walked back and forth around the room punching people with its heavy, sharp end to be sure they would hear what he was about to say.

"Now, I've still got some mad left in me so don't any of you bastards interrupt. You hear?" When there was no answer, he jabbed Skimpy in the belly and tapped Stan on his good leg's shinbone. "I said, do you hear?"

There were nods and even some words that sounded like "yes."

"Well, that's better." Now and then he swung the iron in the air like a baseball bat. "I am a crusader against injustice—especially when I'm the victim. I want all of you to know, if either Miss Mary Schmidt O'Kelly or her father hears one word of this in the form of gossip, written words or any other way, I'm gonna look up your milk cows, your chickens, your kids and maybe your wives, and I'm gonna spank 'em real good, you hear?"

There were quick nods of understanding now.

Bluefeather continued, "And if that ain't enough I'll waylay every one of you and split your bag and run your leg through it. Then I'll really get mean. Now, my Indian ancestors were here thousands of years before anyone else and then one of my other blood brothers—old Columbus—was hired by the Spanish, and he came over here and found the Indians. So you folks are all latecomers to this part of the world. You still hearing me? Huh? Huh?"

Much affirmation amid stifled groans could be ascertained.

He continued, "I repeat. If one sentence, or even a

part of a sentence, gets back to my people, on top of everything else I'm going to do to you, I'll put a Tiwa Indian curse on you that will last through every member of every one of your families for a thousand years. And if that doesn't get it done, with the rest of my blood I'll put out a Sicilian hex that will hold good for ten generations of pestilence, plague and penury."

He calmed down now and put the poker back in its holder with care. He walked slowly around the room kicking each man in the ribs with a light but solid tap to be sure the battlefield contained no dead. He counted his chips twice to be fair and told Skimpy he wanted $6,033. Skimpy pointed to the tin box on the shelf where the ax handle had been. Bluefeather counted the cash twice to be certain it was correct. He didn't want a cent—not one —that wasn't his.

He took the chair out from under the doorknob and returned it to its proper place by the gaming table, which amazingly only had one leg askew. He walked proudly through the storeroom, the whiskey and smoke funnel bar, lifted the bar door lock. As he stepped out into the cold, star-speckled night with a half moon sitting on top of the massive black mountains, he took a deep breath of air and walked toward home.

A coyote was yapping and howling just outside town trying to sound like a dozen. Bluefeather just could not help it. He raised his head and howled right back. He could feel the thick bulge in his pocket packed full with his honest day's work.

EIGHTEEN

MARY, LUDWIG AND BLUEFEATHER WERE WATCHING THE SNOW on Clock Hill almost hourly now. The two remaining drifts were shrinking fast. They had to move swiftly to make the pledged date.

Bluefeather had heard it was against the rules—or maybe even the law—for either the groom or the bride to converse about their matrimonial garments. So he went it alone, although fearful of his choices and ability in this particular endeavor. He had no experience to guide him and hadn't attended a wedding since leaving the family home at Raton.

He had three handsome black suits left over from his gambling days in Tonopah, so he chose his favorite to have cleaned and pressed. He bought a new white shirt and a dress tie. He assumed that bow and string ties, common in houses of chance, might not be suitable for such a grand, if small, wedding party.

Mary, of course, had far more work to do than he because she had the responsibility of getting Ludwig ready and everything packed for the both of them. She also had to dispose of the restaurant. She leased it to the two ladies who had worked for her part-time. The papers were drawn for one year with a two-year renewal and an option to buy after that. This gave Mary the freedom she needed to prepare for the wedding. She spent many anxious hours with the seamstress getting her wedding dress just right.

While Mary was away shopping, Ludwig called Bluefeather over to the house and presented him a bowler to try on for size. Unfortunately—at least in Bluefeather's mind—it fit perfectly. If Bluefeather had not loved and respected jackasses so much, he would have accused himself of looking like one in the silly little hat.

"Ah, yes, my dear Blue, it's an elegant fit to say the least. Yes . . . yes, Mary will be quite proud of you, sir."

Bluefeather said, "I sure do appreciate this, Ludwig. I would probably have had to travel all the way to Denver to find a hat like this."

"Oh, farther than that, my boy. Hats of this quality are only made in two or three places on the Eastern Seaboard."

Bluefeather had moved about town more in the last few days than he had in the ten previous months. People gave him great respect. There was even a fear, an awe. There was no question that something had leaked, no matter how distorted, of his devastation to the gamblers. But no one had breathed a word of it to Mary or Ludwig. That, he would have noticed. However, the intensity and worried concern of getting ready to bind with Miss Mary made him oblivious to this new respect—a respect that can come only in the conquering of very small towns or very large cities. Totally unbeknownst to him, a tiny legend had begun about Bluefeather Fellini.

Then it happened. Ludwig and Bluefeather were in the former's workroom going over the rough maps and other production ideas about the King Tut, when Mary charged into the house shouting with rapture.

"It's gone! It's gone!"

Before thinking the two men chorused, "What's gone?"

"The snow, you idiots. Now, my darlings, we leave on the 8:45 train in the morning." Mary's eyes were filled with the color of a clear, clean sky, and her naturally pink face was flushed to a shade near the color of a ripe watermelon heart. Her excitement radiated out, giving Bluefeather the tingling of a near lightning strike. He was certain the entire world shared their elation.

She said, "At last. At last. At last," throwing her head back and clasping her hands in front of her.

The train ride was quite an outing in itself. Scores of brand-new little streams cascaded in frothy good humor from the crevices in the canyons' sides, dropping finally into the wondrous Rio Bello just as Bluefeather and Mary would merge and begin to assail the world tomorrow. Wet wisps of mountain fog clung here and there. The fog was welcomed by the heavy growth of evergreens and made one's eyes strain to see wild creatures, both real and imaginary, in the primeval-appearing forest. The three were silent in their awe of the vitality of earth, water and trees.

After some two hours the canyon widened and little meadows of new grass were visible. The cows, horses and sheep grazed in these open spaces relishing the tender, green treat. After a long winter of white cold and dry brown feed, the grass was like a before-dinner dessert to them, and they hardly ever raised their heads to look at the chugging train.

Birds were returning from the southern deserts. They flew about constantly chattering love messages and territorial threats before either sound-signal was ready to be consummated.

Mary and Bluefeather held hands, comfortable with each other's silence, absorbing the rebirth of their world all around. Ludwig had blossomed like the timbered canyons. His face glowed with a newness as well. The craggy features had softened and the corners of his mouth and the inner light of his eyes revealed the positive emotions besetting him. He could contain himself no longer. To hell with the lovebirds.

"Look. That's the tungsten mine I found in 1920. See it up the canyon there on the left? See the waste dump? And there, right there below those corrals, that's where my friend Eloy Irick was killed. You remember Eloy, don't you, Mary? Good man, Eloy, but foolish when on horseback. He was chasing a gut-shot lion and tried to jump that dead tree. It's still there," and he strained to look back as a little spot from his past was left behind by the train disappearing in its smoke.

He talked on about the silver find at Leadville, Colorado; the copper prospect outside Billings, Montana; his long-dead dogs; his friends that were all gone now. He included Mary's mother, Ila, in most of his remembrances. He even mentioned, over and over, how hard the decision had been to leave the assaying business. "Hard on Ila and Mary, more than me, because I was out looking and digging up dreams. Little dreams. Broken dreams. Big dreams." Then his voice trailed off and both of the lovers had to strain to hear, ". . . the King Tut . . . yes . . . yes . . ."

The canyon had dried and widened, and ranch houses and homesteads had become more prevalent. Then the ridges spread apart like the handles of a pair of steel pliers, and the wedding party looked at the top of Durango, Colorado.

. . .

Inside the historic Strater Hotel, Mary fussed about in the bedroom of their suite, dressing. Bluefeather was in Ludwig's room across the hall. Ludwig waited impatiently, roaming in and out of both rooms, stopping in front of first one mirror and then another to adjust his vest, straighten his tie or tilt the fedora just a mite more. He liked the feel of the gold watch in his vest and the gold head on what he called his "exorbitant cane."

Finally he knocked on his daughter's door, and she asked him in for a final inspection before the main event. He drew his breath in with delight. "You are divine, my dear. You—especially in that dress and veil—would have made Cleopatra jealous and Josephine rant and rage. Now let me be off to check on our groom."

Bluefeather met him in the hall. He stood and posed. "Well, what do you think?"

Ludwig paused a moment, tilting his head from right to left, inspecting Bluefeather. "As for you, dear fellow, just tilt the bowler ever so slightly. As I see it, that's the only touch I might suggest."

Bluefeather obliged.

"That's right, . . . now back about a half inch . . . ah yes . . . we are ready, I'd say. Ready for the ball."

Mary stepped into the hallway. Bluefeather was speechless at the sight of his beautiful bride-to-be.

And so with an arm on each side of Ludwig, so he could hang the gold handle in the slight bend of one elbow, they marched down the stairs, out of the hotel and along the main street to the justice of the peace.

After the ceremony they were escorted by the maître d' to a private room off the main dining room in the hotel. There was already a magnum of fine champagne chilling and a tray of delicate appetizers awaiting their arrival. Bluefeather had arranged for a private waiter. He was a middle-aged Mexican man with an exquisite, thin mustache and a neatly trimmed beard below a head of iron-black hair.

Bluefeather also had arranged for the music. He imported Ramon Hernandez from the tiny immigrant coal-mining town of Dawson, thirty-five miles southwest of Raton, where he was as highly respected for his music as the Taos masters were for their paintings—even though he was barely grown. Ramon was smiling broadly as he placed the guitar strap around his neck. He not only loved his work but enjoyed every note like a new adventure or gift.

Bluefeather poured champagne for the three of them and yelled at Ramon, "Hey, *compadre,* would you care for a tilt before you play?"

Ramon was pleased by the offer but politely refused for the time being. He was a professional and would drink only when his duty was done. He started playing an old Spanish love song very softly. His music was soul-satisfying and made the fine food taste even better.

Bluefeather didn't really care much for champagne, but he kept this to himself. During the eleven months the three had been together, it had become a ritual game with them to make toasts to many things, but now, right here, was the top time of toasting.

Ludwig had the honor of offering the first one tonight, "To life, love and music."

Bluefeather swallowed the French liquid saying, "To earlier, to later, to now. To my family of the 'forever' world." Of course they all knew there was no such thing as forever, but it sounded right at the moment.

Then Mary raised her glass high and uttered, "For the fine times, and the trying times, but always to our times."

Bluefeather yelled, Ludwig clapped and Ramon

grinned broadly and kept on playing. Their waiter waited.
Their toasts continued.

"To the moon's mother."

"To the father of the universe."

"To all the ships on all the oceans."

"To all the sailors on all those ships."

"To the cactus and the coyote."

"To music of all tongues."

The waiter started serving the meal. Everything was
elegantly presented from soup to dessert—the latter, of
course, being a double-tiered wedding cake. Bluefeather
and Mary cut the first slice together and fed each other
big bites.

Now the mariachi band came in with sombreros, big as
umbrellas, and played. The musicians circled the room
and yelled as they tilted their heads. The music was wild.
The laughter was happy.

Ramon had a drink with them, making his own toast to
the newlyweds, "May your days be filled with work and
laughter, your nights with love and rest, your life with
dancing children of delight."

Everyone clapped and even the mariachi players joined
in the applause. It was their cue to play their way out of
the room, and it was also the cue for the violinist to join
Ramon and play the first dance, but Bluefeather made
them wait as he took the beryl necklace from his pocket
and placed it around Mary's neck. Bluefeather had
planned for this to be presented with some gracious, profound statement, but he couldn't remember the three or
four hundred lines he had memorized then cast away,
searching for a better one, so he said, "Darling, I dug it
up myself."

Mary grabbed him and pulled his head down, saying,
"That makes it so very, very special. I shall never take it
off."

As the groom guided his bride around the table for the first dance, Ludwig stopped them, took out his prospecting glass and examined the gleaming new stone hanging between his daughter's breasts.

He exclaimed, "I found a yellow one once in Colombia, but it was not as lovely as this."

Ramon and the violinist started right back at the beginning as Bluefeather and Mary began dancing slowly, slowly. They held each other and felt the moment with all of themselves. The room turned with the music under their feet, without effort on their part being necessary. It was their private heaven for this little time in eternity, all enclosed with their scent, their touch, their taste and their flesh and souls becoming the same.

Then, as if coming slowly out of a perfumed anesthesia, they awakened and went to Ludwig. Bluefeather helped him to his feet. He took his only daughter, his only known kin, in his arms to dance, but Mary nodded at Bluefeather and he understood that the intoxication of the evening may have been too much for her father. So Bluefeather danced with them.

The trio worked perfectly. Ludwig was held up by them but also was separate and leading the dance. They went around slowly again and again. Ludwig's old heart pumped other songs from long, long ago into his eardrums. The slow little threesome moved across the floor as they patiently circled and finally arrived back at Ludwig's chair. He braced himself against it, and with some risk gave them a bow as gracious and meaningful as grand opera.

One last glass of special imported brandy and the ceremony was closed. The musicians were gone, but the essence of the day and night permeated the air and their hearts like the scent of a mile-high rose garden.

Ludwig was in his bed already sleeping and dreaming

things that were special and known only to him. The La
Plata Mountains were framed in the window like a calen-
dar painting of the Swiss Alps, their white upper reaches
way off behind foothills and the warmth of the room.

The light from a tiny lamp cast a soft, bronze-colored
glow around the man and woman. Bluefeather took her
hands, trying to look and put himself behind her wide,
waiting eyes.

He spoke softly as a breeze from a butterfly's wings, "I
shall love you past history."

And she whispered, "I shall love you longer than memory."

They held each other. They were silent and immobile
for a spell. The man and the woman could hear an old,
old song from before their births—from before fossils.
The ancient melody accompanied them to bed.

NINETEEN

BLUEFEATHER INSISTED, AND MARY AGREED, THAT THEY GET A camp set up before they started digging the crosscut marked on Ludwig's map. He had covered it back up so carefully that a quick look revealed no changes in the overburden.

They chose a small clearing for their campsite, disturbing the bushes and trees as little as possible. These gave added protection from wind, provided more shade and left the clearing's beauty unchanged. A tent held their double bed, and a tarp tethered out in front on strong poles, added to the protected space. A rock-encircled fire pit would take care of the cooking until Bluefeather could get the wood-burning cookstove set up. With a rope, they hung their food box from a large limb to protect it from bears and insects. Some crude wooden shelves in the tent held their utensils. A table, which could be moved easily in and out of the tent for dining according to the weather or their whims, completed the necessities.

He had already cut enough firewood to last a month. His next task was to install a temporary hand pump in a deep hole at the nearby creek, which also held some nice brown trout.

Mary was busy getting the entire place in her own kind of order so she could do her share of the chores as easily as possible under the outdoor conditions. They had gone back and forth to town in the old truck every other day since the wedding, finishing the trip to the camp with the pack mules.

Ludwig wasn't concerned about any of this activity, even though he had experienced these setups dozens of times by himself. He was waiting for the dig. Well, now he would get it.

Bluefeather waited patiently until the sun totally illuminated the opening. Bending down, he narrowed his eyes like an art critic would to check out the patterns of shadows in a painting. At first, he felt helpless. He could discern no difference in the topsoil. Ludwig would have made a top trapper because of the way he could disguise a disturbance in the earth.

At last he saw the very slight differences in the patterns of the tiny shadows made by millions of fallen leaves, twigs, limbs, bird droppings and everything else that had fallen for millions of years in the scattered forest. He was able to see the line of Ludwig's dig, and before he lost its strike, he dug spades of dirt several feet apart. His excitement was growing with every breath, every thought.

Bluefeather dropped the shovel on line with the old cut and went to tell Mary. They had made a pretty good guess. The camp was only twenty or thirty yards from the cut.

"Hey, Mary. I found it. I found the sign."

"Wait for me . . . wait till I finish unpacking these pans. I want to dig with you."

"It's okay. I'll do it."

"No . . . no, I want to help. I want to be there."

Bluefeather knew by her voice she was determined. So he waited. Then they dug the crosscut trench together, scraping down to solid soil with the shovels, then pitching the overburden back to form a trench. They were both perspiring in the still-crisp spring air, without noticing.

Bluefeather constantly tested the earth with his prospector's pick. Finally he heard the unmistakable ring as his shovel blade dragged across rock. He scraped the spot with much diligence and soon had the slightly undulating vein uncovered. He squatted wordlessly, as Mary stared down, digging furiously trying to dislodge a piece of the eight- or ten-inch-wide vein.

A small chunk finally broke loose. The damp earth was stuck to it so that its quality and content could not be judged correctly even after he had rubbed it with his hands and against his pants.

"Come on, let's go to the creek and wash it."

They ran without being aware of the hundred yards to the creek. He stepped into the edge without even noticing its wetness. The swift water helped the scrubbing of his hands. Then he raised up, stepped back on the bank and fumbled to get his mineral glass in focus and adjusted to the bright sunlight. He smilingly handed it to Mary.

She looked and looked. "I can't see anything but rose quartz."

He pointed to the outer edge near one end. "Here. Look right here."

"Oh, yes, there it is. I see it. A nugget. No, it's wire gold. I see the tiny tendrils emanating from it now. My God," she said, "we found it. It's exactly like Daddy's rock." And even though she was a little ashamed at the tremendous burst of elation that encased and penetrated all of her being, she still fell into Bluefeather's arms as he held them open to her. They danced across the forest laughing and giggling as they whirled.

Mary sang like a little girl, "We found it. We found it. We found the pot of gold."

They danced up the hill, around trees, between trees, through the overburden and in and out of strong shadows and brilliant streaks of light. Where the sunbeams touched her hair, they glowed orange; his hair shone as blue-black as newly tempered steel.

Finally they fell onto the soft layer of leaves and grass of the topsoil and rolled over, giggling like children on their first school recess, until stopped by a young sapling. They kissed and loved for the best reasons—the celebration of discovery.

When their breaths were back and their minds had stopped dancing and making love, Bluefeather knew he must find the location of the tunnel or shaft before they confronted Ludwig with the news he had waited for for so long.

The vein seemed headed in the general direction of a suddenly steep, rising slope where a huge boulder hung fifteen or twenty feet above it. They dug there and found it. Bluefeather was afraid if they tunneled under the boulder, it would hold an imminent danger of falling on them or possibly sealing them inside the tunnel. If so, it would have to be blasted apart.

He climbed up and around to examine it with much care and was elated to find that it was lodged between two outcroppings of solid rock. So there was no danger that he could see.

They knew exactly where to dig now, so they carefully covered the crosscuts just as Ludwig had done years before. Bluefeather was extremely pleased that they could tunnel in horizontally instead of having to dig a vertical or incline shaft. There would be no need for a headframe, hand windlass and ore bucket. They could avoid the terrible and constant battle with gravity involved in lifting the rock straight up.

Of course, there was also much to do in horizontal mining: acquiring and hauling dynamite and powder, cutting timbers to secure the entrance or maybe the entire tunnel, and clearing away the dropped ore were among the major things. Right now they would use a couple of large wheelbarrows, but later they might want to lay track and run an ore car.

All this would come shortly, but now they must return the great secret to its first finder, Ludwig Schmidt of Breen, Colorado, who waited with understandable trepidation for their return.

Bluefeather had forcefully stiffened his neck to keep from looking up across the jumbled boulders to the fore of the bluff that had maimed Ludwig. It couldn't be ignored. There it was waiting for him, not quite, but almost, perpendicular. The bluffs had just enough slope to make their climbing seem possible. The protruding sheets of rock would not relinquish their unavowed information freely.

The long-expected good news seemed to make Ludwig grow several inches in height, and the measurement of his bony chest showed a like expansion. He insisted they go out for dinner to the Railroad Cafe where they specialized in huge T-bone steaks. Bluefeather felt a little guilty that they didn't go to Mary's Place, even though it was leased out, but he also felt that the event called for something different.

It was an odd dinner. At the beginning they strained to speak softly and in riddles so that no other long-eared patron would know what they were talking about. Soon though, the game became fun just as their toasting ritual had. The old man seemed about fifty now in his movements and conversation.

They were so caught up in their own private world that Bluefeather had not noticed Stan Berkowitz with three strangers in a booth across the room. He hadn't even felt Stan's presence as yet. A dark sign, indeed.

Stan was talking animatedly to the men as if he had not seen them in a while. He acted as if the people at Ludwig's table did not exist; but once, as he leaned forward across the table, gesturing with his strong hands as he talked, Bluefeather saw Stan shoot them a glance so swift, it could have been the natural movement of his eyes. But Bluefeather's days at the green-topped tables of Tonopah had taught him the difference; Stan was thinking of them under the disguise of other voices and movements.

For just a moment Bluefeather felt a slight irritation. Then his joyous thoughts and feelings dominated any emanations from Berkowitz, and his attention rejoined Mary and Ludwig as the old gentleman raised his glass of brandy. He held it out to theirs. They waited for the game to continue. It didn't. This was a toast too precious for Ludwig to express in words. He held his glass against theirs a long moment, looking from one to the other with a smile that was working itself inward from the surface. His eyes reflected his joy back out to his compatriots. He was filled with total contentment. They would never see him that way again.

TWENTY

THEY WENT BACK TO THE MOUNTAIN TOGETHER, YET APART.
Mary drove the small truck as far as the terrain would
allow and walked the short distance on into camp.
Bluefeather rode Nancy and led Jackknife, packed with
the powder and caps, hand drills, iron bars, saws and just
about everything they would need to open a small operation like they planned.

He dug a small cave around the edge of the mountain,
facing away from their camp. He framed it and built a
door with a lock on it. This was their powder box to keep
the explosives dry and safe.

He started picking at the mountain's overburden until
he could shovel it free to the hard rock and the rich vein.
Now he would have to dig holes for his dynamite and
blast out an even face of rock.

He drilled by holding the forged steel rod against the
rock face and pounding it in rhythm with a broad-faced
heavy hammer. Bing. Bing. Bang. Over and over for
hours. Then he used a longer drill rod called a bull prick.
Hammer. Twist. Remove. Hammer. Hammer. The tiny
holes were placed just right so they would shatter and
drop the boulder into pieces. With a smooth wooden

spatula, he carved a space in the dynamite for the explosive cap. He inserted a short fuse inside the cartridgelike cap and crimped the edges around it; this was then delicately placed in the dynamite and bound there. He placed a stick in each of the holes. The fuses were cut at slightly different lengths, so when he lit them, each would explode a split second apart allowing him time to count and keep track of those that had fired. This was terribly important, because an uncounted round could later blow a man's head off. It took many years of practice to do this perfectly.

If he had planned to mine on a larger scale, he would have used a battery box and long wires to set them off all at once, but here the old ways would be fine.

He set the fuse. He and Mary crouched around the curve of the mountain as he yelled, "Fire in the hole." This was an old, old unwritten law to protect any strangers walking by or workers nearby. With the shock of the first multiple explosions over, the work on the tunnel proceeded rapidly. He soon had the portal braced neatly and solidly with hand-hewn and notched logs.

Now was the dangerous period. They feared someone might unexpectedly walk up while they sorted out the rich ore that had been so clearly visible from the outside. They felt fortunate that no visitors appeared until they were about ten feet inside, where they could separate and hide the rich ore, thus leaving nothing but dead rock for anyone to see.

This safety point had just been reached when a lone prospector came through the clearing and saw Mary, a woman—the unthinkable—push a wheelbarrow out of the mine entrance. His eyes as well as his cringing movements showed his superstitious fears. He spoke but made every excuse to get his burro watered at the creek and remove himself from this dreadful travesty.

Bluefeather and Mary were pleased that the old super-stition—a woman in a mine causes cave-ins or explosions —was still in powerful effect. Bluefeather was certain, and relieved, that word of this madness would spread swiftly and they would be left alone.

They sorted out the richest of the wire-gold ore, put it in gunnysacks and hauled it back to the house in Breen. They always covered it with firewood or some other disguise. They secured it in the cellar, covered with loose straw. That would have to do until they had time to think of something better. They scattered the rest of the rose quartz in front of the slowly growing waste pile, immediately covering it with dead, worthless rock. In effect, their waste dump concealed ore of a secondary, but still valuable, assay. Even though there was no gold visible to the naked eye, a torch or smelter furnace would melt lots of minute specks of the yellow metal from the rocks.

On their third trip home with the high grade, they were surprised to find Ludwig gone. Mary drove down to the restaurant and had coffee. He wasn't there. She didn't bring up his absence because her lessees would have mentioned it if he had been in that day.

Bluefeather saw Ludwig's odd, limping tracks imprinted on the trail to the Rio Bello. He followed them and discovered him sitting on a chair overlooking the river, staring motionless across the waters toward the mountains. Bluefeather wondered how he had gathered the strength and courage to carry the chair, use the cane and arrive safely. He was wearing a topcoat. Bluefeather felt it would be an infringement on the man's privacy to approach nearer. So he sat down, some distance away, and waited.

When the sun tipped the mesas to the southwest, Ludwig stood up stiffly, adjusting his cane, and walked with his permanent limp toward Bluefeather and his home.

Bluefeather dodged behind some bushes and walked swiftly back to the house just as Mary arrived. He felt as guilty as a spy spying on his own country. He told Mary what he'd seen and she became more worried and puzzled.

Soon Ludwig arrived. They prepared dinner and tried to share the day's adventures at the King Tut. They received mostly grunts, headshakes and very little other communication from Ludwig. Every day he returned to the chair and stared across the space between himself and the mountain. He sat almost straight up with both his hands on his walking stick held between his legs.

Mary became so concerned with this strange behavior that she and Bluefeather both agreed she should stay home a few days with Ludwig instead of going back to the mine. She decided her father was just too lonely. It did no good. Bluefeather missed his new bride enormously, and Mary could establish no understandable contact with her father.

The next time Bluefeather returned home, Mary brought him up to date, speaking with confusion and compassion in her voice. "Blue, he just sits out there staring. He doesn't even move. It causes his joints to stiffen up even more, and he can barely make it back to the house. I keep feeling that someday he won't make it at all. I'm afraid he'll fall or something."

"I know. I know. He's having his half-visions, Mary."

"What do you mean, 'half-visions'?"

"Just that. I don't know how to put it in exact words, but . . . but he's not ours anymore, you see."

Then he couldn't explain further; she would just have to feel it for herself. Bluefeather knew the old man was preparing to go away—away to the next stop, to the next beginning that comes to all, sometimes suddenly, sometimes slowly, but eventually to all for dead certain.

Bluefeather knew that Ludwig was one of those few fortunate enough to be so highly honored by the spirits. He was being gifted with a little more time to stare backward at his old trails. It was the order of all things that Ludwig daydream the important times of his life so he would know what knowledge to save and take to his next birth. How could Bluefeather explain to Mary this special tribute that Ludwig had received? This complimentary time meant he could advance to the next dimension without fear of having to return and do more work and penance in the one he currently occupied. Bluefeather was very happy for his friend's unseen prestige, but Mary was suffering, feeling inept and unforgivably helpless.

Bluefeather volunteered to stay home now as well. He tried to convince her that the high grade was all hidden; that there would be no danger to the mine and camp. Mary disagreed.

"Oh, no. You're the one that convinced me of the value of keeping your vows to my father. Now those vows are mine, too. We can't risk anything hurting him in that way. The mine had become his whole life until . . ."

They agreed that Bluefeather would go on back and work the diggings for a week before returning. Mary insisted that they give a week apart, each in his or her own way, to Ludwig. She to his home, he to their mine and mountains.

Early on the third morning of his return to the mountains, Bluefeather was awakened by the howling of three coyotes trying to sound like thirty. He listened raptly, but with no analyzing. He arose, fixed a sparse meal out of habit, saddled one mule and, leading the other, headed for Breen.

He was there by midmorning and found Mary and Ludwig sitting in the music room, drinking coffee and chatting merrily with each other.

Ludwig smiled with all his life's wrinkles and said, "Ah, good fellow, I was hoping you'd come back today. The air has never been purer. The sun will give us seventy degrees and the wind will only whisper good tidings. Have some coffee, my son."

"Thanks, I will."

"I can tell by your bearing that all goes well in the mountains."

"Yes. So far it has been better than one could hope for. We're not even going to timber the mine, only the portal. The rock is solid and safe."

"That is good. That is superb."

Bluefeather suddenly chilled and cringed, thinking for sure Ludwig would ask him if he had checked the continuation of the generous vein high on the outcropping of the waiting cliffs. He didn't.

"Well now, sir, shall we all sin and slip a little morning brandy in our coffee?"

"Sounds better than good to me," said Bluefeather.

"It is ordained then," smiled Mary, highly pleased at the instantaneous and stunning recovery of her father's health and attitude. She moved quickly and poured the brandy, sitting back down so as not to miss a second of this astounding resurrection.

Ludwig tasted it saying, "Ahh," with pleasure. The others did likewise. Then he held it out for a toast, "Here's to the world and all that's in it."

Mary said, "The same."

Bluefeather said, "The same."

Suddenly, with the quick movements of a child, Ludwig gathered his cane and topcoat and tilted his fedora exactly right.

Patting Bluefeather tenderly on the back as he bent to kiss Mary, he jauntily left the room saying, "I feel like a long walk," and departed through the front door.

A relaxed Mary said, "Can you believe it?" She watched him out the window take the path toward the river. "He's walking almost as if he'd never been injured. Come look."

Bluefeather indeed saw that the old man was only touching ground with the cane every other step or so. Then he vanished around Clock Hill.

Mary decided to cook Ludwig's favorite meal—peach pie, pork roast and sourdough rolls. Bluefeather played Wagner and Mozart records, although he did not really care for that kind of music in midday. This was middle-of-the-night music, when a man could be alone or share listening time only with those very few choice people. He didn't ask himself why he was making this exception with Ludwig's favorite composers, he simply acted.

The sun dropped, and the latent breeze came to life moving limbs and leaves in little rhythms. Mary was working as if the end of the world could only be averted by her cooking this special meal. Bluefeather brought in wood, drove in a few barely loose nails around the house and replaced some loose putty on a couple of window-panes. They both seemed to be trying to elongate the day, but nothing stopped the sun from hiding behind the mesa, flaring mightily with shafts of gold fanning out like wagon spokes across the whole of the western sky.

Then Mary stopped working. She washed and dried her hands, took off her apron and got her scarf and coat from the hanger on the wall. She looked with anxious questions in her eyes at Bluefeather, who had already donned his jacket. Neither one said a word as they left the house with Mary's hand clutching Bluefeather's arm. They didn't hurry and they didn't dawdle either.

At the clearing, they could see the figure of Ludwig, sitting upright in his chair in almost a military posture, facing the violet sky and the very last tip of orange on the snow-covered mountain. The beams were dragged out of the sky by the father sun and taken to the other side of the world. The orange tip on the mountain blazed stronger for only a second because of the darkness gathering swiftly all around the other half of the world. The two walked arm in arm up to the figure. They knew.

Bluefeather stopped behind the chair with a hand on Ludwig's shoulder. Mary moved to his front, looking at his face a moment before tenderly touching his eyes. Then she took his face in her hands and said, "Oh father, dear father, we will miss you so."

The cane dropped to the ground as the hands fell limply in his lap. The breeze across the Rio Bello was especially cold for this time in early summer.

TWENTY-ONE

BLUEFEATHER WONDERED WHY EVERY SMALL-TOWN FUNERAL HE ever attended was wind-whipped. Ludwig's was no exception. There were close to a hundred people, he guessed, gathered on the edge of Clock Hill to pay their last respects to the music- and literature-loving mining engineer.

A few came because they admired his intelligence and thought he deserved some last regard. Some were there out of curiosity, wondering at their neighbor's attachment to the man who married his daughter. There were those who thought it good business to be seen among the citizens of Breen country. A very few loved him and were already missing him.

Bluefeather stood with Mary in silence as the monotonous words of the preacher created impatience in the crowd. Mary had already grieved. Now she was simply putting the funeral in its place as a last dignity for a truly fine and feeling man.

Bluefeather felt an invisible disturbance in a shaft of air before he glanced up from the coffin and over the crowd. Behind them, on the hill, he saw Stan Berkowitz standing, staring at him. He was accompanied by the same three men he had had coffee with in the Railroad Cafe.

It was over. Everyone sighed and pulled their coat collars up against the coldness of the late spring wind. Scattering into little groups, they walked to whatever mode of transportation they had.

A hawk dove from the sky, screeched and widened its wings to stop its descent, then whirled and flew south until it vanished somewhere in the corrugated horizon. Just like the wind, a bird always seemed to visit the funerals.

About forty of the crowd showed up at the surviving daughter's home. Several ladies had brought food. Lots of food. People ate, visited and felt free, even joyous, as they talked about what a fine man Ludwig had been. They shared incidents, the loss to the community, but none spoke the dominant truth; they were venting their relief that it was Ludwig underground instead of themselves.

Bluefeather was miserable. He was a man dedicated, almost totally, to a few people who were his friends— those he loved. A surplus of people scattered his emotions. He had been born and reared with close clans just across the mountains from one another. It was one too many for a single human being to handle properly. So he had taken the trail with a few, but very close, friends. The crowds and masses were for politicians, power worshipers, religious fanatics and their foolish soul-shattering followers, not for a man who walked deserts and mountains alone, except for two mules. Not for a man who loved reading fine books and hearing masterful music and who, by the moment, had hundreds of landscapes available to his inner eyes that were painted in his picture-mind by the Great Spirit.

He slipped out the back door and proceeded to the shed to enjoy the company of his longest-lasting friends,

Jackknife and Nancy. They were always glad to see him, even if he placed heavy burdens on their backs and led them to otherwise inaccessible places.

A few days after the funeral, they returned to the King Tut and their labors of love. The next morning Bluefeather began felling trees—all as nearly equal in size as possible—and started building a one-room cabin. He thought this might help take their minds, especially Mary's, off their grief. He had fenced in a bush-encircled meadow for the mules with a spring along one edge so they did not have to worry about them while he and Mary roamed the creek, worked the mine or went into town.

Almost immediately upon their return to the King Tut, they had a surprise visitor. Tracy was a miner for the local company. Mary knew him quite well, but Bluefeather had only seen him about town a few times. Both were inwardly terrified that somehow the knowledge of the wealth-giving discovery had leaked, but their fears were unjustified.

He visited easily over coffee, laughing as he said, "I just couldn't resist a little spying on you, . . ." the two felt their breath vanish, "hoping I'd catch Miss Mary making one of her wonderful apricot pies. Kate and Ellie are pretty good cooks all right. You couldn't have leased the restaurant to better people, Mary, but nobody, and I do mean nobody, can bake a pie like you."

Although Bluefeather agreed with Tracy's compliment, it was hard for him to understand the full reasoning behind this overwhelming desire for a chunk of pie. He saw that Mary was both pleased and embarrassed, but just as puzzled as he was.

Bluefeather decided to test the man, saying, "Miss Mary doesn't have much time for fancy cooking right now. She's been too busy helping me in the mine."

Mary pitched right in laughing a little, "If you can call

it a mine. So far we haven't found enough metal to make a wedding ring."

Bluefeather said, to cover and make Mary's statement seem like the gospel, "There are traces, though, and where traces go you just might find the mother that gave birth. Right, Tracy?"

He had directed the last at the miner, who unaccountably found his coffee cup more fascinating than the rest of the world.

Mary said casually, "Well, I've still got a barrow of rocks to remove." She walked to the mine and disappeared inside.

Tracy watched with total disbelief at what was happening—a woman was actually going into that mine right before his sure-to-be-blinded eyes. The tin coffee cup that had had the miner hypnotized only moments before was now shaking so that he had to put it on the table out of embarrassment. He got to his feet knocking over the heavy wooden bench and fell backward with it. He tried to regain his balance but tripped again over an ore pick, twisting and falling this time on the palms of his hands and on his knees. He was thoroughly mortified, blaming his clumsiness on the cruel spirits that were angry because a woman had broken an inviolate law by transgressing into the mine, thereby sentencing all participants to unspeakable horrors. He slithered off down the trail toward Breen sure that every eye in the world had seen him falling about.

Bluefeather stared delightedly at the receding figure as did Mary peeping around the edge of the portal. They shared a satisfied glance and grin with one another, certain that they would be free from any but the most accidental invader of their privacy from now on. Tracy would spread the threat of doom like a flu epidemic.

.   .   .

This part of early summer became the time of Eden. Bluefeather had made an art out of the blasting. He was using half loads of powder and drilling the shallow holes with a short drill only. He learned how to blast the tunnel face so that the waste rock shook loose and left the vein inwardly sloping on the side called the hang wall. Then, once it was slightly loose from the careful blasting, he could pry the quartz free with a large, steel crowbar. It cut their hand sorting by eighty percent with the same amount of rich recovery. This gave them free time on Harmony Creek.

They both came to care for, and delight in, the many gifts the creek had to give. Bluefeather dug out a seep near camp, rocked it in and made a good well of cool water for all their drinking and cooking needs, but they saved a special hole in Harmony Creek for their bathing.

Bluefeather had never dreamed he would ever make the acquaintance of a person as infatuated with mountain trout fishing as he was—much less marry one. In truth, Mary was better at fishing than Bluefeather. She had as her domain a couple of favorite, deep fishing holes where the water backed up and circled slowly. She would fish an hour or so in one pool, then move to the other. Once she had worms and sometimes kernels of corn attached to her two small hooks, she would sit motionless, patiently, until she hooked one. Then Bluefeather could hear her excited screams no matter where he was on the creek.

He, on the other hand, would slip up quietly to a likely looking spot, hide behind a bush or boulder and some- times hook one as soon as the water engulfed his bait. If ten minutes passed without a nibble or strike from the elusive native trout, he would back off and seek another spot. Sometimes he would walk several miles in a day, climbing over boulders, pushing through heavy brush, slipping, sliding, totally exhausting himself. At day's end,

Mary would usually have more fish and probably hadn't moved over forty or fifty yards the entire time.

Harmony Creek had many varied waters. In some areas it cascaded down steep inclines where the water frothed as thick as whipping cream. In places where the beavers had widened and blocked it with their expertly engineered dams, the water moved slowly. On sunny days the creek turned an emerald green of such beauty it made Bluefeather feel like he could float up like a balloon so high he could look down on the sky.

The first day they had fished, Mary became so excited at her initial strike that she slipped and fell into a large circular hole of water bluer than the deepest ocean. She went under briefly, then stood up gasping and pushing her red hair out of her eyes. The next thing Bluefeather saw, to his surprise and pleasure, was Mary tossing all her clothing upon a smooth boulder.

She said, still spitting out water, "Evidently this hole was made for bathing. We shall hereafter share it with the fish," and she swam about as happy, smooth and free as the trout. Bluefeather joined her and it became a daily ritual.

Some afternoons, after they had sorted the ore, they would simply walk together looking for fish where the water was shallow and clear, reading the signs left by all the animals and birds that habituated, bathed, drank and hunted its sides. Occasionally they would actually see a deer, head high, watching them for a frozen moment before bouncing out of sight into the forest.

There was a special glade with thick grass and no wind where they could lie back and study the sky, the clouds and the birds flying. It was home to lots of chattering squirrels and chipmunks. They scampered up tree trunks and leaped from limb to limb, hiding and peeking at the intruders like little woodland voyeurs.

They could hear the creek softly playing like violins and then increasing in tempo to include horns and wet drums. The creek had become their artery. They ate from it, bathed in it, indulged in many forms of mental and physical recreation with it. It gave life and death, pain and pleasure, like the whole world did. They were the fortunate ones, for it was a treasured liquid trail of near ecstasy for them. They did not own it nearly as much as it did them.

One day as they sat side by side near a gleaming, rippling stretch of the precious creek, Mary said softly, "You know what, Blue? We just have an unwritten lease here along with all the other creatures. Each time one of them becomes extinct the rest of us shrink a bit more, until finally we will shrivel to nothingness."

Bluefeather tossed a little twig in the water and watched it bob up and down, go underwater for an instant, then twist and turn, hang a moment on a rock, break loose and move forward on through a stretch of churning water, and come up on the other side in a quieter pool where it circled and circled, finally finding its way peacefully downstream and out of sight.

"Yes," he said. "Yes. You are right."

She had already forgotten what she had said in her reverie.

Saturday afternoons brought different kinds of entertainment: they drove Mary's old truck into Breen to do their weekly shopping, to hide their high-grade ore in the cellar with the rest of their growing treasure and to attend the matinee at the Lyric Theater. They liked watching the children who attended almost as much as watching the movie. They ate popcorn and yelled for the cowboy heroes just as loudly as the youngsters.

After the shopping chores were done, they would go to

the Railroad Cafe to eat and have cocktails or wine. If they didn't want drinks with their meal, they would go by Mary's Place and dine. Then they would spend the night in the big house playing Ludwig's records or reading. Sometimes both.

Sunday morning would start with an unhurried breakfast and then back to the King Tut in time to get ready for work the next day and hear the coyotes howl.

Their young bodies were hard from all the physical work and play. Health and love and lust and all of life was theirs when and where they chose. They lived a little paradise. The world was a golden smile.

Three days passed before Mary was absolutely sure of something. Then, while things were as near perfect as humans can have them, she decided it was time to tell Bluefeather another great secret. She waited until all their work was done that day and they had eaten an early dinner. The summer sun was still shafting a few soft beams through the tops of the trees. There would be a new moon that night as well.

"Darling, Blue, we're going to give birth. We're going to start a population boom."

He stared and smiled at her, holding in his enthusiasm for an heir and another partner.

"When?"

"I don't know for sure, but I think April or May."

"Just in time for the spring runoff. That's right keen. Now let's see, . . . I think we decided on America Ludwig Fellini, huh?"

"Well maybe, but you see, there is just as much chance at it being Americana Ludwina Fellini, don't you think? She'll be called Cina for short." It was settled. Bluefeather stepped around the table, stood Mary up, patted her belly and then danced her tenderly in a circle singing some made-up madness.

"Roll out the barrel 'cause my baby Cina's gonna smile at me." Happiness flooded the King Tut mine and the Harmony Creek area like an August cloudburst on a field of green corn.

Then one night the coyotes failed to howl. The night birds waited for their signaling sounds, but they too remained silent. There was no perceptive reason for this. Anyway, Bluefeather and Miss Mary and little Cina inside her belly all slept so soundly, they missed the coming of the silence. They got up as eager as the sun, thinking it was the same wondrous world as yesterday. It was not.

The morning of the day the men came, Bluefeather looked up at the bluffs. The sun was washing them with colors so warm they were not only lovely, but enticing. They called to Bluefeather and he heard. They spoke to him of a waiting enchantment. He closed his mind's ears and did not look up at them again that day.

He was eager to get inside the solid walls of the tunnel to sort the ore he had blasted the afternoon before. The carbide lamp revealed the face of the tunnel as solid ore. They had hit a pocket—hit a wide pocket bounty of extraordinary dimensions. The entire tunnel face including the hang and foot walls were solid rose quartz, laced with wire gold in many visible areas.

Miss Mary was busy working on their expense book, so he mucked the tunnel out himself. There was no time to sort the ore from the waste. He had to see if the pocket widened and went down as well as up. He dug his blast holes with the eighteen-inch bull prick and placed the full loads of dynamite. This time he angled the holes so the explosions would break as much rock as possible.

Mary, sensing his excitement, crouched with him around the rise as he automatically repeated, "Fire in the hole."

The earth shook under them and the dust blasted out of the tunnel in a brown cloud. They waited impatiently for it to settle. They each took a carbide lamp and walked inside. The blood rushed through their veins like the waters of Harmony Creek. In the quiet of the tunnel, they could hear their hearts thumping like the drums of a war dance.

There it was under the revealing glare of the two lights. Their minds coursed and scattered around the universe with mighty surges of emotions, thoughts and feelings.

Bluefeather shoveled three or four scoops of ore into the wheelbarrow, but instead of dumping it outside, he decided to do the sorting several feet inside the portal, safe from inquisitive eyes. He tippled the hand-separated richness into a little pile out on the waste dump so the sun could fully illuminate every tiny indentation and projection of the sunflower metal.

They both stared at the ore, bending down, feeling its heaviness, seeing its luxuriance. Thoughts of castles on mountains, privately owned hunting and fishing preserves, great gardens of flowers and shrubs, food and drink from every field and garden of the earth, walls adorned with masterpieces, scores of servants, opulent silks and perfumes were theirs on demand. Demand. Power to control their destinies and those of innumerable others. All.

Then . . . then came the next feeling, simultaneously, to both Bluefeather and Mary—fear. Fear there would not be enough gold to own all these things, not enough to last forever. Fear that others would plot and gather expert and terrible forces to take it all away from them.

Fear of losing their pleasures, their powers. Fear of being murdered, mutilated and, even worse, relegated to shameful poverty with all the earthly demons staring at their ragged, starving dementia, pointing at them in ridicule, with shrieking laughter that caused such shivering that they would turn into little piles of dust out of irresistible fear. Fear beyond time.

All these things and more accelerated through their beings with such speed that they were unable to get any order to their emotions at all. They looked at one another, recognizing that each had succumbed to the ancient call of covetousness.

With a strange, stiff walk, Bluefeather dragged a bench from under the protective awning out into the sun and sat down on one end. Mary joined him on the other. They sat as far apart as the hand-fashioned bench would allow as if each was afraid of contaminating the other with their stricken and avaricious virus. They stared at each other in soul-searching silence.

Mary finally said, "We must not dig anymore. There's enough to last for several years already."

"Yeah . . . we can just live here from snowmelt to snowfall enjoying the creek, the woods . . . protecting the property. Of course, later when we have time to plan, we can decide how to help the poor, the crippled, the disenfranchised. We must do it in such a manner that no one will know."

"Anonymously, of course. There is always our baby to think of, Blue."

"Oh, I am. Believe me, I am. We'll see that he has sufficient funds put aside for any sort of education, in whatever field he desires."

"And we can have a modest but nice winter home in Denver or San Francisco in case she wishes to pursue music or the dance. There's no way she could do that here in Breen."

"No, I suppose you're right there." They were both silent a spell, then Bluefeather said, "We must remember my vows."

"They're mine, as well."

"No. They're mostly mine. I made them only for myself as a gesture to you and Ludwig."

"Just the same, they are my vows too. Now, with the baby coming and, . . ." she motioned at the tunnel, pulling her head back as if a serpent would strike it, "and . . . that . . . in there."

"I suppose you're right. We must not let a single thought of the 'yellow madness' enter us. Right? Isn't that right, Miss Mary? Huh? Huh?"

"That is our vow. Our blood vow." Mary stood up with an entirely different demeanor suddenly suffusing her vital body. "It's all settled then?" She said cheerfully, "I'll race you to the pool."

Bluefeather looked at her, and the concentrated strain vanished from his face and eyes and was replaced by one of challenge—of fun. At this recognition, Mary turned her body, and her long graceful legs carried her swiftly down the trail with a good twenty-yard head start, her hair of fire stringing out behind not quite able to catch up with her momentum.

Soon their many partners of the forest turned ears and heads to listen to the squeals of joyous abandonment as Bluefeather and Mary splashed water over each other's naked bodies, firm and supple as steel cables, and washed the last vestiges of sunflower fever into the purifying waters of Harmony Creek. The mules brayed in such volume that insects crawled under rocks. The forest creatures didn't understand the shouted human words, but they felt their meaning and rejoiced with Bluefeather and Mary.

After their swim, they walked back to the camp slowly, completely relaxed from the cold bathing and warm love-making that followed. There was a look and feel of reple-tion about them.

Bluefeather was thinking how absolutely gifted they were—young, strong, healthy and in love. He envisioned their beautiful baby running and laughing across this spe-cial glade. The baby would stop and turn at the dark edge of the forest, eyes wide with the elation of discovering the world, and wave at them with only the tilting up and down of his fingers as little children so often do. Mary was thinking similar thoughts.

As they returned to their soon-to-be-permanent sum-mer home, Bluefeather felt the bristling of hair on the back of his neck, ever so slight, and an itch on his nose scar like a grass stem rubbing across it. He tried to ignore it, but the tingling was persistent and ·stronger now. There was no sign of the camp being disturbed. Maybe a bear or a lion had passed nearby. That must be it. That would explain it. His ancient survivor's blood was still working, that was all it was.

Then his rock-trained eyes scanned the pile of ore they had dumped on the ground earlier. A chill jabbed at all the skin on his body. He instantly knew the pile was smaller. There were three or four chunks of ore missing. He checked the ground for signs. Whoever the violator was, he had been very careful. Bluefeather could see where he had brushed his tracks out with an obviously heavily leafed limb, but he had missed one tiny imprint of the edge of a rubber heel. Bluefeather didn't miss it, though.

He had to tell Mary about the intruder. He hesitated,

looking over the huge boulder that crowned the King Tut's tunnel portal, on up through hundreds of tons of large rock that had fallen over the aeons from the mountain, concealing the possible strike of the vein, all the way up to the waiting bluffs. Waiting. Waiting. "Oh, Great Spirit, the greatest of us all, it is a terrible thing that may happen here," Bluefeather thought. "If the vein has length, as I'm sure it has depth, it is of such value that men will dig millions of tons out of the mountain's bowels, and the waste and chemicals will fill and destroy the canyons and crevices of Harmony Creek. They will wash and blow down for millenniums, polluting the town and the gorgeous, giving Rio Bello. The wealth will be taken elsewhere, to many cities and many lands, while Breen and its lush forests will only be decimated, until finally even the miners, who will live and prosper until the mountain is gutted, will be gone."

Mary said, "What's that, Blue? I didn't hear you clearly."

He didn't hear her speak as his mind-voice continued, "Oh, what do I do, majestic and wise one, and where is my guiding spirit now that I need him the most? Dancing Bear, you ol' darlin', where do you hide, huh? Huh? Have you gone and left me like an alcoholic husband deserts his wife and children for the saloons? Well, you ol' dancing lush, you better show up or I'll kick your ass until your nose bleeds like a razor-sliced artery and your butt flops in the air twenty feet above your head. Now, you wouldn't like that to happen, would you? I'm sorry, Bear. Of course, I'd never go that far . . . unless you . . ."

"What? Blue, what are you talking about? Have you gone ringy-dingy on me?" Mary's voice finally penetrated. He apologized and told her of the theft.

"My God," Blue answered. "Now that they know about

the ore, they'll kill us for this kind of wealth. They'll kill us for sure, and then the real madness will begin. They'll kill the creek and destroy everything beautiful here."

"What are we going to do, Blue? How can we find them? We don't even know who took our rocks." Mary's anxiety increased.

Bluefeather quickly calmed down and tried to reassure her. "Do not worry your beautiful, little red head for a single second, dear Miss Mary. I'll take care of it for sure."

He momentarily ignored the rest of her questions while he put on his moccasins and tied a rolled bandanna around the long hair he had chosen not to cut that summer. He picked up his .30-30 and checked it for shells, dropping several more into his pocket. As he shoved a hunting knife in his belt, he turned to answer her growing protestations.

He said, "Defilers. Infiltrators of our property and our honor. Desecraters of Ludwig's dream and our work. Usurpers of others' souls, that's what they are. When the devil sinks his horns into your loved ones, his head must be severed."

Mary grabbed him and hugged him. Tears puddled her eyes, as she pleaded with him not to resort to violence. As her belly full of baby pressed against him, his rashness and his madness slowly diminished. He finally promised her that he would strike only to save their lives. He kissed her, held her closely and patted her back, comforting her until she believed him.

He left the camp making a small and then ever-widening circle to seek out the steps of the perpetrator. He regretted his promise, made under such stress in the arms of his love. One did not make those kinds of promises without some pain. He made another silent vow to

keep his last verbal one to Mary. It would not be unde-
manding—this keeping of one's word. It never was.

He moved on, head down, all senses applied to the
hunt now. There was no mine, no Breen, no memory.
Only the enemy to be found and confronted with . . .
with what?

TWENTY-TWO

IT DID NOT TAKE BLUEFEATHER LONG TO LOCATE THE TRACKS. The man had evidently felt no need to cover them after a hundred or so feet. Bluefeather could tell he was a large man by testing the depth of the tracks against his own— of course, making allowance for the gold quartz the thief carried. He also limped on his left leg some, but the regularity of the tracks left by the injured leg showed that the injury was not a new one—the man had adjusted to it.

Now Bluefeather could see by the moisture still oozing from bruised grass and bushes that he was gaining on more than one man. He stopped, leaning his rifle up against a forked limb, cupped both hands behind his ears and listened. It was fortunate he had stopped when he did because he could hear muffled voices coming and going with the gusts of the mountain breeze. He carefully worked his way downwind, at the same time moving nearer to the source of the sounds.

The voices were indistinguishable but becoming louder. He was in thick timber now, occasionally skirting a small meadow. He must move as slowly as a mother cougar after prey to feed her hungry young. With ultimate patience, foot by foot, then inch by inch, he eased closer. If they were on horseback, or worse yet, on mules, and were acute enough to watch their animals' ears, they would know someone was approaching. He would have to risk being discovered, but he felt that his patience and the favorable direction of the wind gave him a good chance of going undiscovered.

He was right. There they were in the meadow, sitting around a small fire with a large coffeepot hanging above it. Bluefeather could not hear any muzzling sounds of horses. They had most likely come in a truck, parked a mile or so below and packed their bedrolls, grub and guns in on their backs. The man he had followed was Stan Berkowitz. He was standing. The others sat on bedrolls.

Stan was saying, "I know you believe your eyes as far as those three rocks are concerned, but I keep tellin' you that they've opened up a solid face of ore as rich as what you're holdin' right there in your hands."

One of the three men whom Bluefeather recognized as having been in Stan's company at the Railroad Cafe and Ludwig's funeral said, "I never seen nothin' like it. Never."

Another said, "I heard about a strike like this over in California somewhere, but I bet it wasn't this rich."

Stan, who moved about agilely considering the stiff leg Bluefeather had given him, spoke now. "What do you think I had you boys come all the way down from Leadville for, anyway? There ain't ever gonna be a chance like this again. We gotta take it. That's all. Take it now before somebody else finds out about it."

"How you figger to do it? That goddamned Indian is a mean son of a bitch from what I heard he done over in Tonopah. Cut a man's head clean off with one swipe and stuck it up on a stick right on the main drag."

The other said, "Look what he done to you, Stan. That feller ain't anybody to . . ."

Stan yelled, raising a large hand for silence. "Yeah, well, he'll damn sure pay for that, my friend. I don't care how much man he is. The smallest .22-caliber bullet made, placed exactly between the eyes, will kill the biggest, meanest, toughest bastard that ever lived."

"Well, I reckon you got that right, but we're gonna have to kill that woman of his, too."

Stan interrupted again, "She's mine. That's another little debt I'm gonna collect. I'm gonna do her special."

"That's just fine, but we gotta get rid of the bodies so nobody can find 'em—not ever. You know there's gonna be a big search when that Mary woman comes up missing. People 'round here sure do think a lot of her. They don't know what to make of that blanket-ass Taos Indian 'ceptin' they're scared shitless of him. Some folks say he casts spells and things."

"Aw, bullshit," Stan protested. "Listen, I know where there's a mine shaft less than five miles from here that's seven hundred feet deep and too risky for anybody to ever reenter, unless they were dead. Couldn't find them bodies in a thousand years. We can pack 'em in on the mules and then turn 'em loose way over there," and he pointed northwest.

There were mutters of frightened approval.

Then Stan cinched his pitch. "Listen, we can mine it ourselves and split it all four ways. In one season we can buy up half of Denver and all that's in it, if we want. You want a stable of racehorses or women? You want big automobiles and the fanciest clothes in the world? You want to eat and drink any damn thing you like and all you like? Well, what do you want? You wanna buy the next Congress? The governor of the state? Well, what in hell? Let's vote on it right here and now."

Bluefeather had seen the rifles leaning on the bedrolls
and the holstered pistols as well. Even so, he could down
them all before they could get organized enough to fire
back. He knew that he would only have to pump five
shells into the chamber of the .30-30 and pull the trigger
five times. He could do that in five seconds. They would
never make it out of the glade alive. None of them. When
they had mentioned Miss Mary's name he had sighted
down on Stan's backbone just behind his heart and fin-
gered the trigger, but he held off because something kept
whispering to him. He wanted to hear it clearly, that
whisper—to know what it said.

Bluefeather was also shocked by the things they had
said about him. He had no idea that anybody around
Breen ever gave him a tiny thought, outside of Stan
Berkowitz and Skimpy Jones, and they did not want to
talk in public much. How could Stan explain about having
his balls mashed like pecan hulls? Bluefeather did not
appreciate them bringing up his trouble at Tonopah,
much less twisting and turning it into something it wasn't.
It was bad enough to kill a man to save your own life
without having some low-quality people spread it around
all out of kilter. He felt the mad enter the back of his
neck, trying to get in deep enough to enter his blood-
stream. If the mad got that far it would be all over. He
would kill the deserving bastards, and then his vow and
prayers to Miss Mary would be ruptured and so would all
the love they shared.

He fought, straining mightily against the mad, but he
was slowly losing as he heard the men's voices vote to kill
him, Miss Mary, the baby, Ludwig's dream, the world.

Then the whispers he had been struggling to clarify
cleared some.

"No. No, dear brudder. Come. Come visit with me.
Here behind you. Follow this voice, dear friend."

Bluefeather turned and rose to a crouching position to follow the blur in front of him; a blur that talked in magnetic tones, enticing him to follow. Finally he walked around the edge of some rocks opening into a small canyon and saw it. The "it" was Dancing Bear, smiling, shuffling about in his moccasins as if he was getting loosened up for a marathon.

"Here we are, dear brudder, all together again. You look strong as an elephant, fast as a deer, miserable as a wounded wolverine. What's a matter? You gettin' the angries cause you cain't kill them sorry folks?"

Bluefeather sighed and sat down, leaning his back and rifle against a big rock. "Where in hell have you been all this time? I been needing you for a long spell. Bad. Why didn't you show up earlier today when I was begging you?"

"I don't know why you white men always ask at the same time two questions, maybe more. Dadburn, it makes answers hard to get."

"There you go, just like always, avoiding the immediate issue, making excuses, making me wait, when I'm near disaster."

"Okeydokey, okay, then. I been over in Los Angeles, California, helpin' a friend get into the movies."

"Movies?"

"Yes sirree, that's what I do. He's gonna make people laugh and fall down doin' it. That is an important thing to do, making people fall down from havin' much, much fun instead of fallin' down bein' clumsy or drunk on whiskey."

"Bear, I don't give a damn about any comedian in Los Angeles. I want to know how to stop a big killing right over there on Harmony Creek. You don't want to feel responsible for that, do you? Did you hear what I said? Say, did you hear what I was gonna do to you back there at camp a while ago?"

"Of course, and for sure, dear brudder. Why you think I'm here? I ain't no dumb Indian spirit guide. I don' want my hind-end kicked way up there in the air where eagles and falcons might tear it in pieces. I say 'no' to any that stuff. I say 'yes' for helpin' my dear brudder Blue Fellini."

Bluefeather felt relieved that Dancing Bear hadn't taken too much offense at his recent threats, but still he had received no answer. His guide had guided him around in circles that got smaller instead of bigger. A few more turns on the trail would finally shrink it down to a dot. He'd seen ancient rock drawings do just that.

"Now listen and listen carefully, Dancing Bear. I can't wait around here visiting with you—as much as I enjoy it. I got to have answers now. There are four men right over this hill with two rifles and four pistols getting ready to kill me and mine. Now, how in all hell am I gonna stop this without shooting bullets of my own? Huh? Huh?"

Dancing Bear was sitting way up in a ponderosa pine on a dead limb looking down at Bluefeather like a great horned owl looks at a mouse. He stood up on his moccasined toes like a ballet dancer, dived off backward and stopped about three feet from the ground upside down just in front of Bluefeather.

"Now, dear brudder, I tell you this. You hearin' me for sure?"

"Yeah, for sure."

"I tell you this again. Go invite them sorry white men to dinner."

As if it had not been difficult enough to listen to somebody floating, resting or whatever it could be called, upside down in the pure mountain air, how could Bluefeather be expected to sit there and consider such an insane suggestion?

"Invite them to dinner?" Bluefeather couldn't believe

what he was hearing. "At our camp? You are crazy, crazy, crazy. Insane, I say. I reckon they are going to come over and enjoy our hospitality so much they'll help with the dishes, apologize for ever having bad thoughts and just walk away."

Bluefeather could have emptied the .30-30 into Dancing Bear's delirious brain, but then he remembered that it was pointless to attempt to murder spirit guides—that was how most of them had gotten their jobs in the first place.

Dancing Bear turned sideways in the air to make verbal visiting easier. "No, no, no, they don' walk away; they run like little rabbits with lions big as clouds and claws longer than pine trees chasin' 'em. Ah, dear brudder, the authorities done sent for poor, poor Dancing Bear. I go work on Saint Louis now. Then I gotta go to London and do the queen's maid," and he was gone.

Bluefeather was puzzled, but his killing mad had flown away. Dancing Bear had helped, but, as always, he couldn't figure how at the moment.

As Bluefeather walked toward the enemies' camp, he started whistling sweet love songs as loudly as he could prior to his advancing into the clearing. They were surprised.

He ignored their hands placed on guns and said in a kind and courteous voice, "Good day, gentlemen. I've been trying to pick up the tracks of a camp-robbing bear for hours. Have you boys seen any sign of one? Well, hello, Stan. I haven't seen you since Ludwig's funeral. How're you doing?" Bear was right. He had asked two questions at once again, but he got more answers than that.

"I'm fine. Just fine, Fellini. Say, I'd like you to meet some of my friends from Denver." He quickly introduced them by their first names only—Bluefeather would never remember. "They're in the lumber business. Thinkin' on maybe puttin' in a sawmill hereabouts. I've been showin' 'em about looking at the stands of timber. Thought another payroll might do the folks of Breen considerable good. You never know when the mines will run out of ore, do you, Blue? They figger on maybe hirin' somewhere between forty and fifty people. Be good for everybody, I figger."

Bluefeather had gotten answers in the neighborhood of three to one on his questions. He felt like that was a good percentage in his favor. His luck seemed to be running. At any rate, he sure did crowd it about as far as a man could. He could hardly believe the purely bizarre words as they emanated from his mouth.

"Why don't you folks come on over to our camp for dinner. We're not far from here. We've got a bunch of fresh trout that are just begging to be cooked. Besides that, Mary's making up a Dutch oven full of peach cobbler. You know how expert she is at makin' those pies and cobblers, Stan."

They all looked around at one another feeling just as amateurish and imbecilic as Bluefeather. Finally Stan stuttered out, "Why . . . why . . . why, I reckon that's mighty hospitable of you, Blue. I reckon we'd be much obliged, huh, boys?"

"Yeah."

"Much obliged."

"Our pleasure."

Stan responded to this "our pleasure" part, getting a gleaming of proper conniving back, "Yeah, Blue, . . . tell Mary it'll be our pleasure."

"Then it's settled. See you about an hour to sundown. I'll have a big pot of coffee ready."

Bluefeather's moccasined feet moved swiftly away,

craving desperately to get his broad back out of rifle range. Even so, he never glanced behind him.

Stan Berkowitz swung his lame leg expertly in a movement that kept his three companions straining to keep up. At each stride, the exultation grew in him at the almost laughable irony of Bluefeather inviting him to dine with them. Yes, these other men were just shadows that he needed temporarily. He realized that now. After they had served his swiftly forming designs, he would dispose of them just as he would the two fools awaiting them beside Harmony Creek. As soon as the mine's reserves were proven, he would be the only one around to watch the great mill be built. There would be no problem with financing—any bank in the world would be delighted to draw interest on such wealth. Instead of being a mill foreman, he would be the sole owner. After a time, he would accumulate so many cash reserves that he would expand around the country, maybe the world, certainly to Brazil where he had heard of great caches of gold to be taken from the Amazon wilderness—if one had the power and guts. He, Stan Berkowitz, would have plenty of both.

He had told his underlings to wait until after dinner to eradicate the male host. He had warned them not to harm the woman. He wanted to be sure her last thoughts were of him.

Now as they moved within a few minutes of the camp, the covert part of his surging blood shoved many thoughts into his brain. Bluefeather had taken the woman away from him so easily, he had not even known that he was permanently damaged by the loss. Bluefeather had beat him in the poker game and crippled him in the fight. And now, now he had casually invited him to dinner. My God, what a final insult. Well, he would be the one counting all the gold and seeing the world with all its creatures in attendance, but before that he would satisfy his prior defeats. He would have that woman in every way his fevered being could imagine, and then roll her over for his underlings to finish off, like the remains of a carcass after the hyenas and vultures had dined. Too bad Bluefeather would not be allowed to witness his retribution, but he was too dangerous and the sunflower metal was too near Stan's grasp to risk it.

Mary had been angry because they—foolishly in her eyes—had only one rifle at the camp. She could shoot as well as anyone. It had been natural. Ludwig had given her shooting lessons when she was twelve, and she had become more accurate than he was in just a few short practice sessions. She had never hunted much, only a few times when they needed the meat, and then only with her father.

Bluefeather consoled her by leaning the rifle next to the cook bench with a gunnysack draped over it. He had the .44 pistol stuck in the back of his belt under a light jacket. Mary wore a sweater. The evenings were cool enough at this altitude to justify them anyway.

Bluefeather was certain that their guests all would be wearing jackets in spite of the warming, mile-and-a-half walk through the woods. It made sense, because of the finality of the situation, that they would come with hidden guns. It would have made a lot more sense if they simply slipped up within rifle range, and with two or more shots blew them down. However, Bluefeather did not expect it to happen in this practical way. It was simple to him at this moment. There was not now, nor had there ever been, anything practical or even slightly understandable about humans dealing with the worshiped metal. The paradox was inconceivable because the metal itself was totally predictable. It was magnificently malleable into any shape of stamped or sculptured glory and would

last in beauty as long as the world. Was there some undiscovered emanation from it that all of mankind's soaring
science had been unable to detect? Had it been chosen
by the great gods as a constant test material of almost
inhuman, irresistible allure as a device to test and try men
and women to the ultimate? If not, what then?

He could not answer these thoughts, but he did not
have to think about his next actions. They just came with
his ancestral nature. He crushed the peyote buds into
powder in a rock mortar with a marble pestle. He added
several dried seeds from the Southwest earth to the mixture as well. He dumped it into the simmering coffee and
stirred it with the long wooden spoon. He set the table
with a large tin coffee cup by each plate. He poured the
cups for Mary and himself almost full of plain water while
she busied herself getting the trout breaded with cornmeal. He took the remains of the cornmeal and cast them
up in the four directions of the compass, up into the sky
and down at the earth. He chanted softly to himself and
the Great Spirit. He burned cedar in a prospector's pan
and whiffed the smoke all about the campsite with a
hawk's feather. An eagle feather was used on most of
these occasions, but Bluefeather used that of the hawk,
which wasn't as strong as the eagle but had more resil-
ience and survival abilities. He gave special attention with
the cedar smoke to the places soon to be occupied by the
guests.

Mary had just put the heavy, iron Dutch oven on the
woodstove filled with the ingredients that would make a
luscious cobbler. The sourdough bread was baking, and
the aroma had already begun to drift on the air. He had
just put the stomped ashes from the gold pan behind the
tent when he knew his enemies were nearing. He could
feel it on the back of his neck and smell them, even above
the cobbler.

Mary added a couple of sticks of cedar to the fire. As Stan and his men entered the camp area, they were hit with the subtle remains of the cedar smoke and the gland-stirring smell of the bread and the cobbler.

"Welcome. Welcome," smiled Bluefeather from his black diamond eyes with the olive-brown complexion surrounding them. "We're almost ready for you."

"I could smell Mary's cookin' a mile before we got here," said Stan.

Everybody exchanged greetings and introductions as the occasion demanded. The atmosphere was absolutely tense with such an abundance of cordiality.

"Here, here, here, Stan." Bluefeather seated them, giving Stan the head of the table, but next to his own elbow. He left his wife's seat open, saying, "The cook must be nearest to the fire." He graciously poured them coffee, chattering on furiously in competition with the birds of the forest. He faked pouring his own, using the same skill he had been taught to deal the cards with in Tonopah— by misdirecting the viewer's vision with an opposite action. It worked.

Mary was tending to pans and all sorts of cookware that needed no attention at all.

Bluefeather was watching all four of the invaders, but mainly Stan, as he knew the mill foreman was the general of this little campaign.

Stan volunteered a polite remark about the "delicious-tasting coffee," and the others nodded and commented just as favorably. Bluefeather was pouring refills by the time they finished their compliments.

Stan's eyes now darted from Bluefeather to Mary. The orbs of all the men were becoming erratic, looking inward a moment and then jerkily outward. Bluefeather knew they all had pistols hidden under their jackets. One guest thoughtlessly touched its bulk under his leather jacket and came within a fraction of a second of dying.

Bluefeather raised his under-filled tin cup with his left hand while he reached to secure his pistol with his right, as if he were scratching his back, which indeed he did as soon as he saw that the man's gesture was a thoughtless one.

Now Stan's eyes lingered on Mary. She felt them and gave swift, hopefully unnoticed, glances at the .30-30 under the gunnysack. Bluefeather saw that these men were now possessed by the vision-buds as far as he could allow.

He slowly raised up and said, "Gentlemen, it's only a moment until you will be served. So, with your permission, I'll play the drums for you before the repast of your lifetime."

Every move had to be smooth. The slightest jerk and the six harmless guns would be put into an action from which there would be death, pain and deadly disruption forevermore.

Bluefeather took the old, hide-covered, Indian drum and beater from where they hung on the corner log support of the lean-to. He squatted without looking at the armed and increasingly befuddled and ominous trespassers. The air was twanging and trembling as it became thinner and harder to breathe.

Mary moved and stood next to the rifle as Bluefeather pounded at the drum with swiftly increasing velocity. He sang now, songs of the Pueblos, the Anasazi before them and the ancients even before them. The sounds vibrated into the air like the noise of a million geese rising in migratory flight.

The men stared at him, mouths slowly opening, eyes flickering as things began to flutter and move in their peripheral vision. Things they tried not to see, but could not hide, nor could they deafen the increasing racket. The trees of the forest were uprooting and flying through the air leaving a vast circle, and the ragged holes they had torn in the earth were filled and smoothed with tall grass. The trees that had moved aside now rocketed upward with whooshing sounds, and the air they displaced whammed against the earth in downbursts of such force that the impact sounded like explosions of dynamite as it shook the earth and rattled all the matter inside their skulls.

Lightning ripped jagged holes in the sky without letup, crossing, crisscrossing and colliding with such force that great balls of whirling blue and orange lights were formed, whizzing so fast the best of eyes could not begin to follow, much less endure the brilliant kaleidoscope of plunging, bouncing lights that inundated everything. The skeletons under all things were visible, even the inner textures of wood and rocks.

Then the lightning stopped in an immeasurable instant, and thousands of tepees circled up and around the clearing and through the forests and fires. Dances and old, old songs were seen and heard separately and together. The lights and sounds filled every twig, every rock crevice, everything. And there on the edge of the circle was Alexander the Great and all his legions astride mighty stamping horses that snorted fire. Their eyes gleamed in blue lights of beauty.

The Roman Coliseum now appeared, alive with roaring lions. A lion, as big as three elephants, slung nude human bodies around like apple boxes in a tornado. A human body made only a single bite for the monstrous creature, and a solid river of blood drained from the terribly beautiful beast's jaws in a stream that flowed in a cresting flood toward the camp.

Thousands of blue-gray souls moved across the opening in silence. Endlessly they came from many directions, moving through one another and finally walking around the great round clearing in the circle of infinity.

All was quiet now except for a low moan never before heard. It penetrated out into the universe and down toward the molten, gut center of the earth. It was the sound of eternity—methodically, ceaselessly marching.

Suddenly the displaced trees all melded into one massive trunk, so high above, it seemed only a twig. Then with a roaring of ten thousand racing trains, it headed toward earth and the campsite. As it neared it became bigger than a town, as big as a city, bigger than anything. Its roots were like mile-long, clutching claws of a gigantic lion. It would, within seconds, be close enough to rip a hole in the earth a mile deep, creating scars like the Grand Canyon.

Stan became unparalyzed. He ran away from the camp, crashing over the table, screaming unheard-of utterances. The other three tried to follow, falling, then scrambling up so fiercely from the earth that they ripped the skin from their palms and the tips of their fingers.

One ran into a tree, crunching his nose flat and breaking his cheek open so that the sides and back of one eyeball were in open air. Another ran into his companion. They fell together, rolling over and over, kicking, biting, scratching at one another, sometimes with rocks and dead tree limbs in their hands until they were crippled and crawled away into hidden places of the forest to die alone like wild animals.

Stan got his good leg hung up in the crevice of some rocks at the edge of a ten-foot drop. Gravity and momentum carried his heavy body free-falling the ten feet to a slope where he rolled until he hit level bottom. All the bones of his good leg were twisted and shattered beyond repair.

After the guests' unannounced departures, Bluefeather and Mary finished off all they could hold of the delicately prepared trout and the hot, buttered sourdough buns. The cobbler bubbled up slightly around the edge of the just-right brown topping as Mary set the Dutch oven out to cool. Ordinarily it would have been hard to wait for such a sweet-smelling treat, but they had lots of time now. There was no doubt in their happy minds that their working and playing retreat would never be perforated again.

They decided to have a cup of the coffee themselves. It would not harm them. They had brewed it. They clanged the cups together for the toast.

Bluefeather said, "Here's to warm campfires and great visions."

Mary said, "To the gods, God bless them."

For reasons that needed no exact understanding, they laughed with the great joy of release, looking at one another's chortling faces as they did so to double their pleasure.

Stan was found three days later, dragging himself with his upper body and a slight assist from the leg Bluefeather had worked on earlier. He was discovered on the eastern road into town by two nine-year-old boys who had intended to spend the morning fishing on the enticing banks of the Rio Bello. Instead, they threw down their poles and ran down the street screaming that there was a crazy man crawling toward town. Indeed they were right. Neither Stan's legs nor his mind ever worked correctly again.

Two days later a man without a face, at least without a recognizable one, stumbled and fell into town, and the most sense he ever uttered the rest of his life was, "There's a long-toothed lion bigger than the state of Texas after all our asses."

TWENTY-THREE

MARY AND BLUEFEATHER DID NOT BOTHER TO SORT AND HAUL the ore from the King Tut tunnel. With the outside threats to their personal province permanently removed, they simply relaxed for a few days. Anyway, whenever they decided to sort the ore there would be no need to mine more for two or three years. They could live abundantly now from their prior work, and a couple of heavy charges in the widened and enriched part of the vein would probably give them ample resources for a lifetime. They could take time to enjoy more music, reading, loving and fishing, without anyone knowing or noticing the difference. Not that the citizens of the Breen area would dare to intrude. There was enough wild gossip and individual imaginings of unknown forces to deal with if one messed around with the half-breed or his lady.

Mary shared none of the blame, but people said things like, "How could she be so blind to this magician of the devil?" Other statements about her were made out of hidden but surely jealous emotions.

The couple now pleasantly planned their quiet but assured future, while enjoying the present warm days, fishing, swimming and walking the banks of Harmony Creek.

They also enjoyed riding the mules down the canyons and around the mountains. They even rode over to look at the Ruby Dove workings and tried to guess which shaft Stan and his boys had intended to toss them into.

A few headframes and some remnants of buildings that had collapsed into great, gray splinters were the only remains of a settlement. Even the ghosts seemed to have deserted the Ruby Dove. But people had lived and died here. There was a weed-covered cemetery to prove it. The wooden crosses had almost all gone to the bugs, and the iron ones had fallen and were mostly covered over.

Two of the old mine tunnels were still visibly identifiable by some odd-shaped rock markers that stood upright and in good order.

Mary pointed to one of them and said, "That's the one they had picked out for me. I can tell by the chamisa growing around it. I love the smell of chamisa."

Bluefeather said, "Okay. That's yours . . . I'll take the other one with the small piñon tree sprouting out of its edge. Piñon is my favorite tree in all the world."

"I think I've seen enough of the Ruby Dove for this lifetime," Mary said, and reined Nancy back onto the trail toward Harmony Creek.

Bluefeather said, "You're right. Those are old, dead dreams and not for people like us who own all the world worth having." He lightly nudged Jackknife in the sides and followed his love.

For a change, that afternoon they sat and had hot tea. Sipping quietly, they stared into the forest filled here and there with the light of the sun forming little temporary, natural cathedrals.

Bluefeather's eyes went up to the waiting bluff. He couldn't stop them. He couldn't grab his eyes with his powerful miner's hands and pull them back down to more peaceful sights. Nor would his will—which was stronger than a thousand such hands—control the orbs either. He could hear it whispering again, growing seductively louder and louder, "Come, dear brother, I'm waiting. Waiting for you to keep your vow. Do not worry. You will conquer my sides as if I were only an infant bluff three feet high. Come, come to me. I'm tired of waiting to show you your desire. Have no fear. You will return to your camp without harm. I am waiting. Waiting just for you. You. You."

At that moment he almost screamed at the bluff to hush before it upset Miss Mary, but she had come over to sit on his lap. She pushed his hair back from his forehead and held his face tenderly in her hands, looking straight into his eyes, saying, "Blue, dear Blue. I want to try to tell you how deeply I appreciate you keeping your word and not letting the . . . the blasted gold possess you. You were right. You were strong enough to whip the madness and you're the only man I've ever known or heard of who has. I have to confess, after all my lecturing, that at the sight of the new discovery—that fabulous face of ore—I had momentary flashes of grand castles and diamond necklaces. I am so ashamed."

"No. No, it's only natural. It's . . ."

"It was over as quickly as it possessed me, because of you. Anyway, I have to tell you now, and I'll try not to bring it up again, how much I admire and respect your willpower."

Bluefeather was pleased almost to tears and so embarrassed that he just gathered her breasts to his chest and laid his head in the comforting bend of her shoulder and encircling arm. Then she said, "Blue, my partner, I love you as much as . . . as . . ." Her voice faded into her thoughts.

They were still and silent in their embrace until the coyotes howled again. And again.

. . . .

Bluefeather arose at daylight, built a fire and put the coffee on to boil. Then he sat by the bed and watched the restful breathing of his Miss Mary. He reached out and touched her hair where it was in very bold relief against the pillow. She was so quietly beautiful at that moment, he almost dissolved. She sighed, smiled so slightly that he nearly missed it and took his hand in hers, holding it to one cheek.

"I can't put it off any longer, my darling. I must climb the bluff today."

She opened her own piece-of-the-sky eyes just long enough to look up at him and say, "Yes, I know."

He had glanced at the bluff surreptitiously hundreds of times and had studied it seriously through a score of sessions. He had glassed it until his eyes and head throbbed, hoping the vein would show up clearly under the magnification and he would not have to make the dreaded climb. There were just too many cracks and crevices to see it any other place, except there on the bluff in the flesh. His.

He worked his way through the tumbled mass of boulders carefully so as not to strain any muscles or ligaments. To get up to the conclusive evidence he would need all his physical powers to help parlay his mental capacities.

He had decided to come at the bluff from an angle he had picked out earlier. It appeared to his naked eye, now that he had neared the spot of resolution, that he could angle sideways and upward, and at the same time avoid the straight ascent that had broken Ludwig. One thing he had spotted with the glass was the flat-looking ledge two-thirds of the way to the top. He had located it earlier in the spring when he saw an eagle land there.

The first going was not so difficult. There were plenty

of indentions for his hands and feet. The bluff angled back ten or fifteen degrees giving his body something to rest against between moves. Already, though, he realized he had misjudged the height; it was much greater when his eye was six inches from the bluff's hard, unforgiving face.

Slowly he moved one hand, one rubber-soled boot, at a time. He could feel the sweat just beginning all over his body, but it wasn't bad as yet for the early morning gusts of wind cooled and helped dry him.

Suddenly he was on the edge of a crevice only about a foot and a half deep and perhaps four feet across. Leaning as far as he dared with one hand out, he still could not quite reach the other side. It was just barely beyond his reach. He would have to retreat and attack again where the indention was narrower. On his attempt at the second step backward, his right foot could find no hold. He moved it about, seeking, touching, scraping it across the rock. How could that be? Where had that foothold gone? He was returning the exact way he had come.

He stretched down as far as possible, straining his fingers, precariously grasping the rock to the limit and pushing the knee of the solid leg hard against the unyielding stone. The sweat came now and he didn't feel the breeze anymore. He was trapped. He could not descend an inch. There was nothing to do but try to get back to the crevice.

He kept one wet cheek against the rock now as he inched back up. Twice a hand slipped from the sweat and his weight. He was suddenly much heavier than he had ever been in his life. He was pulling his muscles tight between all his joints. As he lifted his body, he felt they would rip and twist into the form of steel coils.

The gray nothingness had come upon him, because he was back at the crevice without consciousness of having groped the last few feet. He held a moment to gather what was left of his courage and strength before he leaned out again straining, reaching, until he touched the rock. There was a handhold—just one, but he could not force the extra fraction of the half-hand's distance it would take to reach it.

When he returned to his four-point position he realized that he was in about the most perilous position he could imagine. He could not go down without falling probably seventy feet onto jagged boulders, and the same fate awaited him if he tried to go up. Or there was the impossible choice of grabbing at the single handhold as he shoved himself across the thin mountain air between the edges of the crevice.

Finally, as sweat started trickling down into the corner of one eye, he made up his mind to try it. Once that was done he said in a whisper, "Well, Ludwig, in a moment I may be keeping you company on the hill outside Breen, but here I go." Again he extended his arm across the space with all his force. The far tips of his searching fingers were almost there, but it was the limit at last. He propelled with the other three members, grasping outward for his life. The hand locked into position on the rock and almost ripped apart as the weight of his body struck the bluff. He clawed with his hands and feet for any notch of any size. The fingers of his free hand shoved into a small crack so hard it peeled the hide on his middle finger to the bone. He found another little niche for the toe of his left boot and held. The one leg that hung heavy, loose and unsecured in space, gave him the impetus to claw his way upward through the gray nothingness again.

At last he opened his eyes to the flinty vision he was spread laboriously against. It was strange to him that the granite did look like flint this close up and smelled like old gunpowder.

He discovered he didn't know where he was on this massive outcropping any more than he would if he had been hurled past Mars without a compass. Bluefeather reasoned that there are many ways to break rock: by repeatedly freezing and then toasting it under the harsh sun for several million years, by earthquakes of great magnitude, by encroaching glaciers, by swinging a sledgehammer enough times with powerful arms, and with explosives of devastating power. But one thing he knew for certain, no matter how many ways one could find to break rock, there was still no known way to stretch it. None. That was for sure.

Almost mindless, and certainly mostly blind from the sweat that drained off his forehead, around his eyebrows and into his eyes, he moved upward with a Herculean effort. His hands were becoming so slippery from the wetness, every grasp felt like his last. In contrast, his breath was gasped in and out of his hurting lungs as dry and terrible as desert warfare. Then nothing moved but the bluff. It heaved and moved in wobbly, shaking laughter as he clung to its face. Cold and hot. Weak and strong, but always scared.

Then he said to the bluff, "You deceiving bastard, I know that rock can't stretch. You're not moving except as the world turns. That's all. You're playing little dirty tricks on me. That's for sure. Hey, I'm coming to your ledge, you vain old fool. Your ego can't take it that I'm going to sit right astride your golden vein and take a big, healthy dump right on top of it. How do you like that? Huh? Huh? Why so silent now after all your laughing and taunting? Answer me that."

Bluefeather's rebuttal to the mountain worked as far as his valor was concerned, but his indomitable will could not find a tiny pit for his wet fingers to hold onto. He was stopped here as sure as one of the recent evil imposters in their camp who had run into a tree.

He tried to move one hand up and then the other, over and over, but they would not hold. He was forced to return again and again to the handholds that were deep enough. The increasing sweat made every second more slippery and precarious. He didn't dare drop even the weight of one leg in an attempt to move downward. That much weight would certainly jerk his slick hands loose and hurtle him to eternity.

He could not even see the rock face anymore. Everything was slipping away. Without a conscious precept, he had begun singing the death song taught him by his Indian grandfather, Moon Looker. As he chanted on, the fear began to leave him. He cried out silently for his guiding spirit, Dancing Bear, then several sweet visions of Miss Mary undulated back and forth in the stone—smiling, laughing, beckoning. At this he stilled and braced himself, looking up for the first time. There it was just out of reach. The ledge. There was no question, because he could see the sticks of the eagle's nest protruding out from it. But it was no matter, for he could not move in any direction.

"Well, I'll be a cockeyed, castrated, one-eyed goat. There it is right up there, but it might just as well be in Chicago for all the good it's gonna do me." He didn't actually speak aloud. It was more like guttural rumblings in his throat. His face was jammed against the stone so hard he was afraid even to move his jaws. Even his eyes could only cover about a one-yard circle without tilting him loose. Comparatively this was the smallest piece of real estate that had ever owned him—less than a foot above his uppermost hand to the edge of the rock shelf.

Right here, within a few inches, was the whole world: all the books he had read; all the songs he had heard; all

the fine food and drink he had tasted; all the love he had
felt for Mary, Ludwig, his mules; all the mountains and
deserts he had borrowed from the Great Spirit; all the
deer and bears he had tracked and respected; and all the
coyotes he had heard as brothers and sisters. Here, too,
were the moon and the sun he had followed and avowed,
along with the immeasurable space of the white-freckled
blackness beyond. Water, wind, breath, life of the whole
earth—these things and more were right here this instant. All.

Now he put his thoughts down to his one leg, bent at
the knee, and about even with his waist. He concentrated
with all that was left of him on that one limb. With an
exuberant, reckless and joyous yell, he shoved his body
with that pivotal leg. As he did so, a slab about twelve by
sixteen by ten inches broke loose and plunged downward,
bouncing crazily at odd angles because of its irregular
shape, like the broken club head of a giant warrior's bat-
tle-ax.

Bluefeather reached through space and hung just a
fleeting, horrible second on the edge of the rock above,
with fingertips digging in so desperately the fleshy ends
burst open. Then the elbow of his other arm and one leg
swung over the precipice. He was there. He had made it.
He just lay on the stone as if it were made of goose down.
When he was able to move again, he kissed it like a returning prisoner of war when he first steps upon his
homeland.

Bluefeather said, "Ahh, sweet bluff. You have given me
back my life, so I will cancel my threat to dump on you. I
think my pants are dirtied from the last lunge anyway."

Miss Mary had not looked up at the bluff that had crippled her father and seductively beckoned her life's love.
She ignored it and went about separating the little bit of

muck from chunks that made up their treasure trove. She had put all the waste rock on the dump and piled the high-grade ore next to their camp table so they could sit and replenish themselves while admiring its colored, crystalline beauty in the sunlight.

She was pushing the last barrow load out from the portal when she finally stopped and turned her head to look up for her husband. That's when the sharp edge of the plunging rock struck her. Only a half inch of it touched her.

Bluefeather slowly crawled around the edge of the ledge until he could peer over its back side. There was no vein here that he could find. Of course, he knew it would be weathered and dull. Just the same, he had far better-than-average eyesight and lots of experience for his age at spotting rare rock. He noticed that the back side of the bluff would have been impossible for him to climb; it angled in toward the bottom. No, he had climbed up the only possible way. He must not allow his thoughts to linger on what might have been.

He turned carefully, futilely scratching at the most likely places for the vein with a sharp chip of rock. He failed to find the completion of Ludwig's dream. He had a moment of sadness as he asked Ludwig's forgiveness. He didn't bother to apologize for the fact that only boiling nature could make a rock vein.

He had placed the rope on the eagle's nest. As he reached for it, he realized that the nest was built on the edge of the crevice that had almost consumed him. It took a lot of strength to raise the edge of the large interwoven nest, but he did. There it was. He had found it. He swiftly gathered pieces of rocks and built a stone post to hold up the edge of the nest and crawled under to examine the vein. He chipped at it with his prospector's pick, and when that didn't work he took his pocketknife and cut at it, finally working loose a small piece of gold stuck to a gravel of rose quartz. That was all the proof he needed to show Miss Mary so she would know that all vows had been kept.

Then he noticed that the vein formed one side of the crevice. He peered over and saw that a narrow projecting part of the vein itself had been the singular handhold that had saved his life when he had taken the little leap across the narrow void.

He crawled out from under the nest and removed the rocks. The nest would be ready for the eagle's eggs and a new brood of eaglets next spring. Now that his eye was adjusted to the weathered colorations of the vein, he could see where it wove its way on up in the crevice and disappeared. It was there—solid in the belly of the mountain. Just between his spot on the bluff and the tunnel's face, there was enough ore to mine and supply ten lifetimes. That didn't matter. What counted was Ludwig's dream. They had fulfilled it, and in doing so they had created their own.

"Hey Ludwig, ol' partner. It's done. You can rest easy, ol' boy, on your travels through the other worlds. Bon voyage."

His thoughts left the ledge now. They sailed above the treacherous, tumbled rock pieces toward Miss Mary. He secured the loop over an outcropping, wrapping the rope around his hips and jerking back with all his weight. It would hold. He rappeled down the face of the bluff, having great difficulty taking the necessary care in his descent across the random roughness of the mountain.

Finally he reached grass and bushes with solid dirt underneath. He felt no tiredness from the ordeal. Only jubilation. He rounded the edge of the rise and reached in his pocket as he walked proudly toward the camp. He took out the little sample of truth and held it in his open palm for Mary's eyes.

He yelled, "Mary! Miss Mary! We did it, darling! We pulled it all off!"

He saw her sleeping there on the barrow of gold ore. He felt guilty for shouting. A quick glance around at the ore separated and piled told him that she had worked very hard. She was plainly exhausted from the night of emotion and the day of labor.

He tiptoed up to her, smiling with reverence. He put his arms under hers to lift her up. Her head flopped over, and through the hair the color of fire, he saw the narrow gash just barely cutting into her brain. He knew, but he could not accept, that the blood on his hands was from her body. The cold numbness held him a moment as he talked to her and told her of their victory. He tried to get her to look at the little specimen.

"See, my darling . . . see how lovely it is. Your father will be so pleased. I know he is raising a toast to us right now. He is saying, 'Here's to Miss Mary and Bluefeather, my children who loved me very much.' Can't you just hear him? Huh? Huh?"

It was no use. He got control then. On the way to get a blanket to wrap her in, he saw where the fallen stone had imbedded itself in his homemade cabinet. He vaguely, as if from a time before dinosaurs, remembered the rock cracking loose under him as he made his final leap at the bluff's edge.

He wrapped her tenderly. Then he had an almost overwhelming desire to tear the baby from her—to salvage that part of her breathing life. But he killed the beastly thought. It was too late for that. The baby was not old enough to live anyplace but its mother's belly. So it would have to crash through and travel on with her.

His body turned to pain. The dull but excruciating

throb of sorrow in his breast finally broke loose in long, shuddering sobs as he cradled Miss Mary across his heaving chest.

Bluefeather drove to the morgue. He told the mortician to deliver the coffin containing his wife and baby to the main house. The man tried to get him to sign papers and kept saying things about arrangements. Bluefeather did not answer him. He handed him a large roll of bills and said, "Do what I tell you."

The mortician did.

That night with some difficulty Bluefeather managed to secure the coffin in the bed of the old truck. He drove out into the darkness toward Harmony Creek.

He unloaded the coffin after cutting log rollers, and slowly, with many stops and endless adjustments of the rope and rollers, he finally got Miss Mary to the portal of the mine and then back into the tunnel.

By lantern light, he dug, with inconceivable strength, a large hole in front of the portal. He took the lamp and, scooting through the hole, entered the tunnel. He hung the lantern on an iron spike, then opened the coffin lid, straightened the beryl necklace on her throat and placed the small specimen from the bluff ledge in her hand. Bluefeather looked at his love for a moment. The last moment.

Then he kissed her on the forehead and said, "Someday. Somewhere, my love." He closed and nailed the coffin shut.

Bluefeather picked up an anvil and carried it over, placing it next to the pile of ore. He leaned his rifle against the table. No one —no one on this earth—would be allowed to interrupt his duties to Miss Mary.

He hammered and chipped, hour after hour, until all the nuggets, wires and ropes of gold were mostly free from the rose quartz. It took him the rest of that day and most of the night by lamplight to complete the task. He did not eat, drink or sleep. All the gold was piled on their table now, almost covering its top.

He carried his labors into the tunnel. It took many trips. He scattered the sunflower mineral across the top of the coffin until it was completely covered. Then he got the other lantern and filled it and its companion with fuel. He drove a spike in the other wall and hung one lantern across from the other one where they shined down on Miss Mary's coffin. The tiny pieces of rose quartz caught the minute flickerings of the two flames and sparkled as if handfuls of diamonds had been sprinkled amongst the gold.

Bluefeather was pleased at last. Mary's tomb would be no less than the greatest of Egyptian or Mayan royalty. Considering the clean face of solid ore revealed at the head of her coffin and the just-proven length of its richness, all other tombs in history were amateurish.

He didn't pause now but turned and walked toward the light of the world shining outside Miss Mary's place.

Now Bluefeather was all professionalism. He studied the two rocks that held the huge boulder in place above the tunnel. He hammered and drilled at specific angles and measured his powder charges to his own perceived expectation. He wired it with care and then without hesitation knelt beside the newly acquired charge box, pushed the plunger down and blew the barrier out from the front of the obelisklike rock. It was freed and dropped down into the hole, sealing the tunnel so perfectly it could not have been better planned and executed by an entire family of gods.

It took Bluefeather three days to tear down everything in camp and haul it away. But at last he had cleaned, shoveled and swept with branches until the spot was returned as near to its natural setting as was humanly possible. Then with a hammer and drill he chipped new petroglyphs on the curving face of the fallen boulder.

First he made a cross three feet high; next a peyote messenger bird, sleek and streamlined, flying the message as swiftly as thought straight up to the proper spirits in the heavens; and last he put his own personal sign that he had just invented without conscious thought. It was a circle inside a circle, and then he chipped three little dots in the interior circle. This represented Miss Mary, Bluefeather and their child. The family in the world and universe. He dug up and planted thorny bushes in front of the boulder. Then he watered them and smoothed everything again.

"Now no amount of greed or need will ever allow me to upset the sanctity of this tomb."

He packed his remaining gear on his mules and led them down to drink from Harmony Creek for the last time at Miss Mary's pool. Just for an instant he was sure he saw her body—shining wet, smooth, vibrant, swimming across the pool—and heard her exultant laughter filling the canyon and the woods. Then it was gone.

He mounted Jackknife's back and rode away from the talking waters of Harmony Creek, leading Nancy. Their lease had run out. He did not look back. He couldn't. Ever.

He and his mules wandered in the mountains for several days. Bluefeather was unaware of his actions as he packed and unpacked the animals, automatically making camp and preparing just enough food for bare sustenance. Numbness prevailed.

Then finally, they dropped down out of his beloved San Juan Mountains where he followed a game trail into the northern New Mexico hills. There was a mixture of grasses, sage, cedar and other small evergreens scattered around them as they moved down the curling trail.

He was beginning to notice the tracks and other signs of wild animals again and walked ahead of the mules for a change. Suddenly he saw a movement in an opening perhaps a quarter mile below. Dancing Bear was shuffling about in circles as if preparing, but not quite ready yet, to perform a full-scale dance. As they neared him, Bluefeather raised an arm in greeting and opened his mouth to yell a hello to his spirit guide. In this brief instant Dancing Bear skipped through the air over three treetops, landing on his toes and up again in ever longer leaps, becoming small as an eagle in the growing distance, then he appeared no larger than a sparrow and vanished altogether. Before Bluefeather could shout his dismay at this shoddy treatment, the whole of the firmament before him turned into the face of Miss Mary. The top of her head appeared thousands of miles above him. Her lips smiled at him bigger than the Grand Canyon. He stopped. The mules stopped behind him. He stared, but his keen vision was far too limited to encompass the entirety of the wondrous projection of the loving expression on her face. Was she God now?

As he struggled to absorb the massive transparent vision before him, the various parts of her beautiful face started separating. The cream of her cheeks floated down and became part of the mesas stretching flat-topped across the high desert before him. The crimson of her mouth became part of the iron-blushed streak through the center strata of the mesas. Her sun-flamed hair swept from the sky and joined the barren vermilion hills farther on. Her great blue eyes of such vital mirth and knowing energy fused, dancing and vibrating, to intermingle with the boundless sky. The whiteness of her teeth whirled in a burst of light and motion to blend with the crowning

snows far to the south and east in the Sangre de Cristo
Mountains. Miss Mary's soul impregnated all. All.

A mighty surge of ecstasy inhabited Bluefeather's being. He offered both hands high above him in a silent
thanks to the Great Spirit. Then he leaped down the
game trail, agile and strong as a deer, shouting to the
mules first and to the rest of the world next, "She's in
the mesas, the mountains, the sky. Our darling Miss Mary
is everywhere. Everywhere we look. Everywhere we step.
Every breath we take. Everything we feel. She is around
us, beside us, below us, above us and inside us for eternity. Oh, joyous thanks a billion, a trillion times!"

Then he sat down on a flat rock, and with a smile made
of amalgamated happiness, he stared across the ever-
changing, ever-moving landscape of the earth, the sky
and all its flora and fauna that in their totality were his
very own Miss Mary. He would never be alone again.

PART TWO

~

TRANSITION—MISTS OF GOLD

MISTS OF BLOOD

TWENTY-FOUR

BLUEFEATHER NEVER KNEW FOR SURE WHY HE CHOSE THE small, personal, adobe village of Corrales, New Mexico, on the northwest edge of Albuquerque, for his headquarters. Maybe because it had the same reminiscent qualities as Taos—just as varied, but with a smaller collection of nationalities and artists. It even had the domination of the mighty Sandia Mountains to the east. All this was a plus along with the natural rural feeling. Its small orchards, vegetable farms and pastures were irrigated by the nearby Rio Grande.

He found the exact acreage he needed to keep his two newly acquired young mules happy and a pleasant, well-built, five-room adobe house. But what clinched it all were his new neighbors, Tranquilino Lucero and his family.

He took an instant liking to Tranquilino, and the feeling only increased when he found out he, too, liked and understood mules. It was decided. (Bluefeather would never regret this purchase, through all the times of horror and wonderment that he would be plunged into like a wheat straw in a tornado, inexplicably driven into a telephone pole.)

He settled in, patching up the adobe-mud house with

Tranquilino's expert help. Bluefeather paid him a few dollars that the Luceros were happy to get. Their orchard, garden, pigs, chickens, and milk cow kept them in food, but Tranquilino had to do outside repair work for any extra spending money they might have. It was nice for him to get employment right next door.

It was a pleasant time for Bluefeather. He had the best of neighbors, a place just the right size to go with the house, small barns and outbuildings. Everything was in good repair now. The two huge cottonwoods framing his house were well-watered and healthy. There was an old grape arbor under which he built an eight-foot-long table with benches on each side. He and Tranquilino enjoyed sitting there sometimes in the late evening, sipping beer and talking about mining, ghosts and Hitler's war that was cracking and scorching a large portion of the earth. Or they simply stared out over the lush ditch bank at the elms and cottonwoods across the bosque (the sixty-mile-long cottonwood forest), which hid the fast-growing city, and up at the Sandias turning just as pink as the San Juan Mountains above Breen that he had left almost a year ago now.

Bluefeather had patiently trained his mules for packing and riding, and now the time had come to get on with his life's work. Arrangements were made for Tranquilino to look after the land and see that all was well in the house. He headed into the San Pedro Mountains north and east of the Sandias near the little mining towns of Golden and Madrid where, in the 1600s, the Spanish had taken out many millions in gold.

It felt good to get back into the hills again. He enjoyed the quiet companionship of his mules, which he had named Nancy, after his Tonopah lady, and Mary, after his love in a hidden tomb, or temple, as he liked to think of it. He had made the uncomplicated decision to name all his future mules Nancy or Mary. It was a point of honor, both ways.

He walked and studied the earth and hundreds of chunks of float rock. He assayed samples from many cuts and some old tunnels, but the best he came away with was a little bed of dry placer. Prospecting and mining were his chosen way, but he did resent having to pursue gold right now. He hunted for other minerals but found none that would pay.

He rigged up a good, dry shaker and recovered some color. Since he still had a few funds left from Breen, he did not have to worry about starving or having to hunt a grubstake. He accumulated three small canvas bags of mixed dust and small nuggets, but he could see that the sand would be gone in a few months, and he had found no other pay.

Every couple of weeks, he would ride down from the hills to Golden. He would drink and eat in the combination bar-restaurant and listen to all the war news. That was all anyone talked about anymore. Friends and relatives of just about everyone were scattered around the world fighting or preparing to do so.

He got a letter from his mother in Raton saying that all seven of the Marchiondo boys had joined up. This was admirable, but after Mary Schmidt O'Kelly Fellini, even the war was having a hard time affecting him.

Finally, though, he felt the pull of all these bodies, moving and gathering for the greatest storm of steel the world had ever known. It was irresistible to him. Since Tranquilino had too many kids and was just over the age limit, he would not be going to war. Bluefeather made a deal with the Luceros to oversee the property until his return. His mules could be profitably used and cared for by Tranquilino.

The Luceros did not know what was in the letter

Bluefeather left with them, for it was to be opened only in case of his death. It contained instructions that the adjoining Fellini land would become theirs, along with the mules and the contents of a locked, iron box they were to care for—the box held about $30,000 in nuggets at the current going rate.

Bluefeather, the Luceros and some other close neighbors had a three-day party, a fiesta, a drunk, a feast of red chile in great pots, tamales and posole, and hollow pillow-bread called sopaipilla—made properly only in New Mexico. They drank tequila, beer, wine and even a little brown whiskey. While Tranquilino played his violin like a master, others accompanied him with guitars and dances. Oh, it was fun enough to last the war, he thought the day before he sobered up. Then over many tears and embraces he left to join the army.

Naturally, having knowledge as great as most graduate engineers and a high degree of reading ability that would have made him an ideal candidate to write and prepare general orders, he was put in the walking infantry.

Well, by God, he had done that too. He could outwalk anyone at the Fort Walters, Texas, boot camp and shoot better than anyone he met, but he was too accustomed to being his own boss—answering only to the dictates of mountain lightning storms and three-hundred-pound black bears—to take orders very well. He could have stayed in the army until retirement age and still would have been a private, but he went to war believing it was what one did if one's country, and possibly the freedom of the whole world, was threatened. That's what everyone said, and wrote, and repeated on the radio over and over and over. He believed it with all his soul. Later he was amazed at its truth. Hitler would make five mistakes that would save the entire world from torture, slavery and death.

TWENTY-FIVE

THEY WERE ON THE WATERS OF THE BRISTOL CHANNEL, JUNE 6, 1944, moving in support of the First and the Twenty-ninth divisions already landing and dying on Omaha Beach. Bluefeather's regiment, the Ninth, was an old, old, warring number first organized in 1798. But today the regiment and the world were all brand new to the mining man, who was now a rifleman in Company G, Second Battalion.

The troop ships steamed on out around Lands End and into the English Channel. Selected parts of the division had already landed in engineering and assault units to help their brother and sister divisions claw their way out of the water and onto the land, just as at the very beginning and birth of man aeons ago. The transports of the launching ships for troops soon heard, saw and became part of the biggest military buildup in the history of mankind.

Bluefeather felt smaller than the most minute grain of sand. By nightfall the First, the Twenty-ninth and elements of his division had secured a foothold and moved on past most, but not all, of the initial, heavily armed cliffs.

The night of June 6 and the day of June 7, Bluefeather was so seasick, he truly did not care when they landed or if they sank. Surprisingly, the German air force that was supposed to have been knocked from the sky that day, staged daring night raids. The roar and explosion of bombs, the antiaircraft guns, the flaming barrage balloons and the clattering of flak falling like steel rain on the decks of the ships stretched out in a convoy farther than any eye could see, made the night a circus of power and death; a display so large and unimaginable in scope, it finally became indescribable.

On the beach were parts of men, and in the water were parts of men. A small percentage were whole, however, having drowned as their landing craft disgorged them in water too deep for solid footing. The beach was a caldron of chaos beyond the limbs and bones and scraps of torn flesh mingled with discarded gas masks, useless punctured canteens, broken and bent concrete and steel beach obstacles, erratic piles of smashed and destroyed equipment, and disabled and destroyed vehicles already being reclaimed by the sand and sea. Destruction incarnate.

Many of the seventy-two known elements of the earth, which were of such beauty and sparkle in their natural veined and disseminated forms, were here fused, amalgamated and alloyed into terribly efficient instruments of death. The same elements whose seeking and finding was Bluefeather Fellini's life's work were now particles of booming savagery just before the stillness of death. His sought-after beauty was trying to kill him, but of this he was mercifully oblivious. Violence—violated violence. Piercing, screaming steel, twanging off hard objects and thudding, slicing, piercing softer things, and on impact, blood flying into the convulsed air and becoming a red mist before running in rivulets, sinking into the wet sand searching for the birthing sea. This was the ultimate exploitation of the human wholeness—its severance. The bodies floated facedown calmly now in the sea, moving only as the mother ocean did. On land, the living crawled through the motionless dead and paused over and over next to the nonmovement to gather a bit of sulfurous air into their heaving lungs, and another tad of courage. Then forward again. Again. Again.

Bluefeather saw a lot of this, and none of this, as they moved out of the water into all the above—up little canyons, in the cliffs with sniper fire and artillery harassing them almost every step. Every few yards this harassment also killed someone. But the stench of his own vomit and the excrement and urine in his olive-greens helped disguise that of exploded entrails and the vast nauseating blood-smell strong as a thousand slaughterhouses.

The war was a blur. Like a barroom brawl. There were no great organized plans and brilliant military tactics, no inflamed thoughts of glory and winning of great battles, no patriotic images of heroics and the flags of one's country waving in victory. There was simply a moving blur of frazzled images in a twenty-yard circle. The war, the world, everything, was all in this very small twenty-yard circle. That's all he knew. All he felt. All he realized of existence and nonexistence. All.

They fought their way off the beach through the swift signatory howl and crashing boom of the eighty-eights intermingled with the "BrrrrrpBrrp" of the automatic weapons. The maiming and dying continued.

They moved to the outskirts of the lovely French town Trevieres, with green fields and apple trees and solid old Norman stone houses. The Germans fought like bulldogs, house to house. They actually had to be dug from the cellars before they would surrender.

On to the villages of Saint Germain de Elle and Saint George de Elle. The Germans were desperately attached to the latter because of the good observation posts it afforded and its protection of a major highway. Attack after bleeding attack was launched by both sides. The village changed hands like a million steel Ping-Pong balls. No matter what side was on the attack, the stones of the old homes were blasted until they were mostly powdered, random heaps. Each house cost a gallon of blood and a hundred pounds of powder and steel to destroy—an ancient formula. It stretched out for hundreds of zigzagged miles. Civilians, made up mostly of elders and children, cattle, goats, chickens, pigs and piss-ants, were smashed and pierced to death.

Bluefeather followed, and moved, and fired the M1 whenever he got a glimpse of the gray enemy and sometimes when he didn't. He saw only little movements of the opponent but felt the earth shake like a cow's hide trying to dislodge a bloodsucking fly. He was so far beyond ordinary fear, he became numbly unaware of it.

Now they let the Germans have the ruins of Saint George de Elle and consolidated their lines digging in, preparing for a large-scale attack at the heart of the interior of Normandy—the day and moment unknown.

Men on both sides still suffered and died from intermittent artillery and sniper bullets, but on a much smaller scale. The reduction from intense second-by-second violence to hourly, caused Bluefeather to pause and consider the odds of his card-gambling days in Tonopah, Nevada. If a man listened for the cough of the enemies' mortars, the zapping song of the eighty-eights, hit the ground on time and kept his head below the tops of the hedgerows, he had a reasonable chance to live until the next big charge came off.

The soldiers had a chance now to wash, shave and eat

their first K-rations since the invasion. Bluefeather looked up at the sky and said, "I'm alive."

Now they could look at their living friends and see their gaunt, sunken features, say their names, speak and then a little later make jokes. They also had time to add up the number of missing and really miss them. The generals, the colonels and all the higher officers were meeting, studying maps, casualty reports, the supply situation, the projected remaining air power of the enemy and the growing support of their own uncountable tons of ammunition and supplies moving up.

The thick, stone hedgerows made almost perfect fences for the farmers' fields. Over the centuries the many plants that had seeded there covered the hedgerows with lovely, picturesque foliage. Their roots also wove around the stones with such a strength of possession that each and every hedgerow made a natural fortress. Hundreds of thousands of them stood so strong that tanks had to take long and dangerous time to break through. This was the great advantage the Germans had. Outgunned on the ground and in the air, they still had a new fortress every hundred yards or so for mile upon mile that seemed forever. For thousands it already had been.

A sergeant of infantry, who had been a mechanic in civilian life, solved this greatest strategic problem facing the Allies. He designed and welded a huge, pointed iron ripper on the front of a tank. It worked. Every available engineer and expert in this field was put to work. The idea that a workingman soldier would save uncounted lives and wounds of the flesh was of grand proportions. He should have been as honored as the greatest general, but it was only the dog-faced foot soldiers who truly appreciated the vastness of the contribution, and only a handful of them even knew who had created the smashing design.

Guns were cleaned, oiled. Muscles had a chance to limber and gain strength. Minds and emotions were pulled back together. The second most important thing besides breathing was the mail delivery. They read of home and the special ones there, over and over again, like listening to a favorite song.

Bluefeather said to Pop, "Well, Pop, you think we'll be home by Christmas?" (Every soldier in a long war asks this question, whether it's January or July.)

"No," Pop said, "not even if we live." He had come up as one of the replacements for the dead and wounded a few days before. He was really too old for a front line infantryman. He was thirty-five. Ancient. He looked sixty after a few days on the line.

Bluefeather felt old at twenty-six. Most of the warriors were eighteen to twenty. It has been said that kids fight and old men make the plans. Of course, there was no practical way to reverse it. But here was Pop. Bluefeather wondered how in hell Pop had survived basic training and transport across the seas and on right here to the front. All he had to do was say he had a pain in his chest or his knees were locking, and he would have been instantly discharged. Why was he here? How? Not only that, he wrote poetry in a little book wrapped in heavy waxed paper—poetry, by god almighty, in battle. He was soon known as Pop the Poet.

The child-soldiers were in awe of him and many were afraid. He seemed to them a man far too old to carry the heavy burden of a rifle, shovel, ammo, hand grenades and other gear, under fire, falling, crawling, running, digging into the hard earth they slept on through long days following longer nights. Men who could accept the embrace of violent death surrounding them—inescapable for thousands—were confused and fearful of this simple old man who wrote of tender flowers and steel flak, of happily singing souls and agonized doom—but not Bluefeather.

Bluefeather had known real poets at Taos, and he had felt the poetry of Twining and Harmony creeks and a love for his Miss Mary that transcended even the magnified destruction of Normandy. Instead of awe he felt respect for Pop. Instead of fear he felt a closeness, a kinship. He was certain that Pop had been guided here by Dancing Bear, as his own personal companion and mentor. How else could Pop the Poet be explained?

Pop was small, perhaps 130 pounds of bent weight, five feet, seven inches, and had sunken eyes and a long, thin nose over a mouth curved to kindness. He had much trouble keeping up on the forced marches of battle, and he was usually too tired during the rabid fury of combat to scoop out more than a shallow indentation in the earth. Part of his body was revealed, more vulnerable than others. He didn't seem to care, but now during the time of only small storms of steel, he had a deep foxhole between Bluefeather and Daniel Wind, an Osage from Tulsa, Oklahoma.

They were sitting, smoking and visiting on the edges of their foxholes as Pop quit putting words down and carefully wrapped the notebook with the waxed paper.

Wind watched him with much curiosity, finally asking, "Hey, Pop, you ever sell any of that stuff?"

"Never have," Pop answered. "Nobody wants it."

"How come you write it then?"

"Don't know." He sighed with a tiny smile. "I just don't know."

Wind said, "Well, maybe you're like me. I got ten, twelve dogs all the time. People always asking me what I

do with 'em. I say, 'Hunt.' They say, 'What?' I say, 'Rabbits.' They say, 'Ain't no rabbits in a mile of this farm.' I
say, 'See? Now you got it.' "

Bluefeather wasn't sure he got it either, but he and
Pop laughed as hard and loud as possible without giving
their position away to the foe. Bluefeather had an enormous craving to read some of Pop's lines, thoughts, feelings, but his old-fashioned raising—no personal questions
to your elders—prevailed. His family had carried this unwritten tradition through centuries in Sicily and northern
Italy and three generations in America. Politeness prevailed.

So he said, "For years most folks thought Melville's
Moby Dick was just the wasteful scribblings of a seasick
sailor. It didn't sell over two thousand copies for a decade."

Pop grinned. "So you know Melville, huh?" He
seemed pleased, but even so, he added, "Well, he has me
beat by exactly two thousand copies, and I've been putting this stuff down on paper since I was seven
years . . ."

The shout came down the line, "Air raid! Air raid!"
The three friends, along with many others, fell into their
foxholes.

Two German fighter planes dived at their line, ripping
the earth with machine guns. Then they were gone, roaring up and back to somewhere in France.

"Medic! Medic!" came the now-familiar cry of the
wounded and dying.

"Oh, mama, oh, mama, I'm hit. Oh God. Ohhh God."

Bluefeather and Pop were the first ones out of their
holes. It was Corporal Nye who was wounded. He had
been straddling a slit trench with his olives tucked under
his knees. Pop bent over and dragged him out of the

excrement. The blood from three holes in his stomach was already coursing out through the fingers futilely trying to hold his life's fluid inside a sieve of a body.

Bluefeather jerked his first-aid kit out and opened it. He started to apply a bandage. Pop raised his writing and shooting hand, saying, "Too late." It was.

They cleaned up the best they could by the time the medics arrived. They radioed back for a burial detail. In a little while they carried him away covered by his raincoat.

Bluefeather was numbed by the suddenness of Corporal Nye's destruction. The vileness, the waste, maddened him, but the planes were gone. He was helpless to avenge his buddy. He had known him for nearly two years now. They had trained, and strained, long and hard together. They had been drunk and chased women together and recently fought and suffered together. This made them deep friends. Close—close as humanly possible. Closer than the blood of any kin.

As much as Bluefeather was shaken, Pop seemed more so. He was pale beyond his norm. It was as if his blood had all drained out the pores of his skin along with the corporal's. He leaned against the hedgerow trying to light a cigarette. His hands were shaking terribly, and when he finally got it lit he could barely hold it in his mouth.

Then he said softly as if talking to a sleeping baby, his dark, hidden eyes glowing from within, "We'll never know. Only a few will ever know and then it'll be too late."

Bluefeather took his helmet off and pushed at his dark, sweating hair, staring hard at Pop, wanting to question him, but at the same time having no idea what he would ask. Later, perhaps, if they lived.

Wind said, "Got drunk with the corporal over there at Wales. Gonna miss him many days."

Daniel Wind had spoken for them all, but he was wrong about the days. So many more would immediately follow Corporal Nye's destruction that there would be too much remembering to handle. In combat there is no time for the luxury, and relief, of weeping.

TWENTY-SIX

FOR DAYS NOW IT HAD BEEN RUMORED THAT THEY WOULD MAKE the big push. Their artillery had been firing Time-on-Target for a week. This TOT was set so that every hour the regiment artillery would concentrate on a given spot. The Germans absorbed a great deal of these messages from hell and were supposed to weaken therefrom. Instead they fired back, but of course, in much smaller volume. The last two days, they had picked Bluefeather's Company G Second Battalion of the Ninth Infantry upon which to concentrate their heavy mortar fire. Each time the "carrummmp . . . carrummmp" coughed from the German mortars, they all dropped in their holes like frightened prairie dogs—and suffered waiting, waiting. Then the soft death whisper of the dropping shell and the "ha—whoomp" of the explosions cringed them into the bottoms of the holes as they attempted to bury themselves completely from the ripping, uneven chunks of hot steel. Even so, casualties were always present somewhere on the line.

Pfc Shadow Requenez, a Mexican American from El Paso, Texas, absorbed a direct hit from a mortar shell. He was dug in just past Daniel Wind. He came screaming up out of the earth. One leg was gone at the knee, and part of the bone stuck out, whitish and barren of the red. As he thrashed about in the mudding dirt, he kept jabbing the bone into the ground as if he wished to dig his own grave with the protruding sliver.

Bluefeather and Pop held him while Wind and Sergeant Pack—the lean, almost frail lover of war—tied several first-aid pads over the end of the shattered leg. Bluefeather twisted a tourniquet over the thigh. As soon as the medic arrived he gave Shadow a shot of morphine, but he went on screaming and thrashing about. Finally he quieted, and they lifted him onto a stretcher.

"Carrrummmp!" They came searching again. Everyone dived for their foxholes. It was automatic now. The Germans had the range down perfect. The shells made the earth twitch and bounce. Gravel and spent pieces of shrapnel showered in on them. Quiet. Waiting.

When the numbness of trying to make their bodies amalgamate with the earth eased, and they could gather courage to breathe a little again, Bluefeather listened a moment. Then he raised up, peeking over the edge of the dirt mound. Other heads appeared and saw that the medics were upright now. One was limping badly, a spot of red soaking through his olive-greens just above the knee. Shadow's stretcher was riddled with shrapnel. The motionless, soundless figure of the Latin-American lad dangled the remains of his other leg off the stretcher. The medics stopped, lowered the stretcher, replaced the leg and a dragging arm back on it. They walked away—one of them needing to be carried himself. Pfc Shadow Requenez would never need an artificial leg.

Everyone had returned to their separate earth wombs, except Shadow. He had been Daniel Wind's very best fun-loving, hell-raising, drinking buddy. Even though the mortars came again, Daniel foolishly sat on the edge of his foxhole sticking his trench knife, over and over, into the earth as the shells burst all around him. Not a single piece of shrapnel touched Daniel. When the shelling stopped and the perpetual motion of diving swiftly into holes and slowly easing back up, listening for the cries of, "Medics," "Mama," "God," then looking around with silent relief when none came, then, only then, did Daniel Wind speak, and only to himself. "Hey, Great Spirit, you keep good care of that Shadow man. We got lots of laughs we gotta share someday . . . somewhere . . . maybe."

That night on guard duty, Bluefeather had a sore tooth that finally abscessed. By the next day his jaw was swelled to double its normal size. Every shell that whammed the earth anywhere near him seemed to hit his jaw point-blank. The following day the entire side of his head was swelled like that of a snake-bit cow.

Pop told him, "You better go back and get that infection taken care of."

Bluefeather mumbled and settled back down in his foxhole.

Soon Sergeant Pack leaned his thin face over the hole and said, "Fellini?"

"Yeah."

"Get your ass back to the medics."

"I'm okay, Sergeant."

"Yeah. Well it's sort of embarrassing to insist on this, what with men gettin' their legs and heads blown off, but we're gonna need every man we've got in a few days."

"Okay, I'll be right back."

Bluefeather walked down a lane, each step jarring him so the diseased tooth felt big as an anvil. It was a lonely lane for sure. He walked past a dead black and white cow whose belly was swelled to the bursting point, with all four legs sticking out like posts. There were a few more signs of death, such as a helmet with a shrapnel gash in it that had reached somebody's brain, a riddled cartridge belt and a couple of empty first-aid kits. All these things only emphasized the absolute vacancy of life here. It was as if the lane was poison itself.

Then he knew why. "EEEEeeeeeooooowwww zip, boom!" The eighty-eight shells shrieked down the lane in bunches; an observant artillery spotter had mistaken Bluefeather for a troop movement. Well, it was a one-man movement. He ran sweating, his heart trying to thump his ribs apart, hitting the ground, running, falling, rolling, crouching. On and on for over half a mile. The shells had shaken and jarred the lane to pieces in places, and a pall of dust and smoke hung over it. Not a single fragment of steel had touched him. He had forgotten all about his tooth, but as his breath came back and no more shells pursued him, the throbbing pain returned.

He found the medics' tents in a field shielded by a lot of trees and camouflage netting. It took more courage to walk through the newly maimed and low-moaning casualities and ask to have a tooth pulled than an attempt to catch an eighty-eight shell in his bare hands would have. Only the horribly maimed, or the dying, moaned in this war. It was so strange to see these men hurting so terribly, be in pale pain and swallow their inclinations to scream. He wondered about it as he would many things to come.

The tooth must be pulled. It had to be done. His friend Sergeant Pack, the war lover, had ordered it so. Medics, if they survive, become the most heroic of men. They do, after some time, become weary of imposters with little "nothing" wounds.

It took Bluefeather a few moments to gather the presumption to say, "Please sir, I have a tooth, . . . well, I have a tooth that is giving me, . . . well, I say, sir, could I bother you just a moment? I can see you're busy. Pardon me, sir, but I need a tooth removed. I know it seems like nothing . . . but . . . but, you see . . ." Then he grabbed one medic by both ears, jerking his head so that he had to look at him and said, "Forgive me, but I have orders from a superior officer to have this friggin' tooth removed. There is still some fighting left to do."

A few moments later Bluefeather Fellini acquired some more useless knowledge. First, all available sedatives were for more serious war injuries than his; and second, the roots of an infantry private's teeth are very long indeed—they go all the way to the ankle bone. While two strong medics held him from the rear, another put his knee on Bluefeather's chest and removed the tooth. It was a tragic operation. He was positive that his head had been pulled off along with the tooth. By the time he could stand upright without weaving in circles, someone had stuck his head back on, but he was still a little bit blind and did not see where the medics had disposed of his tooth.

Bluefeather said, "What'd you do that for? I wanted to use that tooth for the head of a prospector's pick when I get back home."

The medics were in no mood for any misplaced jokes, and since that was the only one left in him, Bluefeather spit out a wad of blood, blinked his eyesight back into focus, put on his helmet and took a different route back to the front line.

The rumors of the big bust, later to be known as the Saint Lo Breakthrough, came about. The Twenty-ninth Division was on the right, poised to hit the heavily defended town of Saint Lo face on. He could hardly wait for the order to attack the almost impregnable position.

Hill 192 had to be taken from the Germans as it afforded observation for the advancing Twenty-ninth Division to the orchards surrounding Saint Lo in front, all the way back to the ship-clogged beaches.

They were ready. The tanks were gassed, greased, and the guns were loaded. The dirt-loving fighters hung hand grenades and double bandoliers of ammo on their clothing. The black snouts of the artillery waited, zeroed in. Stacks of shells were laid by, waiting for their controllers to lift them and send them singing through the sky to fulfill the two reasons of their manufacture: money for the maker, death for the receiver.

The little 60-mm mortars were right next to the rifleman ready to be fired. Farther back the heavy mortars waited. The machine guns were loaded with extra belts ready to be fed into the steel jaws that would spit them out in clustered groups that seemed to make the air itself become pieces of flying lead, inescapable in the numbers that spewed forth so fast it sometimes sounded like one continuous solid sound.

The Big It. This day, they were all poised to ride the wire-thin edge between life and death to its ultimate destination. Wherever the hell it might be.

The roar from above came lightly at first, then stronger and louder. The sky was sundered with hundreds of bombers. Their bombers. Horizon to horizon across the sky in such force they seemed to have come from a faraway place where no one on the ground had ever been or would ever know about.

Slowly. Oh, so slowly they moved forward, these mighty dragon birds of war. The smoke bombs had been set all along the front lines, all the way to the left and the right. However, several high gusts of unpredicted wind had blown the smoke back over the waiting soldiers in spots, making it impossible for the planes to drop their bombs with complete accuracy. Nature had always altered even the greatest of battle plans.

The men of this "day of true destiny," feeling smaller than microbes, looked up from the foxholes as the bombers droned, in a solid sound and perfect formation, above and toward them. The wisps of smoke slightly obscured their vision in places. The planes vomited their bombs—tons and tons and tons of them.

The skin of the earth crawled and shook in mighty agitation at this infringement. The earth did not just tremble, it was possessed of a vibration that must have reached to its molten core. It shook. Shook. Shook. The tops of the foxholes actually narrowed, spread and closed and then opened, while much of the abused earth floated in the air. But all the genius of science had failed to a degree. Many of the bombs fell on friendly forces. When they arose to attack, many were as numbed and shocked as the enemy. But rise they did. Those who still breathed.

The artillery, hundreds of pieces, hurled a massive mess of poisonous steel in the sky above them. It crept fifty yards ahead of the tanks. The engineers dropped shoulder charges that exploded both sides of the hedgerows so the tanks could burst through with their newly welded heavy metal spikes. The infantry followed, firing all their weapons. It was synchronized, from the planes in the sky to the creeping artillery, the heavy weapons and then, as always, the man on his belly, the man running, crouching, falling to fire or to die. The footmen had to wrap it up, always. The chatter of the machine guns and the crack of the rifles were lost in the density of sounds—endless, punishing, excruciating sounds. The mind-warping, wanton noise pierced all fibers of being. Every atom of the earth and air above was quivering with it.

As in all great battles, the front lines became staggered. Sometimes the men of the Ninth were out ahead of the main lines among the Germans. Then it became a very personal thing. The war narrowed to each man and the eternal twenty-yard circle.

Private Price of North Dakota died with a rifle bullet in his left eye as he tried to set up his light machine gun. A burp gun pinned the squad behind a hedgerow. Sergeant Mitchell of New Hampshire caught a burst from the burper across the neck. He died trying to give orders, but all that came out was a burbling sound as he choked to death on his private blood.

The Germans had dug tanks into the earth with portholes at the bottom of the hedgerows so that they could rake an entire field with cannon fire. Machine guns were dug in at corners so they would have sweeping cross fire. They were great improvisers, these outmanned, out-gunned soldiers, and they almost made the battle even, with their tenacity and skill. Almost.

Now Bluefeather and the men around him were becoming aware of another sound in the deadly din. The enemy artillery was coming in return, searching through the sky looking for living flesh on the ground.

Lieutenant Noble ran through his men shouting, "What in hell's the matter? One man's holding up a whole company! Come on, we're going to take this nest."

He jerked a pin from a grenade and rounded the corner of the hedgerow at an open gate, hurling it at the enemy dug into a round hole in the hedgerow corner. As the grenade left his hand he caught a full burst of Smeisser shells in the chest.

"Come on," yelled Sergeant Pack. "Come on with me."

Daniel Wind rounded the abutment just ahead of Bluefeather. The lieutenant's grenade had knocked two German parachute troops out of the hole. One was trying to reload. Wind shot him in the head with the Browning automatic rifle. The other raised a rifle and Bluefeather shot without aiming. The M1 bullet hit a rock in the hedgerow and ricocheted into the bridge of a German's nose. The middle of his face exploded.

Sergeant Pack was fighting hand to hand with one of the enemy. He stuck his trench knife in a German's side with such desperation he lost his grip on it. It hung, gradually shaking loose, as they bounced on the hedgerow, each man's hands at the other's throat.

Bluefeather started for them just as Pop the Poet struck the German in the back with the butt of his M1.

"Kill the bastard," Pack screamed.

Pop pointed the gun at him and just stood there. The stunned and wounded German somehow jerked the pin from a concussion grenade. Daniel Wind shot him in the chest and stomach as Pack picked up the grenade and hurled it over toward the other side of the hedgerow. It exploded in air. The blast knocked Pop down and staggered the others, but it was too far away to do critical damage.

A hell of a soldier, Sergeant Pack, from Clovis, New Mexico, where he had been a state golden-gloves champion and a runner-up as a six-foot welterweight in the nationals. It was an amazing accomplishment for one who now seemed so fragile. Bluefeather, observing Pack, began to realize the gods of war do not necessarily choose weight lifters or shot-putters as great infantrymen.

It was all clamorous chaos now. Everyone here in the bloody little circle was so confused and lost, they had no idea whether they were winning or losing this battle. Bluefeather's remaining squad members were separated from the rest of the company. Men from other detachments lay all around.

The spotter for the German artillery evidently saw that the soldiers from many scattered and varied elements of the division had overrun their positions. First the eighty-eights started firing for range. Now they had it, and the high, whining impacts fell among them.

"Medic! Medic!"

"I'm hit! Oh, God, I'm hit!"

"Help me, please, help me."

"Hurry. Hurry. Help. Please help."

"Mama, mama, I'm dying. Oh, God help me."

And those who were mildly hurt said nothing, trying to patch the wounds themselves.

Somehow the medics always came.

It was possibly redundant, but bad wounds, whether on altar boys or atheists, brought out screams for their mamas and their God.

Sergeant Pack yelled, "Come on, we're dead here," and his men, so thin in numbers now, followed.

They came to another hedgerow. Machine-gun fire tore the brush along its top, and the eighty-eights were firing almost flat trajectory over their heads. They moved crouching, hitting the ground as shells burst some forty yards out in the open field behind them. Then Captain Marson showed up with scattered portions of other squads, and the rest of what was left of Company G.

Bluefeather squatted and leaned back against the hedgerow exhausted, awaiting further orders. Three or four yards in front of him, two men slept still and peaceful. He couldn't imagine such casual courage in the midst of the devastation. A shell burst only a few yards out and to his right. A piece of shrapnel banged off his helmet. Others zapped into the hedgerow around him.

He crawled over and grabbed at both the men, one in each hand, attempting to shake them.

"Get over here next to the hedgerow," he shouted, trying to penetrate their ears through the crescendo.

There was no reaction. No movement. There was no blood. No broken skin. The men had died of concussions.

Strangely, after all he had seen of shattering savagery, this was the most repugnant. He was chilled ill. To die without even the honor of a wound was somehow unholy. But then, what wasn't in this maelstrom of purposeful insanity?

A tank clanked past. A squad of engineers fired a large charge of high explosives, ripping a wide path for the tank in the hedgerow. The iron Goliath lumbered around and rumbled into the new opening, with cannon and automatic weapons firing bursts across the open wheat field.

Sergeant Pack yelled, "Up now, all of you! Up and fire!"

Those who could slowly, even reluctantly, rose. Although the enemy was unseen across the field, he was certainly there.

Bluefeather fired on every shadow among the brush-topped hedgerow a couple of hundred yards away. A stranger fired next to him, methodically, as fast as he could empty and reload the M1.

Then as Bluefeather reached for another clip, the man wheeled toward him staring with his mouth open, his lips moving as if to speak. He fell. A bullet had penetrated his helmet. Bluefeather knelt by him and saw that the bullet had struck high in the forehead and come out the back of his skull. His last thought would never be verbalized. Incongruously, he realized that the greatest thoughts of humankind were never written or spoken.

It was very close to impossible for Bluefeather to rise once more, but he did. He peeked as low as he could over the hedgerow, like a squirrel watching a hunter from over a fallen log. Just at that moment a shell struck the tank and fire leaped out from it. A soldier raised the hatch to escape the oven, but the enemies' automatic weapons drilled at him. He fell, hanging half out, half in the tank. He had not felt the fire.

Suddenly, for just a moment, things were very still, like the unexpected brief quiet that comes occasionally between the crashing waves on a long seashore.

Then Captain Marson shouted again, "Move out!"

He had a radioman with him and was receiving orders to continue the attack. The cost had not been discussed. There was no option here. As he led the way through the open gate across the clearing, the same machine gun that had caught the driver of the tank perforated both him and his radio operator. They fell facedown. The captain moved his left leg only once. A private, a new replacement whom Bluefeather had never seen, ran to help the fallen men and died alongside them.

Sergeant Pack held up his hand, signaling a halt at the edge of the gate opening—perhaps fifteen feet across. It was a tiny opening in such a large field, but far bigger than any shell. It was pure, naked space. About every thirty seconds a machine gun fired a short burst into it.

"Get ready," Pack yelled. He raised a hand, looking at his men, waiting.

"Rrrrrrapp . . . rrrrrrrrrrapp."

"Now."

Feeling as nude as the space they ran across, they made it. That is, Pack, Wind, Pop and Bluefeather made it. The next two men were caught. Others succeeded, too. Finally, there were nine fallen men pouring blood in little dirty red rivers across the opening. One had his neck artery shot in half, and a stream of blood spurted in the air at each pump of his heart like a tiny West Texas oil gusher, only it was red liquid, instead of black. Strangely soft moans filled the air that was defiled with acrid smoke, the fumes of burning gasoline, oil and the essence of arteries. The mist and scent of blood was prevalent above all. It dominated even the smell of tons of exploded powder and singed metal.

Bluefeather watched in agony as Corporal Bulto, a heavyset, American machine gunner, tried to outrace the German machine gunner's finger. He almost made it, but slipped in the blood and fell facedown in it, his weapon hurled safely on ahead of his exposed flesh.

"Rrrrrrapp."

He took an entire burst in the side. Bluefeather reached out and grabbed him by both hands and dragged him across the slippery earth up next to the hedgerow. There was no use crying "medic" for Bulto. Following, with the wrong timing, was another radioman. He was shot in the ankle as the machine gun spit out its last bullet before reloading. Pack, alertly and bravely, slid out, jerked him to his hands and knees and dragged him falling, slipping, rising, falling again, in the blood-mud, across the terrible place. He had saved his life, at least temporarily, in the uneasy safety of the hedgerow.

The radio would not work. The German gunner was back at his deadly pastime now. The bullets were striking the dead bodies, moving them a fraction. They didn't care.

"Mortars," Pack yelled. "We've got to have mortars." He raced right back across the opening, almost sliding down, but the German gunner was a fraction too late to get him. A fraction. Now, all up and down the endless rectangles of hedgerows, men were lying, hurt, afraid, dying. And when it seemed they could not possibly bear anymore, the eighty-eights sniffed them out again. The unmaimed dug in.

Bluefeather ripped a hole in the earth with a small GI shovel faster than a dozen badgers. When the eighty-eights were once more quiet, he sat on the back edge of the foxhole looking across the field at a tree with an empty, two-wheeled cart under it. He thought that just a short time back a Norman farmer had rested his team of horses there and had taken his noonday meal. The alterations of war are as varied as fingerprints. Now and then a shell cracked into the tree. It was broken and torn and stark against the sky. The clouds were not real at all. They must surely have been drawn with a huge sky-pencil. No one looked up but Bluefeather. He felt silly and sad.

A soldier came stumbling along. He was blood all the way from the soles of his feet up. One eye socket was empty and left a little cavern in his head. It was obvious an antipersonnel mine had exploded right in front of him. He just stumbled on by, moaning like a long-lost child. An eyeball dangled from a string of flesh down onto his cheek like a rotten plum. One hand flopped loosely, the tendons revealed like white wires. The numbed soldiers tried to stop him, but he walked right across the opening, moaning. The machine gun spat at him and missed. A medic helped him across the last of the opening, kneeling beside him. The man was silent now. The medic took a raincoat and covered him.

Another soldier, without a shirt, casually walked along. He had a hole in his chest from which a thin trickle of blood oozed. Bluefeather stopped him before he hit the opening. The soldier hesitated only a moment.

He gasped, "Look, I'm bleedin' like hell inside. I can feel it. I got to get myself to a doctor. I ain't goin' to last long, friend." Amazingly he gathered the will to cross the opening and made it.

Bluefeather could see where the bullet had peeled the meat away from his back like it would the bark of a small tree.

Then a shell came whipping in from the side. Bluefeather flinched down into the small space he had initially scooped from the earth. He knew that part of his body was revealed. The shell hit in the field with a dead thud. Bluefeather bunched all his being against the impact. It didn't come. It was a dud. He looked to the side where the shell lay. He could feel the powder wanting to burst apart the steel and, subsequently, his body. He stared at it like a field mouse hypnotized by a rattlesnake. It was a long, long time, in battle time, before he could pull his gaze away from the unspeaking shell.

A jeep stopped across the way. It was a medical conveyance rigged to haul the stretchers of the badly wounded and those beyond that. The experienced driver waited for the machine-gun fire, then gave it all the gas he could across the opening. Everyone watched the successful maneuver and gave tiny applause somewhere in their minds. The jeep was on a farm trail perhaps twenty yards out from the hedgerow. As it neared a tree, it just raised up off the earth and blew to pieces along with all the well, the wounded and the dead bodies on it. A mine. Up there in the tree hung what had a moment ago been a man. Strings of shredded flesh dangled, along with pieces of his insides.

Bluefeather stared and stared. He glanced at Pop. He was vomiting. Bluefeather tried to heave but only dried air came up. He looked at the tree once more and then back at the dud eighty-eight. There was Dancing Bear squatted down sitting on the shell. Bluefeather started to scream a warning at him before the dawning of who it was stilled the cry.

"That's perty fair fightin' goin' on around here, dear brudder."

After what Bluefeather had seen and survived in this single day, he was qualified to make a year-long speech if he so desired, but because he felt too weary to work his vocal cords so heavily, he simply said, "Hey, I learned something, Bear. Ground war made me realize that one can breathe blood . . . and nothing is unbearable." He was silent for a while, then he finally overcame his weariness enough to try to be angry. "Where the hell have you been?" He motioned at the carnage around him. "Can't you see this is the worst day of my life? What good are you if you aren't around when the going is tough? Answer me, Bear."

Dancing Bear did a friendship dance around the shell and followed that with one of his famous toe dances right on top of the murderous object. Bluefeather's anger dissipated like an alcoholic's memory. Dancing Bear had presented his message clearly enough in his delicate association with the unexploded shell. Not even Dancing Bear would have blamed him for his flashing thought of suicide. It was just too damn much. However, better judgment did prevail. If he wanted that, all he had to do was raise his head above the hedgerow. The Germans would be delighted to accommodate him.

Instead, he croaked out like a sick chicken, "Answers, Bear. That's all I'd like." He glanced around him guiltily at the motionless forms now slicker-covered. Then he remembered that his voice could be heard by the dancing, maniacal Indian spirit guide.

Dancing Bear slowed down to a shuffle dance now. "You are right. Going is tough all over around here."

"You been around here today?"

"Oh, for sure, dear brudder. I been working my ass off for my clients on both sides."

"You been consorting and consulting with the enemy?" Bluefeather was mortified. "I shoulda known that's why they had us zeroed in all day. That's treason, Bear. You oughta be hanged."

"Whoa. Whoa, to you I say, for sure. They are your enemies for now. Not mine. I don't have any of those.

That's not the way it works when you crash through to this side of the river. Why, just last week I was down in the South Pacific comforting some of my Japanese clients."

"My god, the Japanese, too?" Bluefeather was aghast. "Oh, dear Great Number-One Spirit, banish this bastard straight back to this dimension right here and give me three seconds with . . . three seconds, that's not much to ask for."

Dancing Bear decided he didn't want to hear this kind of talk, so he didn't. "Also I been over in China and Russia doing work. And I been to Brazil and Lebanon and the Philippines and . . ."

"Stop. Stop it. That's enough. I got the idee, kiddo," he said from his mentor, Grinder, without even knowing it. "Don't run it plumb into the ground."

"Oh, no, dear brudder, ground too bloody."

"Look, Bear, I'm sorry. I've just had a touchy day."

"That's all right, young Blue. I get shouts from people having troubles all the time. Everywhere I go. Don't matter. Folks all over think they're the only ones with troubles. They don't think I got troubles over here. Now let me tell you what happened to me in Detroit last April. This woman, she . . ."

"Bear, Bear, Bear, you're forgetting what your position is. What your appointed duty is. You are supposed to listen to my troubles. Give advice, not ask for it."

"Oh. Oh. You're so right there, brudder dear. I haven't slipped up like that since the San Francisco earthquake. Whew. I hope my supervisor was too busy and didn't hear that. I might get sent to Antarctic—barefoot—on that one. I sure hope this tiny, teeny, little-bitty, minute mistake don't get back to the Authority. He would have no mercy, at all. He might even send me to Bakersfield again."

"My god and little dandy daisies, where did you get that idea about Bakersfield? That's good farming country, and now they're gonna drill for oil there. We need oil for these tanks and guns and unruly hair and stuff."

Then Bluefeather realized that he was getting silly and out of line with his spirit guide. They both were over-reacting from a hard day on the job. He decided to be nice and polite and make amends for them both. "Please, dear Bear, I wish you would get me outa here before the Germans do. I've been at this steady, by the minute, for a lot of days now. I'm wearing out. It's getting close to unbearable. What's the answer, old amigo? It's your turn now."

"I say to you the truth, ain't no way for right now to change jobs. You know what the feller said about horses in midstreams, and another one talked something about leaving sinking ships, and then there was the lady in Paris who wrote down about being loyal to your friends. What was her name? You remember her, don't you, dear brud-der? That wolf- and deer-hunting president one time who talked about those good men who get down in the arena. What was his name? What all was it he said? Boy, some-thing is happening to my memory."

"I knew it. I just knew it. All I'm gonna get outa you is questions. Millions of goddamned shit-eatin' questions. I tell you what I'm gonna do, dodging Bear, if you don't help me on past right now. I'm gonna make prayers to the Number-One Spirit, until that entity lets me skip across the river and leap up two or three dimensions until I'm in yours. Then I'm gonna jerk both your ears off because you don't use them anyway. Then I'm gonna jerk your shoulder sockets loose and break your arms in so many pieces I can tie them behind your back in a bow-knot. Then . . . then, hurting Bear, I'm gonna fill all the way up with mad. I think you can tell I'm almost full of mad right now. Huh? Huh?" Bluefeather giggled his position away. He rubbed at the scar on his nose for the first time in an hour and started growling in mock anger. He had so many thoughts he could hardly keep them in his mouth. "Hey, Bear, you know I'm just joking. This day's work was as much fun as a free trip to Hawaii . . . and I'm gettin' paid almost forty dollars a month for it. Think, and be jealous of all these benefits."

"Say there. I heard that one real good in both ears. Give me a few seconds and I'll think of something sweet and soothing for my dear brudder Blue."

One of the most stupid things Bluefeather had ever witnessed was before him now, especially since Dancing Bear had just promised him sweets.

Bear was doing a war dance around the shell. Bluefeather started to scream about the idiocy of this act, considering how many guns had been fired all over the world within the last horrible hour, but no sound issued because he was witnessing some odd and unusual movement, even for Dancing Bear. He had quit dancing, picked up the shell and it turned into three.

Bluefeather suddenly wanted to clap and yell, "Bravo."

Dancing Bear juggled the shells over his back, catching them on one moccasined heel and then the other, and pitched them right back over his head into his masterly hands. He juggled them through and around his legs. He slowly rose in the air, pirouetting and rolling sideways a spell. Even upside down, still moving his head this way, a leg that way, he was still in complete artistic control of the shells. Such dexterity was truly the show of all shows, except, of course, the one taking place down below in the hedgerows.

Then he was so high above the shattered tree, so randomly decorated by the power of gunpowder, that he appeared small indeed. Dancing Bear grasped all three shells in both hands and flung them straight up. They changed into three masses of golden mist that floated slowly toward the earth. The sun, lowering in the west, beamed through the three clouds of mist, turning them such a golden brilliance that the beauty almost blinded Bluefeather momentarily. The three clouds then settled around the tree of life, the tree of death, and dropped into the Norman earth. Six hundred fourteen sunflowers instantly grew nine feet and four inches tall and bloomed, turning their faces toward Bluefeather, shining through the decimating smoke of battle in a red haze. The flowers swayed to some unheard music in lovely peaceful rhythms. For a moment, the floral aroma wafted and washed away the awful, forever-imprinted smell of death.

Bluefeather waved one friendly hand as he looked back in the sky where his Indian spirit guide had been. He was gone. Everywhere Bluefeather looked it was peaceful as a baby's smile, until six British fighter spitfires zoomed across the space. They, too, were gone in just a glance.

Sergeant Pack came back with a 60-mm mortar crew. They set up the guns across from the opening, and the instruments coughed out three rounds for range. The gunners dropped the shells into barrels. Out they belched, arcing high into the sky then down, down, faster, and "carrummmp," right on target. Pack was exultant. He danced around gleefully, reminding Bluefeather of his other-world-across-the-river friend.

It was unbelievable, but Bluefeather took the trouble to ask himself a couple of hard questions. Are we all war lovers like Pack? Or was Pack simply more honest?

The firing ceased, except for long-range 150 artillery from the Allied side. The day's battle was done. There

was no strength left on either side for night-fighting foolishness.

The surviving Germans would magically recover most
of their dead, retreat under cover of darkness and take up
new fortifications by dawn—waiting, waiting for the
metal and men to come again.

TWENTY-SEVEN

ONLY INTERMITTENT ARTILLERY FIRE COULD BE HEARD NOW. The bestial symphony of war had taken intermission.

After cold rations, Bluefeather and Pop were getting in a last cigarette before dark. They talked in lowered voices, seeking anything living to communicate with. There had been so much of death that day.

Pop was writing in his eternal notebook. Bluefeather loved books, even poetry on occasion, but he had a hard time believing that Pop was writing a poem now—not now. And then he handed Bluefeather the book. He strained to read the words in the rapidly failing light, but they blurred together.

"I can't make it out. What did you write, Pop?"

"I don't remember now," he answered, his anemic, bony face standing out around his sunken but powerful eyes. There was a tiredness about him that had nothing to do with the terrible struggle of the past day. It was as if he had finally given up. Not on himself, but on everything else. He looked more than twice his age and a frail weakness possessed his being. He looked so old his nose was wrinkled.

Bluefeather realized, too late, he had taken the wrong

tack in trying to cheer up his blood brother. "You know, Pop, as horrible a defamation as war is to the human species, it's still the greatest adventure we've discovered to date."

Pop looked at him from inside his head. He didn't speak. The cigarette hung unlit from his mouth.

"Pop, why don't you quit?"

"Quit? Quit what? Quit smoking?"

"Quit the war. Just tell Pack you can't go on. Hellfire, pardner, at your age, nobody expects you to go on with all of this."

"It's like the poems," Pop said softly, "I don't know why I write them, and I don't know why I stay here."

"Look," Bluefeather argued, "the odds are out on you. There are only seven or eight of the original men left in the platoon now. It's going to get us all. All. But you can just walk off from here in five minutes. Listen, I'll go talk to Pack myself while you get your gear ready. Okay?"

Pop acted as though he had not heard the last of the plea. "I know the odds are getting short. Don't you think I know that, Blue?"

"Well, then?"

He didn't answer, but said, "You know, I was just thinking about my kids a while ago. Thinking about 'em while I was writing. I was telling myself that maybe they would never have to go through what their daddy did, and that's what I wanted the most. But now I wonder."

"Wonder what?"

"I wonder if it's right they don't know. Somehow they have to know. If I really believed they could understand just a little about it, maybe that would be enough. It's not true, though. You have to be here a long time to understand the tiniest bit."

"Pop, nobody understands. I mean, nobody I've ever known anyway. We just flat-ass haven't learned to love enough, I suppose. But shit, that's nothing new. Well, I take back a little bit. I did love . . . uh . . . never mind. Hey, you know something that just came to my mind?" Pop slowly turned his gaunt face, leaning forward to listen as Bluefeather continued, "Well, we've been up here fighting and killing for nearly two months now, and I haven't heard one man—not a single goddamn one—ask why we keep doing this over and over and over again. What in the hell are we doing here and all over the crazy world destroying one another with all the strength of our beings? It can't just be over land and religion and boundaries and doctrines, can it? We aren't that stupid, are we?"

"I'm afraid we are, Blue."

"What is it then?" Bluefeather asked, realizing he had asked a question of Pop no man or woman had ever satisfactorily answered. He was suddenly ashamed and embarrassed to have spoken of such things. He certainly didn't feel like talking about them, but somehow it had brought Pop back—this terrible pondering.

Pop wrote almost furtively now, glancing up as if he didn't want anyone to catch him at such an embarrassing activity. Not here in a dirt hole—not this instant.

Bluefeather was silent, trying to act like nothingness. Then Pop handed him the page. "It isn't a poem. It isn't what I know. It'll just have to do until I can bring myself to say it."

Bluefeather could tell that Pop intended for him to read this no matter what. He pulled a blanket over them and it took two matches to read the few words.

Bluefeather read. "Hate is equally amorphous with love, every bit as ghostly, as unexplainable, just as mysteriously enticing and alluring. Jealousy can force feed love and activate hate. Both love and hate can be powdertriggered into single or mass murder by the stupidly shameful inferiority of new or ancient defeats, both actual and imagined." Bluefeather sat looking into a cloud of his own creation then handed the paper back to Pop.

"That, Pop, is a whole bunch of something. A hell of a start, but I still don't get it clear."

"I know. I told you. I told you I'd tell you . . . when . . ." Then Pop said resignedly, "I know. I can't put it into words right now. It's more than words. I been trying with these poems and this page." He wadded it up and threw it out over the edge of the foxhole. "I'm just not good enough at it."

"Please, Pop, you should never have owned up to it. Please, I gotta know what you know."

"I tell you, Blue, I can't right now. It's nearly time for me to go on guard."

Pop and the newly arrived replacements, Privates White and Burton, had the first guard. Before they left, Burton came by.

He said to Pop, "I hear you're a poet."

Pop looked up at him, through him and beyond, "No. No, I'm writing imaginary notes for an imaginary audience."

Burton said, "Oh."

Bluefeather was to relieve Burton in four hours. He fell asleep almost instantly in the bottom of the hole.

It seemed like four minutes instead of four hours when Burton shook him gently. He woke up reaching for his rifle.

"It's me, Blue. Burton," he said in his soft, North Carolina voice.

"Anything out?" Bluefeather asked, referring to German patrols.

"Nothing. We've got 'em whupped. They're headed the other way."

Bluefeather got up and walked numbly to his post, on

past the motionless, stiff figures, lying under slickers or blankets with only their feet sticking out to make known they once had been living humans.

It was a long night in Normandy, but a bird sang just at dawn in the shattered tree above the place of the giant sunflowers.

TWENTY-EIGHT

THEY ATTACKED EARLY THE NEXT MORNING. BURTON WAS
wrong about one thing—the Germans had not pulled
back very far. Before nine o'clock they were under heavy
artillery bombardment. They worked their way along,
cringing against the repeated shock of the shells. Most of
them hit short or went over their heads some distance,
but they were there all the time.

It was difficult to segment the enemy's shells from the
Americans' with the guns firing so close behind. They fell
into the ground and rose to run forward and then back to
the earth until it was all of existence: father, mother,
home, life.

Miraculously, Bluefeather's squad escaped any casualties until midmorning. They had not created any either. It
was a duel of the heavy guns for now.

Then it started. The shells came howling in there and
smelled them out. Bluefeather felt the earth toss under
him and his helmet was blown tight against his skull. He
grabbed the helmet as it was nearly torn away and pushed
himself into a slight indentation in the earth.

It seemed endless. Then the cry came—a frail, little
cry. It didn't have words to it, only a message. He tried to

ignore it, but it came again, weaker. It took all Bluefeather's will to raise his head.

Then suddenly he was up and running through the artillery bursts toward the cry. He was too late. Sergeant Pack was already in the shell hole along with Pop. They were working on Private White. His buddy Burton was already gone. A great chunk was torn from White's side, and the shattered ends of his ribs showed where Pack had tried to stop the bleeding.

"I don't wanna die," he gasped. "I don't want to die now. Oh please, please don't let me die now. There's something I have to . . ."

They were done. White and Burton were numbers now. The placid stillness of them made the movement and sound of the living artillery shells sound louder, viciously intruding on the sacred moment of passing.

As always Pack said, "Come on. Let's move out."

And move forward they did—all who were physically able. There were two moving lines on the Americans' side that day. One attacking and another heading back with their perforated skins leaking blood.

The Germans fought tenaciously for every fortressed hedgerow. They crisscrossed their machine-gun fire with the guns dug in under the hedgerows. Even under constant moving barrages of Allied guns, they zeroed their mortars and artillery at every troop crossing. When the Ninth Regiment artillery raised to let the infantry move up, the Germans rose from their foxholes and fought with rifles, grenades and bayonets. Whether a compliment was in order, Bluefeather would never know, but he felt there was no honest way he could visualize a better all-around fighter than the German soldier. The Germans were natural warriors, sensing every weakness, every strength, and moving on them with deadly resolution. The numbers of shells they had to absorb were so great they would finally be forced to retreat so they could fight again. They even fought with tragic effect while in retreat.

Bluefeather and his few old and mostly new comrades paid a very high price for every yard of earth they gained that day in Normandy. Pieces of men, machinery, insects, dogs, cows, horses, birds, wings, bumpers, feathers, chunks of skulls and the insides of all these things were scattered forcibly but randomly about.

That night was very quiet for a while, as it often is in war. The replacements—the new, green men—came up from the rear to take the place of those who had died or had been maimed. They tried to appear brave, but fear came like an ugly perfume with them. Suddenly everything they had been trained for seemed different than they had expected. They were needed intruders in a disoriented landscape.

The unforgettable smell got to them the most because they only made hasty, denying glances at the slicker-covered bodies and the stained, broken pieces of people and their discarded equipment. If they could last seven or eight days, the incoming and outgoing fire sounds would become more familiar than their own breath. They might survive a long spell after that. Few made it through the learning stage. The turnover was great.

"You'll be sorry," was the singsong refrain from the ten-day-or-more veterans.

Most of the new men were sorry to begin with and missed the humor of the statement entirely. Pack always had a line for them—only one—that was different and unexpected by the longtime survivors each time.

From his pallid face—which would make most dead appear vibrant but alive, because of the minute, inscrutable but permanent smile—Pack announced, "You know, men, life would have been miserable for me without hand grenades." Then he surprised everyone by allowing himself an actual outburst of laughter as he scuttled along a hedgerow under fire. He hurled a grenade that silenced a machine gun and calmly strolled back to take two more of the explosive devices from a body under a slicker. It would never be known if this random act of courage gave confidence or shivers to the new arrivals—probably both.

Pop said, "You know, Blue, it's a funny thing. I talked to White and Burton a little bit last night when we were going off guard. They both were absolutely certain they were gonna live through this thing. I swear it. They believed they had some kind of protection. They could feel it."

"They were wrong, huh?" Bluefeather said, feeling rather stupid at such an obvious fact. "Look, Pop, the Germans might break. A man might hold out till then . . . if . . . if it's not too long."

"Yeah, he might."

Then Pop talked about his wife and children, fishing trips to Oregon, his little newsstand business. He asked Bluefeather for the first time if he had a wife.

"I did. She died."

Miss Mary had come visiting in his random foxhole dreams, but mostly he tried not to think of her—not even the wondrous times they had shared. Looking back sometimes made a man look forward, and all he could handle was the day, was now, for now. Pop didn't pursue the conversation any further. Bluefeather was relieved and said, "You know, we should be talking more about fishing and girls and whiskey and dancing and yelling, huh, Pop?"

Pop gave him a little grin that knew too much and started writing in his notebook. Bluefeather dozed off, partly asleep—in the state of half-visions, and he saw the aspens on the Sangre de Cristos back in New Mexico. He saw the trembling of their new, green leaves. They shook from the joy of existence unlike the fearful, quivering leaves of Normandy.

A wispy parade of people with misty smiling faces, some waving their hands and speaking in unheard voices, passed through his vision: his parents; his Raton, New Mexico, friends and kin; old Grinder; Lorrie; Stump Jumper; and there in the parade was a mariachi band. He saw Nancy and his darling, Miss Mary, and his mules. In spite of Grinder's advice—he had a clan. Here in the bloody air.

Now all his friends were marching across the Nevada desert then on to the red-rock areas of Arizona and New Mexico, all smiling and waving at him.

Then there was the spirit of Dancing Bear, and he heard him alone and would never forget what he said. "Ah ha, young man, there awaits you a greater adventure than war. Yes, dear brudder, even greater than that." Bluefeather was protesting and asking when and where at the same time. Dancing Bear continued, "In land beneath the trees where the water burns." Then Bluefeather's half-sleep and his half-vision vanished.

Pop was gently shaking his shoulder saying, "I've never given you anything, Blue, except worry, and this probably won't change that at all, but . . ." and he tore some pages from his precious notebook. "They're not much. I know that, but I had to put it down somehow. It's for you and . . . and all the rest."

GUARD
It was White
It was Burton
It was me
Standing guard by the light of the half-moon.

Eyes dead tired
Bodies numb, aching
Listening hard ahead
88s fiery above
Boom Boom Boom
105s way behind
White he whispered
Burton did too.
That's for sure
They would live.
Long, long night
Staring, blinking, staring
Rifles held taut
On through darkness
To surprising day
Ahead, ahead attack
Into the steel
Burp guns chatter
Cannons belch red
Mines rip earth
Bellies to the ground
Dead flesh smell
One cow here
One horse there
Closing in, closer now
Burton yelled stay
White yelled go
We'd like to live
But we don't know how
The bursting shells
Blow life away
But it's not mine
I'm almost sure
Sweat wet here

Blood wet there
Against the ground
Praying for night
Knowing your buddies
Are too dead to cure

White is gone
And Burton too
It's just me
Standing guard by the light of the half-moon.

It was signed, "For Bluefeather Fellini, my friend in France, forever. Pop Marsten."

My God, he had even forgotten his friend's last name. Bluefeather wanted to cry. He tried, but the best he could manage was a tiny sniffle in his left nostril. A great loneliness came over Bluefeather. He could not imagine, ever, how Pop had gathered the strength to write about fate throwing a detour in the path White and Burton had been so sure of following. It had wiped Pop out, all right, for he was sitting up asleep in his foxhole.

Bluefeather wanted to say something, but couldn't bring himself to disturb the exhausted old figure. Pop looked older than any attempt at measuring time. He was as still and lifeless as a dead car battery.

Bluefeather crawled over to Daniel and said softly, "Hey, Wind, do you know what an old, worn-out cowboy from Taos once told me when I asked him what thirty years of that kind of work was like?"

Wind said, "No."

"He said it was just shit, hair, blood and corruption."

Wind thought a moment and said seriously, "He left out canvas and leather."

Bluefeather took a little time now, then speaking to

himself he put their words together, "Shit, hair, blood, leather, canvas and corruption." He whispered it several times before he reached in the foxhole and patted Wind on his perpetually tilted helmet. "Hey, Wind, you're a bloody genius. That ain't only a fine description of cowboying, but that's a damn near perfect description of this little old war we're in here right now."

About then, a light machine gun started firing bursts a short distance down the hedgerow. They all grabbed weapons and leaped up, except Pop, who slept on. The rest stared out across the uncut wheat field, expecting a night attack.

The gun fired an entire belt and then a noise came; a crying noise, but not human. It was a minute or more before Bluefeather realized it was the dying bleat of a flock of goats. The Germans had herded them out into the field, and the new man on the machine gun had become trigger happy.

Some of them bleated all night. It upset the men far more than would be expected. The goat incident cost them some casualties the next day because of loss of sleep. Bluefeather heard several soldiers mention the fact that they couldn't get the sound of the dying creatures from their minds. This was odd, since the cries of dying men were all around.

About noon they were held up by heavy automatic fire. Their artillery seemed unable to dislodge the Germans from a strong gun emplacement.

Sergeant Pack's tall, emaciated figure ran by, hunkered down just below the top of the hedgerow at least part of the time.

"Dig in," he ordered. "We're launching a tank attack in about five minutes." Bluefeather was astounded to see the rapture glowing from Pack's sallow, war-loving face.

They welcomed this chance to burrow into the mother earth.

Pop had only enough strength to scoop out a shallow hole, that might, or might not, cover his entire body.

As Bluefeather dug he thought, "The damned old fool, he's going to get it today. There's not a chance. He's done. Why'n hell doesn't he go back?" It was driving him crazy, all this unnecessary worrying about the old man. Everyone wanted him to take his goddamned notebook and go home to his wife and kids. Everyone, of course, except Sergeant Pack. If a man could raise one arm and open one eye, he figured he should be able to shoot a gun. Damn the crazy old man. He could be out of artillery range in fifteen minutes. Safe. Everyone would silently applaud.

Pop was throwing Bluefeather's survival rhythm off, and he was talking serious crap to him when he should have been concentrating on nothing but escapist fare. All who had survived more than ten days in heavy combat knew that heroics and cowardice were from the same mold. Survival is the only bravery after the odds have thinned far enough against you.

Angry from his love for the old man, Bluefeather dug furiously up against the brush and rocks of the hedgerow. He dug deep. Some insects were bothering him, but because of the clanking roar of the tanks coming across the field, he ignored them.

The enemy had held up their artillery for a couple of hours. The six U.S. tanks ground out onto the field firing ahead at German emplacements. Then from higher ground the eighty-eights came. There was no firing for location now. It was a perfectly executed trap. The shells whammed all around and into the tanks, in one grand explosion. At least ten or twelve cannons must have been concentrated on the field.

Bluefeather hit the hole with shrapnel zipping across the edge into the hedgerow—very close, for the thousandth time. Then the insects covered him. He had dug into a wild beehive. In a moving mass, they covered his hands, his face, even his closed eyes, ears, mouth, and buzzed under his helmet. Bluefeather almost panicked and raised up out of the foxhole, but there was no choice. Nothing could bare itself to the hail of steel up there and live.

He made prayers in Pueblo Indian, Sicilian and English. He lay perfectly still and made more prayers and promises of bribery. He told all the great spirits, no matter what their religious preference, "If you'll let me survive these bees, I'll go and accomplish that great adventure under the trees by the burning river. I swear it on the souls of all my grandparents as far back as the Sicilians and the Tiwas go. Even further, if needed, Dear One."

Not a single bee stung him. Not one. And after a while they all left at once. It was a very difficult thing for the young soldier to believe. He had seen much in life already, that was for sure, but this deliverance made him humble, profoundly so. He surely would attempt to fulfill Dancing Bear's prophecy and his own wild promises. But he didn't have much time to repeat his vows; the shells came on all that day. My God, how the Germans fought for land that wasn't even theirs. Vire, France, only a few miles away where the Twenty-ninth fought, had been conquered by the Germans, and now the GIs of the Second Division had to go on dying until they took it away from them for good. The town wasn't theirs, either. For a moment Bluefeather lost sight of the rules. Who in hell was refereeing here, anyway?

Finally, in between bursts of the eighty-eights' coordinated fire, he could stand it no longer in the bottom of the visionless hole. He raised up and took a quick look. All six tanks were knocked out, their hulks torn and rent and burning. The smell of cooking flesh was almost unbearable. Bluefeather felt guilty thinking that the smell was probably as mouth watering to the gods of war as to the early-rising inhabitants of a hunting camp.

Bluefeather wished he were someplace else. Say, right on top of Taos Mountain with a gallon of wine and Ramon of Dawson playing his old Spanish love songs for him. He would feel so good to be there that he would do one of Bear's toe dances all the way to the Rio Grande, where he would go fishing. These were nice, little, foolish daydreams, but one wish of all his buddies was granted an hour before sundown. The P-38s came.

They dived on the heavily fortified hill and dropped bombs and fired rockets. Ah, what a sight of splendor. For the first time since the beaches, they all stood up in their foxholes and cheered at the beautiful life-taking, lifesaving sight. Bluefeather wondered if the German infantrymen had done the same when their artillery had demolished the American tanks a few hours earlier.

Bluefeather told Pop about the bees. Pop grinned weakly and said, "I promise you I'll laugh out loud, later."

The next morning they moved on to the crushed, but still heavily fired upon, city of Vire, seeking to cut off and entrap the entire German army there. Sergeant Pack, Daniel Wind and Bluefeather were the only ones left of the original squad. They walked on, and fought and dug, and were thirsty and scared, and sick and cowardly, and brave and lonely.

The battered Twenty-ninth Division held Vire. The Second relieved them late one afternoon and moved toward a high spot in the powdered town. The Germans shelled the living hell out of them as they took over the bunkers. They were good ones. In spite of the shelling, the protection they offered gave the gift of light casualties through most of the following day.

Pack sent Pop and Bluefeather to get two cans of water from the supply depot to the rear, and if they felt they could carry them, some dry rations.

They moved down the main road—clear, but pulverized now. It had once been blood and stones, but the red stains were not visible; the shell-shocked earth had settled over it as dust. The street was a deserted Sahara, made of even finer grains.

They got the water and half a pack each of C rations and struggled nakedly back up the street. Now, several more GIs from different platoons were on water and food details. As the war gods would have it, they all met next to a bombed-out building with a cellar still partially revealed.

Pop put his water can on the edge of the cellar, moved down some concrete steps and sat down, saying, "I finally have to admit it, I gotta rest a minute. Blue, come on down in the shade and let's have a smoke and talk about fishing in Oregon."

Bluefeather had heard, since the first hour he entered the army, that you never hear the shell that gets you. Well, they must have been talking about small-arms fire, because he heard the "boom" and then the heavy, rustling "swoosh" of the shell from a railroad gun, displacing air like a runaway train. He, of course, didn't hear it hit about ten or twenty yards away.

Bluefeather woke up blind. He flailed his arms out to his sides in the rubble in the bottom of the cellar, desperately seeking to feel what world he was in. Then with great trepidation he put both hands gingerly to his eyes. Maybe he was dead. Maybe that would be better. If he was dead, why wasn't Dancing Bear there to quiet him with the glowing white light. No . . . no, there was wet flesh around his eyes—probably his brains—but how could he have these thoughts if his brains were blown out of his skull?

"You okay, Blue? Speak to me, Blue."

Well, at least he wasn't deaf, because he heard Pop's voice as he pulled the entrails that once belonged in some other GI's body from around Bluefeather's face and eyes.

Bluefeather sat up. Then he stood and then stumbled to his knees. His head hurt beyond anything he had ever imagined, and the world whirled so fast the dizziness made him throw up. The world slowed. He could finally stand. He was bleeding from the nose, the mouth and one ear. Only one tiny piece of shrapnel had hit his forehead. He rubbed it, pulled it out and stuck it in his pocket for a souvenir, like a child keeps a pretty rock.

Pop washed his face with a little of the precious water from his canteen, saying, "You'd better head back to an aid station."

Bluefeather knew that he probably should, but he had spent so much time trying to get the old man to go home that now a stupid, stubborn streak possessed him.

The other GIs would need no medics. Bluefeather had been blown about twenty feet out into the basement, and he couldn't see a whole part of any of the others—anywhere.

It had been two days of miracles. Pop had been below the main force of concussion and steel. His water and food were intact. Bluefeather sent him on saying he was going to get a checkup at an aid station and would catch up later. What he did was go down and trade in his shredded can—that looked like a cheese grater—for a new one full of water.

He delivered the water and rations to Pack and a new corporal. Pack said, "What took you so long? You been takin' in the sights?"

Pop pointed at Bluefeather and said, "Sergeant, you oughta send him back. He got a concussion that blew him almost across the basement of a big building. Look, he's bleeding from the nose and ear again."

"Hey, Pack, don't listen to that worn-out old bastard. I'm all right or I wouldn't be back already."

Pack's entire life was spent running yellow lights. It was the way he had been made by two relatives copulating his final genes together in some dark jungle ancient times ago. So that's all Pack had to hear. Anyway, men with Bluefeather's experience were scarce around Vire, France, that day.

The next morning, August 9, the Ninth Regiment and the rest of the Second Division attacked out of Vire, toward Linchebary. They did not know it then, but the main line of German defense had been broken. They only knew the twenty-yard circle, but the immediate result of their foray across Normandy was the crumbling of German resistance in the sector, and ultimately led to the crushing out of the Normandy Peninsula and the end of their first great war campaign in France. They did not know what they had done at the moment, and the few of them left did not much care.

They attacked. It was the usual battle of attack, the enemy retreating, fighting back, on and on. By August 13 they had taken Linchebary. Immediately thereafter the division was notified to pull out of the line and prepare to head for Brest, France, and the Brittany Peninsula. There a hardened group of German paratroopers had received orders from Hitler to fight to the death. Some of his select SS soldiers were also dug in to help enforce and inspire his wish. It was a crucial submarine base, and a little piece of the Führer's pride still left intact, on the French coast.

On the day Linchebary fell, the Third Army moved north from Le Mans around the southern flank of the German positions in the direction of Argentan. At the same time the British, the Canadians and a Polish brigade swept in from the opposite direction from Caen toward Falaise. These pincers created a pocket out of which over one hundred thousand German troops were captured— on top of the multitudes of dead and wounded—and millions of tons of enemy armor and trucks were smashed along scores of miles of fields and roads. To the generals, the politicians and the composers of news headlines, this was a great victory. To those walking men with rifles, it was the same little bloody, twenty-yard circle. That's all.

TWENTY-NINE

THEY WERE MOVED BY TRUCK ACROSS NORMANDY TOWARD Brest. Riding was new to them. They had run, walked, fallen and crawled every step from Omaha Beach to Linchebary.

As they crossed Normandy, the signs of war were everywhere. The shell-blasted fields, the artillery- and bomb-shattered towns, the absence of people on the roads, all gave evidence of the struggle just past. The loss to the inhabitants as well as the invaders was stifling. However, as they moved into Brittany the feeling changed. Except for a few bombed railroad stations, the countryside was green and peaceful under the late summer sky, so peacefully blue. The people had been liberated from the Germans by the rapid dash of General Patton's army. They came out en masse along the roadways, waving almost hysterically in their relief.

The Brittany faces showed only a portion of the strain the Normans' had. The people still laughed. It was good for the soldiers to see. The fresh beauty of the young women was almost too much to bear, but the trucks rolled on. And then they began to notice, there were no young men; only old men and children were scattered among the French flesh. Yes, war was here just the same.

On to Brest they rolled in a great snaking line of wheeled vehicles, moving in a constant grinding roar— moving men to fight and die sooner.

Pop was weak and listless. Bluefeather could not get him to talk, and he was worried about his health. But there was nothing to do but wait and hope. This thought seemed somehow foolish to Bluefeather, no matter how true. He would not ask any more stupid questions of Pop about "the answer" now. He felt that he was the only soldier in the world so dumb he could even have dreamed of a partial answer to this madness. Then he became dizzy for a spell. Since the railroad shell explosion, he had been having these sudden attacks. He hid them well from the others, but now, as he withdrew into himself, he had these imaginary debates and questions. Damnit.

He could stop the talk with Pop, but he couldn't stop his own thoughts. The parade of friends started by. It was the time of half-visions again. They all formed a partial circle around him, smiling and muttering things he still couldn't hear. He spoke anyway, "There is only one General Eisenhower who is the leader of the Allied Forces. Not a hundred. Not three. There can only be one Number One. Why can't all these religions, which have never, ever, stopped hating and killing one another, realize that just because their prayers are said differently, they nevertheless all pray to the same commander in chief?"

Bluefeather waited for his father to answer, his grandfather, Moon Looker, Lorrie Friedman, old Ludwig, Miss Mary and all the others. He looked from one to the other, but they just smiled and chattered on all at the same time.

He tried again, "How, oh, God, oh, Muhammad, oh,

Buddha, oh, Jesus, oh, greatest of Great Spirits, can they
be so bleeding dumb and ignorantly blind?" He pleaded
to Old Grinder now, "Are we really that goddamned in-
fantile? Is vengeance a disease in the genes of entire na-
tions? Huh? Huh?" Then they all moved, skipping,
whirling lightly in single file over the top of Sandia Mountain and out of his vision.

The trucks stopped. They had moved as near to the
new front as they were going to. The men unloaded stiff
bodies, packs, rifles and all the weighted things it would
take to make a new little war.

They expected the battle of Brest to be over in a week.
A rumor spread and grew that they would soon be relieved for garrison duty, guarding prisoners of war. How
foolish. Generals did not pull strong, proven divisions
from the line for lesser duty. The better they fought, the
tougher the front line they would be thrown at, and the
more they would suffer. Nevertheless it was a silly little
hope they wished to survive on.

In spite of Hitler admonishing the Brest garrison to
battle to the death, General Herman B. Von Ramcke had
set his holding mission there at ninety days. He had at his
disposal troops ranging from the highly trained Second
Parachute Battalion and select storm troopers to civil service workers and naval personnel. He had ample weapons
and deep concrete defenses. The antiaircraft guns were
skillfully set so they could fire both air defense and flat
trajectory against ground troops. The German forces controlled the high ground and were dug into some of the
strongest concrete bunkers ever built. They had been
told that every shot fired at them by the enemy was one
less fired at the Reich. The defenders believed these
words and fought accordingly.

In every major battle ever fought, somebody occupies
the main hill looking down on their attackers—throwing

rocks, sticks and spears; shooting with bows and arrows then with caps and balls; and finally, up there on hill 154, semiautomatic rifles, fully automatic burp guns, mortars, machine guns and cannons. It had taken only a short while to graduate from the bow and arrow to the machine gun, and it was not done to put meat on the dinner table either. Methods of killing humans were escalating with vast speed.

Hill 154 had eight concrete bunkers and many and varied guns. Besides those, circular trenches were dug all around its base. The hill had to be taken before any progress could be made on the approaches to Brest.

The Third Battalion attacked that day near the end of August, moving in single fashion, Indian style, taking cover anywhere they could: in slight indentations, in clumps of grass, behind rocks, behind fallen bodies—wherever.

Finally two men from L Company, equipped with a bazooka (a hand-held rocket launcher), crawled forward and knocked out a self-propelled gun that had held the entire battalion to almost a standstill; but because of at least twenty-five heavy machine guns, many high-velocity flat trajectory weapons, as well as mortars and small arms, the hill remained in enemy hands throughout the first day and night. Casualties were heavy on both sides.

The battalion was finally completely pinned down, and in spite of heavy fire from the U.S. tank destroyers it was up to one man to break the battle open.

Infantry Sergeant Carey crawled forward. He shot down a German rifleman at forty yards with his own rifle and crawled on until he was able to finally lob a grenade into the mouths of the main pillbox. Although severely wounded, he continued to do so till he died. This was one of the few, true heroes of war. A very dead one.

Bluefeather's company was moving around the edge of

the hill while others took the top. But in his twenty-yard circle nobody knew the others had succeeded. The fire of cannon and many sorts of weapons seemed to come from all four directions and the sky itself.

Bluefeather had to lift and half drag Pop along several times. After the two days of heavy battle, the gun and pack he wore were just too much for his weary little legs to hold up.

Over and over, Bluefeather picked him up and said each time, "Enough, you old goat, haven't you had enough?"

Pop just created a thin smile of thanks and weakly staggered on. It was rapidly becoming one additional burden that Bluefeather, and their little circle, could not handle. They were pinned down.

Men were scattered all over. Some would never move themselves again. Others shoved themselves into the lowest spots they could find on earth. At staggered moments, one, two or three soldiers would rise up and charge forward only to fall, never to stand again.

Sergeant Pack was rolling, crawling, gathering hand grenades from the dead. As he neared Bluefeather and Pop, he handed Bluefeather several.

Then the eternal cry of battle came from nearby just ahead of them, "Medic! Medic!"

Pack and Bluefeather moved up, their bellies dragging heavily from the weight of the extra hand grenades. A medic was somehow there, and then another. It was a waste of precious time and risk. The man they had crawled over to help had his entire lower jaw blown off, revealing only a burbling hole down into his body. There was just enough lower jaw left to hold two dangling teeth on one side. Bluefeather had an irresistible and futile impulse to pull them free before the dying man could swallow them and choke. He pulled them loose just as one last gasping spurt of warm red liquid gushed over his hand. The final bubble broke. All that remained was a hole with the lungs underneath bubbling up little red froths and a rattling sound. Then nothing.

Bluefeather stared numbly, turning to look at Pack, who also stared. Then it happened. Bluefeather felt the scar on his nose burn as if it had been painted there with acid. If the hairs on his neck had been long enough, they would have been standing up like the quills on the back of an agitated porcupine.

Pack whirled toward Bluefeather, his usually calm blue eyes filled with rage. This rage was so great that some of it lopped over and penetrated Bluefeather's already lambasted being.

Pack yelled for the thousandth time, "Let's get the bastards, Fellini."

Bluefeather followed like a simple, unthinking servant infected with some of Pack's own frenzy. They charged through shells and bullets, crawling, firing at the enemy's emplacements, grinding into the trembling earth, spurting ahead like track stars only to fall, jolting the joints of their bodies loose but feeling none of the pain.

Others rose at Pack's cries of relentless inspiration and fired and fought blindly in the new little circle. The fire from the emplacements cracked at them, and Pack's usable troops were bloodied and thinning rapidly.

Pack yelled, "Stay, Fellini." He dragged two wounded men through the storm of steel to a swale and stanched their blood, tying it off so they could remain alive. He did the same three more times on his way back to Bluefeather, who had been happy to obey orders and lie with face and body as thin against the earth as fear could force them. The little bit of fury that Pack, and the blown-open throat, had imparted to him was gone and he felt like he had been in this losing, pounded position for years; whether he lived or died, he never wanted to move again. But Pack did. When his rifle ammunition was all gone, he crawled and screamed Bluefeather along with him. Now he hurled the grenades at the bunker openings. They were so close that the enemy couldn't lower the line of fire of the machine guns enough to touch them.

One bunker became silent. Pack had demolished the living there, and one of his beloved grenades had exploded on the edge of a dirt emplacement and trench. He was fixing his bayonet to charge when a shot came from somewhere and Pack fell.

This brought life back in Bluefeather, and he threw a grenade at the emplacement himself. Before he could reach Pack, the maniac was up and charging, blood streaming from his forehead into one eye. Bluefeather followed, so afraid that his legs buckled several times. Pack shoved his bayonet through the chest of the last enemy soldier on this Nazi machine gun. Stabbing with lethal precision, he killed two other riflemen.

He wiped the bayonet on the side of the trench, saying softly under his silently heaving chest to Bluefeather, "Well, Fellini, ol' partner, we sent several of them to the kingdom of all wishes." Then from a curve in the trench a concussion grenade was thrown at Pack. It dropped into the trench in such a way that part of the exploding force was absorbed by the earth, but enough was left to knock the sergeant down and into blackness.

Bluefeather crawled over the edge of the emplacement just in time to catch a small part of the blast. He ignored the light concussion and threw his last two grenades down into the curving trenches. One German soldier was blown up on the edge of the trench with the side of his neck gone—two vertebrae dangling loose. The fire from this particular bunker, in this particular little circle, was silent.

Bluefeather knelt by Pack. The bullet appeared to have grazed his head just enough to take away a tiny furrow of bone and leave the lining of his brain untouched, but he had no idea what the concussion grenade had done to Pack's insides.

Bluefeather was the one to yell now, "Medic!"

The soldiers rose from below and moved on up and took over the conquered trenches. Then Pop just rolled over the edge and lay there prone, looking into the pale, pale face of another hero, Sergeant Pack of the Ninth Infantry. Bluefeather could not decide who looked worse, Pop or Pack.

They came and took Pack away on a stretcher and Bluefeather felt empty, lost and lonely. He just patted Pop on the shoulder softly and sat there speechless, too tired to be thankful he was alive and unmaimed—on the surface at least.

He thought, for the moment, that most heroes of war are created by the acts of men gone mad, but of course, he too, now qualified. Many of the great fabrications of man had been instituted by people thought to be crazy at the time, and often thereafter, most were.

After the Third Battalion had topped out on the "killing hill," the three attacking divisions, the Twenty-ninth, the Second and the Eighth, straightened up their lines and began preparing for the major assault on the port city.

Bluefeather's depleted company moved up into their part of the line. There was a small, delaying party of Germans along the other side of the next hedgerow. They held the company pinned down temporarily, but the 60-mm mortars silenced their fire. There was no return fire now. The riflemen loved the 60-mms when they needed them desperately, but at the same time feared their sound because they almost inevitably drew return artillery and mortar rounds. The 60s were the bastards of infantry, but they had allowed Bluefeather's company to advance one more hedgerow.

Bluefeather cautiously raised up, and to his surprise, a German soldier jumped out of a hole and started racing erratically across the field right in front of him. Bluefeather figured the mortar rounds had knocked the German's senses loose. The high moan of the German eighty-eights, and the flatter tone of the American 105s, drowned out the report of Bluefeather's M1. The German's knees buckled. He fell forward, then rose again.

Bluefeather eased off another shot, surprised at the sudden deep pain of guilt he felt toward killing a man who a moment earlier had been trying to kill him. The German whacked against the earth facedown. One foot twitched and that was all.

Then, at last, they settled down for a few days of hot food and some rest. The Germans only fired at large troop concentrations or patrols now as their lines were being straightened again. They were conserving their ammunition for more numerous game soon to come. The men were beginning to spit bathe, shave, laugh a little, write letters home and start dreaming of all those July 4 celebrations, white Christmases, their wives and girlfriends, or those envisioned to become so. Pretty little songs were being played all around the world saying for sure these dreams would come true.

Bluefeather kept thinking of the dead German lying out there in the wheat field. He could see the dirty, gray uniform above the stubble between the shocks of wheat, like a big, dead rat.

Finally on the fourth day he could stand it no longer.

He passed the word that he was going out to the soldier. He slid over the hedgerow and moved toward the stiff figure, even though his body cringed at the thought of enemy fire concentrated on him alone. No bullets came his way. None.

The instantly identifiable stench was already there, aided by the summer heat. The flies had done their dirty work, and the body was turning the usual gun-barrel black. He could see the round holes in the German's back about three inches apart. Bluefeather was only briefly revulsed at his good marksmanship. He grabbed a shoulder of the uniform and pulled the German corporal over on his back. The entire front of the dead man's uniform was blood-covered—some dry, some sticky wet where it had been between the clothing and the ground.

He extracted the wallet carefully, for half of it was blood-soaked. He was later amazed at his disappointment because the man had no valuable ring or wristwatch or gold teeth. My God, had he become more vulture than human? Was he so jaded and empty that the man he had killed was meaningless? Was humankind a joke the Great Spirit had pulled on the universe? Was mankind just a big, bloody laugh for deities, war lovers, warmongers and eternity as well? If so, even memory itself never had been.

These thoughts came later. As for now he was more troubled by the little photos he found of the man as a civilian having a joyous-appearing picnic in a park with his wife and two small kids. They were all smiling, and one little two- or three-year-old girl was waving at the camera. The poor unlucky son of a bitch had loved and lived the same things as everyone else. Ah well, he should have had the sense to surrender instead of trying to escape across an open field.

Bluefeather felt better when he saw how many thousand franc notes were in the wallet, and he was glad the soldier hadn't carried Reich marks, for they were worthless to the GI.

Bluefeather walked purposefully back to the foxhole he had covered over with bundles of wheat. He carefully extracted the notes from the wallet. They were all stuck together at one end with blood. The other half was perfectly clean. He poured a canteen of water into his helmet and cautiously dipped the bloody ends of the bills into it. Then even more delicately he laid each out to dry. The bills had the odor of the dead, but he was sure that the combination of water and sun would take it away. He lay back against the hedgerow and took one of his rare smokes, waiting for nature to do its work.

He dozed awhile. When he awoke, he inspected his newly acquired wealth. The first bill he picked up looked almost clean. He decided the others would pass. He could hardly control his anticipation as he walked swiftly down the hedgerow to a poker game going on there.

"Hi, fellers. Got room for another sucker?"

"Come on in," said Private Jenkins from Texas.

"Money's money," said Sergeant Gallagher from upstate New York.

Corporal Kreuger from Wisconsin said, "Feeling lucky, eh?"

"I am lucky. Whose deal?"

Bluefeather stacked the money in front of his folded legs. It was wrinkled from the fast drying of the hot sun and would not stack neatly. Bluefeather pitched one note in the pot. It was the equivalent of a twenty-dollar bill in 1944.

He played carefully because he didn't know the cards yet, and he would have to play it straight as long as the others did. He had just robbed the dead, but he would never be able to bring the skills of his cousin "The Bookkeeper" from Chicago, or his Tonopah, Nevada, tricks to use here against his own men.

Every time someone took a pot, he would ante the soiled French note. It was repeatedly pitched back into play until Bluefeather wondered what in hell was bothering these guys. The game got quieter. At dark it broke up.

Early the next day the game continued. Bluefeather lost all the change from the first note and managed to get a second in the pot. The players tossed it back in over and over just as the day before. The dampness of all their hands seemed to make the odor exude from the bills even stronger. Now it was Bluefeather's turn to ante up, and he, too, pitched the stained bill back in the pot.

The three remaining players stared hard at the note. Bluefeather tried not to acknowledge it, but even he couldn't help noticing the pinkish stain across one end. His eyes kept moving from the dirty end to the clean one. Back and forth. He shuddered suddenly and felt like the pink stain was spreading over all his body. The other players got up and walked away. He sat alone. Jesus H. Christmas Christ! He was becoming immune even to the blood of the dead—by his own hand, no less. He had to stop this numbing of his soul before it was too late. Too late?

Bluefeather got up slowly and crawled over the hedgerow. He looked out where the burial detail had just that morning removed the corpse. He walked slowly toward the dark stain and smashed wheat stubble where death had overtaken a son of the führer. A little to one side he dug with his bayonet and buried all the money. Then he walked slowly back and picked up a V-mail letter and wrote his parents way, way off in Raton, New Mexico. He told his father to go down on First Street and give a twenty-dollar bill to the worst-looking bum he could find. He would pay him back and explain later. He never did either one, but somehow felt better for now. He also felt a little cleaner than he had for many hours.

Pop finally decided to shave. His whiskers had been out about half an inch in thin patches that made him appear older and more worn than ever. One could hardly see his eyes now unless directly in front of him, but this morning he had received letters from his entire family and it had pepped him up. His hands were still shaking, and he had cut his face in several places with the razor.

Bluefeather said, "We attack in the morning, you know?"

"Yeah, that's what I hear."

"It ain't too late, Pop."

Silence.

Bluefeather went on with his seemingly lost and grinding purpose. "Well?"

Pop said, "The only way out is to plunge right in."

Bluefeather almost held his breath as he tried hard yet again. "There are just so many times an old tire can roll over on a rutted road. We're travelers with thin-soled shoes."

Pop thought a moment, rubbing at his clean face. "A few days back I didn't have enough air left in me to blow up a balloon, much less a concrete fortification, but today I'm ready to wipe up the town," and he made a casual wave in the direction of Brest.

If Bluefeather had known Pop in peacetime he could easily have strangled him. Well, there was just no use trying to help him anymore. They both felt pretty good this day. Might as well try to enjoy it. Pop was also exuberant because he had somehow bribed a mailman to send all his notepads of poems to his sons. He, like Bluefeather, had seen many causes for disillusionment in the last few weeks, but he still believed they had to go on fighting this war for their country and the children of the world. Naive, of course, but true as well.

Pop said, "When this is over, I'm gonna take you fishin' up in Oregon. I know a . . ."

Bluefeather didn't hear the last; he had become obsessed watching a bird that had landed in a bush on top of a rear hedgerow. He could see the bird raise its head to sing, but he wondered why he couldn't hear it and what the bird was doing this close to the front.

Then they heard a German machine gun rattle three times in the distance, the flat crack of an antiaircraft weapon and then the returning song of American 105s searching for the sounds to bring them to permanent silence.

Pop the Poet said, as he made himself consciously listen, "You know, Blue, . . ."

Bluefeather waited.

". . . all things make music if you listen. Water, wind, even war."

"Yeah, yeah. The cottonwoods of Corrales and the Rio Grande make music—music together from the wind. It is like having your own private chimes big as mountains, big as forests. You are right, Pop, all you gotta do is listen. Really listen."

"What kind of town is Corrales?"

"Oh, it's what might be called a little Mexican town in the Southwest. If you're poor, you're Mexican American. If you're rich, you're Spanish. 'Course, all that'll be changing, I suppose, after the war. Some people think they'll even let Indians drink in bars someday. Corrales looks a little bit like a spread-out Indian pueblo, too. The gringos are mostly involved in the arts some way. I like it there, Pop. My old mining mentor, Grinder, said a man had to have a headquarters so he could dream about returning to it. You gotta have a place to keep your mules. I like mules, and I like little towns to live in, and big ones to go to."

"Having good neighbors sure counts a lot," Pop agreed.

"I got the best, . . . the Luceros." Bluefeather proceeded to describe every detail of the Luceros. He left no praise unspoken. They were the most loyal people on earth. They had the most beautiful and brightest kids ever to eat chile. Tranquilino's violin could accompany the music of angels. Their garden produced the sweetest tomatoes in the whole valley. That's the way Bluefeather felt about the few people he loved.

Pop said, "We've got this old bachelor, Dave Boston, right next door. Gripes all the time. The bastard's personality is so sour he'd give a buzzard ulcers. Turn right around, and there's hardly a week goes by he doesn't bring the kids some kind of unique present. Car breaks down, he's right there to give you a pull or a lift into town, griping all the time. We wouldn't trade him for a dozen do-gooders and four church deacons thrown in.

"Our mailman is prejudiced against everybody that didn't come over on the Mayflower. As if that bunch of thieves were his kin, Blue. He was cussing some nationality or other and said, of course, that didn't apply to a white man like Mr. Boston. Mr. Boston yelled back at the letter carrier, 'You prejudiced son of a bitch, I'm not a white man, I'm half Irish.' "

These two friends went on like this for a couple of hours, sharing, laughing, living for a moment with the folks back home.

Then Pop inadvertently broke the spell, "We got a new lieutenant named Cohen."

"Yeah. Well, he won't last till noon tomorrow without Pack around to show him the game."

"Probably not, but he survived three days before the lull."

"It seems to me it takes about a week to get your sea legs of battle. How many lieutenants have we already gone through, Pop?"

"I lost count, and you've been here longer than I have."

It was true. An infantry lieutenant was the most exposed of creatures. Few ever had a chance to learn the different voices of the shells before one of them blew his breath away.

"Pop, we don't have to worry about that. We'll never make lieutenant. You and I will be privates till the day the war ends."

"Yeah, you're right there, Blue, unless we're the only two left. Then we could promote one another. Say, I overheard Lieutenant Cohen and Sergeant Gallagher talking, and you're up for a Distinguished Service Cross."

"I'm what? What in hell for? I haven't done anything but survive."

"That's not the way they figure it. The sergeant said the report quoted some soldiers saying you saved a bunch of wounded, blew away a machine gun and antiaircraft cannon and bayoneted several German soldiers. Hell, I don't know what all. Cohen was feeling bad because they hadn't put you in for the medal of honor."

"Oh dear . . . dear Number One Above, forgive us all. God uh mighty, Pop, I didn't do nothing. I just followed Pack out of pure-ass insanity. He did it all. All of it."

"Shhh, Blue, quiet down. You'll wake up the enemy."

"I don't give a shit if I wake up the whole damn SS Corps. This is crap. That medal should go to Pack. I didn't do anything but throw one grenade after it was all over."

"They've even got a recommendation from Pack, soon as he comes to."

"Well, it's a hell of an embarrassment to put on a man who's half coward and half . . . well, half something . . ."

That put them back in a good mood again, and Bluefeather scouted around in bombed-out cellars until he found a half bottle of Calvados.

When he returned, smiling big at his scavenging victory, Pop said, "I was getting worried. Thought maybe you'd gone back to the reservation."

They had just enough Calvados to get a little drunk and laugh at all the nothing things they said to one another. In fact, for a couple of hours they were not only already on their way home, but were two of the world's greatest humorists.

Then Bluefeather looked into the sky and said, "I haven't caught on to all I know about this world."

They started laughing again.

Pop gasped out, "One good laugh will cure a thousand tears."

Bluefeather replied with great difficulty between spasms of mirth, "Our souls are scattered about like glass from a wrecked auto, but we have . . . we have . . . what? What in hell do we have, Pop?"

Pop said, looking at the almost-empty bottle, holding it right in front of his eyes, "I'm sorry you forgot the little jewel of wisdom, but I'm glad we've got one big drink left each."

"Hallelujah, amen, and forty fast Hail Marys."

They drained the bottle, crawled into their foxholes and slept.

THIRTY

THEY DIDN'T GET TO TALK ABOUT ANYTHING BUT BLOOD AND ammunition for several days. The enemy occupied their time quite well. The Ninth Regiment moved relentlessly on toward Brest, just the same. Every field was costly, but that's the way with wars.

Finally, the enemy was contained within the fortified city itself. Few buildings were totally intact. The artillery of three divisions had made it a ghost town, and even the ghosts seemed to have left. But the German soldiers, with their uncanny, even unholy, ability to improvise on any spot, made the Americans pay with many limbs lost for every yard gained. The Germans were particularly adept at inventing diabolical devices of death; booby traps and mines filled with charges of powder up to three hundred pounds infected everything. Some were made from 75-mm artillery shells with pressure igniters dug into the roads. They also had pulled torpedo heads forward from the naval yards and rigged them with trip wires and pressure devices, along with antisubmarine mines. Several road junctions had been mined with over a ton of explosives. It was said, by a division historian, that here the infantry and their engineer units found the most horrendous concentration of explosives on the European continent. The infantry engineers and mine platoons suffered and paid their dues uncounted, terrorizing times during the next three days.

Bluefeather knew some of these things in a foggy way, like struggling to get out of a bad dream and back to a reality that's even worse.

The Americans breached the fortress of concrete and buried powder, and were ready for the final assault. The units consolidated their positions once more. So did the Germans. There could only be one assault left. It only took one to die.

Already, up and down the line, men were talking about a long leave and the war's end for their outfits. This invention of wishes came about because they had been under fire for almost three and a half months now—those who had been there since the beginning. A small arms bullet killed a man just as dead as a thousand-pound bomb, but it was the hundreds and hundreds of shock waves, over mile after mile of hedgerows, that shook more than a soldier's body loose. It was the never-ceasing artillery barrages that finally made him grasp blindly at the earth in a silent pleading for succor.

They injudiciously believed they had done their fair share, somehow forgetting the old, old, knowledge that war was the very last place to seek fairness. Justice belonged to the lucky. To compensate for this mistake the troops figured the least they should get was a long-deserved rest before being transferred to the new front in Germany itself. They were looking forward to a real shower bath, some play and a short time without shell burst. At least this. A man might even find a woman if he had some loot, or was lucky—or both.

These thoughts were what made it so hard on them the morning of the Big Do—and this was one reason why the commanders didn't like their soldiers thinking too much. They knew it would be, at most, only two or three more days of deadly conflict before a reprieve.

Bluefeather was especially nervous this morning as they advanced into the heart of the city whose soul was out to the nearby sea. The windows and doors were the vacant eyes of the dead, until a sniper fired from one and brought life back to the building by sending death into the street. Sometimes the hollow buildings, with walls standing so precariously, belched forth such resistance that the Americans had to hurl phosphorous grenades into the streets to disguise their sprint from one side to the other.

Bluefeather moved with the others on past the body of Lieutenant Cohen, a child officer, who had not lived long enough to gain the necessary experience to go on living. Bluefeather fired at movements in the building, and he hit some, but he had no adrenaline left for the lust of battle. He just wanted to live. One sniper's bullet struck the corner of the doorway he was peeking around, less than three inches above his helmet. Three inches. It was the same sniper who had shot Lieutenant Cohen in the chest, puncturing his heart. No inches there.

Then G Company's firing on the city almost ceased. Intermittent only. The tank destroyers that had moved in ahead of them had done a fine job of explosive ferreting. It was said that General Ramcke was negotiating a surrender. Bluefeather—recklessly now because of possible booby traps—rummaged around several ruins hoping to find a bottle of wine or Calavados for a little victory celebration with Pop and Daniel Wind. He thought about Sergeant Pack, too, and then remembered he was hospitalized. Pop followed along as he tried to plunder futilely. There was nothing left but tiny remains of papers and pipes, empty or broken cans and bottles. It was mostly pulverized. Waste.

Then, as they exited a corner building, on the opposite side, Bluefeather saw the German private's body. A tank destroyer shell had struck him right at the belt buckle. He was blown completely in half except for a few strings of flesh on his right side. His severed ribs stuck out, and the inside of his chest cavity was almost empty. His arms were flung back as if he had reached out for something compelling with all his strength the instant of his death.

Bluefeather stood, staring and staring, somehow never getting used to it. The suddenness. This one had moved his arms up and out in a desperate grab, in a minute, immeasurable, split part of infinity.

Pop walked around the edge of a caved-in wall saying, "What's the matter?" before he saw the hollow body.

Bluefeather pointed.

Pop stared too.

They had seen many hundreds of fractured bodies, but now, here at the end of this battle, far apart from the main ones, on a French peninsula in the month of September, on a clear and lively day away from the city, they were both hypnotized by the fragmented form that had once been like themselves.

Pop began to shake from something other than exhaustion and fear. He quivered like an old Model-T Ford that had been started for the first time in months. His paled face turned pink and his breath came short and hard.

"Look," he said, moving with the sudden agility of youth. "Look at that! You see now, don't you?"

Once it seemed, long ago in a land made of trances, Bluefeather had wanted Pop's answer. Now this day, right here, he plain didn't give a shit. It was as unstoppable as it was meaningless, he thought.

Pop made sort of a dance in front of the body, agile,

but pitiful, too. Then he bent down to look inside the corpse. He suddenly, shockingly, straightened up and leaped into the air with grasping hands. Then he ran about grabbing at air with his flexing fingers.

"Where is it?" he shouted. "Where, oh where has it gone?" He made a motion as if he had caught something out of the air, and he ran back to the hollow part of the body and pantomimed shoving the "something" inside it. "It won't stay," he shouted. "It won't return. Ohhh, ohhh, where has it gone?"

Then he ran around in a circle looking under stones, bricks, slivers of wood and peering into the crumbled corners of the building. "Is it here? No. Maybe it's over there. No? It is gone. Gone. Gone. It is gone and no one knows where."

Bluefeather was possessed by an impulse to grab Pop around the neck and hold him until he shut up. Instead, he stood still, silent.

Pop raved on, "What was it? Where did it come from? Where did it vanish to? Ah, my dear friend, Blue, we don't know, do we?" Now softly, almost whispering, he went on, "We don't know what it is." His voice rose again. He shouted so that Bluefeather thought Pop's mind was altogether gone as well. "It is so simple. We don't know what we are. Remember the goats? Remember, just remember, how upset we all were. Well, that's because we know what goats are. Don't you see?" He pleaded desperately, standing crouched forward with his arms waving, begging in the air.

Then the hands stopped and he slowly spun around and settled to his knees and his face fell forward on his chest as if he were praying. His arms hung limp as he rolled slackly over on his side.

For a moment Bluefeather was paralyzed, then he ran to his buddy. There was a black hole under each temple.

A tiny bit of red began oozing from one, but it was from gravity that he bled, because the blood Bluefeather saw had no life pumping it. It had none of the element he had but a moment ago grasped so frantically for.

Bluefeather heard a rattle of friendly small-arms fire a short distance away. The sniper was now on the same trip as Pop.

Bluefeather straightened him out, took the raincoat from his friend's pack and found in it a lost, unmailed letter to his family back home. He covered as much of him as he could with the raincoat. Tenderly. Then he walked back toward the rear. He had to mail the letter as quickly as possible. He had to find Sergeant Pack and Daniel Wind and tell them about Pop. Then he remembered that Pack was gone. The first ghosts were already returning to Brest. The port was never used by the Allies.

THIRTY-ONE

THE CITY FELL AND THEY TOOK A LOT OF PRISONERS. BLUE-
feather was amazed at the arrogance of the defeated SS
officers. Most other armies would have executed them
without hesitating. Hitler had done such a masterful job
of brainwashing his SS children that, for centuries, psy-
chologists would be entertained, and other dictators edu-
cated, by his feat.

The portable shower baths were enjoyed, relished. The
first hot food in weeks was gulped as if it were gourmet.
As he stood in line for his first meal, dangling his mess
kit, Bluefeather remembered his late grandmother Fellini's cooking. She had been from the Calagari family of
Lombardy in northern Italy. She always kept Franchia
cheese, with its brown line over the top, for snacks and
dessert. He could see her hands now, as she made
crespelle cheese pancakes, mixing the three cheeses. He
could taste the sharp tanginess of the provolone cheese
that she used in everything possible. She mixed the flour,
eggs and nutmeg for the pancakes, then, with expert, loving hands, she poured the cheese batter inside them. His
heart was full of the nostalgic smells and tastes of his

grandmother's house—but then he wasn't there any longer. He was here—near Brest—waiting, waiting, as soldiers had forever done.

The laughter, the sleep, the letters to and from home were exulted in.

Bluefeather won a pocketful of money in a poker game and invited his one remaining close war buddy, Daniel Wind, to a nearby village for relaxation. It was the time of fun.

The place was loaded with GIs who had had the same thought before them. It took quite a spell for the two friends to get drunk on the cheap wine. The villagers kept what good stuff they had hidden. Wisely so, for they knew its rare and precious vintage would grow in value almost hourly. They would need all the resources they could muster to rebuild their steel-shattered land.

Finally, Bluefeather put up enough money, a lot, for a bottle of the good stuff. It was the time for remembering.

"Dan'l, ol' pardner of the storm," Bluefeather said, "here's to those who died and to those who lived. Here's to the worlds that have come and vanished and to those adventurous ones yet to be. And here, Dan'l, ol' foot soldier, here is a brimful glass to the poets. God rest their scarce hearts."

Daniel wiped the wine from the corners of his mouth and said, "Yeah," and poured the balance of the bottle into his empty glass and drained it just as fast.

It took all the rest of Bluefeather's poker money to find them a woman. The few women available for this sort of social contact were outnumbered by the partying GIs by at least fifteen hundred to one.

Bluefeather had more money left than most, so he cut a line short. They got this very important relief and pleasure over with, even though they had to share the same lady.

"Buddies to the end," Bluefeather told Daniel right after.

Daniel replied, "For sure."

Way into the night, they started stumbling, drunkenly, back toward the company bivouac. Somehow, they went astray off the road and wound up staggering across a railroad bridge high above some body of water—a stream, or pond.

Bluefeather never considered the ocean to be in the reckoning. He had never heard of anyone building a bridge over an ocean. He wondered how it had escaped bombing and was about to ask Daniel Wind what he thought about it when he heard a splash down below.

He muttered something to himself about that crazy Indian going swimming at this time of night and went on doing an imaginary stomp dance in his picture-mind.

About noon the next day, Sergeant Gallagher woke Bluefeather and told him that Daniel Wind had evidently fallen off a bridge and drowned. Some E Company boys had seen him floating on top of the water about a mile from camp.

"Well, I'll be damned," Bluefeather said, wiping at his dehydrated eyes. "Say, Sergeant, have you got a drink of water on you? My canteen's empty."

All around Brest, back in Normandy, out on the South Pacific Islands, down in Italy and over in Russia, the worms, the ants, the dung beetles, the roaches, the flies and millions, billions and trillions of insects waited in the earth, the grass and the bushes for the juicy parts of detonated flesh to come to them. They could handle the meat of any size mammal, from the elephantine to the micro-

scopic, as long as it was dead or dying. They grew glutton-
ous and fat. These were days and years of surplus riches
for the under-earth.

As soon as the troops had healed their exhausted bodies
and minds enough to start getting into trouble, the commanders knew they would fight again. This sort of knowledge is what had gained them their power to begin with
—and end with. The ability to get men to fight and die
for you took a special talent. Custer had understood this
long before he attacked the twenty thousand Indians with
two hundred fifty men. He was already a minor hero,
after dashing and driving hundreds of soldiers to their
deaths in the Civil War, and as the fate of fractions would
have it, survived unscathed. He, in the end, outdid them
all. He accomplished his goal of world recognition. What
did he care if he was infamous as well, and they all died
to the last man?

It was the time to return to battle. The commanders
passed down the orders. Part of the Second Division
made the trip to the Ardennes Forest and the Siegfred
line in old boxcars, stopping at every railway station along
the way. Others were moved through France and the
edge of Paris by motor convoy along the Red Ball Highway, made famous by motor drivers of the Red Ball Express. They were mostly black troops and made both the
highway and the convoys famous. The rest walked the
seven hundred miles.

Before the new choices of travel had been made for
them, a fresh replacement asked Bluefeather, "Which
method of transportation will we have?"

Bluefeather smiled and said, "Guess."

The walk into the foothills of the Ardennes was
through mud as thick and sticky as half-set concrete. The
rain came on down, good for the trees and brush. They

slept in the water until it turned to snow and then slept in that. They took up positions along a thin, thirty-mile front. Here Bluefeather had just passed completely across the land of his admired Balzac and had not seen a single volume of his work, nor would he have had the time to read an opening chapter if he had seen one. Now, here he was in the country of Bach and Wagner. At this time in history it seemed impossible that the beauty of their music had made it around the entire world and the conquering dreams of Hitler had not. He had to listen to the chants of the erratic music of the screaming meemies (German short-range rocket launchers) and to Hitler's vaunted V-2 weapons. Eight hundred twenty-nine bombs and twenty-six rockets were recorded—most of them on the way to rear areas. The total damage from this great expenditure of energy was two minor wounds and two trailers crippled. Then the buzz bombs came, looking like small planes as they flew over, adding to the symphony with ear-shattering noise on their way to England. At night the music continued, seen and heard as streaks of roaring fire in the sky. Some flew in circles and dropped on the Ninth Regiment, while others returned to their sender. The music makers played on.

Bluefeather told the new lieutenant from Beverly Hills that he was going to have to assign him some help. "I'm wearing out running through this forest, pushing trees apart, making a path for German rockets."

To amuse himself even more and keep his mind in tune, he did some mathematics. Bluefeather figured that in Normandy and Brest he had dived to the earth a minimum of thirty times a day. Figuring at the low end of three months and ten days, he had whammed into the earth three thousand times, at least. This, loaded with a full pack, as well as ammunition, grenades, rifle, canteen of water, a bayonet and a GI shovel. He had dug at least three foxholes every day. So he had moved enough dirt to have created a massive meteor crater. The molecules of his body had absorbed the continuing shock of enough exploding bombs, artillery shells, mortar rounds and concussion grenades to turn granite boulders into prisoners-of-war soup. Yet he felt pretty well and anticipated fulfilling the prophecies of his spirit guide having these great adventures to look forward to "after the war."

There was still much pain for many here, beyond the explosives. The snow melted and froze over and over. The infantrymen had to put a layer of sticks in the bottom of their foxholes every two or three days to stay ahead of the water buildup caused by the living warmth of their bodies. Some had frozen feet and toes. Some lost them to trench rot or black foot.

He had survived long before, and long after, Burton and White. He believed now. Dancing Bear had given him notice of the great adventure to come "below the trees where the water burns." The division patrolled, and occasionally fought, in three countries—Belgium, Germany and Luxembourg. Sergeant Pack came back. His presence assured Bluefeather of a close friend and war mentor all the way to victory and home. No doubt. Pop was gone. Daniel was gone. Burton and White were gone, and . . . and . . . and . . . but Pack was back.

The division went through the Battle of the Bulge, the Rhineland and on to Pilsen, Czechoslovakia, to greet the Russians. Bluefeather went methodically on, but since the deepest snow of December in the Ardennes, his spirit had returned to roam the red mesas of the great Southwest in the company of two amiable mules, and he heard the voice of his Tiwa grandfather saying, "Oh, wah, ha, water, wind, breath, life of whole earth." The sonorous song of comfort drifted across the fields and foothills of

Taos Pueblo, vanishing in the struggle to reach the top of the sacred mountain.

Then he heard someone else singing that old-time favorite, "Wake Up and Dream, You Sleepy-Headed Bastards."

He was home before he got there.

PART THREE

~

NEW FRIENDS—NEW FOES

AND THE RETURN TO TAOS

THIRTY-TWO

IT WAS THE TIME FOR FAMILY, FRIENDS AND FUN. THE PROPHE-
sied adventures of Dancing Bear would just have to wait
for their space on the turning wheel.

The Luceros had taken great care of his place in Corrales. In fact, the garden was like a small farm now with
spaces for tomatoes, chiles, squash and corn. Bluefeather
could not believe the size of the children. Had it really
been that long? They were all big enough to chop wood,
and Tranquilino was joyous, heavier and even more lov-
able.

Bluefeather brought each child a souvenir: an SS belt
buckle, a small Nazi flag with bullet holes in it and a
German paratrooper's knife that had multiple uses and a
blade that would spring out of the handle by pressing
a small lever. He also brought a ten-pound bag filled with
every kind of candy he could find for sale. He gave Tina a
shawl, a silver comb and a mantilla to wear during special
Mexican-American ceremonies.

Tranquilino stared, puzzled at his gifts. The goodies
were in a large box divided into two sections. The top half
held dishrags, dishtowels, dishscrubbers and a cuckoo
clock. Tranquilino received his gifts, with Tina's great

black eyes pouring tears of laughter as she slapped her left leg over and over with both hands. The kids even forgot about their own presents and joined their mother, Bluefeather and, finally, their father in the laughter over the surprising idiocy of Tranquilino's presents. He had never washed dishes in his entire life. The second section of the box was a little more to Tranq's liking. There was a bottle of very scarce brandy, a fancy and complete shaving set, an eighteen-karat gold pocket watch and a paid-up certificate for a new John Deere tractor as soon as it was available. Now appreciation gleamed from Tranquilino's eyes, and he drank about a fourth of his liquid present to show it.

Later, after a great meal of Tina's enchiladas—made from Verlarde chile—Tranquilino and Bluefeather went out to see the mules. Tranquilino had them both brushed and in the pen. The sun caused bands of light to glisten across their sleek bodies. They were too well cared for—too fat.

Bluefeather exulted in the smell of the corral, the hay, the oats, as well as the animals. He would have to get them out in the San Pedro Mountains and walk them lean and tough again. He rubbed their necks and their foreheads. He felt certain they knew him. Mules never forget a kind friend or an abusing enemy. Never. Then he put his arm around one lowered neck, and silent tears flowed from his body and out his eyes. Then his chest heaved in mighty silent sobbing. He was home.

Tranquilino walked out of the corral and examined the garden with great care, keeping his head down. All of Bluefeather's grief for lost loves and dead buddies had been necessarily repressed for years now. The mules' scent, their living warmth, their environment and their loyalty finally released the pressure and it was eased.

·   ·   ·

He bought a secondhand truck and loaded it down with gifts for his parents, uncles, nephews and nieces at Raton. He wanted to give everyone he loved the world and would have done it, too, if the Great Spirit would have sold or traded it to him. He hugged and kissed so many people that he had to get drunk to keep going. His mother and father and sisters all tried to love and feed and drink him to death. He told his cousin Mario that surviving the war had been easy, but an Italian homecoming was damn near impossible.

His Italian blood pulled at and nearly, but not quite, magnetized him into falling into the comfortable womb of protective family love and expectations. It was hard to leave the constant rolling talk, hugs, laughter, and the promises and suggestions for a great future in the mines awaiting a war hero. There also was the ready-made wedding, planned all the way through his honeymoon, kids, grandchildren and beyond, to where he would meet the Heavenly Father and a family of waiting Fellinis and their kin for thousands of years on into eternity. It was terribly tempting.

He was amazed that all seven of the Marchiondo boys had returned home safely. His mother had saved him a copy of the *Life* magazine they had been written up in. Finally, he could stand it no longer. He would have to go back to Corrales to see his mules and rest. He would also have to cash in some of his gold nuggets to maintain all this loving, eating and drinking.

Then his mother had to take him to Taos to visit his grandparents, his uncles and cousins. He was required to get drunk at least once with Stump Jumper and Smiling Dog. The venison from the mountains and the hot loaves of bread from his grandmother's *horno* were as enchantingly delicious as all the finest nectars.

All this multiplied love only led him to remember the

words that he had promised his mentor, Grinder, never
to forget. How was it exactly? "You are not half-Indian.
You are not half-Italian. You are a whole Bluefeather.
Bluefeather is Bluefeather. Blue is Blue, and you are
you." He was almost certain that was it. The words. It
didn't matter. It was the essence of the meaning, and he
would travel his own trails just as he had given his word
to the old prospector of gold and truth. He would make
new trails. He would invent them, if necessary. Here too,
the Bear Clan was strong—very strong. Again, he had this
easy temptation to stay under their protection in the
shadow of the blessed mountain.

Soon he returned to Raton and took a room at the El
Portal Hotel. The family condoned the time of change
that was here. They left him alone unless he wanted to
see them. He loved the old hotel with territorial furniture
in the rooms and dining area.

His friends Charlie Musso and Charlie's sister, Rose,
would occasionally neglect their business and join the
sporting activities. Mugs Moss and Pal England from the
village of Hi Lo, about halfway between Raton and Clayton in a southeasterly direction, moved into the hotel.
Both had been shot down on the same bomber just after
crossing over the English Channel and had parachuted
into the waiting clutches of the German troops. They had
spent over two years as prisoners of war and had, what
seemed to them, a small fortune in back pay. They were
obliged to try and spend it all. They finally got it done,
but before they did—with much help from Bluefeather—
the party, the laughter, the wildness of freedom possessed them. No one seemed to mind.

Mugs fell in love with Rose, and for a while it was
beautiful, but Rose finally left for Denver. It was too
much for her. Her family had already planned her future,

and it was apparent that the only thing this bunch wanted was endless fun.

It *was* fun, too, until it ended. When Mugs and Pal had used up their back pay and then their credit, the imaginary bullets and crashes of their dreams slowly dissipated along with the cushioning haze of total abandonment and alcohol. The old, old reality of new obligations to themselves, their families and the new world slipped into their beings and took over. Ambition itself helped crowd the war into second place, then third . . . then way back, for the great majority of them anyway. For a few, of course, their real lives ended with the signing of the peace treaties—they stayed at war as they grew older and weaker. They could imagine no other adventure that could ever touch it, and consequently bored people to death till their own demise talking about it. These were truly the exceptions, though.

Something finally ended for Bluefeather as well. He realized he could play Ping-Pong the rest of his life between the Indian and the Italian clans and have a lot of fun doing it, but he had promises to keep and dreams to fulfill. He decided to go study mining engineering at New Mexico Institute of Mining and Technology in the Spanish-gringo, high, dry mountain town of Socorro, eighty miles south of Albuquerque. He was a student of great perception when on field trips, but the chemistry of the classroom did not suit him. Even so, his grades were good, and he held himself in place there, mainly because it was an easy drive back to Corrales for the weekends.

He dated some women, as nature demanded. Occasionally he would go on a weekend ripper of a party, dancing, yelling and, once in a while, having a little fistfight, if someone insulted a friend. It was purely for fun and did no harm at that time in his life, at that time in history, at that time in New Mexico. Times change. It also just wasn't quite exciting enough. He became involved in a minor mercury smuggling operation out of Old Mexico. Nothing too important, and not illegal, in his eyes. Bluefeather was not clearly aware of it, but he was moving about hoping the spear of Dancing Bear's prediction for the rest of his life would pierce him and activate the greatest of all adventures.

About three months before he was to graduate, he packed up his mules and headed for his placer spot in the San Pedros, but someone had cleaned out all the remaining gold while he had recently been otherwise busy. Somehow he resented this, but at the same time, he was relieved that the mine was emptied. He put it immediately from his mind.

After World War II, most of the prospectors used jeeps and all kinds of four-wheel-drive vehicles for prospecting. They only searched for massive deposits of ore and overlooked small rich ones. Bluefeather was aware of this, and he sampled the little, tiny, overlooked veins of silver hoping for a modest discovery to keep him and the mules busy and alive. He, like Grinder, could smell gold, but he did not want any more of its scent of constant disaster. He didn't find the silver either, because he had unknowingly limited his avenue of searching. The prophecies were still in his mind. He knew they would start being fulfilled, but he didn't know when.

Half of the gold he had stashed was cashed in and spent on indifferent prospecting, assays, food, drink and fun when he was back in town. There were three bags left from all the riches he had found at Breen and at his other small strikes. He also still had the three specimen rocks: two from Breen and the one from old Grinder. He would starve before he would let them go. It didn't make good financial sense, but he borrowed money from the bank to survive rather than cash in the last of his stash.

He had paid his own way through school, but he could have applied for help from the GI educational program and gotten his degree. Somehow this seemed redundant to him and a step backward, whether it was true or not. He could go back, way back, to the mines at Trinidad, Colorado, or for that matter, almost anywhere in the world. Among the many things Grinder the Gringo had told him for sure, was that a man had to have his own headquarters to fulfill himself. By God he believed it when he had first heard it, and he believed it now, but he was just about to put his at risk.

He would make up his mind to do something about this situation in a couple of days, but he didn't know what in hell it would be. Of course, there was no way he could visualize, without the unpredictable help of Dancing Bear, that the new world he had so lightheartedly thrown away was going to abruptly change.

THIRTY-THREE

BLUEFEATHER SAT ON AN ORTIZ MOUNTAIN PEAK RESTING AND contemplating while his mules grazed nearby. His eyes wandered way up north past Santa Fe and the Sangre de Cristos, down to the Jemez Mountains to the west and to the San Pedros and Sandias to the south just outside his current hometown of Albuquerque. It was a magnificent view encompassing over a million acres and four different mountain ranges. However, he didn't give the awesome sight its proper concentration. He only saw it with his outer eyes; his inner eye was practically blind to the spread of beauty. He had just discovered that someone had trespassed and dug out his placer mine during the three years he was in the armed services. It created a multitude of emotions.

At first there was a sense of loss and betrayal. How dare anyone—anyone on earth—take advantage of his patriotic absence to loot his claim. For a few moments his nose scar seared, and he wished to feel the perpetrator's neck encircled by his hands.

These feelings began to vanish as he sat staring across the land. He mused hopefully that someone with a large family to feed had worked the dry placer, or maybe it was an old veteran from the last great war. Anyway, it was only a nice little survival claim. No one had gotten wealthy from it. That was for sure. He decided he was lucky. He still had three bags of ninety percent nuggets and gold dust stashed back at Corrales.

The last of his ill feelings had disappeared and full acceptance of the situation had set in, when he first heard the distant "whack whack" of a helicopter. Before he could pinpoint its location and direction, the whirling blades almost blew his old leather hat off. It circled in the opening between two peaks less than forty yards from him, almost level with his gaze. His surprise kept him from getting a good look at the two occupants. The machine clattered on around the peak again and slowed, hovering about thirty yards out.

A young woman looked straight at him, smiled and waved. Suddenly his heart filled the entire cavity of his chest and seemed to be struggling to burst out of his body. It restricted his breathing so that he had to gasp the high-altitude air into his lungs. It was Miss Mary! How could she have reincarnated so soon? No, it couldn't be. He waved feebly back at her and realized that it was the auburn hair and the red, full lips that had fooled and stunned him. No, it wasn't Miss Mary. This woman had higher cheekbones and a leaner jaw than his last love, but the totality of her coloration was shockingly similar.

He stood up, having trouble keeping solid footing in the wind wash from the chopper propellers. Smiling, he removed his hat and graciously bowed toward them. At that, the male pilot and the lady clacked off through the air toward Santa Fe.

He sat back down and watched them move out of sight over the hills. What were they doing out here? What could they possibly want from him? Why did they go to the trouble to take an extra look at this lone prospector,

Bluefeather Fellini? Maybe it was a simple joyride.
Maybe they were uranium prospectors. Maybe. Maybe.
Maybe. Whatever, he would always remember that face,
that woman.

He tried to cajole Dancing Bear up for one of his confusing, puzzling answers, but the emotions of finding his
mine had been robbed, and the initial shock of having
seen a Miss Mary facsimile, had left him without the energy.

By the time he got back to Corrales, he had decided to
leave his relatively new team of mules at home for a time.
He had named them the same as his other mules: Nancy,
after his first notable love at Tonopah, Nevada; Miss
Mary, for the love of his life from Breen, Colorado, and
Harmony Creek.

He told them, "Do not worry your beautiful heads,
inestimable ones. In my absence, Tranquilino will treat
you like the queens you are. I will make the trip as brief
as possible. Please, bear with me and grant me patience.
The excitement of making it back home from the war to
my loved ones has caused my mind to vacate. The pleasure of celebration, and haphazardly—mainly in fun—
prospecting with you, my dears, has created a meagerness
in our funds. Forgive me for this oversight. The only excuse is our enjoying the wandering too much. We only
halfheartedly sought those earthly treasures we so expertly know how to sniff out. I have erred against the
advice of my mentor, Old Grinder, and put our property
here—our homestead—in slight jeopardy. But do not allow my meandering voice to dismay you, sweetest ones. I
shall increase our stash soon and all will be well. Do you
hear and get my offerings clearly?"

They looked at him with shining eyes of velvety softness, large as a doe's, and understood.

"Good," he said. "Good."

Then he proceeded to the house, picked up the heaviest of the three bags of gold, and got into his already-loaded jeep with a canvas top. Previously, he had visited, dined, had drinks and jamboreed with the Lucero family, so now he was free to make another run at the world and continue what began when he had met Old Grinder in Trinidad, Colorado, and fortunately had fallen for his yarns of gold and glory that were as true in his mentor's mind as a church steeple.

He started the jeep and drove toward the main city on the south side of Sandia Mountain. He had to cross the Rio Grande and finesse his way through the city traffic of Albuquerque.

He stopped at the office of a dentist who had always paid him cash for his gold. As he left, he wondered if Dr. Dingel illegally melted it down to make crowns for his patients' teeth.

He circled around the east side of the mountain past Golden, on to the old coal-mining town of Madrid, and then to the tiny outpost of Cerrillos. Nearby, before there was any other nationality on this part of the earth, the Indians had mined turquoise and many before him had sought and found some gold. Even Bluefeather had accumulated enough gold near here to allow this trip. Cerrillos had been bad to some, good to others. It had always been comfortable and lightly rewarding to him. Why not start his next and continuing quest here? Why not, indeed?

The hills moved by as fast as fence posts as he elatedly spurred the jeep toward his destiny.

The Cerrillos Bar had the usual smoky mirror, western prints and beer advertisements scattered about on the walls, a jukebox, three or four customers and that same old smell. It was unmistakably an icon of the great Southwest. It was also a sort of restaurant. Customers could eat at the bar—if they weren't slobbering drunk—or they could choose one of the seven tables scattered all the way across the forty-foot room. Blessedly, the kitchen was next to the bar. The restrooms were in the far northwest corner. For utility purposes, the jukebox was halfway between these two rooms of the absolute. The tables circled around a small dance floor. All in all it was an establishment to succor the body and replenish wounded souls, with a touch of ancient history in its often stale air as a bonus.

The owners, George and Mattie Gull, handled the entire operation. He tended bar and waited tables part of the time. She cooked and waited tables part of the time. He was big and hairy, with a laugh that would have startled a charging rhino. She was also big, but deft and skillful in her work. Her laugh was not big. It was a light, almost continuous, titter for convenience' sake. The Gulls knew how to please without condescension or arrogance. They were the power in the village of perhaps a hundred living bodies. This power element was simple: they had control of the necessities of life for this sort of land— namely booze, bread and music.

"One could do worse," Bluefeather thought as he sat drinking a cola and looking out the only window into Cerrillos's mostly empty main street. He had casually observed the uranium prospectors at the bar telling Big George about their claims. They were holding "hot" rocks next to their Geiger counters, thrilling at their buzzing the signal of radioactivity in the specimens. They carried and handled these instruments with the same pride a Texas Ranger had in his badge. These "hunters" —for most of them had so little experience one could not justifiably call them prospectors—were scattered by the hundreds of thousands throughout the valleys, mountains and bars of Colorado, Arizona, Utah and New Mexico. They were from every state in the Union and several foreign countries, searching for the bonanza of "yellow cake" that could be turned into power enough to blow up the world. None of them thought of this. Druggists, accountants, farmers, grocery store owners, gas station attendants, all kinds were obsessed with the glorious riches to be found and the glorious worship they would receive from their neighbors back home when they found them. It was only an idle curiosity to Bluefeather. The uranium fever had escaped him. He was aware that countless little restaurants, bars and motels across his part of the world had found a lucky bonanza of business.

While Bluefeather mused about going back to the New Mexico Institute of Mining and Technology to earn his degree in mine engineering—it would only take him about six months—he saw a man walk past the window. There was something that emanated from the figure right through the glass to Bluefeather. He rearranged his chair so its back touched the wall. He sipped his cola, watching the bar entrance.

The door opened. A combination of light and shadow filled it. After tipping his tweed cap to the bartender, saying, "A good day to you, George Gull," he walked straight across the room toward Bluefeather.

"Why, why, hello there, Dr. Godchuck. How're you doin' today?"

The man ignored this as he moved on. He was dressed all the way in perfectly fitting tweed. A tan silk ascot encircled his neck. The thick showing of white hair underneath his cap had a sheen to it even in the soft light of the Cerrillos Bar. He wore a perfectly trimmed white mustache exactly one-eighth inch in width and two inches in length. His brisk walk was accentuated by a cane that was somehow part of his being, but obviously not needed for any type of physical impairment. His left hand carried a briefcase, or a leather valise, at least. The bottom was flat, ten inches wide, and the single piece of leather on each of its widest sides sloped up and came together with a hole in both forming a perfect handle. It had gold-buckled pockets on all sides. It was different and elegant, just as the man.

He sat right down at the table in the corner next to Bluefeather, placed the odd-looking walking stick on the table and removed his cap, placing it very correctly atop the handle of the cane. The briefcase was pushed up against his right leg. He had hardly finished these move-ments before Big George placed a glass of ginger ale in front of him and poured the liquid into a glass as if it were rare French wine.

"Thank you, George Gull."

"My pleasure, Doctor."

The man raised the glass now, his piercing dark eyes looking directly at Bluefeather, and said, "And a good day to you, sir."

Bluefeather stuttered, "Why sure . . . sure enough, and an even better one to you."

They drank the toast. A swallow each. The man stuck out a hand smooth and spotless as the butt of a fresh-powdered baby, saying, "I'm Dr Merphyn Godchuck."

Bluefeather took the soft-looking hand and almost winced at its crushing strength as he replied, "I'm Bluefeather Fellini. Pleased to meet you."

"Ah, ah, ah, let me guess. Bluefeather Fellini. Yes, that would be Indian-Italian ancestry, I believe," he said with just a trace of the Old South in his voice.

"Yes, sir."

"Fine, fine people. Are you here prospecting for ura-nium, Bluefeather Fellini?"

"To tell you the truth, I was just thinking about going back to school for a few months and getting my M.E."

"Good, good. I'm glad you're not a follower of the uranium tide. These poor creatures will have to sell their claims at a price the big companies choose. You see, these corporations have the only permits to mill and process the ore, and most of them are merciless. Of course, only one in a million or so of these hill climbers would know a worthy deposit if they found it."

"Well, it's good for local business," Bluefeather said, motioning to the bar.

"Indeed, it is that. Also good for the sellers of penny stocks."

Bluefeather agreed and added, "There are always more sellers than buyers in the mining business."

Dr. Godchuck seemed highly pleased at this statement and said so. "You display considerable wisdom of how the great metal scam works, Bluefeather Fellini."

Another blur moved past the window.

Dr. Godchuck cleared his throat and motioned to George Gull, who leaped around the bar and politely opened the front door. A young lady of perhaps thirty or maybe thirty-five years entered with a silver tray balanced on the bent palm of one hand. It held an elegant, old silver teapot and four teacups with saucers. She pranced delicately across the room toward the doctor and placed the tea ensemble on the corner table just as caringly as he had placed his accoutrements. Dr. Godchuck rose and stood until she was seated.

She was something, all right, but Bluefeather could not figure exactly what, except of course, woman. She had a short pageboy cut to her light brown hair and a 1920s hat —one of those soft-looking kind with one side curving down over her left ear. She wore a fine silk dress the color of her hair. It fit tightly over her lower breasts, revealing the upper portions of the smooth, creamy flesh as she bent over to pour the tea. Her mouth was almost painted in a cupid's bow, and her dark brown, gleaming eyes seemed to exude liquid sparkles of joyousness. She expertly poured a cup of tea for Dr. Godchuck and herself.

Bluefeather stared back and forth from one face to the other. His hunter/prospector eyes could not discern a single wrinkle on either face, although the doctor had to be sixty or older in spite of his agility and smooth hands. There should have been at least the first sign of smile wrinkles around the lady's face, but he could see none. Both of these people moved with such expert quickness that the two cups were correctly filled and properly placed before she glanced at Bluefeather.

The doctor caught her swiftly moving eyes and thoughts, saying, "Ah, ah, ah, this is Mr. Bluefeather Fellini, dear. Bluefeather Fellini, please meet my aunt, Tulip Everhaven."

Bluefeather stood up, bowing and kissing the tender rose-water-scented hand of Tulip Everhaven. He was certain the doctor had meant to say "niece" instead of "aunt." It had to be. He was almost stunned at his sudden courtliness when he said like a practiced Kentucky colonel, "It is a great pleasure to meet one of such delicate beauty."

She put one hand to her cheek, blushing—or feigning one better than a great actor—smiling with red and white profusion. "Oh my, you are such a gentlemen. Tea?" The southernism of her speech was undeniable. There was no exact location to it.

"Thank you, I will."

"Good, good," she said as she poured the hot liquid and smoothly moved the saucer and cup to the space on his table an inch from his hand.

"Mr. Bluefeather Fellini is a mining engineer, Tulip."

"Oh deah, how exciting. My third husband, Franklin Debonshire, was an engineer of some kind . . . or was it my fourth, Wilby Strick, Merphyn?" She set her cup down and tried to make wrinkles of thought on her forehead. The puzzle was so great that Dr. Godchuck deigned to solve his aunt's quandary.

"No, Tulip, it was your seventh, Farmley Casino. He wasn't an engineer exactly, more of a . . . a caretaker of floors."

"Oh, that's right, Merphyn deah. He was the one who electrocuted himself by . . . by . . ."

"Lightning struck him while he was emptying a pail of mop water in his client's hedge."

"Of course. I sometimes get them mixed up and especially how the deahs departed. Eight of them, you know." She smiled in confidence at Bluefeather. "Whistle-Stop Everhaven was the last, of course. He was a fighter for prizes, but alas, one too many blows to that precious head and it exploded inside. He was blessed, though. Never knew what hit him. He had been out on his feet for three rounds. God does have his ways, you know."

THIRTY-FOUR

BLUEFEATHER HAD BEEN SOBERLY CONSIDERING HIS NEXT MOVE at the perpetually challenging world when these two—these two individuals—had simply, elegantly barged right into his thoughts—his being. Just a few moments ago he was seriously considering finishing his education, when an older man with the skin of a healthy baby and a weirdly gorgeous young woman finely attired in flapper fashion that had ended twenty-odd years ago had suddenly become part of his space. He felt as if his previous world had suddenly been moved over, like a chair, but a thousand or so miles away.

For a young man, Bluefeather felt that a sufficient number of adventurous experiences had befallen him to make him at least somewhat worldly. He had grown up in two strong but separate cultures. He had been fortunate to have a great, a trusting, a loving mentor in Old Grinder. He had placed his life in jeopardy countless times on steep mountainsides and in carelessly dug tunnels. He had gambled at cards and dice against the best. He had fought for his life in bars, at gambling tables and in a mighty bloody war. He had loved, by varying degrees and ways, a few fine women. He had experienced assorted spiritual initiations and involvements with a dancing spirit guide who gave erratic advice.

Yes, he had been places and done some things. Now he felt inexperienced, even amateurish, at life. These two people—within less than five minutes, but what seemed like several eternities—had invaded his person, his place on the planet, and somehow taken it over. The "deah this" and "deah that" of Tulip Everhaven, and Dr. Merphyn Godchuck consistently calling everyone by his or her full name, had temporarily thrown him off balance. Everything seemed to be reversed, and yet somehow promptly and properly normal. Even the doctor's clothes, which were more suited to a lord of a Scottish castle than a little worn-out mining village in New Mexico, seemed as natural as onion breath, as did this aunt of his, who dressed like a playgirl flapper and seemed to be about thirty or more years younger than her nephew.

Dr. Merphyn Godchuck had been talking a while now, and he continued in his smooth gentlemanly way. "I can see by your demeanor, Bluefeather Fellini, that you are a strong-willed man and indecision is against your nature. I sensed before I entered George Gull's place that I was about to have one of those rare, gifted and fated meetings."

Strangely, Bluefeather now felt the same way. He had told them he was deliberating about renting a room in Cerrillos or possibly going on up to Santa Fe. They both offered and insisted, with such diligence, that they had a special, unused room for him. Not only that, their home was only two blocks from where they presently sat. He could not bring himself to refuse.

Ordinarily, he would never have accepted such an unheard-of offer but did so now without hesitation, feeling at home with these people and their house before he had ever entered it. Rare, indeed.

Now they had an easy, comfortable visit and talked of many things. Bluefeather told them of his relatives at Taos Pueblo and his Raton family and some of their ways. They each in turn related scattered incidents from their past lives and how they had lost their plantation to robber barons, rapists of good people and purveyors of tax bills so huge they would have been unpayable by the Rothschilds. The proud Godchuck family had been shamed beyond repair. All, except the good doctor and his flexible aunt, had found ways to depart the accursed land, hangings, alcohol, train wrecks, and murderous constipation from eating too much red-eye gravy and shortening bread.

Tulip let out a soulful sigh, reaching out to pat one of Merphyn's hands with tender remembrances, uttering with pity, "Deah, deah, it seems like only this morning that we moved the bed to the center of the room for Merphyn's birth."

Dr. Godchuck explained to Bluefeather that the left side of his body was born in Louisiana and his right side in East Texas. He made a motion with one hand down his middle. Tulip picked up the descriptions where she had left them. "You see, deah Bluefeather, the Louisiana and Texas state lines ran exactly through the center of my deah sister's bedroom. You understand of course, why everything, and I dare say, my deahs, I do mean everything, had to be centered. It did pose a slight difficulty since Merphyn's mother was in full labor, but with the help of several hired hands and a tape measure we managed to deliver deah Merphyn in one piece but in the two states of Texas and Louisiana." Tulip smiled and looked wide-eyed—very wide-eyed—at Bluefeather for approval.

He gave it. "An extraordinary achievement indeed, dear Tulip. Few men have had the great fortune to be related to an aunt who realized the importance of being born in two states at one time. Why, it enlarges one's homeland by several million acres and gives a special stature to the recipient of such a majestic privilege."

While she was shyly thanking him for his appreciation of the special event, he realized he was already beginning to sound like his brand-new friends. He would have to be careful and stop this unintended imitating right now.

He had little time to worry because the man from two states was talking, using his smooth unmarked hands to emphasize. "Everything, everyone, takes many jagged, seemingly random detours in this life, but you can draw a straight line right down the middle of your final existence, from your mother's womb to your last breath, and that will be your life. By the way," the doctor continued, "I believe that a normal life span should be between 135 or even 150 years." He paused a beat, then said, "All a reasonable-thinking person has to do is take a glance at sweet Tulip," and he smiled affectionately at her as she coyly accepted the compliment as her due, then clasped her hands together in front of her upper cleavage and beamed her pleasure at her nephew's words at Bluefeather. She had evidently agreed with her nephew somewhere near one hundred percent.

After about third or fourth thoughts, Bluefeather backed up to what the doctor had said about the "seemingly random detours" and saw much truth in the simple declarative statement. Hadn't his cousin Hog Head changed Bluefeather's direction drastically by slapping the arrogance, vanity and other things out of him with one fateful blow? Hadn't his meeting Old Grinder, by pure accident—or was that fated, too—led to his searching for his own dreams of gold instead of digging those of others? If Grinder had not fallen, killing himself, would he, Bluefeather, have left Taos, or would he have wound up with Nancy, the grand lady of gambling? Would he? If he hadn't killed the man in Tonopah—even though it was in self-defense—would he have gone to Breen where he met Miss Mary, the love of anyone's life? Would he have moved to Corrales and eventually on up to work the placer mines south of Cerrillos? If he hadn't heard about all seven of the Marchiondo sons going into the armed services would he himself have joined up, fought, bled, puked and felt horrors and loves beyond description? Would he?

It must have been the influence of the powerful spiritual number seven. Certainly it had worked for the Marchiondos. New Mexico governor Mabry had invited the parents, Anna and Tony, to spend a day and a night in the governor's mansion. Both the state and American flags had been flown in their honor. The next day Governor Mabry presented the proud parents and entire family the American flag, saying, "In a small attempt to repay and show appreciation for an Italian immigrant family who offered the lives of their seven sons in World War II, I hereby give this symbol of freedom." A true miracle.

Yes, like he, they had all returned, battered but alive and free. The *Life* magazine cover story as well as a pictorial feature in *American Legion* magazine about the immigrant family had made Bluefeather feel good and offer up many prayers of thanks.

But now he continued his cogitation of his own fate and destiny. And without Old Grinder's early company, love and advice, he never would have had the patience to enjoy his present delightful, eccentric companions. Without all the previous events having happened, including the robbery of his last mine, he would not be sitting here with these two wonderfully preposterous people right now. The old-young Dr. Godchuck spoke eternal truths. His life, any life, of seeking and purpose was linked to another, like a tapeworm tied in a bowknot at its ends. And now the voracious worm had fed itself into a growing new link for Bluefeather—the doctor and his aunt. It was all tied together just as the doctor said. Simple.

Tulip poured them each another cup of tea, since the cola and the ginger ale were all gone, saying, "I hope Mr. Barkitch and his son are on time for dinner. My tummy tells me I'm neglecting it woefully."

"Patience, my Tulip," said Merphyn as he took a heavy gold watch from his tweed vest, "it's only an hour yet."

"Oh, that's wonderful, deah. I do hope they come in faith."

Bluefeather's head was clear in spite of the odd company and thoughts surrounding him, but he felt it a miracle on its own that Aunt Tulip could speak with such a southern accent and still not drop many of her *g*'s and *r*'s.

Merphyn pushed, just once, at his vast array of crowning white hair, stroked his perfect moustache, just once, and said, just once, "I'm frightfully delighted, Bluefeather Fellini, that you're going to be there to lend your strong emotional support when I make my sacred presentation of ideas of actuality to John D. Barkitch and his attorney son, Joseph S. Barkitch."

Bluefeather swallowed in embarrassment at this show of faith. "I won't know what to say since I don't know what you're going to present."

"Do not be concerned. I don't need words from you. I have millions of words of my own. All I need is the support of your mind, the force of your will and the presence of your special spirit."

"Well, if that's all, you've got it."

It was the time of silent giving now. All three seemed to hold a quiet moment of support for whatever the upcoming struggle might bring.

Then Bluefeather saw her. He was almost certain the

woman in the helicopter had just driven by in a Cadillac convertible. He leapt up and ran around the table, leaning into the recessed window, anxiously staring down the street. There she was at the gas station getting out of the car. With her was a huge man with a scar completely angling across his face—a deep scar, for he could discern it from where he stood. The scar-faced man exited the other side and stood leaning against the door looking up and down the street without stopping, as if both Chief Joseph and Geronimo had singled him out for attack.

Bluefeather said, "Excuse me, please. I'll be right back."

Before his new companions could answer, Bluefeather dashed to the door and outside, fully intending to accost the woman. However, the fullness of the scene made him stop and look around for the great Indian warriors himself. The attendant, Rocky Ames, pumped the gas, wiped the windshield and then checked under the hood of the sleek blue car.

The woman walked several steps down the street, where she had a dead-on view of the high-desert sunset. The warm, pink-orange afterglow caught her features as she stood raptly absorbing the solemn event, hands on Levi's-clad hips. For just that moment, the sinking sun found one last opening between the spearlike clouds, giving her a burst of illumination that made Bluefeather feel he was intruding on a sacred moment of a goddess. He walked back toward the bar, reached to open the door, then took one last glance at the divine vision. She was looking straight at him with a smile that beggared quick description. He swiftly reentered the Cerrillos Bar feeling as if he had spied upon the birth of Christ.

As he sat back down, Dr. Godchuck spoke in a voice so smooth it would make silkworms go into jealous tantrums. "Bluefeather Fellini, you have just gazed upon

Korbell's only daughter. The man with her is head of his security."

"Korbell? The one we read about doing all this business around the world? That Korbell?"

"That Korbell."

Bluefeather suddenly felt helpless. There had been some unknown bond in the air between them. The link was there between them, even when she was hanging high above him in the helicopter in the Ortiz Mountains, and now again as she enjoyed the late-day explosion of color in tiny Cerrillos. Korbell. Just the name had damaged the invisible binding that stretched between them.

"What is a woman like that doing in Cerrillos?"

Dr. Godchuck answered, "Something, for certain. The Korbells never do nothing."

That made as much sense to Bluefeather as he felt he was going to get.

With the tips of her exquisite fingers, Tulip touched the edges of her brown hair and unconsciously covered her cleavage with the other hand, volunteering, "I visited with Marsha, Marsha Korbell, for a few exhilarating moments. She is a lady of charm, grace and decisiveness. She is also beautiful in a . . . a fresh-air way."

Merphyn reached over and patted her hand, saying softly, "That is generous of you, Aunt Tulip Everhaven, but she is not nearly as alluring as you, my dear."

She gave him a beatific smile, replying, "Oh, deah Merphyn, you do use such honeyed praise. Of course, that's why you have always been my favorite."

Then the Barkitches came. There were only two of them, but the floor seemed to shake and the walls to quiver at their arrival. They both had fattish faces with slitted eyes and widespread nostrils that somehow reminded Bluefeather of a pig's snout—although he would never mean to insult that noble creature. They both wore the same dark gray suits, ties slightly askew. In fact, nothing exactly synchronized here. Their hips were too wide for their shoulders and their hands too small for such large-boned wrists. But they forced smiles with ease as the introductions were completed and they were seated. They were in the heavy construction business—highways, bridges and such. Surprisingly, few people questioned how they seemed to always bid their jobs just a very few dollars under second place.

"Well now," said Barkitch the elder, "how about some drinks? What's this tea service doing in Cerrillos anyway?"

Mattie Gull had come tippy-toeing and twittering up, appearing to float her substantial weight in between her dainty steps. She passed a menu to each and then said, "Care for drinks first?"

The junior Barkitch motioned to Tulip, "Lovely young ladies first." His eyes stayed on her, roaming back and forth from her cupid lips to her milky, soft cleavage. She felt this, and after careful thought ordered a dry red wine. Both contractors desired bourbon on the rocks, and to make it simple, Bluefeather chose a bar Scotch with water and ice. It was understood with the establishment that Dr. Godchuck would order Irish whiskey aloud, but would be served ginger ale and ice.

The drinking was on. Mattie would not let their glasses stay empty long. She would wait just the right amount of time to take their dinner orders.

After silly small talk through two drinks, Dr. Godchuck said, "Gentlemen, I assume you've perused our documents and are ready to talk business."

The elder Barkitch said, "I leave most of that to Joseph. I've got to get something back from all that money I spent on his law school." He laughed at himself, alone.

Joseph became so serious, one would have thought he

had just been notified of the death of the world. He said, "Well . . . well now, the patent on the sage oil is only good for a few more months. We feel there's too little time left . . ."

Dr. Godchuck had spent a lot of the "time" Joseph spoke of with him and his father already. Precious time. "I believe that I explained this clearly at our last meeting, Joseph S. Barkitch. If we set up our processing plant ahead of any competitors we will be so far ahead that . . . certainly you can't deny the gingivitis cures?"

"We must be cautious, Dr. Godchuck. Our finances have come about the hard way. We've had to outperform and outbid all competition. We can't just gamble on any project, no matter how promising."

Tulip gracefully chimed in, "My nephew's invention is not just 'any project,' sir. It can lead to great benefit for all humankind, including yourselves."

"Well yes, we're taking all that into consideration, Miss Everhaven. May I call you Tulip?" Joseph's eyes gleamed rapaciously at the overall softness, smoothness and classiness of Tulip Everhaven. His father, observing his son's obvious weakness for Tulip's delicacy, reentered the fray.

"I tell you what, Dr. Godchuck. Why don't you just run the deal down step by step, and then we'll make our decision after we eat. How's that, huh?" He beamed around at everyone, feeling in control now. He was gratified.

Dr. Merphyn Godchuck did not hesitate a second. "I first heard of the wondrous curative powers at your old home, the pueblo just north of the town of Taos, Bluefeather Fellini. During the terrible flu epidemic of 1918 and 1919, people were dying like the black plague was upon them—over three hundred in the small village of Taos itself. However, a shaman of some grandeur ordered the Taos Pueblo tribe to boil the leaves of the sagebrush and drink it several times daily and inhale its wondrous curative vapors. The death rate was nothing in comparison to the rest of the land. I was already practicing medicine then. It was only a couple of decades back that I could force myself to start my experiments. It's very expensive to have a chemist distill small amounts. That's why, John D. Barkitch, we need the pilot plant now."

"Yes, yes, I understand the urgency of that all right, Doctor."

"Now you've had in your possession records of over four hundred cures of gingivitis, and when taken orally with two other herbal compounds the sage oil relieves ulcers almost instantly. The common cold, if caught early, goes in remission in less than twenty-four hours. I have already quoted you an endless succession of enormously promising cures and other remissions such as . . ."

In spite of Bluefeather's dedicated interest in Dr. Godchuck's elixir, he felt an unknown but powerful force toward the bar. He could not stop himself. He turned his head and eyes and there sat the huge, scarred man and Marsha Korbell. He could swear she was staring at him and had lowered her eyes just as his lined up with hers. But it was so swift, he could not be sure it actually happened. He was pushing his chair back, preparing to go introduce himself, in spite of her gorilla companion. Then they arose and walked out, nodding and speaking unclear words to Big George as they exited into the darkness. In a moment he heard the convertible start and saw the headlights flash on the bar's lone window as they made a U-turn and drove toward Santa Fe.

Bluefeather felt a strange loss at his unnatural inaction. He forced his attention back to the business at the table. Joseph had just said something to Tulip as an excuse to place his hand on her warm, soft arm. He was conjuring how those silken arms could enfold him and crush his back in ecstasy.

"Ten thousand seems a little high for just five percent of such a risky deal," said Barkitch the elder.

"Well, I can't see how we can build the pilot plant for any less, John D. Barkitch. We have to gather the sage leaves first as well. That takes wages for the pickers and, again, time. Time, you see, is all we own. Everything else is on lease or borrowed. Everything. We must not waste the one single thing that the great mystery has deigned to grant us to use as we please. We may waste it joyfully on occasion so we can better use it wisely the rest of our lives. Now is the time for wisdom, for vision, Mr. John D. Barkitch. Now, if ever."

"Well, I dunno. What does that legal mind of yours tell you, Joseph?"

The lawyer removed his arm from patting Tulip on the back and said, "Oh well, I think we need more time . . . a few more meetings." Bluefeather saw Junior's telling glance at Tulip as he said this last and continued, "Why don't we dine now? Is everyone as starved as I am?"

The doctor would have no more waste of his precious gift of time. He said in a voice that eradicated any thought of interference, "Very well, then, John D. Barkitch and Joseph S. Barkitch, I will give you a demonstration of another of the oil's wonders. If this won't convince you, then I withdraw my own offer."

He bent over and took a small bottle of sage oil and a box of kitchen matches out of his unique valise and set them on the table in front of him. Then, methodically, he opened both the matchbox and the bottle of sage oil. He held his smooth, unblemished left hand out flat in front of everyone. With his right, he struck one of the kitchen matches and held the flame under his left middle finger. All were transfixed.

Bluefeather forced his eyes from the burning sacrifice and watched the impassive face of the doctor. However, when he saw the jaw muscles knot up in pain he turned his eyes back to the match. Dr. Godchuck held it until it extinguished itself against the forefinger and thumb of his right hand. Then he turned his left palm up and there on the obviously burned finger was a spot almost swelled to a blister.

He took the bottle and, with the dropper suction cap, applied a tiny drop to the burned spot. Then with the two fingers he had singed while holding the match, he rubbed it into his burnt skin. The oil vanished almost instantly.

"It takes so little because of its unheard-of penetrating power," he said.

Throats were cleared. Glasses of alcohol were emptied and unbelieving eyes stayed on the finger now. The swelling diminished and disappeared. There was only a slight pinkness left to show where the flame had burned.

"Think. Just think of the ramifications for saved suffering, scarring and death all over the world from this one use alone."

The elder contractor laughed dryly, saying, "You are a magician. A real good'un, Doctor. That's some trick you pulled there. You really had me goin' there for a minute."

Tulip sat straight up with the palms of both her hands on the table and said, "Any faker of small skills can be a magician, but only the chosen can make real magic." She stared at them with a look so proud, and hovering anger so dangerous, that the contractors both swallowed three times almost simultaneously. But they could not allow their control to be lost.

However, before they could think of a put-down, Dr. Merphyn Godchuck sat as straight as his aunt. His white, glossy hair seemed to capture power from a source above his head relaying it down through its roots and into all the elements that went to make up the body of the doctor.

"Sirs," he said, "I shall point out one last series of verification for you. The last one. Look at the skin of my hands—smooth, full fleshed, no brown spots. See if you can." As he leaned forward toward them, he said, "Examine my face with care. Can you spot any lines, wrinkles or blotches natural to a man seventy-four years of age?"

They leaned forward to examine him like a jeweler does a diamond. Then they reared back trying to think of the thing to say. Their minds were not that quick.

"I speak to you in truth and faith, Joseph S. Barkitch. Since you are next to Tulip Everhaven, look at the full handsome breasts."

Barkitch did so willingly for the fiftieth time.

"Examine with your own hands the firm skin under her arms."

He did so eagerly as the rest watched enraptured.

"Now, Tulip, turn your face full at Joseph S. Barkitch and let him try to find a wrinkle around those wondrous eyes or the corners of those luscious lips."

Joseph S. looked hard, all right. He looked willingly.

"Ah, ah, ah," said the doctor, "before her startling beauty blinds you, did you find a single fault when you examined her as I instructed?"

"Well . . . well, no, Mr. . . . Doctor. She's a beauty all right, but we've all known that since our first meeting. What does that have to do with our deal?"

"Have to do? Have to do? Why, everything. Have you ever seen a seventy-four-year-old man and a ninety-six-year-old woman, like me and my dear aunt, with such skin? Well, it came from the smallest application of the sage oil mixed in a lanolin base applied lightly twice daily."

"You folks look pretty good all right, but you cannot be

a day over sixty, and you, Mrs. Everhaven, must be an expert with heavy makeup to make it look that smooth. I've seen 'em do it in the movies," said the elder Barkitch.

The younger Barkitch spoke decisively now. "You must be crazy, Godchuck. Plumb raving, wall-butting nuts. This pretty little thing here you call your aunt couldn't be a week past thirty, if that. Now isn't that about right, honey?" he said, grabbing one of her dainty hands.

She spoke softly with a coy glance as she moved her hand so that his missed hers. "Well, I do color my hair a wee bit."

The lawyer said, "Are you people putting us on? The only reason I'd advise Dad to invest in this phony deal is if you went with it, Tulip. What kind of suckers do you take us for, anyhow?"

Bluefeather's nose scar was hotter than the demonstration match the doctor had burned up. He was clenching his jaw so hard he felt the tops of his teeth had been mashed down even with the edge of his gums. The only thing that stopped damage from occurring was Tulip, dear Tulip, opening her purse, casually taking out a little vanity mirror and redoing her lipstick with expertise. She touched the hair that bobbed out so evenly under her 1920s hat, turned a smile on the two enemies that would have charmed a snake that had just swallowed a baby porcupine. She spoke in a syrupy voice, barely above a whisper, "Snakeshit, you bloodsucking soul snatchers. Remove instantly your fat, stinking asses from the exalted presence of my deah nephew and our most esteemed associate Mr. Fellini. You and your kind only meet with 'givers' such as ourselves to steal time and take advantage of those you know to be your mental and moral superiors. It makes you feel almost equal for a moment to toy with the grand thoughts of grand people." And then louder now, yet smooth as catfish skin, as deadly sharp as a cottonmouth's fangs, she finished, "Away assholes! Away!"

They had scooted their chairs back from the table and had risen, no doubt, to say crude and insulting things, but on observing Bluefeather standing, feet spread to leap, his finger to his lips motioning, "shhh, shhh," and the honorable doctor poised with his pointed cane like a swordsman, they were caused to knock both their chairs over, and three others as well, as they hurried from the premises talking to themselves in unknown tongues.

In a voice without rancor, but of solid certainty, Dr. Merphyn Godchuck said, "Taking into consideration our few geniuses and near geniuses along with our uncountable idiots, I cannot visualize the collective intellect of the entire human race being sufficient or deserving of its permanent survival."

Bluefeather and Tulip Everhaven thought and nodded in agreement.

As they sat back down, in order to hasten the forgetting of the Barkitches, Bluefeather said, "I've been meaning to ask you about that distinctive cane, Doctor."

The doctor handed it to him saying, "It is a bull's prick cane. Here, take it and examine it carefully. You'll see where my friend, Luz Martinez, the great wood-carver of Taos, made the handle from walnut."

Bluefeather was amazed at how it had been carved, waxed and fitted so one could hardly tell where the bull started and the tree parted. "Excellent work here, Doctor. A prize cane for sure. I've never seen one before. I'm honored."

"I'm pleased you like it. If we can manage the time maybe I could get you one made. After the penis is removed from the bull—at a slaughterhouse, of course—it must be dried properly in the sun. It takes quite a spell for proper curing. Then, of course, Mr. Martinez is a perfectionist, and he uses up several days and nights for his part of the construction."

"Well, I won't mind waiting."

"Let us, as gentlemen, consider the deal done then."

"Agreed."

Tulip said, with near happiness, "I'm so terribly delighted that we made some kind of deal tonight. Would it be unreasonable to suggest we order our dinner now before it's too late? And if you would join me, Blue . . . may I call you Blue?"

"You already have. Please continue to do so, Ma'am."

"Thank you. I was going to suggest that you and I share a carafe of dry red wine. It's too early for my deah, deah, nephew to have his allowable two bedtime bourbons."

Dr. Godchuck said, "Please, let us proceed."

They did with unabashed joy.

THIRTY-FIVE

IT HAD NOT TAKEN THEM LONG TO RETIRE FROM THE CERRILLOS
Bar to the Godchuck home as Bluefeather drove his jeep
up and moved in. It was a comfortable six-room adobe
house decorated with a strange combination of Navajo
and Persian rugs. There were prints and paintings of, and
by, southwestern artists as well as English fox-hunting
prints.

While the doctor poured one of his two bedtime bourbons and settled among the colorful pillows on a colorless
old couch to enjoy it, Tulip swiftly poured Bluefeather
and herself a glass of dry red wine—make unknown,
since there was no label on the half-gallon jug.

Bluefeather followed Tulip, paying the usual respects
to each room. She saved the doctor's office for last. His
degree from Columbia and a few photographs were displayed. In one of the doctor's graduation photos, Tulip
pointed out so many attending family members that
Bluefeather lost track, but he did discover Tulip looking
almost exactly the same age as she did now. He was again
startled, although only a moment ago he was still accepting her as the world's youngest ninety-six-year-old.

At his voiceless consternation, she, without looking directly at him, said, "It was only a few years after this photograph that I became Merphyn's guinea pig. He's made oh so many experiments on me. I've enjoyed and survived them all quite well, don't you think, Blue?"

"Oh my, yes, you most certainly have."

They glanced at one another with mutual respect and, of course, Tulip added to her wide-eyed glance of innocent expectation one more little dash of spice—flirtation. There was an old examining table and other medical artifacts that Tulip proudly pointed out, adding, "Of course, deah, you can appreciate the lack of patients in such a small and healthy place as Cerrillos, but deah Merphyn has a respectful clientele who occasionally drive down from Santa Fe or up from Albuquerque. You see, it's enough to care for our necessities, but not sufficient to progress onward to the pilot plant. It takes so very long for an individual to obtain a medical patent. I'm sure you, being an engineer and all, understand this better than I do."

"Well . . . I . . ."

"That's why Merphyn chose the gingivitis patent first. It was the easiest to prove and therefore the fastest to get registered, but there are so many far more important cures we've proven to ourselves that must have patent proceedings finished and others begun. That is, in order to benefit the world. Don't you see, Blue? You do realize the urgency is to get a sufficient supply of sage oil on hand from the pilot plant in order for Merphyn to prove his findings once and for all?"

He was trying to think how to properly answer her when she said with a powerful longing that was also somehow a pleading, "Don't you see, deah Blue?"

"Yes, Tulip, I believe I do better than most."

He realized she had been pitching a perfect con at him, but he felt it was sincerely unintentional. The few belongings he had with him certainly made him look like he was unemployed, and there was no way she could know about the seventy-eight hundred dollars in new hundred-dollar bills in his billfold. No, it was simply her love and belief in her nephew's work and vision that gave such a passionate chime to her velvety voice.

They rejoined the doctor. She was her demure self again. It seemed she either chattered in long discourses, made short pungent observations or remained smilingly, enigmatically silent, seeming to absorb every sound and sight around her with acute awareness. Bluefeather thought this Tulip woman was so full of life there was enough to slosh over and spill on those in need of the elixir.

The doctor had put on a soft smoking jacket and was comfortably enjoying his allowable second Kentucky bourbon.

"I see Tulip has bored you with our humble abode, Bluefeather Fellini."

"No, Doctor, quite the opposite. I thoroughly enjoyed the all-too-brief tour," Bluefeather said as he sat on a couch opposite the doctor.

Tulip refilled their glasses and joined him on the couch making a slight gesture of pulling the short dress over her knees. It was only a movement of habit, but the little movement served to draw the eye to the graceful, even sensuous, legs protruding thereunder.

Bluefeather made the first toast, looking past the burgundy-colored liquid at Tulip's oversized brown eyes, then to Merphyn's dark ones. In the soft lighting of the room his eyes appeared as black as the center of a cannonball and just as penetrating.

"Here's to a night of new friendships. May it be one to remember as warmly as its actuality."

"Well done, Bluefeather Fellini. May those precious thoughts increase a thousandfold for you as they are certain to do so for us."

Tulip simply whispered, "Agreed."

And they all took a sip in perfect unison as if they had trained a hundred years to do so. The three were attuned in soul and possibly deed. Bluefeather suddenly felt that he had done enough talking in the presence of such exemplary company. He would speak a few more words and then go into action, rightly or wrongly. It was his true nature.

"I beg your forgiveness in advance," he said, "but could I have a match and the bottle of oil for a moment?"

The doctor surprised him by saying almost eagerly, "Of course you may."

Tulip volunteered her services and obtained them for Bluefeather. She placed both on a hand-carved coffee table in front of him. He carefully took the lid from the little bottle of light golden-colored liquid, opened the matchbox and removed one. Then he held his left hand out, palm down, just as Dr. Godchuck had done. He struck the kitchen match on the box and placed the resultant flame under his middle finger. The first second he didn't sense the burning, but then the pain came. He could feel his eyelids wanting to close in agony, and his lips screamed silently to curl away from his teeth and pull tight to the sides. He controlled this somehow, although the effort made his breath feel like it would explode his chest into the four eyes of the anxious observers. His only flinching was the uncontrollable clenching of his jaw muscles, just as Dr. Godchuck had done before. It was beyond the comprehension of a snail how long the match burned. Again, just as Dr. Godchuck had, when the flame neared the end of his fingers, he tipped it so the flare would continue until it singed itself out on the tips of his right thumb and forefinger. All three were holding their breaths, eyes transfixed on the tiny diminishing blaze as if watching a tornado disappear in the distance. Then it flickered out. All breathed in unison again.

Bluefeather tipped only a tiny bit of oil onto the fingers that had held the match and began to rub the swelled spot on his testing finger before it could break into a blister. For the hundredth time this night, he was pleasantly surprised. The pain was reduced with almost the same speed as the swiftly penetrating oil disappeared through the skin pores to begin its soothing healing. In a few minutes the main swelling was gone, and there remained only a pinkish residue of injury and a slight combination of both warm and cool feeling.

Now at last, he raised his eyes to the expectant ones staring at him, awaiting his decision with both confidence and a slight, understandable uncertainty.

Bluefeather said, "Dr. Godchuck, you and your aunt are among the rare chosen. Your formula works beyond words. Congratulations."

They were all so suddenly overjoyed at the wonder of mutual understanding and respect that they silently drained their respective glasses.

Dr. Godchuck arose with a new agility and went to pour a third forbidden drink, saying, "One must become a fool occasionally to appreciate rare moments such as this."

As soon as the doctor was seated, Bluefeather took out his thick wallet and swiftly counted out six thousand dollars on the coffee table. "Please honor me by accepting my minor partnership for this pitiful amount. I shall do better as we move forward."

"Ah, ah, ah," said the doctor. "Blessings be tendered to

us all. Tomorrow we shall move into La Fonda de Santa Fe. That's where the funding for our pilot plant shall be acquired."

Tulip clasped her hands over her cleavage and beamed. "I deahly love that hotel lobby."

THIRTY-SIX

BLUEFEATHER SAT AT A FAMILIAR TABLE IN THE LA FONDA
dining room awaiting the arrival of his two compatriots
for brunch. It had been over three weeks since they had
loaded his jeep and the Roadmaster Buick belonging to
the Godchucks and settled into the hotel. The load, in
volume, had consisted mainly of the doctor's many varia-
tions of tweed and her mostly flapper-era wardrobe. Besides the necessities, Tulip had insisted on taking
Merphyn's framed diplomas, awards and her favorite picture of their family, whose members were now scattered
somewhere amidst demons or angels. Bluefeather's wardrobe was easy to handle, consisting of one blue-gray suit,
several pairs of Levi's, a dozen or so white shirts as well as
some plaid Pendleton ones. He had two pairs of prospecting boots, two pairs of shoes and one pair of rubber
galoshes that could be worn over either. Today he wore
pressed Levi's and a white shirt.

The doctor had acquired a two-bedroom suite for him
and Tulip. Bluefeather's room was directly across the
hallway from Tulip's door. The suite's living room area
was furnished with heavy, territorial-style furniture, a
mirror with a hand-worked tin frame, a short bar, and it

had a view across adobe house rooftops to the Sangre de
Cristo foothills. Tulip kept the multiple-use area dotted
with a few green plants, chocolates, snack chips and nuts
of various kinds. These items were not only for their pleasure, but for the occasional interviewee who would be
subjected to the mildest of suggestions that it would be
wise to invest in the development of the oil of sage and its
vast restorative qualities.

The doctor acted as adviser and Bluefeather as front
man for their presentations. Bluefeather soon learned
that other medical men were skeptical and often ridicul-
ing. This was confusing to the young entrepreneur, because Old Grinder had told him that doctors and dentists
were the most inclined to take gambles. This group actually seemed afraid of Dr. Godchuck. It was a while before
he realized most of them were possibly jealous of
Merphyn's courage and felt insufficient around a man of
medicine who was, and always had been, more than willing to give up the private clubs, the golf, the tennis, the
many comforts of mercilessly combining the gods of
medicine and money. It was a fear of an unknown terri-
tory that they would never dare to tread upon.

He had raised five hundred dollars from a truck driver,
a thousand from an insurance salesman and fifteen hundred from a sheep rancher. The profit was not as much as
he would have liked because it had taken many steaks,
cocktails and wearing conversations to arrive at these
small contributions.

Dr. Godchuck had told Bluefeather to avoid the elderly, or the second-generation rich and the wealthy from
inheritance, as they would mostly just take up his time
and use up his soul for their own entertainment, then
pass, saying, "My accountants have turned the deal
down," or "I have an enormous tax burden coming due."
One woman of this kind had surprised him by speaking

straight and saying she understood real estate but had no knowledge of the sagebrush that sometimes covers it.

At his admitted failure with this play-it-safe-at-all-costs group, the good and great doctor said, "If you insist on wasting time in the effort of acquiring inherited money, get a group of them together. They don't mind gambling a little if they all do it together. That way if the deal turns sour, they can all laugh in chorus. No one person is singled out as the fool. You do understand what I'm telling you, don't you, Bluefeather Fellini?"

As yet, Bluefeather had been unable to get more than two of these types of people together at one time. However, today he had meetings with several prospects: a Ford car dealer, the manager of a grocery store and an admitted cow thief. There was one order that Dr. Godchuck had handed to him with much sincerity. He was told that the lovely woman of the helicopter and the Cerrillos Bar was also staying at La Fonda. The woman of shocking beauty and forceful feline movement, the adopted daughter of a real, self-made, world-class power, Marsha Korbell must be approached for bigger things.

"Now, listen carefully, Bluefeather Fellini," the doctor said, "Korbell is the kind of man we want to join us after we have properly used our pilot plant. We must not waste a man of his caliber on small stuff. He would not be interested. We must tap into his funding through his daughter for all the hay in the fields—for the factory, the worldwide distribution and the advertising."

Bluefeather replied, "Then I should wait to approach her until we have succeeded with the pilot plant?"

"Ah, ah, ah. No, oh, no. Make the run when it feels right. We must get started with Korbell, for he will check us out right down to the exact count of the pores in the skin of our big toes."

Bluefeather said, "That will take some time."

Now as he sat in almost, but not quite, half-vision, the woman of his thoughts was standing, talking to a couple of men in the dining room entrance. She shook hands with each as they turned to leave. She was then guided by the Spanish hostess to the table next to Bluefeather. He looked around instantly for her entourage of guards, or whatever they were, but could recognize none. It was the right place, at the right time, as the song went. He waited impatiently, surprisingly nervous, for her to get her order in. He did not know how, but knew he had to make a move.

"Excuse my rudeness, please, but aren't you Marsha Korbell?"

She placed the coffee cup back on the table, turned her head full at him and smiled inquisitively, nodding "yes."

"My name is Bluefeather Fellini. Would it be too much of an imposition if I joined you for just a moment? There's a question I'd like to ask you."

She hesitated, then making up her mind motioned toward a chair opposite her and said, "Please do," in a tone that removed his doubt, calmed his nerves and caused him to trip over his own chair in eagerness as he followed the route of her casually directed hand to the seat at "the table" with "the woman."

"Thank you. Thank you very much," he said.

"Have you ordered yet?" she asked.

"No. Actually I'm waiting for Dr. Godchuck and his aunt to join me."

"You mean Tulip Everhaven? I've visited with her casually, of course. She is a charmer."

"That she is. Please don't think me impertinent, but recently I think I saw you fly right by me on a hill in the Ortiz Mountains."

"Fly? How do you mean?"

He could not help but choke back a laugh. "Oh, you were in a helicopter, and the pilot held position while you looked right at me."

She calmly took another sip of coffee as the waitress waited to fill her cup, saying, "Oh, it's possible. I fly all over the state checking out state land for oil or other mineral possibilities."

He was a little let down at her appearing not to remember him. He sure as hell remembered her and how he had felt the invisible rope that tied them together. She obviously had not recognized him or the connection.

He was uplifted some, however, when she unexpectedly shared her current work with him. "As I'm sure you're aware . . . you are in minerals, aren't you?"

"Yes. I have been."

"Well, as I started to explain, I'm sure you know that New Mexico holds monthly auctions of mineral rights on state land."

"Yeah. Sure."

"Well, that's what I do. That's why I'm here. We're looking to bid on oil possibilities only."

At that moment Bluefeather regretted deeply that he had not majored in oil geology instead of mining at the Institute of Mining in Socorro, and oh, how he wished he had finished. Here was the opening everyone would dream of charging. Well, he had not majored in oil geology and he had not earned his degree. He would just have to get his mind back to Dr. Godchuck's project where he was obligated, and forget stupid, wasteful regrets with a vital vengeance.

"Folks say you're Mr. Korbell's troubleshooter."

"They do? Well, what a compliment. I've never felt qualified for such a title, but will accept it as great flattery."

"Oh, I'm sure you measure up, all right."

For some reason they both laughed as she said without any vanity showing, "My measurements have sometimes led to embarrassing situations, mostly to the measurer."

Bluefeather reserved any more comment. She had somehow made him just as comfortable as he had been hesitant earlier. He no longer doubted that he could bring up the oil of sage without being ridiculed or insulted, so he decided to be just as open as she was and see what happened.

"I was curious about seeing your lovely eyes out in space in front of me and my mules on the little peak, and I also noticed you looking at the sunset in the streets of Cerrillos and later in the Cerrillos Bar having a drink. I have also pleasantly observed your movements in and out of La Fonda and a couple of times here in Santa Fe while you were shopping, but right now I have a serious business venture I would like for you to take a look at. It, too, is oil. But a different kind."

Well, there it was, he had made a speech. A goddamn speech. However, it was all truly felt. He waited.

She looked at him straight on and said, "Shoot."

He did not remember the words as they poured out, because of the intensity of his feelings about Dr. Godchuck and his work. She interrupted now and then with sensible questions about the quantity needed, overall plans and other things so rational that she made the pitch easy for him.

Just as he asked her if she would present the larger view to her father, if he could prove to her beyond any doubt at least one of the oil's possibilities, they were approached by the doctor and Tulip.

Bluefeather and Marsha both stood up as Marsha said, "It's so nice to see you again, Tulip. You look wonderful."

Since the citizens of Santa Fe had always dressed in any manner they chose without undue alarm, Tulip's short red dress and wide-brimmed red hat could legitimately be called charming, Bluefeather supposed. That was the word almost everyone seemed to feel suited the ninety-six-year-old flapper.

"Why, thank you, deah. And this is my nephew Dr. Godchuck."

"So good to meet you at last, Doctor. Tulip and Mr. Fellini have both spoken so highly of you."

"I am as pleased to meet you, Marsha Korbell, as I am to hear about the kind words of my associates."

Marsha insisted they join them at the table. Through bits of conversation, all managed to order again. Surprisingly, eggs Benedict was the mutual choice. Dr. Godchuck insisted that their Saturday brunch be accompanied by a bottle of chilled champagne. It was agreed.

The food was better than usual, the champagne was better than ever and the conversation was somehow lost in the enjoyment of it all.

Bluefeather's keen hunter's eyes were now in their proper mode of observation. There was nothing false he could find in the warm welcome Marsha was attending them. Her charm and beauty matched those of Tulip. He felt that invisible cord pulling at his chest and other portions of his anatomy in a sultry touch that infused his entire body, his heart and his highly pleased mind in a glow of beginning fondness.

After the successful meal, Marsha surprised them all by ordering another bottle of champagne.

Tulip said, with the usual hiding of her cleavage with her clasped hands, "Oh, deah Marsha, what a delightful suggestion."

They had fun. Tulip hesitated to take the last glass, saying as she did so anyway, "Oh my, my, I'm afraid I'll be dancing on tables."

The doctor smiled, touched his flowing white hair as if

to assure himself it was still there and said, "Please do, my dear. Remember the last time you enjoyed that particular procedure?"

"Why yes. Yes, I do, Merphyn. It was right after Schoozie Felts's funeral, wasn't it?" She looked apologetically at Marsha, continuing, "Please forgive Merphyn and myself, deah, for talking about an event neither you nor Blue attended. You see . . ." then she turned with great seriousness to the doctor, "Schoozie Felts was my third husband, wasn't he, Merphyn, or was he number five?"

"Felts was sixth."

"Oh, oh," she was thinking, counting mentally, "but of course, he was. My precious, redheaded number six. Oh, that Schoozie was a dandy dancer, I can tell you. Smooth as glass he was for certain. That's how he died—just started on a dancing drunk in Baton Rogue, danced right on through Mardi Gras at New Orleans like that's all there was or ever would be. Schoozie died shuffling both feet, holding one hand around my waist and snapping his fingers with the other." Tulip raised a hand, snapping her own smooth fingers, and then pointed at the floor. "Poof. Just like that. He was on the floor dead as a seventy-year-old dream. Now, deah Marsha, isn't a beautiful death like that something to dance on the table about?"

"I can think of many reasons and excuses for such celebratory activity, Tulip, but none better than you've just described."

Now they all laughed in joyous vision.

In spite of the easy fun they were having, Bluefeather caught the doctor's signal as he changed positions with his cane and gave Bluefeather a look so swift a barnyard cat would have missed it. However, before he could start his deal-closing remarks Marsha said, "That's a remarkable-looking cane, Dr. Godchuck. What kind of . . . what is it made of?"

Tulip saved the doctor from having to explain his favorite accoutrement. She was good at it. She spoke now very softly, as she often did. "The cane is made from a bull's prick. A Jersey bull. They have the biggest ones, you see. They're also the most dangerous."

Even in the jaded, ancient city, nearby heads turned, chairs grated and half-suppressed giggles ensued. Tulip was oblivious to these onlookers and Marsha didn't seem to care either.

Without hesitation or frustration Marsha replied, "Perhaps the danger and the size go together," and she looked at Bluefeather with one of those "almost" smiles of hers. He felt naked as a porcupine with no quills.

Tulip belatedly said, "Why, of course, my deah, they do both go together."

Bluefeather and the doctor realized they were about to lose possible great gains to a happy time of camaraderie. Bluefeather took the situation over, saying, "Marsha, while we're feeling good, I'd like to demonstrate something of vast importance." He asked the doctor for the objects from his always present wide-bottomed case. The doctor was surprised and pleased that Bluefeather would suffer this act himself for their cause.

As he moved painfully through the match, burned skin and oil trick, Marsha watched with unblinking, unmoving eyes. When the flame was out, she took his hand, examined it with extreme care, then closed the fingers, holding on a moment more in silence before saying, "Draw up a proposal and I'll present it to Korbell." Suddenly she was all business. She got up saying, "It has been a pleasure dining and visiting with you. I have a meeting in fifteen minutes. Enjoy."

They all muttered nice things to the delicious, decorative force moving so enticingly away from them.

Bluefeather held his hand, not feeling the burn, but still feeling the touch of her hand.

Twice now in just three weeks, Dr. Merphyn Godchuck had broken his rule of drinking alcohol even though he had only had two glasses of champagne. Nonetheless, he was in high spirits.

"I'm not one for complimenting in advance, but you gave our project a big boost today, Bluefeather Fellini. Your presentation to the extremely intelligent Marsha Korbell was first-rate."

"Thank you, Doctor, but it was simply spontaneous. I won't be doing the finger-burning part again."

"I understand. One can only crowd luck so far. An overburn would take two or three days to heal and the observer wouldn't be around to see it."

"Precisely."

"Then I have my notes to work on while you two celebrate the victory, minor though it might appear." The doctor took his cane and custom case and prepared to exit the dining room.

"Why, thank you mightily, my deah," Tulip said. "I'll share a carafe of wine with Blue . . . if he'd be so generous with his time."

"Granted," said Bluefeather. "As long as you wish." Then added, "Tulip, why don't we remove our bodies and place them in the bar for convenience' sake."

She happily agreed. So they did just that. They ordered the wine and looked at one another in satisfaction for a chore well tended.

"You are quite taken with her, aren't you, Blue?"

He was surprised at her unfamiliar familiarity. He stuttered, "Well . . . I . . . she . . . seems like a very intelligent woman . . . and she . . ."

"She is lovely, too, huh, all the way up and down?"

"Sure, but . . ."

"I'll not meddle anymore, Blue. Merphyn doesn't like me doing this, but Marsha is a thoroughbred, a strikingly beautiful thoroughbred, and she's rich, just terribly rich, my deah Blue. Don't ever sell that rarest of combinations short." At his growing discomfiture from her so very true observations, she changed the subject and continued, "We must forgive Merphyn's single-mindedness for now. He's so terribly, terribly torn about which curative source of the oil to pursue next. You know, several skin cancers he treated disappeared in less than ten days. Of course, he's been experimenting with different mixtures of herbs and other chemicals with the sage oil for years now. He feels it is equal—with proper development—to the perfecting of penicillin. Possibly greater."

"You don't have to sell me, Tulip. I'm one of the team, remember?"

"Oh, deah me, I'm rattling on like an idiot. Forgive me, will you, Blue? It's just that we've given ourselves to the concept for so many decades."

"It's okay. Hellfire, I've had obsessions too, and I made them work . . . but then . . ."

A small Mexican band was set up now. They could play, and did with expertise, popular music as well as Latino. Bluefeather and Tulip listened without speaking for several minutes. Tulip was inwardly glancing back at moving people and objects from her long past. Bluefeather was thinking some of his two new associates, but mostly of Marsha Korbell. He still imagined he felt the touch of her hand on his. He knew he was being childish at the tingling that rippled through his body at the thought of her, but he didn't care. Yes, he was af- flicted with an almost embarrassing puppy love, and it showed. Tulip had not put it in exact words, but they both were aware that she knew. Of course, he'd had considerable experience in this area, but nothing to compare with her eight husbands, and even the great mystery in the sky might have difficulty keeping track of her flirtations.

They were both surprised when the group started playing "Begin the Beguine." Bluefeather moved, taking Tulip's soft hand, then her soft body in his arms. They danced—or rather they flowed. They were in such unison that they moved as smoothly as water over glass. She felt he was Bluefeather at the beginning, then Herman Slats, her first husband, during the rest of the dance. Bluefeather would have been amazed at her suppleness if she had been only nineteen, but for ninety-six, she was one of the world's great wonders. Someday, when he needed it, he must remember to ask her for the exact formula of the sage oil she had been taking for over forty years.

He soon forgot about all that, and he too imagined she was Nancy of Tonopah and Miss Mary of Breen. Then she metamorphosed into Marsha Korbell and seemed to stay that way through a dozen dances and another carafe of wine. Their intermittent but almost continuous dancing caused them both to perspire slightly, thereby creating a reason the two bodies were sticking closer and closer together as they danced. Her breasts against his chest, her thighs pressuring against his and all the movement in between caused their breaths to increase in volume.

Just when Bluefeather felt he was dancing alone outside a tropical cabin under a damp tropical moon with Marsha Korbell, Tulip said softly in his ear, "Come with me now. Let us have one flirtation. Just one, deah, to do me the rest of my life."

As she led him to the elevator, Bluefeather's half-vision was still in the tropics with Marsha, and they were going hand in hand to the cabin covered with bush-green jungle growth. The adrenaline-jumping acceptance of their project by Marsha, the champagne, the wine, the whirling dances, holding the sensuous transcendental body of Tulip Everhaven against his own and his orgiastic imagining of Marsha Korbell had left him weak and susceptible.

He followed her to her room. They entered from the hallway door. He followed her to her bed where they both disrobed and eased into one another's arms and he into her in a warm soft glow of hard and tender flesh. They were both easily and subconsciously in earthly heaven for this moment.

Then the action from the ageless Tulip "Began the Beguine." During these blissful moments, the strongly built territorial-style bed held together in spite of a ninety-six-year-old who would have severely tested the talents of a world champion bareback bronc rider. Bluefeather was to be commended for his skill, strength and courage. But all the lastly named attributes began to shatter as Tulip Everhaven screamed like a badly wounded elephant or several chimpanzees fighting over a banana. She made other rug-curling cries that were so loud they could be compared to nothing less than a pen full of male dogs with an equal number of females in heat at the same time. His ecstasy was stentorian. Bluefeather was simply hanging on now in great fear as her cries became verbal, and he was certain she was awakening everyone in the hotel and maybe even other nearby hotels.

"Skin! Skin! I haven't felt skin for sixteen years," she shouted to the world. "Oh, Herman, sweet Herman, I love you, Herman! Herman! Ohhh, Herm . . ."

And then she was so still and silent, Bluefeather was sure her uncontrollable desire had killed her heart dead. He hurriedly jerked on his pants, clutched at his unbuttoned shirt, grabbed his untied shoes and was in the process of fearfully taking Tulip's pulse when he heard the knocking on the door and concerned voice of Dr. Godchuck.

"Aunt Tulip? Are you all right, dear? Answer me, please. Tulip, do you hear me, dear? Now, listen here, no more of this . . ." There was a frantic twisting of the locked doorknob.

Bluefeather was startled as the lovely sweating body bolted to a sitting position in the bed, pushing at her hair trying impossibly to pat it into neatness, saying, "Everything is fine, deah Merphyn. I was just having a dream. A beautiful dream of Herman Slats, my first husband. We were in the first throes of our honeymoon night. Ah, Merphyn, what a beautiful dream it was, deah. It seemed as real as roast beef. Do you hear me, Merphyn?"

Bluefeather exited swiftly, guiltily, into the hallway before he could hear the doctor's answer. The closing of the heavy door sounded like the clanging of a prison door on a man condemned to death row. He leapt across the hall to his own room, but before he could enter, the house detective and the night manager descended upon him. Three other doors were now open with people who had been shocked awake, staring down the hall wondering if a vile and bloody murder had taken place.

Bluefeather kept one hand on the doorknob and raised the other outstretched palm to stop the two unsettled men. He took the initiative, which was his nature to do.

"Whoa, there. Stop right there. The lady has had a bad dream about the demise of one . . . of her late husband. As you know, her nephew is an eminent physician. He's giving her proper care at this very moment."

"But . . ." said the house detective.

"What? How do you know?" asked the night manager.

"Listen. Let me warn you that any uncalled-for or unnecessary disturbance at this critical time could open this establishment—and you as individuals—up to a very large lawsuit."

"Well . . ."

"I don't know . . ."

"You can hear the silence now. Don't jeopardize it and yourselves. Get back to work while all is quiet and you're still safe."

They stood, mouths slightly open, in massive puzzlement. Bluefeather turned loose the doorknob momentarily and took a step toward them, pointing a decisive arm back down the hallway, silently saying, "Go."

That was the decision maker. They both halfheartedly slunk away, mumbling under their breaths to one another but prudently in very low voices.

Tulip stayed in bed for three days. She was not ill, rather she was festive. She simply liked her bed more than anything else.

THIRTY-SEVEN

While Tulip was in bed reliving her extreme ecstasy or letting her vocal cords heal, or both, and while the doctor worked on his formula notes, Bluefeather staked out the lobby for Marsha. She didn't show. So after reading the *Santa Fe New Mexican,* the *Taos News* and both the *Albuquerque Journal* and *Tribune,* he wrote her a note: "Marsha Korbell. Stop your march to glory in time for dinner at El Nido. Seven o'clock tonight. Good time guaranteed. Blue."

El Nido was a fine restaurant a few miles north of Santa Fe. It was owned by a French couple who, oddly enough, specialized in popular American food such as steaks. Of course, they also had a few French specialties disguised as purely American.

Bluefeather walked out of the hotel and started around the plaza. He stopped as he passed under the old portal of the first governor's place, to study the jewelry, rugs and pottery that the various Indian tribes had displayed on blankets on the brick sidewalk. He went down Palace Street to the New Mexico Museum of Art. He found a special exhibit of the Taos masters there. He got a feeling of great nostalgia when he looked at a painting done high in the aspens of Twining Canyon, featuring two of his uncles and their horses. He felt he was talking to them as if they were still alive. Well, they were on this canvas by Joseph Sharp for immeasurable time. He was proud.

He moved on through the painted landscapes, adobe houses and mystical mountains painted by the sun, the moon and the clouds of an invisible brush wide as a county. He had walked on these mountains. There was a Blumenschein mountain that climbed up in cubist tiers that was his favorite at this show. He wondered why the Taos artists were always stuck with the title of "realists" when so many of their works were so highly impressionistic. These "tags" must have been invented by people who had seen only a few of their paintings. He decided that en masse they would fit any designation and average out with the greatest of schools. The Joseph Sharp painting of Twining Canyon brought back a tearing image of Old Grinder as well as a warm missing of his elderly kin. But the Berninghaus with one rider high up Taos Canyon imaged his mind's eye with young Lorrie Friedman for a moment. He didn't know why he was momentarily sad. They had enjoyed only the finest times of flesh and photography up this particular canyon. He brought himself out of the nostalgic musing by reminding himself that not all was from the past. He presently knew and liked many Berninghaus descendants, the Brandenburgs, and on and on.

He ended his tour feeling fortunate to have been a tiny part of that area and era hanging there on the museum walls, and went across the street to the Palace Restaurant and Bar. He was relieved that nobody approached him while he finished off his green chile omelette. He was thinking deeply about the doctor's vision and the great possibilities to help lessen the many perpetual pains of the human race, but no matter how he struggled to keep his mind there, it kept disjointing and flashing on the woman of the auburn crest and the cerulean eyes—Marsha Korbell.

He finished his meal long after most of the business-men had returned to their offices and the politicians had retired to other negotiations. He had three coffee refills then decided to go back to the museum.

He passed by the Taos paintings and wandered slowly through the other rooms, absorbing the land he worshiped from the palettes of others—many who were not born upon it as he was, but who had parts of their souls imbedded in that same earth and repeated in oils, water-colors, ink and many other mediums for everyone to see and enjoy in the head and heart. How lucky he was to be able to sponge up these wonders both in the vast lands and on these canvases that were just as widespreading—if one knew how to look. Here in the whispering silence of the museum, he was both sad and happy to know that these works of art would show how it once had been in spite of the scarring of the land that was sure to come.

It was closing time at the museum. He was pleasantly shocked at how long and involved his visit had been. When he got back to La Fonda, he went straight to the desk. Marsha had taken his note and left one for him. His heart beat like first love as he unfolded it. Her note said: "Well, Bluefeather, I must fly to Lea County for consulta-tions with geologists. The bids come up next week. Our timing is off today, but some mañana? Dinner at El Nido soon. Marsha."

He felt like he was walking on the breath of friendly dinosaurs as he skipped the elevator and bounded up the two flights of stairs and knocked on Dr. Godchuck's suite. The doctor was glad to see him but was preoccupied at the same time, ordering room service for just the two of them, saying, "Tulip has been eating in bed all day."

Then they turned to business, took a few moments to add up their finances and realized there was just not enough to gather the large amount of sagebrush leaves, build the pilot plant and at the same time keep their fund-raising going. They had been selling a quarter-percent share per thousand-dollar investment, but they had not raised enough to realize a surplus. They were not acquiring the needed extra funds, but were giving up parts of the whole rapidly.

Bluefeather volunteered to approach Marsha with the problem upon her return, but Dr. Godchuck nixed that instantly. "No, my dear Bluefeather Fellini, we must risk it all. Even if Marsha Korbell could persuade her father to invest the funds for the pilot plant we would have used up our one source for the big 'run.' We must not risk him while we are risking everything else. He just won't be interested at this stage. I have known these big club-wielding types all my life."

"He might do it as a favor to his daughter."

"No, she would know better than to pressure him at this time, unless I've vastly underestimated her."

Bluefeather put up no more argument. The dinner was served and, shortly thereafter, the two men were friendly and comfortable enough to sit in silence. Bluefeather suddenly made his mind up. He would go to Corrales and get his next to last bag of gold. According to the figures they had just perused that should be enough, with what they had on hand, to gather the sage, build the pilot plant (really a large whiskeylike still) and process enough of the oil to continue proving up the patents pending. He'd do it!

"Dr. Godchuck, why do you insist the sagebrush be gathered at Taos?"

"Ah, ah, ah, well, your own ancestors proved it worked on respiratory ailments long ago. We must not risk lower-altitude sagebrush until I've got all my formulas and my herbal mixture correct for the Taos sage. Then . . . then we can start experimenting with the sage at other altitudes."

There was no way Bluefeather understood the exact differences these altitudes would make, but Taos it would be.

The next day he drove his jeep to Corrales, visited briefly with the Luceros and his mules, then moved on with decisiveness. He pulled up the floor in a crowded closet and looked at his stash. The three gold rocks he would "never let go of"—or so he thought—and the two leather bags of small nuggets and dust were all that were left. He took out the largest one, leaving a single small one behind, and headed for his dentist friend to cash it in. He was on fire with true purpose now and puckered up tight to win.

THIRTY-EIGHT

BLUEFEATHER WAS NOT READY TO RETURN TO TAOS UNDER THE present conditions. It was possible to be laughed out of the state by the majority of Spanish Americans for picking sagebrush. Once, they had probably known of some of its medicinal qualities, but for now he would have to somehow come up with another reason for its procurement. Long, long ago, the old Spanish dons, who were mostly sheep barons, had overgrazed the grasslands so that the sagebrush took over. The result was a lot fewer sheep and a lot more artists around Taos. Just the same, it was not like harvesting corn or picking cotton around here. The gringos would join in the laughter as well, maybe with even more hilarity than anyone else because they would understand it less. Even though some great medicine man had used it so effectively back during the massively murderous flu epidemic, Bluefeather was somehow afraid to tell his true duty here to even his closest kin. Of course, his uncle Stump Jumper was the exception.

After a short visit at the pueblo, he and Stump Jumper moved into the Sagebrush Inn a little over two miles south of Taos. A favorite cousin, Smiling Dog, wanted to

join them. It was difficult for Bluefeather to refuse, but
they could not risk his fondness for alcohol and his actions thereafter.

The inn was a large adobe establishment inspired by
the real pueblo. It was a fine place recently bought by a
short, fat, bespectacled fellow, Myron Vallier, and his
wife. The lobby was one to remember as long as one had
any sight at all—and maybe after that. The north wall was
at least half picture window, and what a landscape it
framed.

The blue-green sagebrush mostly hid the highway into
town so that one could see the plants for a considerable
distance, enhancing the sight of cottonwood trees and
glimpses of adobe walls before the great Taos Mountain
seemed to boom up and take over. The picture was different by the minute as the clouds and light changed
dramatically. The window alone brought visitors from
around the world to headquarter their exploration of the
Taos area from here. Those fortunate enough to have
lived or visited there at a time before that inevitable scarring would occur were blessed indeed.

The lobby was filled with Mexican carved furniture
around a massive fireplace. On the walls hung paintings
by some of Taos's finest while the floors were decorated
with Navajo rugs. It didn't matter, summer or winter, the
warm feeling of the lobby and the bountiful views for the
eyes and souls bequeathed by the window were truly beyond compare.

Just off the lobby was a large dining room of pure
southwestern decor and delectable food. A small, inti-
mate bar joined it. One could hardly drink there without
somehow striking up a conversation with a stranger and
often making a lifelong friend. The patrons ranged from
local day workers, artists and writers, to Texas oilmen, or
often international celebrities, from politicians to sym-

phony composers. It was extremely eclectic in its clientele.

At the time Bluefeather and his uncle moved in, Jay, the only black bartender in Taos County, ran the small corner of delight. The setting was one of the finest on earth, and their duty was one of possible wondrous contribution to all who lived on that same earth. The pressure of finances made it a requisite that they keep this endeavor to themselves. Any interruption could doom the project. That part would be a struggle, for Stump Jumper's natural reticence around strangers would—after a half a bottle of alcohol—turn to unlimited information about the world and all that was in it.

They got settled in their double bedroom, then got back into the Jeep and drove immediately west about two-thirds of a mile to a little farm surrounded by a three- to five-foot-high carpet of the material they sought. Emilio Cruz owned the place and clawed out a living with a medium-sized flatbed truck, hauling anything from furniture to garbage. The Cruz family kept a milk cow, pigs, chickens, goats and a garden to supplement his small earnings. His wife, Elena, had borne six children—three were still at home. Bluefeather had known the couple as long as he could remember.

They sat down at the kitchen table of the extremely clean, four-room adobe house. The only modern appliance was an electric refrigerator. It was given a place of honor in the modest room. In the living room was a small area of worship on top of an old, carved chest covered with a hand-crocheted scarf. Candles in small, red glass holders burned at the base of a statue of the Virgin Mary and two *santos* (carvings of the saints). There were some pictures of Christ on the cross hanging in a group with a couple of *retablos*.

"Hey, Emilio, I got a good job for you."

"Need some ore hauled?"

The question didn't surprise Bluefeather because once Emilio had worked the mines north of Taos at Moly Corporation.

"No, no. Don't need any ore hauled." How in all hell could he say it? It was a scary statement that had never been made outside the Taos Pueblo in the history of the West. "I want to rent your sagebrush and hire you and some of your *compadres* to pick the leaves."

Emilio stared at him like he was a dog puking on the kitchen table. Elena dropped a spoon that rattled on the floor like tiny machine-gun fire.

"You want to lease the sagebrush, not the ground?" Emilio finally asked, wide-eyed with a silly half-smile on his face.

"That's right. Just the brush itself . . . and for only a few weeks."

"I never heard nothing like this before. What do you want it for? You gonna make something and sell it to the tourists, huh?"

Bluefeather had to give some kind of answer to Emilio's question without telling the truth. He twinged because he was afraid that the true use of the plant was buried deep in Emilio's mind and he might dig it up.

"No, Emilio, we just want the leaves. We'll pay good wages. You can hire your brothers to help harvest. Stump Jumper here will oversee the operation."

"Well, I don't know how to do a deal like that. I just haul stuff, you know that. Like cows, horses, manure, anything I can load and get paid for, but I don't know nothing about dealing like this here. I never heard . . ."

"Look." Bluefeather counted out five twenty-dollar bills. "Here's a down payment. We'll work out the details later. Gather a lot of gunnysacks full of the younger leaves. We want the leaves hand picked. Then when we get a truckload of full sacks, I'll pay you again for hauling them all to Cerrillos."

"Whew," Emilio said looking at his wife, hoping for some kind of silent advice from the expression on her face. He got no help. She was moving about wiping at things that were already spotless. Her kind heart pounded out strange rhythms in her chest at this one possible bounty of their entire life.

Emilio said, "Whew," three more times then went on. "Well, it'll take me the rest of the day to get my brothers and maybe two *primos,* huh? Yeah, that's okay. We can get started first thing in the morning, say seven o'clock."

"Now, you got five brothers and you're gonna use two cousins, so with Stump Jumper that makes a crew of eight. Elena, you think you can handle the noon meal for that many? We'll pay two dollars a person."

For that kind of money she would have taken on a hundred diners. "Yes, ah yes. I feed 'em good—beans, bacon, tortillas, chile . . ." and she went on counting long after Bluefeather had agreed to the deal.

Emilio followed them smilingly out to the jeep, having great difficulty keeping from laughing out loud. It was the hot feel of the hundred dollars in his pocket that kept him under momentary control, but as they climbed in the vehicle he just had to ask, "I know it's none of my business, Bluefeather, but what you gonna do with them sagebrush leaves, huh? They're not good for nothing."

"I know you're not gonna believe this, Emilio, but my clients are going to distill this stuff." There now, he had told the truth and had not given anything away.

Emilio nodded his head in agreement and understanding. "You mean distill them like run them through a whiskey still, huh?"

"Yeah, only bigger."

"Well, I'll be a . . ."

"See you early in the morning. Be sure you get the sacks and the hands gathered. We don't have any time to fool around."

"Okay. Okay, old *compadre*. We'll be ready," and strangely he started trotting to the house holding one hand over his mouth. Before Bluefeather and his cousin could get turned around they heard screams of laughter coming out the open front door, windows and cracks.

Emilio said to his wife, "The goddamned fools are goin' to make wheesky! Sagebrush wheesky! Ain't nothing but a crazy artist would ever drink that stuff. Goats won't even eat it 'less they're starvin' to death. Goats won't even . . ." and then he and Elena could not utter words for a moment for their hilarity. The last thing Bluefeather and Stump Jumper heard as they sped over the corrugated dirt road was, "We are gonna get rich on sagebrush wheesky. God is good."

"God is getting better."

Before they were out of hearing range Stump Jumper, who had shown exemplary control, suddenly burst apart with long wails, cackles and guffaws too pent up to control any longer. He was trying to say something, but couldn't squeeze it out.

Bluefeather drew back one hand to hit him in the mouth and then remembered he had sworn off violence in 1945. In spite of a valiant struggle he soon joined his uncle in howling humor so drastic he had to brake the jeep to a halt. He could not see the road for the tears.

THIRTY-NINE

BLUEFEATHER DECIDED HE WOULD WORK ALONG WITH THE pickers until he was certain the operation was moving smoothly, even though Dr. Godchuck had insisted his time would be more valuable promoting the project than in the field.

The workers had all lined up a few yards apart. Holding their gunnysacks in one hand, they started picking at the pungent sagebrush leaves with the other. In varying degrees and minutes, they all learned things about sagebrush they had never even thought about, even though all had been born and raised near hundreds of thousands of acres of it. First, the leaves grow gracefully on the ends of the stalks in an umbrellalike formation, giving the appearance of ten times the actual amount of leaves. Second, the leaves do not pull clean like corn, cotton or green beans; it took more time and more care. Then they found that it took far longer to cover even the bottom of the sack than they had thought.

Emilio was the only one who thought to bring gloves. By noon everyone but him had sore, bleeding hands, so Bluefeather sent Stump Jumper into town for leather work gloves for all. It took another two hours of work before Bluefeather realized that the leather gloves were too tight and stiff—the pickers were dropping half of their production on the ground. Now he sent Stump Jumper to town again for gloves made from cotton that were much better. They could feel the leaves and handle them much more cleanly, but they found that they wore out a pair every other day. So they bought out the entire town's supply of canvas gloves.

All these delays and learning processes had slowed the gatherers greatly. By the fifth day they only had ten fully packed bags. Bluefeather had long-ago forgotten about promoting. He labored, cheering on his workers.

"Do not worry, amigos," Bluefeather encouraged, "we'll get it done if it takes a month."

The sun beat down in the supposedly cool seven-thousand-foot altitude of the Taos area like a symbol from hell. The dust from the sage got into their eyes, ears, pores and noses, causing alternating sneezing and watery-eyed spells among the men in the fields.

Two brothers and one cousin decided to quit at the end of the first week. Bluefeather heard one of them say, "I'd rather starve for five years than spend one more day at this work for fools."

Brother answered brother with, "I agree. This is work meant only for prisoners or someone being punished for some terrible deed."

Bluefeather wisely called it a payday and said, "From now on you will be paid in cash, plus two ice-cold beers at the end of each workday."

It was a delicate balance between the daily pay and cold beer, against the itching, sneezing, back-tearing, sweat-soaking, sore-handed work. However, Taos had long been a hard place to make the barest of a living. So the longed-for treats at day's end kept them going—for now.

At night, Bluefeather and Stump Jumper showered, put on clean clothes, had a couple of drinks with their meal in the inn's restaurant, then fell into bed half dead and asleep. Bluefeather was so exhausted he didn't even dream—none that he could remember, anyway—and he was a man of many dreams, mostly memorable and all in full color.

Bluefeather was proud of the way Stump Jumper was performing. He worked harder than anyone and took most of his money home to his wife and two sons. And he hadn't even looked at the bar. Of course, there was great wisdom in that action for him. Temptation. Stump Jumper was sometimes misunderstood. He had attended Bacone College in Oklahoma—the college that had graduated many Indian notables—intending to make his clan happy by becoming a grade school teacher. He had done well in his studies, but the confinements of a schoolroom were not for this Indian. What he liked was fishing, hunting, alfalfa-hay farming and occasional drinking. The last would create small problems on rare occasions. Contrary to popular attitudes he was by no means an alcoholic or even a so-called periodic drunk. He might go six months without a drop or he might get zapped two weekends in a row. What made his drinking seem like a continuing event was his total enjoyment of it from the time he made up his mind to do it until he slept it off. The impression of his having fun was so strong that often people would see him acting in the same happy, crazy manner and would assume he was always like that. A mistake.

However, things—little things at first—began to occur in the harvesting fields that could cause even a man of total control to take to strong drink. At first, there was just one carload of people driving slowly down the road next to the slaving sagebrush harvest hands. Then two.

Then three. They drove so slowly, staring hard in amaze-
ment, that the drivers often ran off the narrow dirt road.
At first they were just onlookers making little gestures of
diversion to one another. Then finally a pickup from Arroyo Seco drove by with three passengers in front and
three in back.

One melodious voice boomed out across the field. "I
wanna go back to them old cotton fields of home. Away,
Dixieland, away."

They all chorused, paraphrasing the old song.

"I wanna go back. I wanna go back to them dear old
sagebrush fields of mine, away Dixieland, away Taos land,
away."

Then a carload of beer drinkers joined in the musical
competition and switched songs. They drove back and
forth singing in reasonable harmony, "Bringing in the
leaves, bringing in the leaves, we shall come rejoicing,
bringing in the leaves."

As if the stupid singing wasn't enough, they began
shouting things like, "Hey, amigos, why don't you get a
hay baler and save all the work?" or, "I got a million acres
for you to clean up soon as you finish this little job."

Mostly, though, they just pointed and said unheard
things, gigging one another in the ribs with their elbows
as they broke out in insulting mirth.

The constant travel churned up the hard ground of the
narrow dirt road so that there was a permanent fog of
choking dust in the air, which settled on the sage to further discomfort Bluefeather and his men. The difficulties
of the hand-tearing labor were enough without being
joked to death about them. The men made quick shameful glances toward their kibitzers at first, but as nerves,
bodies and fractured souls were kibitzed almost ceaselessly, the glances and mumbling became angry.

Bluefeather realized mutiny was at hand. So, after paying the pouting men that late afternoon and waiting for their two-beer allotment to take effect, he suggested they dig a ditch across the road. All cheered up and pitched right in.

The sage was so thick on each side of the road, all were certain the ditch would stop the traffic dead. They scattered the dirt out on the open land so that a driver would be upended in the trench before he knew what had jolted him unconscious.

For the first time they could hardly wait to get to work the next morning. It was a day of little progress. Everyone kept raising their head from their task to look and listen for an automobile engine. Bluefeather was biting big enough slices of flesh from the inside of his cheeks to enrage a sloth. They were losing precious time and money. Dr. Godchuck's money. Well, it had once been Bluefeather's, but now it belonged to the maker of great medicine. The waste of effort and energy in anxious anger galled him meanly, which was against his postwar vows. The scar on his nose burned in such controlled fury that he could not keep from rubbing it. That action filled his eyes and nostrils with sage dust so he could hardly see, and he had fits of sneezing that would have done justice to a blacksmith's bellows.

Reprieve. There was the engine just around the hill. The workers stopped now, looking, their expressions changing from extreme anxiety to hopeful anticipation. It was a big old rusty gravel truck with only two passengers in front. As they crept forward, the driver started honking a tune of mockery. They ground slowly along now, closer and closer to the ditch.

Bluefeather took command. The driver's eyes must not spot the ditch in advance. He shouted at his troops, "Smile, wave, dance, do anything to divert the driver's attention."

Oh, what a performance the sweating, long-taunted, long-suffering men put on. One sang "El Rancho Grande." Another danced an artificial flamenco. Others whirled about clapping their hands above their heads like Greek celebrants. Bluefeather and Stump Jumper simultaneously started a war dance, chanting and yelling and making motions of stabbing with spears. Not only was this action courageous, but it was also somewhat hurtful, as their movements were greatly, painfully hindered by the now-hated sagebrush. They persevered, gaining momentum as the truck neared the ditch. All eyes were wide and eager. Mouths were ready to fly open in hee-haws, and hands itched to slap knees and their companions' backs with vengeful glee.

The truck was within inches now. All breathing of the workers stopped, so did all motion. Their eyes riveted on the coming crash. The truck stopped just on the very brink of the hand-dug trench.

The driver waited while his companion got out and looked at the ditch with such lingering care, one would think it was his first visit to a bordello. Then ever so slowly, he unbuttoned the fly of his pants and relieved himself in the ditch as he watched a couple of ravens fly across the soft blueness of the summer sky. Then he shook his apparatus several unnecessary times and buttoned his pants while still showing the intense interest of an ornithologist in the flight of the birds. He then walked slowly back to the truck looking into the distance at different mesas, mountain ranges and various species of smaller birds, as well as a couple of cumulus clouds forming over Taos Mountain. If the word "forever" had any meaning at all, this was a time and place where it applied. When he took out a cigarette and lighted it, using six matches to do so, Bluefeather could see with his eyes closed and feel with his back turned, the blood baking in the arteries of his hired hands, who now had become friends through their shared responsibilities.

He raised one silent hand that held them back momentarily. As the casual one climbed back into the truck and took three slams to get the door closed, Bluefeather could sense the danger of his compatriots bursting forth and dragging the men from the truck and tearing them into such small bits that only the hardy desert ants would be able to find the pieces.

The driver backed the truck up. Its reverse gears resounded across the land as if metal were eating metal. He stopped, put it in a low forward gear and plowed a new deviant road around the ditch through the sage and back on the other side to the old road. He drove on toward the highway next to the Sagebrush Inn, honking clever little ditties as they rolled past.

Even though it was only eleven o'clock, Bluefeather swiftly declared it was time for lunch. He led the way back toward Elena's kitchen, walking through stripped sagebrush that looked like dying plants on a dying planet. It did nothing to ease the terrible joke the "saints" had played on them by making a latrine of their ditch.

In spite of what the moguls, the greedy, the evil politicians and the first-rate accumulators of the world might collectively believe, there exist a few things that money cannot buy. One was right here and now at the home and in the fields of Emilio and Elena Cruz. These men were not going to go back to work for any amount of money that Bluefeather could afford. The humiliation of having their ditch pissed in, and their certitude of the tables of mirth being tilted away from them, were simply too much to endure. No reasonable human being should expect more from them without some sort of uplifting compensation.

Bluefeather had long ago proven he was a fast thinker

in desperate situations, so now he said, with all the conviction he could draw out of his limping genes, "Men, I have to go to the inn and make an important phone call. Wait here at the house for me after you've enjoyed Elena's delicious repast."

Grumbling.

"No matter what," he continued, "stay here in the shade of the porch and enjoy in advance your after-work beers. No more work until I return, you hear?" Grumbling. "Now promise me again not to leave this site until I return."

With a swift glance and nod to Stump Jumper indicating he was to stay and take control, Bluefeather swiftly moved to the Jeep and took off before his workers could ask questions that might expose the possible vacancy of good news. It burned his ass some more to be forced to follow the bumpy trail of the gravel truck around the ditch, thereby helping make a permanent detour in the road, further defiling and insulting this patch of desert.

The first thing he did upon entering his room was call Dr. Godchuck at La Fonda.

The answer came over the phone purring like a madam's cat, "Dr. Merphyn Godchuck's laboratory."

"Tulip?"

"Blue?"

"It's me, darling. Are you having fun?"

"Why, of course, deah boy. That has been a custom of the Godchuck descendants for centuries."

"Good. Good. Keep it up for my sake. Is the doctor present?"

"Oh, no, he isn't. He's in Cerrillos composing his plant. He insisted I stay here and take phone calls until he's all done down there. Why don't you just call the bar, deah. The Gulls are such nice accommodating people, I'm sure they'd be more than pleased to conduct Merphyn to the phone."

"Aww, it's okay. I just wanted to pass the word on that we should have the hay . . . I mean sage picking and sacking done in ten or twelve days. You can pass the words on to the doctor if you wish, and I'll just get on back to work. Oh yeah, before I go, have you seen Marsha?"

"Yes, we had tea day before yesterday. She was asking about you. In fact, she seems curious beyond the ordinary. That's good news, deah. I know you've forgotten my telling you not to resent that such a fine specimen of femaleness is going to be terribly, terribly rich. That's a rare combination, deah. In fact, it's just as hard to find an all-'round woman among the poor as the rich. You do understand me, don't you, deah Blue?"

"Right down to the rabbit's hole. I must go now . . . and give Marsha my . . . my . . . best."

"That will do quite well then."

"Bye, Tulip."

So she had asked about him, huh? That made Bluefeather ready for his next move to save the sage. He went to the lobby and had a visit with the owner, Myron Vallier. If he could have dug up the courage he could have mustered at least a small smile at the irony of the Sagebrush Inn's name. Everything had suddenly turned to sage or thereabouts.

Now the square and roly-poly Myron imagined himself as a helpful and trusted nonmember of the CIA, the FBI or any other semisecret organization that was supposed to protect the sanctity of the good old U.S.A. and protectorates. This attitude probably came partly from his having served with the OSS in the war. He was as sincere about this as a guard dog, and even more ready to freely serve any cause for his country. That was the feeling Bluefeather drew upon, and in fact, took no little advantage of. He assured Myron that the gathering of sagebrush leaves was heavily related to experimentation that had a lot to do with the welfare of America's citizenry. It must be kept hush-hush for now, but later he would explain in detail, for he knew Myron was one of "us." That did it.

Myron immediately discerned that Bluefeather was in the secret service of his country and said, conspiratorially, "I understand. Is there any way, any manner at all that I may help?"

"Well, now that you've broached the subject, maybe, just maybe, there is a way you could be of service. We would be most grateful," he whispered, taking a quick glance around to be sure no one could hear the vital secrets. "I've let it drop, Myron, that we are going to make sage whiskey from these leaves. Can you believe the workers fell for it? Can you believe? What am I saying? Of course, you can. You've had the training."

Whatever all this meant, if anything, Myron took it seriously. His entire fat-laden body became tense, strong and ready to assist in the cause.

Bluefeather continued, "Just to keep their minds from wandering and possibly endangering our cause, I thought it would be prudent on our part to throw a little diversion. Say, food, drinks and music for just one evening out here in the patio," and he made a motion out toward the large space enclosed on three sides. "Diversionary tactics worked quite well in fooling Hitler at the Normandy invasion. As I'm sure you well know, having been in on the planning personally."

"Well the OSS did have a role. Yes, they played their part." Myron seemed to be stretching upward, now taller and much thinner. He was ready to do duty. "I'll talk to my wife and the staff immediately. When do we begin the . . . the diversion?"

"Oh, if it's all right with you, say an hour before sunset tomorrow."

"Done."

Myron clasped the deal-closing handshake with such surprising strength that Bluefeather's sage-picking hand was numb for a bit. That was a good sign that patriotic and sacrificial adrenaline was flowing freely in Myron's previously Jell-O-type body. Bluefeather was certain that handshake was the most physical act Myron had extended in a decade or more. Bluefeather was highly pleased, at least for the moment, with his unthinking, inspired actions. Instead of the coldness of dread, he now anticipated facing his men with the happy news, face on, full force.

He drove now toward the Cruzes' with a heart that sang with violins, guitars and the warbling of meadowlarks and canaries. The air had suddenly turned to a fine champagne mist, and the corrugated road caressed the wheels of the Jeep like velvet-palmed hands. Oh, glorious day of days.

In his relief, he felt all and nothing. He saw much and little. That's the way of sudden deliverance from almost certain disaster.

It was a quarter of a mile before he realized that sometimes there was a transparent figure poised on the toes of one foot on the hood of the jeep. Then the figure leapt from the vehicle to the ground landing a few yards in front of him. He jammed his foot on the brake pedal so desperately and with such force that not only did the jeep come to a jarring, skidding halt, but also the motor died. There, thirteen inches from the radiator, stood a smiling Dancing Bear.

"Lookee here, dear brudder, at this." He did a side shuffle and a couple of whirls with an imaginary partner. "Fred Astaire and Ginger Rogers," he said.

Then he did a single dance of great action, whirling back facing Bluefeather and shoving his arms back and forth to the sides dancing in place. "Gene Kelly for sure, dear brudder." Then he did a tap dance with so many accurate steps and tricks that Bluefeather forgot to be agitated. Even though his spirit guide had been absent lately when he was so sorely needed, Bluefeather's mood was so elevated that he welcomed Dancing Bear's presence.

"Who is that?" Bluefeather asked.

"Roosevelt Martin Luther Jones."

"I'm not aware of him, Bear. Does he do movies?"

"No, dear brudder, not yet. He ain't been born yet. Forty maybe fifty years to go. Watch for coming attractions. Watch this. He's gonna be the best for . . . I betcha a hunnert years."

Bluefeather thought he was about to be bored with another toe dance representing the upcoming reincarnation—not so. Dancing Bear whirled so fast at times, he nearly became invisible. At other moments he took circular steps on the heel of one foot and the toes of the other at the same time, and that was hard to do. Then he zipped back and forth, changing the position of his feet from front to back in the process, and finished with a whirling leap and six knee bends with each leg. He then bounced up and stood stiff as a flagpole with one arm angled straight up and out to his side while the other made wild circles at the exact same angle, only downward. Then he got his crazy dancing self together. Smiling, he bowed as if a half billion people were applauding. One was.

Bluefeather jumped out of the jeep, clapping to beat the half billion and said sincerely, though unthinkingly, mocking his guide, "Bravo, dear brother. Wonderful, terrific and downright done good."

"Ah ha. Thank you, Blue. Thank you very much. I have to practice the Go, Ho, Hey dance all the time. The authorities will not tell me where on earth Mudball Eclair is going to reincarnate."

"Mudball Eclair? How did he . . . I mean, how is he going to get a name like that?"

"Well, when he first comes around this dimension here that you're hung up in, he is gonna be first born in Florida swamps. He's gonna learn to dance in the mud 'cause there ain't no other place to do 'er. Understand? Huh? Huh, Huh?"

"Makes all the sense in the system to me, Bear. Say, ol' missing-when-I-need-you pard, how have you been? Where have you been? Have you traveled a lot lately?"

"Just like always, you ask more fast questions than my slow ears can hear. I'll just finish up, maybe, that Korea war is going on, you know? There's lots of folks staring at one another across the invisible line. Guns all cocked and eyes peeled like fancy grapes. Both sides been gettin' the nervous jerking disease. I been plenty busy. Say, how come you ain't over there? The Second Infantry Division is right on the front line right now this beautiful day."

"I've done been, Bear. More than I can bear. Forgive that awful pun, okay?"

"Okay. Ain't much to forgive."

"Right. Well you must know I've sworn off all violence."

Dancing Bear began to laugh and tramp his knee-high Apache moccasin boots into the dust over and over. Bluefeather could not see for the life of him and all of Taos County what was so funny.

"What's so funny?" Bluefeather asked with annoyance.

"You done said it just like everybody else. Since I been working for the high-upper folks—kings, dictators, generals, politicians, ax murderers, serial killers, wife beaters,

husband beaters and retired combat marines—" Dancing
Bear laughed heartily, "they all say," still laughing, "the
same thing. Ever' time, I tell to you. It's so sad it makes it
funny to me. All these no-gonna-do-no-more-violence-
anymore kind of folks, all these I-been-born-again-to-be-
a-pussycat folks. All these . . ."

"Whoa! Whoa! I got it. I got your feelings clear. But it
doesn't make any difference to me. I've got proof. If
you'd been around the last few days you would know that
I had many justifiable reasons to commit dismemberment."

"Chure. Chure. There's always excuses aplenty."

"You're not getting it, Bear. I didn't do it. You hear
me? I did not do it when it would have been allowable."

"I hear now perty good, but if you had not talked to the
fat FBI man over at lodge, maybe you don't keep away
from dismemberment violence. See what I mean? Huh?
Huh? Huh, dear brudder?"

"All right, I concede a little there. Say, what are you
doing listening in on secret service conversations without
letting me know you're around, anyway?"

"Sometimes it much better when folks don't know too
much. Savvy the burro, kid?" he kidded.

"Bear, I like to have fun as much as you do . . . well
almost, but you know this oil of sage business is serious. A
lot of pain, and maybe even lives, could be saved with Dr.
Merphyn Godchuck's inventions and formulas. Why
don't you take a little time off from your other chores and
help us when we need it?"

"Well, there's too many lives scattered 'round places as
it is. No way I can take care of just my little share. No
way, brudder. Believe it, dumb ass."

"You don't need to be calling me names just because
I'm seriously concerned about the success of our project."

"Sometimes people don't listen to politeness. Sometimes the world is full of gaps. Sometimes fences have water gaps. Teeth have gaps. Sometimes dreams have gaps, and sometimes, great inventions have gaps."

Before Bluefeather could ask him to decipher those "sometimes," Dancing Bear changed the subject, chuckling almost evilly, saying, "Dear brudder, I hear from my fellow guide amigos that you been lookin' hard at almost redheaded lady. I hear she is tough and tender like steaks from two different cuts. I hear she got so many smarts between her ears that her eyes are wide apart like a good quarter horse. I hear she got a daddy with enough money to buy . . . to buy . . . well, to buy maybe Hong Kong. I hear . . ."

"For once, Bear, I want to thank you for overhearing these things from your spirit guide friends, and I want to thank you for telling me what you did. I'm gonna level with you, Bear. I think I like her a whole bunch. Now, after all the trouble you've gone to, straining your slow ears to hear all these things for me, why don't you just haul off and tell me what to do about her. I'm adding a little-used and very special word to my request. Please, Bear, please, please, please, advise me about the almost red-haired woman. She is red when she's in sun or bright indoor light. Red as fire. Red as a ripe tomato, red as . . ."

"Hey, hey, you beginning to sound like me," Dancing Bear said. "Hokay, hokay. I see you don't quite understand about gaps. So, I say enjoy yourselves together between the gaps."

"If you think I don't understand, why do you keep using the word over and over? Why don't you explain it to me in clearer terms?"

"Beat a frog with the same stick long enough and he'll finally piss. Hey, dear brudder Blue, I just got a commission to save a senatorial candidate from gettin' the clap. That's a real emergency. Bye-bye, Bluebird."

Then with a little one-toed whirl he became less and less visible until he was gone. Bluefeather walked over and looked where he had last stood. There was a perfectly round hole in the hard roadbed. He did not try to guess how deep it was. He crawled back into the Jeep with the not-quite-understood but well-taken suggestion that he and the almost-redheaded woman, Marsha, should "enjoy together" each other in spite of gaps. Whether he had decoded his spirit guide's message properly or not was of no matter. He intended to fulfill that "enjoy together" part with all the power of pleasure he had.

He drove to Emilio Cruz's place as the bearer of multitudes of joyous tidings. The workers were given the rest of this day and the next off to prepare for the little entertainment.

FORTY

IT WAS THE TIME OF WAITING. MRS. VALLIER SUPERVISED THE
tables and bar being set up in the patio. Except for a few
clouds guarding the highest points of the Sangre de Cristos, the sky was a blue of great purity. The sun gave warm
blessings on all the area, and the breeze across the desert
was just enough to make breathing effortless.

About three o'clock in the afternoon, Stump Jumper,
who had showered twice trying to rid himself of what was
to many the enticing aroma of sage, finished wrapping
the two plaits of black hair down the back of his head, put
on a heavy silver and turquoise bracelet, a black shirt and
clean trousers, wrapped the folded white bedsheet
around his waist Taos Indian style and headed, without a
word, toward the bar.

The hired hands, with wives, girlfriends and a few extra
"cousins," started arriving about an hour or so before
sunset. Jay, the bartender with a gleaming white smile of
great anticipation on his black face, started serving drinks
assisted by Jack "Rattlesnake" Sowers, who had volunteered to help out.

The women wore every kind of apparel from Levi's to
squaw dresses. The men were mostly in Levi's and plaid

western-style shirts, but some had on their best suits and
neckties. Many wore silver Indian jewelry and bolo ties.
This was not a diamond and ruby crowd. But there was
sparkle—and color. Lots of color. A spirit looking down
would have sworn the crowd was a large moving flower
garden.

The buffet was laden with a variety of sumptuous delights: cheeses, fruits, sliced meats and Mexican dishes.
Many took their food and drinks to tables, while others
stood around in handshaking, hugging, kissing and happily chattering groups. Neighbors who lived only a small
farm or house away acted as if they had not seen one
another for years.

It was supposed to be a festive, relaxing event, and it
was. Of course, Mr. Vallier had used his connections with
the forces of law and had Sergeant Leach and Officer
Gallegos on hand. All knew them. In fact, the policemen
had several kin here themselves. They joined in, visiting
as casually and comfortably as if they were at a family
picnic; however, as Myron had so keenly foreseen, it gave
the crowd the freedom of fun without the worry of violence.

Bluefeather held back as long as possible, then headed
for the bar figuring to have a quick drink before joining
the main party. As he entered the bar he was greeted by
Stump Jumper in a manner to create thirst.

"Hey there, Bluefeather. Here's my nephew
Bluefeather I was telling you about. Remember? The
mining engineer and manufacturer? Hey, Blue, get over
here and have a drink with these fine folks from Texas."

These "fine folks from Texas" consisted of a group of
seven from Dallas and Forth Worth. Bluefeather never
did understand who they were, what they did or exactly
why they were here, because too many people were talking at once. Happy. Happy. Happy. Rattlesnake, the sub-

stitute bartender, was frustratingly trying to keep the swiftly emptied glasses refilled and had already given up on keeping tabs and correct change. He just served.

"Hey, Blue, these Texas people are coming to the party with us. Hey, bartender, give 'em another toddy all round to get 'em in the mood."

Bluefeather downed two drinks, and in the midst of the babble headed, at a speed just under a trot, for the great outdoor patio. He was fondly greeted from so many different directions, he was momentarily confused as to how he should respond. Then he remembered that when Tulip Everhaven did not feel like making small talk, she just smiled and nodded lightly. It worked. Of course, he felt glad that his vow of nonviolence was sanctified as he shook hands and visited awhile with a quietly beaming Myron and his two brothers of the law.

Then Bluefeather was shocked to find here the guitarist Ramon Hernandez of the Dawson mining camp from over near his birthplace of Raton. He had not seen him since Ramon had played so sensitively for his marriage to Miss Mary at the Statler Hotel in Durango. Their mutual embraces were deeply felt. What better frosting for the cake of fun than to have a man of such giving music in attendance.

Ramon then introduced Bluefeather to the other guitarist who had been hired for the evening. He was stocky, curly-headed Antonio Mendoza, who had recently arrived from Old Mexico. Antonio exuded a love of music and life that was a privilege to absorb. Here were two true givers. Oh, how they played. Oh, how the listeners danced. Oh, how they all ate, laughed, yelled, clapped and loved, and later on some—like Dancing Bear—did their own private dances.

Myron Vallier's importance and connections were mostly underrated by everyone but Bluefeather. Myron was that rare human being—he delivered—and he and his wife had delivered in high style here.

A photographer and reporter moved about, mixing in the crowd. Myron quieted Bluefeather's concern with, "Don't worry. It's all taken care of. You'll be proud when you read the paper."

Bluefeather had danced with every woman there. At this moment, at this time, in this patio with these friends, it was all first cabin. Bluefeather felt inspired. As the awestricken quietness of a short-lived, blazing sky turned the night a soft blue-green, with a three-quarter coyote moon, Bluefeather let out a triumphant howl of fulfillment. He was certain it could not get any better than this.

Oh, but it could, for instantly following his jubilant yell his eyes were whipped in the direction of the lobby door as if directed by a powerful beam of energized light. Through that door stepped Marsha Korbell.

She stopped, looking widely about until her blue eyes sighted down the invisible beam straight into the coal-dark ones of Bluefeather Fellini. Her smile of radiance dimmed his of stunned delight. They moved to each other. He took her in his arms and they danced. She smelled of incense from the Orient, rosewater from the Deep South, frankincense from the Mideast, flowers that grew someplace far away in the sky. She smelled of the female Marsha—blood stirring and distinct from all others in the world.

She whispered in his ear, "I heard you asked after me."

"Yes."

That's all they needed to say.

As they moved smoothly past Ramon, his guitar strings seemed to turn to fresh clover honey, and he nodded at Antonio with knowledge. Antonio also expressed his utmost feelings and stirrings of love on the guitar strings.

Bluefeather did not dance. No, he simply moved with

Marsha in warm air a foot above the patio. His face had already melted and joined with her cheek and shoulder. His slow but heavy breathing was filled with musk and mystery. It was the divination.

Then she spoke softly. He felt his feet on solid material once again and pulled his head free to look into her eyes. She put two fingers from her lips to his, and he somehow heard her words, "I must go now. It's a long drive this time of morning back to Santa Fe. It was a wonderful time."

She walked toward the lobby door, paused, turned her head back, giving him a smile that could have projected through a mile of darkness. He started to raise a hand to wave good-bye but decided that would have been super-fluous. She was already gone.

He slowly made his way through the swiftly thinning crowd to the bar. Rattlesnake was sitting in a chair un-conscious from serving and participating at the same time. Jay could handle the crowd alone now, anyway.

"What'll it be? A nightcap?"

"Yes, Jay, thank you. A brandy, perhaps."

Jay reached under the bar and lifted a bottle of Courvoisier. Then he brought up a snifter and poured three fingers of the golden liquid.

Bluefeather leaned on an elbow on the bar saying, "It was a great one, wasn't it, Jay? A truly great party."

"Yeaahh, that it was. That it was."

Surprisingly, Myron came up and asked for a nightcap himself. His last drink of the night was also his first. He and Bluefeather raised their glasses in a silent toast to Jay and then clicked them together for themselves.

Myron said, so pleased at his efforts he actually smiled a bit, "To the cause."

Bluefeather replied, "To the cause, forever, sir." He finished his brandy, set his glass down with a fifty-dollar bill showing from under it, turned and walked with deliberate steps to his room. Ramon and Antonio were putting away their guitars as they saw him retreat.

Myron said, "A fine American."

Jay appreciatively pocketed the fifty and said to his boss, "He is that," and began to close his bar.

The sagebrush gatherers, at least those fully conscious, had gone home happy and honored.

FORTY-ONE

AFTER THE PARTY A DAY OFF WAS CERTAINLY NEEDED, BUT THAT afternoon the clouds spread away from the mountain and inundated the valley with rain, making it impossible to work in the desert clay, anyway. However, the weekly *Taos News* could be delivered. There was a big headline: "Secret Government Sagebrush Project May Bring Prosperity to Valley." There were captioned photos of the festivities and a shot that included Bluefeather and Stump Jumper, who were named as heading up the work. Myron Vallier had taken all this to his officious heart and almost overdone his job.

It turned out quite well, though. The American Legion, along with a few local police, volunteered to protect the workers from the dust-raising traffic and eyes of possible foreign agents. The workers now felt honored. They really went about their leaf picking with diligence. Emilio's small barn was almost filled to capacity with the full gunnysacks. He had informed Bluefeather that in a couple more days his truck would be loaded to the limit.

Bluefeather, now satisfied that this end of the venture was a success, left Stump Jumper in charge and went to the inn to catch up on his phone calls. Besides, the successful ruse of secret government work had certainly nullified any chance he might have had in selling shares. He was looking up the number of the Cerrillos Bar when his phone rang.

He picked it up with anticipation, saying, "Hello."

The sweet voice came back at him. "Bluefeather," Marsha said, "I might as well get straight to it. Korbell turned down the proposal. I know you want to know why."

"Well, yes, I suppose I do."

"His turndown has nothing to do with the potential of the various formulas using the oil as a base. He thinks there are great possibilities eventually." Bluefeather was silent. "Are you there?"

"Oh, yeah. Yeah, I was just waiting for you to finish."

"Oh. Well, he simply thinks it will take too long to do the research to prove up all the patents. He's only interested in projects he can move on right now. He's always been that way. I am sorry."

"Don't worry about it. I figured—and so did Dr. Godchuck and Tulip. We all knew it was a long shot."

"I must say I am relieved at your attitude."

"No worry."

"Good. How is the leaf gathering proceeding?"

"Fine. We'll have our truckload day after tomorrow."

"You'll be coming back south then?"

"Be back in Santa Fe and Cerrillos in four or five days. You gonna be around?"

"I don't know from one minute to the next right now. We've been checking out a large parcel of state land to see if we want to bid on it. Please, call anyway, and we'll get together the first time we're both free. Promise?"

"Promise."

They said good-bye and for the moment the turndown by Korbell was secondary to her insistence on his calling. He was truly thrilled in a childlike manner just thinking of being with her again. Then it slowly seeped into his being that he must call the doctor and break the bad news to him. He wanted to run to the mountain behind the pueblo and hide like a rabbit. He craved going on across the mountain to his kin in Raton and absorbing their healing love. He could go into the bar only a few seconds away and forget the unpleasant duty for a while at least. He decided against that. He would just face it and get it over with.

He picked up the phone and called Cerrillos, asking Big George Gull to please seek out the doctor. He did.

Dr. Godchuck's voice was almost instantly on the other end of the line, "Ah, ah, ah, Bluefeather Fellini, what a pleasant surprise. We must be near a truckload."

"Day after tomorrow. I . . ."

"Fine. Delightful. We've just an hour ago finished testing the plant with some local sage and it's working perfectly, I'm happy to report."

"Well, that is great news, doctor," he swallowed, turning a little numb, and continued, "but I'm afraid I have some not quite so good news for you. Korbell turned us down. However," he crowded in, "he did say he thought we had great potential." Bluefeather waited for the doctor to have a heart attack, a cursing fit or a show of terrible disappointment, but instead he seemed somewhat jovial at the information.

"That's good, Bluefeather Fellini, very good. I never expected him to come in now. No, no, his kind waits until all the gamble is taken out of it . . . then . . . then they move in like stabbing rapiers. It's all just as I expected, dear boy. Congratulations on your fine work."

Instead of complaints or reprimands, he was being complimented for what he considered a failure. It was a feeling of relief, but he could not believe he and Marsha had delivered. He decided to make a quick trip to Raton, leaving a note of explanation for Stump Jumper.

The drive through Taos Canyon was one of sweet nostalgia as he remembered Lorrie Friedman and their many visits there. But now Marsha dominated his mind almost equally to his thoughts of the healing elements of the oil of sage. Banished was the massive effort it would require to make his thoughts go on over the mountain to Eagle Nest, Cimarron and then home to Raton.

There was a big family dinner that night as he was loved half to death. His mother remembered well the life-saving uses of sagebrush. Surprisingly, she was seriously concerned whether it was the thing to do.

"But Mama, it will ease burns, arrest colds, cure ulcers, slow the aging process, and that is just the beginning of what can come to mankind with the oil used as a base with other herbs and lotions."

"Well, of course, son, that is probably all true, but will it work without the blessings of the tribal council?"

"They would never give it. You know that. It would just get lost."

"Well, I do not know whether it's right or not."

"But Mama, millions of ailments and lives could be helped."

"Not if the Great Spirit hasn't approved."

Bluefeather was so knocked back that his mother was, as yet, even after all her years away from the pueblo, still set in concrete when it came to the old ways. He simply changed the subject to Hog Head's adventures in Chicago and how mine production was going in York Canyon. He had wanted to tell his mother that anything so good for the Pueblo Indians should be shared with everyone but was glad he had dropped the subject because when he did the family camaraderie returned immediately.

His father got him out on the back porch—alone, except for a bottle of good red wine—and wanted to know all about the venture. It was all quietly discussed, but when Bluefeather casually mentioned he had been associating with Marsha Korbell, his father slapped him on the back so hard he felt like his spine had joined his chest bone.

"Korbell's daughter, you say? Well, now . . . now there's some real handy work you've done there. Congratulations, my son. Who would ever think a coal miner's son would be hitching up with the likes of the Korbells? Wait till I tell your Uncle Alberto. He'll celebrate for a year, huh?"

Bluefeather tried to tell his father he had only been with her three or four times, but he was so overjoyed he would not listen and insisted they empty the bottle as a toast to his great accomplishment. They did.

His father said, "I think I have a feeling she is part Italian. In fact, I know it. I know it in here," he said quietly and pounded his chest. Then he jerked Bluefeather to his feet with surprising strength. With his arm around his son's neck, he led him back into the house, proudly and loudly announcing the upcoming joining of the Fellini family to the Korbell name.

Bluefeather was embarrassed and did his best to deny it. He might as well have tried to swim the Pacific Ocean with lead weights tied around his neck and feet for all the good his protesting did. It was a done—very well done— deal to his family that night in Raton, New Mexico.

The morning arrived in a few minutes.

It was completed. The gathering was finished until later, when much bigger acreage and many more workers would be needed. The field looked like a half-plucked chicken, but it would swiftly grow to normalcy.

After the truck was loaded and tied securely with ropes, Bluefeather paid everyone off with a little bonus he couldn't afford. They all thanked him sincerely, shook hands, happily volunteering to be first in line at anything he might need them to do.

Years before, Emilio had hauled ore from a mine in Cerrillos, so he knew exactly where and how to go. He drove away with the load. Bluefeather went over to the porch where Elena stood waving after her husband. He gave her a hug of thanks, reminding her, as he had many times, how vital her cooking had been in keeping the strength and mood of the workers up. He also slipped an extra twenty-dollar bill into her palm, in spite of her protests. He walked away with Stump Jumper, refusing to take it back.

The last words he heard from her were, "May the saints bless and keep you."

He drove Stump Jumper to within a half mile of the pueblo. He let him out, explaining to his puzzled look, "I don't have time right now for any more family celebrations. We've got to get this thing on the way, savvy, Stump?"

Stump Jumper did not savvy at all. He had forgotten they had already celebrated at the Sagebrush Inn all night long. That event no longer existed. He was ready for fun now. Everybody was supposed to celebrate the finish of any harvest or hunt. It had always been so.

"Hokay, you go on and work like a white man. I'll celebrate enough for everybody."

As Bluefeather drove toward the hotel to pick up his clothes, he had a moment of remorse knowing he was going to dearly miss some wild, crazy fun with his uncle. Ah well, such is the life of inventors and men of medicine.

FORTY-TWO

HE STOPPED IN A SHOP ON KIT CARSON ROAD AND BOUGHT A vase in a shape that pleased him. Then he took the twigs of spruce he had cut at Palo Flechado Pass, between Raton and Taos, and the few select sagebrush twigs he had left in the Jeep from Emilio's field. He drove to the little graveyard near El Prado, got out and knelt at Old Grinder's gravesite. He tenderly placed the bottle with its spruce and sage next to the headstone. The sage and spruce represented what Grinder had loved most, besides silly fun—the mountains and the high desert. So did Bluefeather.

"Hey old pardner, I've been mining sagebrush for gold. Bet you don't believe that one, huh? It turned into quite a bit of fun, but I'm sure you were poking around somewhere and know all this anyway. Now I got to go see about milling the blue-green ore. Miss you old buddy, but you're always with me anyhow. Bye for now."

He got up, took a quick look at Taos Mountain and the pueblo, got into the Jeep and headed into his other worlds looking forward to every change of weather or turn in the road.

· · · ·

He checked in with Tulip, whose old-young skin and wonderful round brown eyes radiated good cheer and excitement at the pilot plant actually having been assembled and distilling the potent Taos sage.

"Oh, just think, deah Blue, at last Merphyn will have enough of the oil to finish the research to secure his patents. Isn't that the most stunning feeling?"

"It is indeed, Tulip."

"I always had faith it would happen, but these last few years I'd begun to have some concern for poor deah Merphyn. He's spent most of his life, you know? There's not much left in the purse."

"Yeah, well, now no matter what, he'll have the necessary material to finish his experiments. What's more, I'm going to see to it that he has enough money to go along with those materials," he said with an urgency in his voice.

Bluefeather hurriedly finished lunch with Tulip and excused himself from the table. He called Marsha and left a message. He started scouting the town for prospects to whom he could sell small interests in the one patent that existed. He felt the pressure of time, but he just was not clicking yet. He had been too long in the rhythm of the fields to just instantly switch over to the rhythm of sales. This did not slow his trying, though, for he believed the more effort extended now, the sooner he would reach his best form. He was a long way from that ideal now. All he was getting from his prospects were strange and doubtful looks and the proverbial promise of "I'll think about it" or "I'll talk it over with my associates" or "We'll talk it over with our accountants" or "Just got to talk it over with my wife."

He counted the cash he had left. It added up to $482.68. He checked at the front desk and was pleased, at least, to find they were paid up for another week there.

He was disappointed when he found Marsha had not answered his message. He felt guilty at this feeling because he knew she tended to business before she played. Just the same, he missed her more by the hour. It was a longing.

He forced his mind back to Dr. Godchuck. There was no way to know without asking—which he would soon do —what the doctor's financial predicament was. There could not be much left after hiring help, renting the garage, buying parts and constructing the plant.

He decided to drive on down to Corrales and check on the Luceros, his mules and the gold in his last precious bag. He would cash it in immediately. He planned to hand most of the money over to Dr. Godchuck. The last bag was the smallest of all and weighed out only forty-five hundred dollars, but maybe, just maybe, it would be enough to distill an ample supply to finish all the experiments. If so, he would somehow work, promote or rob, as a last shot, to see that the dedication of this rare man would be fulfilled.

Tulip was thrilled that Bluefeather was taking her with him to Cerrillos. She said appreciatively, "Deah Blue, how thoughtful for you to ask me on a little outing. I'm dying to see Merphyn and his machine. Just nearly dying."

Bluefeather drove the Roadmaster. Tulip chatted the entire way about everything from mint juleps to a Basin Street jazz joint where the music was so grand that "one is simply transported."

Then, in the casual manner he had learned to expect under the most trying situation from the two remaining members of the Godchuck clan, she suddenly tossed him a lap full of live hand grenades. "It is so wonderful that deah Merphyn will have a chance to go right on with his other patent applications since the one on gingivitis runs out the third day of next month. What fortunate timing for us all."

He did not run off the road as she so lightly tossed all his efforts for them away. He did not grind his teeth or turn pale with fear. He did not even glow with anger. He was simply numb and cold somewhere deep inside the stomach area.

She went blithely on, "I do hope he pushes forward with the age-slowing process. We know that works. Just look at the two of us. Of course, Merphyn only applies it externally, while I've taken it both inside and out for decades now. I've never noticed any side effects, except in the beginning; I felt slightly queasy when I danced all night, but aside from that, . . ." and she talked on and on with total sincerity.

They pulled into Cerrillos. Bluefeather slammed on the brakes right in the middle of the street and leapt out. Bluefeather's lower-mind showed his eyes a disjointed, distressing sight.

Tulip said, "Deah, deah me, it looks as if we've suffered an incident."

There in front of them stood almost the entire population of the village, surrounding a capless Dr. Godchuck, his necktie uneven and his mane of white hair turned anywhere from lamp black to dull silver, blown awry as if he had just walked through a tornado bareheaded. Smoke and soot smears covered his face, his moustache and his tweeds, as well. Several other persons were in the same condition.

A man stepped back from the doorway with considerable strain and hacking. "The fire's under control, but we gotta get them smoldering bags of sagebrush outa there."

Bluefeather rushed up to the straight-standing, perfectly controlled doctor, breathlessly asking, "Are you all right?"

"Of course, Bluefeather Fellini, of course," and with his bull's prick cane he pointed, smiling, at the two safely packed drums at his feet, saying, "We have two pure quarts here."

"What on earth happened?"

"We'll never know for sure. Something stopped up the distillate machine and the pressure built to an explosion."

Bluefeather ran and looked in the building. It was a mess. The large still was distended, distorted and destroyed. The coiled tubes looked like a den of dynamited snakes. It reminded him of a direct hit by an eighty-eight-millimeter artillery shell. Men were dragging the remaining sacks of sage out a back door. Some of the sacks were giving off an acrid smoke.

He went back to the doctor. Tulip stood calmly holding one hand on his arm as if they were about to enter a Broadway theater presenting a Shakespearean play.

"Was anyone hurt?"

"No, no. We were lucky. Only a few little burns and bruises. Nothing to cause concern. The building is mostly intact and we have two quarts of pure liquid gold." He glanced endearingly, still smiling, at Tulip. He patted her hand and then stood even straighter-appearing than a healthy pine tree, his walking cane by his side as a decoration only, and continued, "We shall proceed forward." He then asked Bluefeather, "Would you be so kind as to take Tulip back to the hotel? I will get this slight delay straightened out and join you both shortly."

Bluefeather hesitantly agreed to obey.

He drove—neither one spoke. They stopped a moment to check for traffic at the main highway to Santa Fe. Tulip sat still, and her eyes were motionless but looking inward.

She said, finally, "Merphyn is a brave and totally dedicated man."

He answered, "None more so." He glanced at her and

instantly saw through the smooth ivory skin and body, like a living ghost. He could visualize the ninety-six-year-old woman underneath. A silent tear followed the lovely contours of her face as she whispered in a cracked voice he had to strain to hear, "So very, very brave."

FORTY-THREE

IT WAS THE TIME OF UNCERTAINTY. THE FIRST DAY HE FOUND out that Marsha was still in the southern part of the state in Lea County. The second day Bluefeather called Merphyn at Cerrillos because he wanted to return to help him. The doctor said everything was going well and that Bluefeather should remain in Santa Fe and keep Tulip company.

This became very hard to do after she told him, "Merphyn is selling our property in Cerrillos, deah Blue. We're especially pleased that our deah friends George and Mattie Gull are the purchasers. Such a peachy couple, don't you think?"

The third day, Bluefeather called Merphyn again to talk about the money.

"Look, doctor, I forgot to tell you, I've got several thousand to get us started again. Should I bring it down?" He acted as if he didn't know the doctor was selling his property.

"No, my dear Bluefeather Fellini, the gods have suggested other approaches. I'll be done here in a day or so and apprise you of the situation. My heartfelt thanks, however. Love to Tulip, as well." He was gone from the line.

Bluefeather took Tulip to dinner at Claude's up on Canyon Road. The food and wine must have been excellent, as always, but he really didn't notice. He did not notice enough to remember much of their conversation either; just a few lines of hers and none of his own.

"My deah Blue, how loyal you've been to us. But you must not let our endless endeavors come between you and Marsha. I've had much experience along those paths of roses and thorns, you know? One can conquer armored dragons with one who fits. That's the secret of life and love, my deah. Two who fit. So simple, isn't it?"

He halfheartedly looked for investors in and around the many and colorful watering holes of old Santa Fe. Excuses. Promises. Then that did not matter so much. He waited for Marsha's return. He was ecstatic to find a message at the desk saying she would be back sometime the next day.

He got up at dawn, had breakfast and drove around the hills north of town looking down on it, feeling the centuries of oxen, mules, horses, Indians, Spaniards, gringos, traders, artists, gamblers, business people, politicians, soldiers, madams and princesses who had fought, frittered and loved away centuries here, just as he himself was doing today. The costumes and transportation were the only differences.

After a while, he drove back down to take Tulip to a late lunch. He decided to go to his room and take a shower first, for he was certain that later he would be with Marsha. There was a little framed photo and an open letter on his desk. The picture was of a woman looking almost exactly as Tulip did now, holding proudly, with a smile, the baby Merphyn. His usual steady hand

quivered some as he picked up the letter on La Fonda
stationery, and read:

Dear Bluefeather Fellini,

If during a lifetime one can truly help twenty people change their lives or work for the better, then
that person is truly a fine and fortunate individual.
You have two on that small list in Tulip and me. You
have given of your most precious possession—your
time—and you have given it unselfishly and with
faith and dedication, as well. You have delivered.

Remember always, my son, that you have partici-
pated in a grand medical movement first proven by
your own ancestors during the terrible flu epidemic
of the First World War. The three of us together
have given it a momentous kick into the stratosphere
and it will forever move until someday it will enter
someone else's brain and soul. Then it will be carried on, and then perhaps on again, to its fruitful,
life-enhancing destiny, with our labors being im-
proved upon over and over. Radio came to first attention, and then invention, from the amazing mind
of Lee Marconi to be passed on to Edwin de Forrest
and thence on for more key improvements to Howard Armstrong until eventually the wireless could
send voices and music—some of great importance
and renown—around the world. Entrepreneur
David Sarnoff made the relay of inventors' dreams
and work "his" and spread the use and sale of radio
around the world through a company called RCA
and finally NBC, as well. We were able to communicate from shop to shop, from ship to shore, from
land to plane and nation to nation. Then in 1939 we
moved on into television, and I'm sure someone is
continuing the perpetual motion right now, moving

on to molecular transport and perhaps finally to complete the earthly circle, with teleportation, so that the supernatural will once again become the natural.

So, you see, Bluefeather Fellini, that our part of the medical movement is no less significant than the parts played by any of the above named. You have helped move a little goodness forward for others. That alone makes you blessed.

We are off to Brazil to study combining Amazonian forest herbs with the sage oil. I shall concentrate my next patent process, for expedience' sake, on skin revitalization. Most people feel that looks are more important than health.

> In faith forever,
> Dr. Merphyn Godchuck and
> your Auntie Tulip Everhaven

For a moment the letter caused him to blanch like an atheist at the sight of the archangel and to feel as uncomfortable as a dog plagued with diarrhea. Then he perused the letter again and yet again. With each reading he felt more merited, more complete, and finally filled with a warm truth of major accomplishment. He had done his part. His molecules all returned to their proper position, relaxed, joyous even.

With a confident and purposeful stride he went down, crossed the lobby and, as he knew he would, found a message from Marsha saying she was back. He rang her room from the lobby. No answer. No matter.

He strode out, walking around the portals of the plaza. Then he saw her inside a curio shop examining some heavy silver and turquoise jewelry. She was so enraptured, he slipped in and stood back making as if he was interested in a rack of knickknacks, but he was looking at her, and his heartbeat and breathing changed pace almost instantly.

Then he saw the dealer reach under the counter to a hidden shelf and pull out an old squash-blossom necklace. Bluefeather could tell it had been created with exquisite hands and much love. It was a very special piece, just as Marsha was.

He walked up and whispered in her ear, "Buy it."

He moved with smooth but swift steps on outside where he faked studying the window display as he watched her try on the necklace. Then she turned to him for his approval through the glass. She waited for his decision as the saleslady looked back and forth in puzzlement. He nodded "yes."

In a few moments she walked out the door, wearing the piece, and said, "You have very good taste, Mr. Bluefeather Fellini."

"Yes. Yes, I believe I do."

"If you're free, we can finally make our long-awaited dinner at El Nido," she said, tilting her head slightly to the side and giving him a flirtatious smile.

"I'm free for a lifetime."

"Meet me in the lobby at six o'clock then."

She walked away. He moved away from the window to appreciate her elegance more clearly. Both males and females stared at her as she came toward them and then looked back as she passed. Maybe the average man and woman on the street were smarter than he gave them credit for. At least they saw, smelled or somehow felt when they were in the presence of a true princess, no matter how brief the encounter. He wanted to rear back and crow like a fighting rooster.

She stopped just before entering the portal and looked through the moving crowd to find him staring at her as she hoped he would be. She smiled with an overwhelming expression that spoke to him, radiated along the invisible connector between them, vibrating into his wide-open soul. She tossed her hair back with a movement of her head and vanished from his sight into the hotel.

It was around four now, by clock time. The next two hours would seem an eternity. It was one he was happy to spend. Bluefeather Fellini of Taos and Raton, New Mexico, danced a little jig forward, sideways, then forward again, as his whole body smiled.

Two Navajo jewelry makers passing him noticed his happiness, and one said without rancor, "That crazy man there looks like some kind of Indian I never seen before."

"Cannot figger it. He dances like the original white man."

"Maybe he eats locoweed."

"Maybe he is in love."

"Same thing."

It was the time of anticipated ecstasy. Bluefeather Fellini danced on to many kinds of music. He laughed out loud—twice.

Crafted with all the beauty and wonder that has earned him numerous awards and high praise from his peers, Max Evans continues his grand celebration of the American West in his second novel chronicling the adventures of . . .

BLUEFEATHER FELLINI IN THE SACRED REALM

The mystical deserts and mountains that shape the Southwest region's character serve as the backdrop for a tender love story in this magical land. Evans illustrates his firsthand knowledge of the broad cultural terrain of the Southwest, turning his piercing insight on the creatures, both domestic and wild, that inhabit this vast landscape of the soul. On our travels with Bluefeather Fellini we discover the Indian belief in the Underground, the power of the stars, and occasional interference from the gods, all mixed with a gritty reality salted with humor. Ultimately, *Bluefeather Fellini in the Sacred Realm* offers a wondrous, revealing look at what might have created this beautiful and strange world—and what threatens to bring it to a tragic end.

Turn the page for a preview of *Bluefeather Fellini in the Sacred Realm,* a Bantam Domain paperback on sale in July 1995.

2

Ordinarily, Bluefeather would have enjoyed the ride up through the scattered piñon and cedars decorating the foothills. The mighty Sangre de Cristos dominated the horizon above, making the world seem very big. There was glass between him and Marsha, the driver. He did not use the intercom to speak, nor did she.

As they rounded a curve, the house was revealed. It was surrounded by a ten-foot-high adobe, concrete-plastered fence partly disguised in the trees. There was a huge iron gate ahead at the entrance, but it, too, was painted earth colors. The sight certainly jarred Bluefeather out of his comfortable musing, for it wasn't like any house he had ever seen before.

The first impression was of a medieval castle, but the lines of old-modern southwestern architecture dispelled this impact. The curvature and soft edges of the massive structure could only be adobe. It was multistoried like the Taos Pueblo main building, but faded back in more compact layers of levels. It exuded a sense of strength, permanence and, yes, power.

If Bluefeather had given any prior thought to it, this would be the kind of house Korbell, by his nature, would obviously occupy. One heard all the rumors of his financial manipulation. There was gossip, of course, that he was in oil, mining, manufacturing, arms shipments and on and on.

Bluefeather couldn't remember a single interview with the man in print or on radio. However, now and then, one would see a photo of him at some exclusive international gathering with several lovely ladies surrounding his imposing presence.

Bluefeather, using his mind-voice, said, *The son of a bitch is a mystery all right, and it was one created by his own choice.*

When Korbell had moved to the Southwest, the local papers, and some national ones, had simply stated—without giving reasons—that he had decided on this part of the world for his permanent home and hinted at the fact that everyone in the state would all be better for it. Personally, Bluefeather had paid little notice to the latter. It had been his minor experience that the move of big money always created that same initial reaction, even if it was later found that the wealth came to pour concrete over the hills and hide the natural horizon with all kinds of look-alike structures.

Bluefeather had been trying to quit smoking for over a year now, but he suddenly reached for his security pack in his coat pocket. He hesitantly put it back and wiped his suddenly dampened palms on the sides of his legs.

The great gate swung back in front of the limousine. Now after entering the acres of compound, Bluefeather's practiced eye saw the hidden guard boxes on each side of the gate and scattered every hundred yards around the entire estate. He had no doubt that they were being watched with careful interest.

The security commander was a huge man with a deep scar angling like a steep mountain trail carved into his face. By their subtle gestures, Bluefeather could tell that the man and Marsha were somehow close. Then he remembered seeing her with him in the Cerrillos Bar south of Santa Fe before they met.

She said, "That's Fontaine. You'll meet him someday. Now, Blue, don't go into any fits or questions. Just calm it all down and I promise you it will all come clear in the future."

Well, he might as well play along with this plot, game or whatever it was. What, really, did he have to lose?

They drove upon a circular graveled driveway bordered by arranged groupings of piñon, sagebrush, cacti, yucca and other plants indigenous to the region. The limousine stopped. My God, he was about to meet the man. His brain turned into a cement mixer.

The lady opened the limousine door, waiting, still smiling. "We're here."

Bluefeather exited, giving a weak thanks.

As they walked along toward the large antique doorway,

Marsha talked casually and comfortably, but he didn't remember a single sentence she uttered. He hoped he had answered if questioned, but he didn't know for sure. The door, like the front gate, swung open before they reached it. Bluefeather truly expected a polished, British butler to greet them, but instead there stood another elegant woman of indeterminate youth, smiling.

Marsha introduced him thusly; "Elena, this is Mr. Bluefeather Fellini."

Elena shook hands in a solid way and said, "It is so nice you could come. Korbell is expecting you."

Bluefeather noticed she did not preface the name with the usual "Mister."

"This way, Mr. Fellini."

Bluefeather followed, glancing back for Marsha, but she was walking away down the long, tiled hallway without having said another word. However, the vision moving ahead of him was sufficient to hold the attention of a lobotomized lizard. Elena's long, ballerina, graceful legs floated under the flowing gown that intermittently clung to and outlined her entire body. The gown had Aztec designs of varied hues from top to bottom. Maybe Rembrandt could have given proper attention to these works of art clinging to her surfaces. Bluefeather could only think of the Great Spirit's art underneath.

She stopped at another large door, smiling as she opened it. Bluefeather was struck by the glowing whiteness of her skin and the delicate but strong chin under the slightly arced crimson lips that curled invitingly around teeth whiter even than her skin. Her hair was blue-black like the barrel of a new gun, with a large silver comb placed so that the long strands snaked around and over a shoulder, just reaching one of her slightly revealed breasts. Bluefeather had an urge to dive into the two pools of eyes that matched her hair and to swim straight to heaven, if he didn't drown first. What was wrong here? He was thinking like a beginning madman.

Then the man, Korbell, was walking across the room, smiling of course, as if he were meeting the Pope or a king, but it was just plain Bluefeather Fellini.

Elena said, with the purr of a little tiger, "Korbell, this is your Mr. Fellini."

"Ah, what a pleasure to meet you in person, Mr. Fellini. Of course, I've heard about you from Marsha." He grabbed

Bluefeather's hand and gave it a shake that would have torn limbs from a great oak. He turned it loose just as swiftly as Bluefeather muttered, of all things, "Howdy, Mr. Korbell. It's sure good to meetcha."

"Korbell. I prefer just Korbell."

Bluefeather would never forget the last statement even though his present retention was being shattered like a dropped clay pot.

Korbell was at least a couple of inches taller than Bluefeather, probably six three, and as lean and tan as a tennis pro with Aegean Sea eyes and a long Sherlock Holmes nose over a wide, thin-lipped mouth. His hair was, to use an ancient description, shining silver, of course—it would have to be. His age, like Elena's could not be determined. Bluefeather guessed it could be either side of fifty. Korbell, too, had the same perfect teeth that gleamed from the ladies' mouths. Bluefeather ran his tongue over his own rather common ivories and then figured that maybe he could get a recommendation to their dentist, if nothing else. To top it all off, Korbell wore a very casual umber smoking jacket.

"You've met Elena, my adopted wife?"

Bluefeather's voice-mind clicked in again. *Horseshit and smothered onions,* he thought, *an adopted wife . . . he actually said that.*

Bluefeather swallowed and decided he had better just enjoy the show before he got lost in the mezzanine.

Elena vanished. Bluefeather was seated in a luxuriously soft chair as Korbell took a matching one to the right of him, angled so they could look at one another without twisting and both could comfortably gaze out a ten-foot picture window across miles of rolling hills rising through blue-hazed timber to barren, snow-covered peaks. Right magnificent.

"Well, now, Mr. Fellini, do you feel like a drink?"

"Blue. My friends mostly just call me Blue." He had to do something in self-defense. He added that he would be delighted to have a drink with him.

Another striking woman quietly appeared. In contrast to Elena, she had on a simple, tailored dress. Her brown hair was done up in a neat twist on top of her head. Bluefeather felt better when he saw that she had one tooth slightly out of line. She waited, smiling. After the introduction failed to come, Bluefeather heard her say, "Brandy?"

"Perfect," he answered, aiming to oblige where possible.

As she poured the drinks in a distant corner, Korbell looked at the boundless panorama, sighing contentedly, "What a perfect setting for our first meeting."

Bluefeather said, "Leonardo da Vinci would be honored."

Korbell chuckled slightly, adding, "Very good, Mr. Fellini. Very good, indeed."

Bluefeather thought, *The bastard has got me snake-charmed already. I'm almost ready to rise up out of a basket and start weaving to the music of his flute.*

The brown-haired lady came with a large tray holding the brandy and a box of Havana cigars. Bluefeather took the brandy and placed it on a hand-carved Spanish table next to his chair. The lady hesitated just a moment, so he took a cigar along with a gold-embossed match box. She served Korbell. Bluefeather waited. Korbell lifted his snifter. Bluefeather lifted his.

"To our potentially highly rewarding association."

"Whatever that might be."

Korbell gave his underplayed chuckle again, and they drank. It was very fine stuff. Bluefeather expected Korbell to speak of some exclusive, expensive brand name, but he was fooled again. Korbell lit his Havana. So did Bluefeather, wondering when the Philharmonic would enter.

"I do so like to mix business and pleasure, Mr. Fellini. More so all the time. Much more so." With that he reached down by his chair and picked up a flat, leather folder, opened it and began to read. Bluefeather knew for sure now that the game had started. A change came over him. He was no longer overwhelmed. He knew a contest was beginning between the two of them. Overmatched? He might be, but he was prepared to challenge the odds. What, really, did he have to lose? He was ready. Excited.

Korbell read, muttering at first, "Now, uh huh, yes. Born 1914, Raton, New Mexico: Italian father . . . mine foreman, now retired; Taos Indian Mother, has become a fairly successful traditional water colorist of Indian art." Korbell continued to read, "B-student, baseball and track star in high school; assistant mill foreman before you were twenty; became gold prospector; bought property and moved to Corrales; went to war, Europe, three major campaigns . . . aha awarded a Silver Star a Brest . . ."

Bluefeather swallowed some high-priced cigar smoke and

coughed out, "No, that's all wrong. It was a mistake. I didn't deserve it . . . I swear . . ."

"I like modesty in its place, Mr. Fellini, but this is not the place. I can fully read and understand a commendation. I was myself in the OSS for four years, you know?"

Then he read on briefly in silence. "I see you left the School of Mines a few months before graduating . . . setting third in your class at the time. Oh, well, it's not my concern why. I see you've hidden the fact that you did a stint of mercury smuggling out of Mexico recently. Not that it concerns me, but is that why you left school?"

Bluefeather had hidden the last even from himself. There would be little he could hide from this man, so why bother.

"Yes. That is why I left. I think you've already figured that. At the time the mercury movement was faster than a quarter horse track, and a hell of a lot more profitable."

"I see. The short-range profit motive overcame the long-range solidity for a degree as a mining engineer."

"I've never witnessed any solidity in the mining game."

"Game. Game did you say? You might have been . . . no, let's forget this part." Korbell shuffled the papers and continued, "You did have a very successful early life considering the choices you made. You survived the Great War in good shape and were building up your investment property just outside Albuquerque. Then things started to go to hell. What happened, Mr. Fellini? What in this world happened?"

"Several markets broke, including mercury. I became jaded and careless, that's all. It won't last. I won't let it."

Korbell continued to read, "You were married briefly. Your wife, Mary O'Kelly, expired from a mining accident near Breen, Colorado. What, I pray, young man, was a woman doing mining?"

"She was very good at it. It was just a . . . a freak accident. I'd rather not speak of it again."

"As you wish. Forgive my impertinence, but I have to know certain things. Oh, oh, I almost overlooked this. You killed a man in Tonopah. Self-defense. That's good."

How could this man go on so casually about the major events in his life? He decided to fire back. "Before we go any further, I want to know why you turned down the presentation on Dr. Godchuck's sage oil. It could have stopped a lot of suffering. And Marsha said you thought it was a good deal."

Korbell looked up from the papers, smiled and said, "Maybe so, Mr. Fellini, but you see I have something that is far greater than that of the good doctor, and the time is now. You know, one may be fortunate enough to have great wealth, but it will not purchase him a single second more of his allotted time. I have things to be fulfilled and my hope is that you'll see your way clear to help." Then he returned to the reading. "Let's see, where was I . . . ? Your father is now retired from the mines and your mother has become a successful watercolorist of Indian art. You phone her on the first Sunday of every month," Korbell was smiling so slightly that Bluefeather had to strain his $^{20}/_{20}$ eyes to see it.

This last personal piece of information was just a little too much. Bluefeather was sure the man knew the brand of toothpaste he used. He decided to end the inquisition. "Well, it looks like you know how many times I fart each day. Let's cut the crap and get down to the deal."

"Deal?"

"Yeah, you said you needed my help. And I know you haven't invited me here for my scintillating conversation, have you?"

Korbell chuckled again, finished his brandy and relit the Havana. Bluefeather did likewise. Waiting.

"Forgive my intrusion into your personal life, but I have a delicate proposition to make you, and one needs to know with whom and what he is dealing. I hope you understand."

Bluefeather countered with, "How about another brandy?"

Korbell raised his right hand and said softly, "Nedra."

The brown-haired serving girl entered the scene from around a latticework and they soon had their brandy. She exited.

Korbell stood up, brandy in hand, and said, "Please come with me."

Bluefeather followed him, warming the amber liquid with the palm of his hand as he walked. They wound through a hallway down a curving iron stairway beneath the house. They went through another heavy, iron doorway that opened smoothly at Korbell's touch. Everything seemed to be machined perfectly around here. Everything.

Bluefeather followed him perhaps twenty steps to a like

door. Korbell touched it as lightly as one might a frozen windowpane to test the cold. It swung silently open. They were in a vast wine cellar. Maybe it was average to Korbell, but it was mammoth to Bluefeather.

Korbell did not hesitate now, but strode purposefully past rows upon rows of worldly wines without even glancing at them. At last he turned and started down another aisle. Here he stopped by a tall, small-topped table that reached above their waists. He smiled around his teeth, white even in the dimly lighted cellar, and lifted his brandy to Bluefeather in a silent toast. He acted like he was in a library full of sacred tomes. Their glasses touched ever so lightly, making a ringing sound in the underground stillness.

Bluefeather followed Korbell's lead as he placed his glass on the odd-sized table. With delicacy and practiced skill, Korbell took a bottle from its resting place and very carefully placed it upright on the table between the brandy glasses and whispered, "Read."

Bluefeather bent down in the dim light, somehow knowing not to touch the old bottle. He read aloud, "Mouton Rothchild—1880." There was more fine print that he could not make out in the poor light.

Korbell whispered now as if he stood before the open casket of a dearly beloved. "That, Mr. Fellini, is one of the great wines of the world. And just as important, it pleases the palate like no other. The Rothschilds have refused to sell me another. They value each bottle in the thousands of dollars. Many thousands. It would do no good to offer more. Each year, at the end of the grape harvest, one—only one—bottle of this is opened in honor of the eldest of this noble clan. It is a priceless product to the Rothchilds, and to me. Do you understand?"

"I don't believe I do . . . unless . . . unless it is craving something one cannot buy, can't have just for money."

"Ahhh, you are partially correct, but you see I can have it . . . more Mouton '80 than even the Rothchilds have left in their cellars."

Bluefeather could only stare at him.

"Mr. Fellini, have you heard of Joshua Tilton?"

"The famous mining man?"

"The same, indeed." Korbell explained, "Joshua Tilton struck it very rich in mining between the two great world wars. He built large homes all over the Southwest and lavished friends with many, and varied, gifts. He was known as an eccentric—mainly, I felt, because he spent his wealth publicly and opulently on parties for renowned people from all over the world."

Bluefeather was aware that both Tilton and Korbell had become legends, even though their public approach to life appeared to be exactly opposite.

Korbell continued, "At the time Hitler invaded Poland, Tilton had become obsessed with the concept that the dictator would truly conquer the entire world. Tilton was reported to have gathered a great store of gold and silver bullion and hidden it in one of his mines. Great fortunes and many lives have been spent in a futile effort to find this treasure. If the reports were true, or if the treasure has been found, I've not been able to verify it."

He paused a moment, watching Bluefeather, his piercing eyes showing his enthrallment with the story and his curiosity at its effect on his visitor.

"Tilton's unsolved murder in a Silver City hotel during the height of the bombing of London only added to the mystery. It became a notorious incident since the head was missing from the body and has never been recovered. All the forces of the law were expended in a futile attempt to solve the case. Every lead, no matter how vague, was followed. They all petered out. Right now as we visit, someone, somewhere, is seeking the fabled fortune."

Bluefeather was aware that Tilton's bullion had become almost as famous as the lost Adam's diggings of the Superstition Mountains near Phoenix, Arizona. Elusive dreams or hard facts? The thing is, people wanted to believe in its existence, so they searched on and on.

Korbell sighed, looking at the Mouton '80 and spoke again, "I'm sure, Mr. Fellini, that your mind is racing with whirlwind thoughts of Tilton's lost bullion. Well . . . that is a strong rumor, but a rumor nevertheless, you see. But, a mostly unknown fact is that Tilton did hide sixty cases of Mouton '80. Sixty cases, Mr. Fellini! Do you realize what a treasure that truly is? Perhaps a million dollars' worth of Mouton. Maybe more. Who knows what the careful disclosure and handling of such a find would accrue. But, you see, that is not its true value, is it? Far from it. It would be like owning half interest with the French nation in the Mona Lisa. I have the old shipping and arrival bills, proving without a doubt, that this wondrous shipment was delivered only a short time before Tilton's demise. The wine is here. Somewhere in finding distance."

Korbell was breathing like a milerunner at the tape. His eyes were staring through mountains. An obsession had possessed his being. Then Korbell recovered and got right down to real business. Real for Bluefeather at least. He informed Bluefeather that Tilton was certain to have secured the wine underground to keep an exact and constant temperature. Bluefeather was surprised by Korbell again when he admitted that the very cellar they now stood in had already been dug by Tilton and the foundations of the great house had already been poured and most of the walls laid at the time of his decapitation.

Korbell praised Tilton for his choice of this location and admitted that it was his exhaustive research on Tilton that had led him to this most perfect of all places to build his final and permanent residence.

Korbell explained that he and Tilton were of the same stand of timber; all that remained to be done was the finding and glorious consumption of their Mouton '80.

Now he led Bluefeather out of the expansive wine cellar and up to his sanctuary. It was a room almost as large as the cellar—a room hung with paintings of the old and new Taos masters: Sharps, Couses, Phillips, Berninghaus—the whole drove and more. There were the originals of world-famous Indian artists such as Woody Crumbo and R. C. Gorman's landscapes and varied styles of Andrew Dasburg, Howard Cook and Fremont Ellis. There were long shelves of southwestern titles from such authors as Mable Dodge Luhan, Willa Cather, Oliver La Farge and many, many others that Bluefeather recognized at a glance. It was difficult for Bluefeather to listen to more talk of lost bullion and wine when the mentors of his mother's birthplace hung about the adobe castle as casually as an old hunting dog.

Korbell forced him to return his attention to Tilton's legacy. He showed him maps of all the mines in New Mexico that Tilton had either owned, prospected or leased, as well as the dates they had been opened, or closed, or abandoned.

Then the deal was pitched. Korbell would pick up all Bluefeather's overdue payments, thereby saving his home and land, and pay him a generous retainer for six months, renewable at Korbell's choice. If Bluefeather found the wine, he would pay one-half its immediate market value. He wanted the wine. Simple.

It did not take Bluefeather long to make up his mind. He was on the verge of losing everything that had taken so much real blood and love to accrue. It wasn't just the monetary worth of his loss. It was old Grinder's advice that was being downgraded. Anyway, he loved the Corrales place, his mules, his neighbors. The place had to go on existing for those from the past. It hurt to think it might not be there for some future . . . future . . . ? What the hell! He might as well admit it. He had goofed. His balls were in a red hot vise that was rapidly closing. Another thing that shot through his system with a surge was Marsha. He would be with her, because she definitely was part of this strange equation unfolding like the wings of a giant butterfly. Without hesitation, Bluefeather gave Korbell a powerful handshake. The act would indeed change his life completely.

Korbell held Bluefeather's hand a moment, looking through his forehead, and probably beyond, saying, "I expect the same dedication to our great cause from you that I myself have given and will continue to bestow. Do you totally understand me, Mr. Fellini?"

Mr. Fellini said, "I do." And he did.

"Fine. Fine. Now let us retire for cocktails and dinner."

3

They sat about the great room of their first meeting. Elena, Marsha, Korbell and Bluefeather talked about current painters, potters and musicians of a local bent. It was easy-flowing conversation with no interrupting or domination of the talk. Nedra served the drinks and appetizers smoothly, without any wasted apologies or fuss. Bluefeather felt it was an omen that he and Marsha both asked for J. B. Scotch. The world was made of small likes and dislikes.

The hiding sun was turning the snow-peaked mountains watermelon pink. The Spaniards had long ago designated this last light of day as *sangre de cristo* — blood of Christ. The valleys and hills had already become part night with misty blues and purples that made one think of long ago and the possibility of eternity.

The mellowness of the booze and the relief from many suffocating debts had put Bluefeather in a pleasant torpor. They all seemed to sense that. Korbell, as well, was a happy and relieved man. Marsha's eyes and rosy skin beamed like summer sunspots. She sipped her drink casually, occasionally pushing a random strand of auburn hair back from the side of her face, giving him looks that he was sure had deep meaning. Of course, those looks could only be special for him, no matter how brief. He was right. She *was* studying him, wondering how Korbell could trust him on such short acquaintance, even with all the prior information he had gathered and her own short acquaintance with him. Well, they would all soon know what his capabilities were.

As Marsha looked at Bluefeather's strong features again, she was embarrassed that she felt a quickening of breath. My God! She was feeling like a high school sophomore and praying it didn't show. She could not let him know that—not until she could explain, someday, why she had left him in Santa Fe without an answer.

Elena listened to whomever spoke with a rare raptness. As the natural outdoor light receded, her white skin again drew Bluefeather's gaze. Her large, dark eyes fastened on him like those of a master hypnotist. He wondered for an instant if they had hypnotized him—this Korbell group.

No. The mountains, now becoming one with the sky, were real. The drink he held was real. He took a small, cool swallow to verify. He pushed his own thick, black hair across his scalp. It was his own head he was inside of, for sure. Well, whatever. A few hours back, he had arrived here with one leg hanging in space above a chasm of darkness, and now both feet were planted firmly on the Indian-rugged, tile floor. Solid. Even though he felt it unnecessary, he was certain he could elevate himself to the ceiling like Dancing Bear, on command

At the instant of this thought, the aquarium of tropical fish that he had noticed in a far corner moved toward them. It slowly circled the entire group, stopping for a fraction of a moment in front of Bluefeather. The multicolored fish swam about in little liquid rainbows, nuzzling the bottom of the aquarium among pebbles and swaying vegetation. One large, white fish looked arrogantly at Bluefeather a moment, knowing all. Then the aquarium settled down and moved on four little wheels to the great window and stopped. Bluefeather looked about—casually, he hoped—at the other faces. They had taken no notice at all; their current attention was on Korbell, who was expounding his admiration for Maria Martinez's San Ildefonso Pueblo pottery. Nedra, smiling, served as the aquarium now smoothly rose up and floated to its former place.

Bluefeather thought, *My God, how they all smile. Did rich and powerful people take smiling lessons, and . . . and ignore magic aquariums as if it happened to be their due?*

Bluefeather was confident that he had maintained his composure as Korbell spoke, "Ah, yes, Mr. Fellini. I forgot to apprise you of one more item. My adopted daughter, Marsha, will be your assistant on our little venture. I trust you will find that satisfactory, as she is extremely efficient in many fields."

Bluefeather looked at her teeth lined so perfectly back of her luscious lips and said, "If you say so, sir." This was one of the closest six or seven times in his life he had ever come to dying of both shocked surprise and pained pleasure.

Marsha controlled the jumbling and jangling of her nervous system, emitted a sigh of acceptance and nodded her head so casually it was almost imperceptible. Oddly, everyone in the room watched her minute indications of acceptance.

Dinner had been, so to say the least, grand. The wine was of such a bouquet that the young guest wondered why in the holy hangdogged hell a man ever needed to give a thought to Mouton '80. They had duck à l'orange that chewed and swallowed itself. There were many more courses, but Bluefeather blanked on what they were. There are only so many goodies a man can swallow at once without choking. He did not, however, resist when Korbell insisted that he stay the night. They all had brandies except the elegant, somehow aloof, Nedra.

Bluefeather was happy when he was shown to his room with a bed big enough for a basketball team. He was wondering about the adopted wife, the adopted daughter and, no doubt, adopted serving girl as he pulled the silken covers over his shoulders.

He thought, *By God, maybe the obsessed bastard will adopt me, too.*

He was just trying to think of a single disadvantage to this as a coyote howled off toward the north, answered by one farther on, when he realized a figure stood silhouetted against the window, backlit by a rising moon. It was a female. No doubt about that at all. The scent of a subtle perfume from some far-away island wafted about and mixed with the Scotch, brandy and wild dreams in his head.

She crawled into bed beside him. He couldn't make out her features, nor did he have a chance, for her smooth, warm arms folded over and around him. Her breasts had his chest captured and enraptured.

He croaked out, "What are you doing here?"

The unrecognizable whisper came soft as the first breeze of autumn, just as her hands found him.

She whispered, "Well, the Orientals say there are one hundred and one ways."

Bluefeather lost count at six or seven.

Later he realized he was alone. One of the three adopted ladies had permissively raped him. It was too late to care. He was too lusciously tired to stay awake and ponder.